COLLATERAL DAMAGE

ALSO BY H. TERRELL GRIFFIN

Matt Royal Mysteries

Bitter Legacy
Wyatt's Revenge
Blood Island
Murder Key
Longboat Blues

Thrillers: 100 Must-Reads
(contributing essayist)

COLLATERAL DAMAGE

A Matt Royal Mystery

H. Terrell Griffin

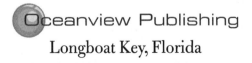

Oceanview Publishing
Longboat Key, Florida

ISBN: 978-1-60809-026-6

Published in the United States of America by Oceanview Publishing,
Longboat Key, Florida
www.oceanviewpub.com

2 4 6 8 10 9 7 5 3 1

PRINTED IN THE UNITED STATES OF AMERICA

For Kyle and Sarah

Dishonor will not trouble me once I am dead.

—Euripides

ACKNOWLEDGMENTS

A book doesn't just happen. At least, my books don't. I need a lot of help, and I always get it. First and foremost are the readers. I've only been writing for the past six years, but I've been an avid reader my entire life. Books have given me pleasure beyond reckoning, and I think it is my duty as a writer to provide the same good feelings to my readers. I learn a lot from the feedback I receive at book signings and other events and from e-mail sent by readers across the country. I appreciate it all and I take it to heart. My readers' comments make me a better writer.

I have the good fortune to have three friends, Peggy Kendall, Debbie Schroeder, and Jean Griffin, who read my books as I write them and give me plenty of advice. Most of it is good. For example, Jean Griffin is the one who came up with the idea for the character J. D. Duncan. I hope I have made J.D. believable and likeable.

Oceanview Publishing is a wonderful organization made up of outstanding people who support their writers with understanding, advice, and the occasional pat on the back. Bob Gussin, Pat Gussin, Maryglenn McCombs, Kylie Fritz, Frank Troncale, and Susan Hayes work hard to make our books better and to get them into the readers' hands. We miss Susan Greger and Mary Adele Bogdon, but I know they are truly enjoying their retirement.

Finally, there is my college roommate, Jean Griffin, who married me when I was a student and has put up with me all the years since. She encourages me, edits me, supports me, and forever makes me smile.

COLLATERAL DAMAGE

CHAPTER ONE

On the last morning of his life, Jim Desmond woke to the sound of the gentle surf lapping on the beach, pushed by the onshore breeze that barely rippled the surface of the Gulf of Mexico. Early light reflected off the water, the angle of the sun hanging over the mainland to the east giving the seascape a flat appearance, as if much of the color had been leeched out of the vivid hues that usually paint the southwest coast of Florida.

Desmond snuggled a little more deeply into the bed, a sheet and light blanket covering his naked body, protecting him from the cold air blowing from the air-conditioning vent in the ceiling. He knew it was already hot out on the beach, the June humidity lying like a damp shroud over the entire island.

A hand slowly reached over him, caressed his chest. He felt breasts snuggle against his back, a long leg cross his. Heard a slight snicker, felt a wet kiss on his shoulder, the warm breath of his wife against his skin. He turned toward her, kissed her smiling face, and began to make love to the woman he'd married the day before on the beach in front of the Hilton.

Later, they lay in the bed, her head on his shoulder, her blonde hair tickling his nose. They were sated for a time, their physical need for each other slaked. Two people on the cusp of the future, a long life of success and children and growing old together stretched before them. Happiness was their due, for they were the children of the baby boomers, the generation that had known tranquility in their world, enjoyed the fruits of their parents' success, gone off to college and joined fraternities and sororities, partied and studied, and moved into the wider world where they expected no less than life as they had always known it.

Jim kissed his bride on the forehead and padded to the shower. He dressed in running shoes, shorts, and a white T-shirt bearing the logo of his alma mater, the University of Georgia. His wife had made coffee in the small coffeemaker provided each room. She poured him some in a Styrofoam cup, and standing nude, smiling, held it out like an offering to the god of love. He sipped the coffee, kissed her chastely on the mouth, and went out the door for his morning jog. She never saw him again.

CHAPTER TWO

My buddy Logan Hamilton and I were having lunch at Mar Vista, the bayside pub in the Village on the north end of Longboat Key. The year-rounders, those of us who don't go north in the spring and return in the late fall, know better than to sit outside in June. The heat and humidity, while not as bad as August, is brutal. Even the sea breezes that blow across our island don't bring relief. It is just hot air. Logan said it reminded him of trial lawyers, my former profession. I never argue with him when he's right.

We sat at a table next to a wall covered in currency of every kind, much of it American greenbacks. Many of the bills had messages scrawled on them from people who had left them along with their names and the dates of their visit. I wondered what made otherwise sane people tack good money to walls or throw coins into fountains. Like much of the human condition, it was a mystery to me.

Logan and I were planning a fishing trip for that evening. We thought we might have some luck after dark anchored off the north end of the Sister Keys just outside the channel. And if the fish weren't biting, we had beer and a lot of lies to tell. We'd get to Moore's Stone Crab Restaurant before closing and have a drink or two with Debbie the bartender. Maybe a nightcap at Tiny's. Not a bad way to spend a hot evening in Southwest Florida.

I was having the Caesar salad with blackened shrimp and Logan had ordered his usual, deep fried scallops and a Dewar's and water to wash it down. I felt the heat as the door to the parking lot opened behind me. Then, a voice. "Matt Royal, there you are." Cotty Johnson. I turned and saw my eighty-something-year-old neighbor coming toward us. "Hey Logan," she said.

Logan and I stood. Cotty pecked us both on the cheeks. "Join us," I said.

"No, thanks. Shirley Beachum is on her way. We thought we'd see how the vodka stock is doing."

I laughed. "Sit until she gets here."

Cotty took the chair next to Logan, across from me. "I guess you heard about the guy getting shot on the beach this morning."

I hadn't. Cotty knew everything that happened on the island, and often knew it before anybody else. No one ever figured out how she knew so much so quickly.

"Shot?" asked Logan.

"Yes. Apparently a high-powered rifle. The police think the gunman was in one of the condos just south of the Hilton. Got the guy right in the chest. He was dead before he hit the sand."

"Who was he?" I asked. "A local?"

"No. Some guy from Atlanta. Got married yesterday. He and his bride were staying at the Hilton. He went out for a jog early this morning."

"Any witnesses?"

"Not really. There were a couple of people on the beach who heard the shot and saw the guy hit the ground, but nobody saw where the shot came from."

"Any leads at all?" Logan asked.

"Not that I've heard. Bill Lester and that new detective J. D. Duncan are still at the Hilton doing whatever it is they do."

Bill Lester was the Longboat Key chief of police and J. D. Duncan was a detective who had recently joined the force after fifteen years with the Miami-Dade Police Department.

I felt another heat blast as the door opened again. Shirley came over to say hello and she and Cotty went to the bar and took seats. By the time they left, all the island gossip would be told and retold. As good a way as any to spend a hot afternoon.

Logan sipped his Scotch. "What do you make of the shooting?"

"No idea. I wonder who the victim was."

"The Chamber of Commerce isn't going to like this. They'll be afraid the publicity will scare the tourists away."

"I don't know. It's not like people regularly get mowed down on our beach."

"You're probably right."

Our conversation turned back to fishing. We put together a plan that mostly involved the question of where to get the beer and bait. We decided on Annie's in the settlement of Cortez across the bay.

CHAPTER THREE

My home is Longboat Key, Florida. More specifically, Longbeach Village, long called simply the "Village," that takes up the north end of the island. My cottage backs up to the bay, giving me a view that brings real estate sales people to their knees. Tropical flowers are abundant in the yard, and I pay a guy more than I should to keep them blooming or whatever they're supposed to do during any given season.

Longboat Key itself is small, about ten miles long and less than a half-mile wide in most places. It lies off the coast of Southwest Florida, south of Tampa Bay and about half way down the peninsula. Once you leave the south end of the key you cross some bridges, another island and end up in downtown Sarasota. On the north end you'll cross the Longboat Pass Bridge, part of Anna Maria Island, then Cortez Bridge, and find yourself in the city of Bradenton.

The island is my slice of paradise. I'm not old enough for retirement, but I'd been to war as a young man, then college and law school. I'd practiced as a trial lawyer in Orlando for a number of years and despaired of the business that the profession was turning into. I began to drink too much and take myself way too seriously, plowing into the law practice with a single-minded devotion that left little time for the only woman I'd ever loved, my wife, Laura. She finally gave notice that our marriage was over. She moved to Atlanta, remarried and died a few years later.

I gave up, sold everything, and moved to Longboat Key. If I was careful, I had enough to live on for the rest of my life. I'd pretty much achieved my goal of becoming a beach bum, living in a small community with lots of friends and time for fishing, walking the beach, drinking in the salubrious bars that dotted our island. I'm not sure how healthy all that drinking was, but the lifestyle gave me a peace that I'd not been able to achieve in all the years before Longboat.

I stayed in shape, worked out with a martial arts instructor a couple of times a week, ran daily on the beach, and always found time for a round of exercises that kept me young. Or at least younger than if I'd become one of those people whose only daily exercise consists of moving from the TV to the beach, then to a bar and back to the TV.

I'm six feet tall and maintain the same one-hundred-eighty pounds I weighed when I was a soldier. Gray has not yet crept into my hair, and I have what I describe as a ruggedly handsome face. Most folks just laugh at me when I say that. They say that I'm, well, pleasant looking. Soldiers do not think of themselves as pleasant. Tough, rugged, even mean as hell, but never pleasant. Oh well, I am what I am, and I'm reasonably satisfied with that.

Logan and I sat in the cockpit of my boat, fishing lines out over the transom. We were off the main channel a few yards north of the tip end of the Sister Keys that separates part of Sarasota Bay from the north end of Longboat Key. The twin two-hundred-fifty-horsepower Yamaha outboards purred quietly, idling in neutral. My anchor light was on and some illumination slipped from the small cabin. We were easily visible to any boat coming up the channel.

We were drifting slightly in the current as it ran toward Longboat Pass and the Gulf of Mexico. The tide was going out, but in our area of Florida the tidal range is not great and the outgoing tides are gentle. The engines were running in case I had to move quickly to dodge a sandbar or another boat.

It was nearing ten o'clock in the evening. An onshore breeze brought the scent of the Gulf's brine, a pleasant tinge redolent with the hint of the beauty of the ever-changing water that lapped gently on our beaches. The lights of *Dulcimer*, a dinner cruise boat owned by a local restaurant reflected off the dark surface of the bay as she made her way slowly north toward home, full of satisfied diners who'd taken the evening dinner cruise. *Dulcimer* was one hundred-ten-feet-long and twenty-eight feet on the beam. She was big and slow and stately and looked like an old Mississippi

River steamboat. She was powered by diesel engines and the paddle wheel at her stern was just for show. She was about two hundred yards south of us, running the narrow channel to the west of the Sister Keys, chugging along at ten knots or so. As she neared, strains of music floated across the water, a pleasant counterpoint to an almost perfect evening.

The channel that runs north and south along the western edge of the Sister Keys doglegs around a sandbar that has pushed out from the lagoon that separates Longboat Key from Jewfish Key. The captain on a northerly course must turn about thirty degrees to the east and then back to the west. We watched as *Dulcimer* made the turn to the east. She kept coming. No turn back to the west. She was on a collision course with my boat.

I jumped to the helm and pushed the throttles forward, moving swiftly across the bow of the oncoming vessel. I knew there was a sandbar lurking just behind where we'd been fishing, and if the captain didn't get back on course in the next few seconds, he'd be piling up on the bar.

I turned to my left, paralleling the course of the larger boat. The pilot house was dark, but the decks were lighted. I could see people sitting at the tables, walking around with drinks in hand, leaning against the railings of the open upper deck. The music was still playing, an old rendition of "La Vie En Rose." I wasn't sure if it was Edith Piaf singing, but it sounded like her.

As I passed amidships of *Dulcimer,* she went dark. The lights and the sound quit at the same instant. No lights on the decks, no running lights. Nothing. A ghost ship was slipping by my port side, dark and foreboding. The sounds of surprised guests getting louder as panic set in.

The boat came to a shuddering halt. It had found the sandbar. I heard tables and glassware shifting and breaking. Screams of panic and pain drifted over the water. I'd been reaching for my radio microphone when the lights went out. "Mayday! Mayday! Coast Guard Cortez, Coast Guard Cortez, this is *Recess.*"

The radio jumped to life, a calm female voice at the other end of the ether. "*Recess,* this is United States Coast Guard Cortez. What is your emergency?"

"This is *Recess.* I'm at the northern tip of the Sister Keys. The *Dulcimer* dinner boat just ran hard aground. I can hear screams coming from the passengers. It looks as if several are in the water. I'll try to pick them up."

"I'm sending boats, *Recess*. Stand by on channel sixteen."

"*Recess*, standing by sixteen."

I was shining my spotlight on three heads bobbing in the water. I eased *Recess* toward them, put the engines in idle, and drifted. Logan was at the stern, the transom door open, the ladder down, a boat pole in his hand. He helped bring the waterlogged people aboard, told them to sit down on the cockpit floor. Logan dug into the bag of towels in the cabin and gave one to each of our passengers.

I kept the spotlight moving, but didn't see any more heads. Some of the passengers had apparently gone overboard from the open deck when the boat ran aground. Several of them were standing near the bow, the water up to their knees.

"The Coast Guard is coming," I called to them. "Stay where you are."

Less than ten minutes after my radio call to the Coast Guard, I heard sirens whooping in the distance. I looked to the north and saw two boats, blue lights flashing, racing toward us. The Coast Guard station was only a couple of miles north of our position.

I picked up my microphone. "Coast Guard Cortez, this is *Recess*."

"*Recess*, this is United States Coast Guard Cortez."

"Coast Guard, this is *Recess*. I have three people aboard, no casualties. I'm standing by near the stern of *Dulcimer*. I see your boats approaching."

"Standby, *Recess*.

"Roger, Coast Guard."

I turned to the people we'd brought aboard. "What happened?"

"I don't know," said a middle-aged lady, shivering in a towel-draped sundress. "We were on the top deck when the lights went out and the next thing I knew, we were in the water."

The other woman and the man with them murmured agreement.

I watched as the Coast Guard boats pulled alongside *Dulcimer*. Men in blue uniforms boarded carrying flashlights. I waited, playing with the throttles, keeping *Recess* in the middle of the channel, awaiting orders.

After a few minutes I heard a motor turn over, the sound coming from *Dulcimer*. Then the lights came on and music again played over the water. One of the Coasties had gotten the generator working. The music stopped. The gay evening was over. Time for the work to begin; to find out what happened.

I heard a siren and saw a boat coming from the south, blue lights announcing another law enforcement vessel. It was the Longboat Key Police boat. The cop at the helm recognized my boat and pulled alongside.

"What the hell happened, Matt?"

I told him what I'd seen and that I'd picked up the three passengers from the water.

"I've been listening on the radio," he said. "I've got ambulances coming to Moore's. We can offload any injured at the docks there."

"You've got some people in the water up by the bow," I said. "They're going to start getting cold."

"I'll go get them. Why don't you get these folks names and take them to Moore's so the paramedics can take a look."

He went around me and moved slowly into the shallows to pick up the people on the sandbar. I crossed the channel running almost due west, past the southern tip of Jewfish Key and across the lagoon to Moore's Stone Crab Restaurant. I saw a sea of flashing blue lights in the parking lot. I maneuvered into the dock and cut the engines. Logan and I helped our passengers off the boat and turned them over to the paramedics.

"You ready for a drink?" I asked Logan.

"Damn right."

I picked up the microphone. "Coast Guard Cortez, this is *Recess*."

"This is United States Coast Guard Cortez."

"This is *Recess*. I've dropped my three passengers off at Moore's with the paramedics. I'll be inside in case your people need to talk to me."

"*Recess*, did you get their names?

I gave them to her, told her my cell phone number, signed off, and headed for the bar.

CHAPTER FOUR

It was late by the time the Coast Guard accident investigator called me. He'd had to drive down from St. Petersburg. He told me that they'd inspected *Dulcimer* and didn't think there was any structural damage. Just a bit of bottom paint scraped off the bow where it ran up on the sandbar. They'd kept the passengers aboard and were going to tow the boat back to its dock at the restaurant. Other than a few scrapes and bruises, there did not seem to be any casualties, except for the captain. He'd apparently had a heart attack or a stroke and died at the helm. The investigator said he'd call me the next day and come by and get a statement.

It was midnight and my friend Debbie the bartender was trying to kick us out. Logan and I had been joined by a few other villagers who were interested in all the commotion out on the waterway. We filled them in on what we knew, and after I talked to the investigator, they all knew as much as I did.

Logan paid our tab and we walked down to the dock and boarded *Recess*. I pulled away from the dock and threaded my way around the sandbars and idled toward my cottage. We could see the activity over on the Intracoastal where two small towboats were hooking up to the bow of *Dulcimer*. They'd see her home.

"I wonder why they don't just take her home under her own power," I said.

"Gotta pay the towboat captains anyway. Might as well make them work for their money."

"Probably makes it easier to justify calling them out in the first place."

"The bureaucratic mind," said Logan, "never fails to amaze me."

I slid *Recess* into her home berth, tied her off, and told Logan I'd wait until morning to wash her down and flush the engines. "I need sleep."

"Me too," he said. "I'll check in with you tomorrow."

Logan went to his car, and I opened the back patio sliding glass door and went in to bed.

My cell phone rang, waking me from a troubling dream of soldiers falling off boats into subtropical waters. Daylight was creeping through my windows overlooking the bay. I looked at my watch. A few minutes after six. I rolled over and picked up the phone.

"Matt," a soft voice said "this is J.D. May I come by with the Coast Guard investigator and talk to you?"

"Sure. When?" I was puzzled as to why she was calling me so early.

"Now. There's been a bad turn on the *Dulcimer* grounding."

I sat up in bed, a little surprised. It had seemed pretty routine last night. "Give me ten minutes to jump in the shower and put some coffee on."

"We'll be there in fifteen," she said, and hung up.

J. D. Duncan was my friend and Longboat Key's only detective. She'd spent fifteen years on the Miami-Dade police force, ten as a detective, and the last few as assistant homicide commander. When her mom died and left her a condo unit on the key, she'd decided to leave the stress of Miami and join us in paradise. She'd gotten the job with the Longboat Key Police Department a few months before and had quickly become part of our island community.

I took a quick shower, put on a clean T-shirt and cargo shorts, and set the coffee dripping. My doorbell rang. I opened the front door to find J.D. standing next to a tall man in civilian clothes whom she introduced as Chief Warrant Officer Jacobi. The Coast Guard accident investigator.

The dectective was in her late thirties, stood five feet seven inches tall, and wore her dark hair just short of shoulder length. Her green eyes could stare down a criminal or crinkle in happiness. She had a smile that made you just want to get up and dance, a straight nose, laugh wrinkles bordering her eyes, and a complexion that could only have been the result of good genes and skin care products. She was slender, small waisted and long legged with full breasts that could not quite hide beneath her clothes.

I invited them in and poured coffee for each. We sat in the living room. Jacobi was a couple inches taller than I and weighed thirty pounds less. He wore civilian clothes, was about forty years old, had a head full of brown hair with some gray starting to show at the temples. His nose was a bit small for his angular face and his chin had that tucked in look that you get with a large overbite. A chipped left upper incisor would have given him an odd smile. He seemed to be a serious man and I doubt that he smiled much.

"We've got two murder victims on *Dulcimer*," J.D. said.

That brought me upright. "Murder victims?"

"Yes," said Jacobi, his voice rumbling in the deep register I'd heard on the phone. "They were both knifed and thrown overboard."

"What's going on?" I asked, trying to get my head around this new piece of information.

"Did you see anything that looked out of the ordinary?" he asked.

"You mean other than a hundred-ten-foot boat running hard aground and throwing passengers into the water?"

"You know what I mean," he said.

"If you're asking if I saw any bodies, the answer is no."

Jacobi looked hard at me for a moment. I suspected he had practiced that stare in the mirror, the better to intimidate witnesses. I wasn't impressed. I looked back passively, waiting for another question. He broke eye contact, looked over at J.D., shrugged.

"One of the victims was the husband of the woman you fished out of the water," J.D. said.

"What do you know about them?" I asked.

"The husband was a fifty-two-year-old lawyer from Jacksonville named Peter Garrison," said J.D. "The other victim was a twenty-five-year-old woman from Charlotte, North Carolina."

"When did you find them?"

J.D. took a sip of her coffee. "A few hours ago. When the Coast Guard got *Dulcimer* back to the dock, we let the passengers off. No reason to hold them. The paramedics brought the woman you picked up," she paused, looked at her notes, "Mrs. Betty Garrison, from Moore's over to *Dulcimer's* berth. She couldn't find her husband. It seems she'd gone to the upper deck to have a cigarette and left her husband in the dining area on the second deck. She was leaning on the rail and when the boat hit the sandbar, she was tossed into the water."

"Where were the bodies?" I asked.

"Washed up on Sister Keys, right near where *Dulcimer* went aground."

"Who's the young woman?" I asked.

Jacobi broke in. "According to her driver's license, she is Katherine Brewster, single, lived with her parents. I had to break the news to them about thirty minutes ago."

"Any connection between the girl and Mr. Garrison?" I asked.

J.D. leaned forward in her chair, reaching again for the cup sitting on the coffee table. "We haven't had time to establish anything except that Mrs. Garrison never heard of her. Katherine had come to the area by herself and was staying at a small bed and breakfast on Anna Maria. We found the key in her pocket. We'll check all that out."

"How did you know she was missing?"

"We didn't," said Jacobi. "We found her body while we were looking for Garrison."

"Any evidence on the boat?" I asked.

"The crime-scene unit from Manatee County is going over it as we speak," said J.D. "I doubt they'll find much with all those people tramping through it."

"You said the bodies washed up on Sister Keys. Do you think they were in the water when I was picking up those three people?"

"I doubt it," said Jacobi. "It actually looks as if they were thrown overboard and may have been washed up on shore by the movement of the boats trying to get *Dulcimer* off the bar and underway to her berth. They weren't in the water very long."

I sat for a beat, thinking. "Do you see this as a crime of opportunity, random, or what? It seems awfully coincidental that the grounding gave the murderer the opportunity to strike in the confusion."

"We agree with you," said J.D. "The medical examiner will do an autopsy on the captain today. He may not have died of natural causes.

"Look," she continued, "I know you didn't see the bodies, but give me a minute-by-minute description of what you did see. There may be something there that'll give us a lead."

I took her through the minutes from the time I saw *Dulcimer* making her way up the channel until I pulled into the dock at Moore's.

J.D. was quiet for a moment. "You said the pilothouse was dark before the other lights went out. Isn't that unusual?"

Jacobi and I both shook our heads. "No," he said. "The captain would have kept the pilothouse dark so that he could see better outside. His instrument lights glow red, so even they wouldn't have been visible from Mr. Royal's vantage."

J.D. nodded her head, accepting the explanation. "How long after the lights went out did the boat run aground?"

"Seconds," I said. "No more than a minute. I was still running alongside at idle speed. She was moving at maybe ten knots. She would have gotten by me quickly if she hadn't hit the bar. When she stopped, I was still beside her, back near the fake paddle wheel."

"Was she still moving at the same speed?"

That stopped me. I sat upright in my chair. I was thinking about the exact second when *Dulcimer* grounded. It had been quiet except for the nervous chatter of the passengers. When the music died, so did the engine sounds. That was the reason I thought of her as a ghost ship as she was sliding by me. The big diesels were quiet.

"The engines had been shut down," I said.

"When?" asked Jacobi.

"I don't know. Let me think."

I closed my eyes, trying to get back to the very moment that I became subliminally aware that the engines had shut down. "Just as I crossed her bow, I heard the engines race, as if someone was pouring the fuel to them. Then, just as suddenly, they stopped. Somebody shut them down. She'd gotten a little burst of speed, and then drifted onto the bar. She hit pretty hard, though, so she had some speed on."

"How much time elapsed between the time the engines were shut down and the boat went dark?" asked Jacobi.

"Immediately. Or almost immediately. I think whoever shut the engines down did so by turning off the ignition and probably reached over and turned off the generator. It was that fast."

"And how long before the Coast Guard boarded and fired the generator back up?" asked Jacobi.

"Let me think. I radioed Cortez as soon as the lights went out. In the few seconds it took to get a response, *Dulcimer* grounded and the screaming started. I'm not sure I even got the transmission off before she hit the sandbar. I think it was probably ten minutes before the Coasties arrived on scene and boarded. Somebody apparently went to the pilothouse and kicked over the generator. I'd say fifteen minutes tops, but the Coast Guard log will probably give you a better time line."

"I've already ordered that," said Jacobi. "We'll match the log to your recollection."

"You might want to talk to Logan Hamilton," I said. "He was there the whole time."

"We will," said J.D. "Anything else, Mr. Jacobi?"

He shook his head. "I think we're through for now. Thank you, Mr. Royal."

They stood, shook hands, and left.

CHAPTER FIVE

I took my paper and coffee onto the patio. It was getting warmer as the sun rose higher. I was starting to feel a sheen of sweat brought on by the high humidity. Soon it would be too uncomfortable to sit outside. It was time for my morning jog on the beach.

I was just tying my running shoes when my cell phone rang. The caller I.D. told me it was J. D. Duncan.

"Good morning, again," I said.

"You had breakfast yet?"

"No. I was just going out for a run."

"If you'll join me at the Dolphin, I'll buy."

"Does this include Chief Warrant Officer Jacobi?"

"No. He's gone back to Cortez to finish a preliminary report or something."

"You're on. What time?"

"Right now. I'm just pulling into the parking lot."

"See you in five."

I put on a ball cap and drove out to Broadway, took a left on Gulf of Mexico Drive, and rode south. The royal poinciana trees that lined the road were in bloom, providing a canopy of red blossoms that brightened the island, a neat juxtaposition to the foreboding cloud that had encapsulated my paradise.

I turned into the Centre Shops, a small plaza set among seagrape trees, bougainvilleas, banyans, and other local flora. The Blue Dolphin Café was housed there and during the summer served mostly the local population. In the winter, during what is known as "The Season," snowbirds flocked there for breakfast and lunch giving the place a buzz that was absent in the doldrums of summer.

J.D. was in a booth near the front door. She stood as I approached. She was wearing a short-sleeved blouse, blue slacks, and low-heeled navy pumps, what she called her detective uniform. Her hair was pinned back from her ears and she was smiling. Her belt held a holstered Glock 19 semiautomatic pistol, a small case for her cell phone, and the gold detective's badge. A handheld police radio sat on the table.

She gave me a perfunctory hug, the kind that our islanders almost always give, a token of friendship, no more. J.D., whose real name was Jennifer Diane Duncan, and I had become good friends in the months since she had come to our key. We'd share drinks with friends at Tiny's on the edge of the Village or Mar Vista or the Hilton or Pattigeorge's, the occasional lunch or breakfast, and sometimes we'd go off by ourselves to one of the local restaurants or take my boat to Egmont Key for a day at the beach. Our relationship never progressed beyond that, even though there were moments, like now, when my heart skipped a beat at the sight of her.

She'd been very professional that morning at my house, and I had expected nothing less. She was working a case and had a colleague from another agency with her. It would not have been seemly for her to hug the witness. She was seeking information, but she also knew that I would be more forthcoming over a leisurely breakfast than in a staring contest with the Coast Guard.

We took our seats and the waitress brought me a cup of coffee and a glass of water. One thing about the Dolphin, they knew their regulars and what the regulars liked. J.D. was already half finished with her first cup. I knew she had a large capacity for coffee, perhaps a legacy of all those years in the cop business.

"Sorry about Jacobi," she said. "I just met him this morning when they called us out about the bodies they found."

"Not a problem, cupcake."

"Cupcake?"

"Um, Detective?"

"There. Isn't that better?"

"Sounds kind of formal."

She grinned. "Yeah, but it won't get you shot. 'Cupcake' just might."

"Point taken, Detective."

"I wanted to make sure you haven't thought of anything else about last night before I go talk to Logan."

"No. I gave you and Jacobi everything I remember."

"Okay. Just checking, Studmuffin."

"Studmuffin?" I asked.

"You don't like it?"

"No. It fits."

She smiled and my heart jumped up and did a little jig. "Right," she said and gave her attention to the server who'd come to take our breakfast order.

"Is Jacobi going to be investigating the murders?" I asked.

"No. That'll fall to me. Jacobi is an accident investigator. His job is to find out what caused the boat to go aground. Since the Sister Keys are part of the Town of Longboat Key, the murders are my jurisdiction."

"Do you see any connection between the shooting on the beach and the knifings on *Dulcimer*?"

"No. Well, at least not yet. There may be. I am curious about one thing you said this morning."

"Yes?"

She took a bite of her scrambled eggs, chewed for a moment, sipped her coffee. "You're pretty sure *Dulcimer* was making the dogleg when she went dark."

"Yes. She made the turn to the east, but never came back westerly."

"Okay. It was about that time that she headed toward you and the bar and just seconds later the engines died. Right so far?"

"Yes."

"Almost immediately after that, the generator shut off."

"Right."

"Somebody had to kill both Garrison and the girl and dump their bodies overboard in the time between when the lights went out and the Coast Guard got the generator running."

"I agree," I said.

"Assuming these weren't just random attacks, the killer would have had to stick close to the victims so that he'd know where they were when the lights went out."

I saw where she was going. "There had to have been at least two people involved. One to take out the captain and the other to kill the victims."

"You're pretty good at this," she said.

"Then we're assuming the attacks weren't random."

"Yes. I think if the killer had just been on a rampage, he wouldn't have had a buddy in the pilothouse."

I thought about that for a minute. "It's kind of circular reasoning, but it makes sense. Unless there was a connection between Garrison and Katherine, the killings were random. But, the very fact that there were two bad guys aboard, and the confusion on the boat was planned, would militate against the assumption of random killings. There must have been some connection between the two victims."

"Probably so. We just don't see it yet."

"What about a connection to the dead guy on the beach?"

"Same problem. If there is a connection, we can't see it yet. Desmond, the man on the beach, was from Atlanta, Garrison was from Jacksonville, and Katherine was from Charlotte. Katherine and Desmond were in the same age range, but Garrison was old enough to be their father. Mrs. Garrison had never heard of either Katherine or Desmond."

It was a puzzle that would not be solved that morning. What I didn't know was that it wouldn't be solved over the next month either.

We finished our breakfast, catching up on island gossip and speculating more about the murders. On Longboat Key, a detective's job is mostly about investigating car break-ins at the North Shore Road beach access or the occasional home burglary. Homicide seldom intrudes on our cosseted island, but murder was no stranger to J.D., and I knew she'd handle these with the same intensity she'd brought to her job in Miami.

CHAPTER SIX

It was the middle of June and still chilly. The last of the snow had finally melted and little green shoots of grass were tentatively poking their heads out of the newly thawed North Dakota dirt, as if sniffing the air to make sure the temperature had risen to the point of survival. The large man was bent over a tire, snapping it to the rim. He'd finish and put the tire on the car, tightening the lug nuts and handing the keys to the lady sitting in the small waiting room.

He was glad to see spring. The frigid hours in the unheated garage with only a small electric space heater to break the grip of the freezing air were over for a few months. He was tired, his back starting to bother him already, months before his twenty-third birthday. What would he be like at fifty? Old? Like his dad, a man wasting away in this little garage in small town America, a forgotten village in a corner of the upper Midwest.

He finished the tire, went inside and took a credit card from the woman who'd taught him in fifth grade over at the town elementary school. They chatted a bit, mostly about other children with whom he'd grown up. Some had gone off to college or the military, and others had stayed in the dismal little town, eking out a living farming or working construction, what little there was of it, or carrying a badge, working for the local sheriff.

He'd always known that he wasn't college material. He just didn't have the head for it. He'd learned the mechanics trade at the knee of his father who'd run this one-man garage since he'd returned home from military service. It was now a two-man operation, with the old man working as hard and as long as the son. The business provided a modicum of income, enough to keep his mom and dad in food and shelter and now to pay a salary to the son. The boy had worked in the garage part-time since he could remember, and on the day he graduated from high school, he became a full-time employee.

The young man, whose name was Marcus, was looking forward to the evening. He'd been dating one of the Osburn girls for several months, the younger one named Riley, and today was her twenty-first birthday. On their last date the unspoken promise had been made, that on the day she turned twenty-one she would offer him her virginity.

He'd taken off early the day before and driven down to Minot, the nearest town with a jewelry store. He'd bought his girl a ring with a small diamond, bargaining with the owner and striking a deal that he could afford, agreeing to make weekly payments directly to the store. It was not an obligation he assumed lightly, and he would make those payments even if he had to forego food.

Marcus had been raised by parents who valued honesty and hard work and he'd learned the lessons they taught. Like his father, he was an honorable man and would pay the jeweler every penny owed.

The young man went to the bathroom and used something called Goop to clean the grease and dirt from his hands. His nails were cracked and jagged and grease seemed to accumulate under them with a vigor that even Goop couldn't overcome. He shook his head. Riley didn't mind. She had told him once that the grease was the mark of honest work, and a man couldn't do much better than that. He smiled at the thought of her, and of the promise the night would bring.

The teacher with the bad tire was the last customer of the day. Marcus closed up the shop and walked the two blocks to the house he shared with his parents. They liked Riley and would be happy to know they were to be married. He knew he'd have to find another place to live. His meager salary from the shop would supplement Riley's salary from the town's only restaurant where she waited tables. They could make it, but would have to put off babies for a few years.

Spring days are long in the northern latitudes and the sun wouldn't set until nine thirty. He showered, shaved, and dressed in a clean pair of jeans and a plaid long-sleeve shirt. The temperature was in the low sixties and would drop further when the sun went down. He pulled a worn windbreaker over the shirt, slipped into his gym shoes, and walked toward the house where his girl and their friends waited.

It was only later, when Marcus didn't show for the party, that Riley and her brother went looking for him. They followed the route along which he would have walked on the way to Riley's parents' house. And it was there, in the gathering dusk of a cool spring evening in the far north of America, in a ditch beside the road, that they found his lifeless body. The hard-working, honorable young man who loved a girl named Riley had been shot through the head.

CHAPTER SEVEN

I was sitting on the patio of my cottage staring at the bay. It was early on a Monday morning near the end of July. The sun had barely risen over the mainland, the heat of a summer day lingering just over the horizon, the air not yet soggy with the humidity that would come with the sun. This was the favorite part of my day, a time to sip my coffee, read the morning's paper, and enjoy the slight breeze blowing over the water.

The lead story in the Sarasota paper was about the murders that had taken place on our key six weeks before. There had been no progress. The police had no clues, no suspects, and no indication that the cases would be closed anytime soon.

I'd kept up with the progress of the cases during my regular visits with J. D. Duncan. She was stymied. She could find no connection between any of the victims. As far as she could tell, none of the dead had known any of the others. There was no reasonable place that their lives would have intersected. Garrison was an aging lawyer in a silk-stocking firm in North Florida who handled real estate matters. Katherine Brewster was a waitress at a Hooters Restaurant in Charlotte, North Carolina, and Desmond had just finished college and had been accepted at the Georgia State University Law School in Atlanta for the fall semester. He hadn't made up his mind to enroll and had been looking for a job in the Atlanta area. His brand-new wife was from Savannah and was planning to teach at an elementary school in the Atlanta suburbs.

The captain of *Dulcimer* had been murdered. Somebody broke his neck. The first people on the scene didn't pay any attention, thinking that since there was no blood, he must have died of natural causes. As soon as the medical examiner took a look at the body, he realized that the captain's neck was broken. The autopsy confirmed and the official cause of death was listed as "mid-level cervical fracture caused by a person or persons unknown." Death had been instantaneous.

The island had been quiet, the gossip trailing off as the mystery of the murders wore on without solution. The days became hotter, the humidity more pronounced, the sun brighter. Summer on Florida's southwest coast is a time of aimlessness, the people lethargic and huddled in their air-conditioned homes. The brave ones venture out to the Publix market or lunch in an air-conditioned restaurant. The outdoor dining areas, aswarm with snowbirds during the season, were empty. No self-respecting Floridian would dine al fresco in the summer heat. Time itself seemed to slow, the earth's rotation sluggish in its daily movement, the heat only slightly diminished by the afternoon thunderstorms that prowled the state, regular as a Swiss timepiece, bringing the deluge that caused the pavement to steam and the air to hang ever more heavily over the sweltering peninsula.

I looked out over the bay, a flat gray expanse of still water, not a puff of wind to disturb its quiet surface. *Recess* sat quietly in her berth, no movement, the lines holding her to the dock were slack. A brown pelican sat in repose on a piling, still, as if not daring to move for fear that the heat would overcome him. A fish jumped nearby and the pelican took no notice. A kind of torpor had settled over the island, bringing with it a stillness of body and mind. I sat and watched and tried to summon the energy to head for the beach and my morning jog.

My doorbell rang, a strangely discordant note in the early morning quiet. I looked at my watch. Not yet seven o'clock. It was either bad news or a friend who knew I was an early riser dropping by for a cup of coffee. That is not as unusual as it sounds. It's part of the island rhythm that we have adapted to, friends visiting at odd hours, knowing that if you didn't want to be disturbed you'd simply ignore the doorbell. Feelings would not be hurt.

I left my coffee and paper on the table and walked barefoot to the front door. I was wearing a white T-shirt with the Grady-White boat logo on the breast pocket. The back of the shirt featured a picture of a twenty-eight-foot boat and the name of the dealer, Cannon's Marina, owned by my friends David and Lucille Miller. Khaki cargo shorts completed my skimpy summer attire.

I opened the door to find a stranger fidgeting uncomfortably on my front stoop. He was about six feet tall, lean and fit, a head of gray hair, the planes of his face sharp and creased by years of tension, bright blue eyes, good teeth showing when he smiled. He was wearing a pair of taupe slacks, white golf shirt with the logo of an Atlanta country club on the pocket, cordovan loafers. I could tell by the contours of his body that he was younger than his face and hair made him appear.

He smiled, and held out his hand. "Long time, L.T."

L.T. The universal appellation given by soldiers to the young lieutenants with whom they serve. I'd once been a nineteen-year-old lieutenant, back at the tail end of the Vietnam War, back when I wore a green beret and killed people who were trying to kill me. I'd led some of the toughest men on earth, an A team of U.S. Army Special Forces, the storied Green Berets, as we prowled the jungles seeking our human prey. We became closer than family, closer than anyone who hasn't been part of a small group of young men engaged in mortal combat can understand. It has often been said that soldiers do not fight wars for honor, or country, or policies dictated by governments in faraway capitals, but for their buddies, the ones who share their danger and their fear and their disgust, who understand the emotional damage done to one who kills another human being whose only crime was wearing the uniform of the opposing army, who identifies with the necessity of the kill, because that other soldier would have killed you or your buddy for the same reason.

My mind flashed back to a time when flies buzzed in the heat of a quiet day, the high sun baking the plain on which I lay, the sound of gunshots in the distance giving substance to the combat that was about to come. I lay in the tall grass near a line of trees that marked the beginning of another jungle-like expanse of Southeast Asia. My left leg was afire, the result of the bullet that had gone through my calf, fired by some scared kid in the Viet Cong unit ensconced in the trees.

My men had moved on, attacking, going forward to clear the area of the enemy. Our medic had stayed with me, wrapped my leg, and told me not to try to stand. He thought the slug had nicked one or both of the bones in the lower leg. I ignored him, tried to stand, and fell back when the pain struck, a sapling taken down by one stroke of a good ax. Blood was running down my leg, warm and bright in the harsh sun.

"Goddamnit, L.T., you don't listen good."

"Okay, Doc. I'll stay here. You go on. The guys might need you."

"They'll be fine. I'm getting you back to the LZ."

The landing zone was three miles away, and I didn't think I'd make it back without a stretcher. We'd improvise that when the team reassembled. And Doc was right. The men would be fine without him. Most had been cross-trained as medics and could handle things. All of them, including Doc, were Rangers and infantrymen. Doc had taken extra training in medical matters back at Ft. Sam Houston, Texas, so he was designated the team's medic. But at heart, he was an infantryman, and in the end, he would act as one.

We sat quietly, neither of us saying anything. The pain was getting worse, but I didn't want morphine. I needed to stay coherent. When I took the bullet, command of the unit had fallen to Master Sergeant Jimbo Merryman, the most capable soldier I'd ever known. My men were in good hands. I had a walkie-talkie, a small radio with limited range, but I could talk to Jimbo if I needed to.

I heard the occasional snap of rifle fire in the forest, but much of it was muffled by the thick vegetation. An hour passed and the air came alive with the sound of gunfire. A machine gun chattered in the distance, then the whoop of mortar rounds.

Jimbo came up on the radio. "L.T., Charlie has moved in behind us in force. I don't think we can get through. I'm going to have to go forward, get through these woods, and find another landing zone so the chopper can extract us. Can you move?"

"Go for it, Jimbo," I said. "We're on our way back to the original LZ. It's too hot here to bring in a chopper."

"Can you walk, sir?"

"I can, Jimbo. You take care of the men. Doc's with me. I'm fine."

"Will do, sir."

I put the radio down, looked at the soldier sitting beside me. "Get out of here, Doc. It's going to get hot as soon as Charlie starts coming out of those trees."

"Yes, sir. We got to go."

"You go. I can't walk."

"I ain't leaving you, L.T. You remember what they did to Ronnie Easton."

Easton was one of us. He'd gotten separated from the team the week before and disappeared. Late that night, we'd snuck up on an encampment in the bush that was full of black pajama clad Viet Cong, fifty or more of them. We heard Easton start to scream. He screamed for a long time, longer than any of us wanted to contemplate. The men begged for permission to go after him, but Jimbo and I kept them hidden. We wouldn't help Easton by getting ourselves killed.

Finally, the screaming stopped. We waited out the night and moved in at first light. The VC had left, and all we found was Ronnie Easton hanging by his feet from a tree, his body badly mutilated. He'd suffered greatly and died in a trackless jungle about as far from his South Carolina home as he could get. He'd died terribly, and we'd all heard it. We cut him down and brought his body out, back to what served as civilization, our putrid base camp at the edge of the mountains.

"I remember. I've got a loaded rifle, and I know exactly how many rounds are in the mag. I'll save the last one for myself. Go. Lieutenants get to give orders. That's one right there."

"I'm going, sir."

He squatted beside me. "Now, listen up. You ever hear of the fireman's carry?"

"Won't work, Doc. Too far to go."

"I'm going to put you on my shoulders and we're going to move. It ain't going to be comfortable, but I'll hold onto your right leg so you can move the left one a bit when the pain hits."

He lifted me onto his shoulders. I was wrapped around him like a stole, my right arm around his chest, my left over his shoulder, my left leg sticking straight out from his left shoulder. He held onto my left arm and right leg and we set off. He'd slung both his and my M-16s around his neck and they banged against his chest as he walked. It was going to be a rough afternoon.

It was slow going. We'd walk for fifteen minutes and take a five-minute break, sip from our canteens, and rest in the knee-high grass. Doc checked my calf and on the third stop redressed the wound. We were five minutes into the fourth leg of the trek when he came to a stop and set me down. "We got Charlies coming out of that tree line," he said.

I looked back out over the plain. "I see them. They're pretty far back, but coming fast. You've got to get out of here."

"There's a dry creek bed about five minutes in front of us. It's got some big rocks that'll give us some cover. Let's go."

"Five minutes with me on your back is going to slow you enough to give Charlie a chance to catch up."

"Then we'll attack."

I laughed. "There's got to be a hundred of those guys coming our way."

"That'll make it a fair fight. Ain't a one of those pissants got a green beanie."

He picked me up and started toward the creek bed. We'd make it, but we had two rifles and a lot of ammo against a hundred rifles and a lot more ammo. Not very good odds.

We had moved about a hundred yards when we heard the distinctive *whomp whomp* of a chopper. The enemy didn't have helicopters, so it was one of ours. Doc set me on the ground and stood, waving, trying to get the pilot's attention. The radio on the ground next to me came alive.

"Squatter six. This is Birddog four."

I picked up the radio. "Squatter Six."

"What's your name?"

I knew the pilot was making sure that we weren't enemy soldiers trying to lure him close enough for a shot with a rocket-propelled grenade that could bring him down. "Matt Royal," I said.

"Hometown?"

That wasn't information found on the dog tags and was another layer of security for the pilot. "Sanford, Florida," I said.

"What do you want to be when you grow up, son?"

"Fuck you, Flyboy. Get down here. We sure do need a ride home."

He laughed. "There's a shitpot load of Charlies on your six coming out of that tree line. They're moving fast. They must know you're out here."

"Yeah, we saw them," I said. "They're about five hundred yards behind us."

"I've called in a fast mover. He's due in less than two minutes. Drop smoke on my say-so. As soon as he makes his pass, I'll set down right where you are. Be ready to load quick. I don't want to wait around."

"Roger that."

Seconds passed and then I saw it on the horizon, angling down, moving fast, the twin intakes of the F-4 Phantom barely visible in the distance, the ordinance slung under his wings menacing.

"Smoke," rattled the radio.

I threw a smoke grenade toward the advancing VC. Its red trail would mark us, so that the F-4 jock wouldn't plaster the good guys with whatever he was carrying. The jet was moving over us not two hundred feet up, the sound of the straining engines roaring around us, the sound of death to the VC who were turning and running back toward the tree line.

I saw canisters drop from the plane and then a terrible roar as fire engulfed the struggling troops. I hoped they were the ones who had tortured Ronnie Easton, that their deaths would be as painful, if much quicker, than Ronnie's.

The jet pulled up and began a two-hundred-seventy-degree turn, coming back across the scattering troops. The pilot dropped more canisters, this time between the fleeing VC and the tree line. They were caught between the lines of fire, the heat blast warming the air around Doc and me. I could hear the men screaming, terrible screams of pain, not unlike those of Ronnie Easton. I chose to believe that we were taking out the same men who'd killed him. Maybe we were.

The smell of gasoline wafted over us, the residue of the burning napalm. The F-4 did a barrel roll just above us, waggled his wings, and climbed into the waiting sky, gone in an instant.

I watched the Huey descend at a sharp angle. The red cross on the white background was clearly visible on its nose. A med-evac. I don't know why they wore those crosses. Charlie didn't cut them any slack because of it.

Doc loaded me onto the chopper and crawled in. We were taken directly to a field hospital where the medics found a clean, if painful, wound, no fractures. They promised I'd be back in shape in a couple of weeks. Just as we landed, the pilot told us that he'd heard on his radio net that our team had been safely extracted with no casualties. I breathed a sigh of relief.

Doc went back to our base camp to wait for the team's return, and I was shipped to Saigon to an army general hospital and spent three weeks recuperating. Jimbo Merryman caught a chopper ride down to visit for a day and assured me that the team was doing fine. They had been pulled from regular patrols and were getting a little downtime themselves back at the base camp. Two of the guys had flown out to Hawaii for R & R, relaxation and recreation, which meant they'd drink a lot and find women willing to trade a bit of their virtue for stories of soldiers at war.

I returned to the unit to find it intact, except for Doc, who'd been transferred into some extra secretive unit that had no name. We'd heard rumors about it, but no one actually knew any specifics. I never saw him again, until that July morning on Longboat Key when I opened my front door and found him standing on my stoop.

CHAPTER EIGHT

"Doc," I said, "Come on in."

We shook hands, hugged, and he walked into my living room. I choked back some emotion. "Man, it's good to see you, Doc. How the hell have you been?"

"Okay, Matt. I've seen better days."

"Let's get some coffee and sit out back."

We went into the kitchen, and I poured a mug full of the black coffee. "You're still drinking it black, I suppose."

He grinned. "Damn right. No cream in the bush, L.T."

We went to the patio and sat in two wicker chairs with cushioned seats covered in a floral pattern. A light breeze moved across the bay, barely touching the water. Out by my dock, a fish jumped, a mullet probably, running from a predator. The sun was up, hanging a few degrees above the horizon, painting the bay in pastels of orange and ochre and crimson. It was quiet, the only noise coming from the splash of the diving pelicans that lived on nearby Jewfish Key. Doc and I were quiet too, each in his own thoughts, remembering those long ago days when we were young soldiers doing what we thought was right, trying to survive, dreaming of the big PX that was the United States, of going home and living out the rest of our lives. Mine had turned out well. I wondered about Doc's.

"How did you make your way to my door, Doc?"

"Do you remember my real name?"

"Of course. Charles T. Desmond, aka Chaz. Hometown, Macon, Georgia. Graduate of Willingham High School, class of nineteen seventy. Had a girlfriend named Julie."

"Damn. You're good."

"I remember them all, Doc. Every last one of them. I knew them, their hometowns, their hopes and dreams, the ones who came home and the ones who didn't. Not a day goes by that I don't think about you guys."

"The same thing happens to me, Matt. I'll be in the middle of something, concentrating on whatever it is, and one or all of you guys will come traipsing across my brain. It's almost supernatural, but it usually gives me a smile. I get a little warm feeling deep down in my gut, even when I think about the ones who didn't make it back."

"They all made it back, Doc. We never left a man."

"You know what I mean. We got them all back, but some of them were just cold meat. Jimbo Merryman told me about you."

"Good old Jimbo. I go fishing with him now and then, down on Lake Okeechobee."

"He told me. He also told me you'd become a lawyer and were living here on Longboat Key."

"I'm sorry it took us so long to hook up, Doc. Back in Nam, when I got out of the hospital, you were gone. Nobody knew exactly where."

"You remember what they did to Ronnie Easton."

"Cut him up like so much fish bait."

"He was my best friend. I wanted some revenge. More than we got with the napalm that day in the grass. I'd heard about this deep-cover unit that assassinated the VC top dogs. I went down to Saigon and rattled around until some colonel decided to listen to me. He checked out my credentials and the next thing I knew I was part of the secret world. I became part of a group of special-operations types, soldiers, Marines, and CIA people, called Operation Thanatos, after the Greek God of Death. We went after the leaders, and we took them out. It wasn't bad duty, if you didn't mind killing up close. I didn't. I kept thinking about Ronnie Easton and how those bastards butchered him."

"Did it do any good?"

He smiled ruefully. "No. I still hear Ronnie screaming sometimes in the night when I can't sleep. When I first got home, I went up to Mc-Cormick to visit his grave. It didn't do anything for me. There was just a slab of concrete with his name on it, sort of lost in a big cemetery behind a church. Some of those graves had been there for over a hundred years.

There were crypts that had fallen in on themselves from lack of maintenance. The inscriptions chiseled into some of the older stones were mostly
obliterated by age. Ronnie had a few wilted flowers. Somebody had
planted a little American flag at the head of his grave. That was all. I
couldn't feel anything. And I knew that in a few years, in a time after we're
gone, when the memories of Ronnie are lost forever, his grave will be as
meaningless as all those others. And maybe the screams will finally stop."

"I'm sorry, Doc. I am so fucking sorry."

"I married the girl from high school, you know. Julie. We had a son.
I named him James Ronald Desmond, after Ronnie. He grew up into a
fine young man, married a pretty girl from Savannah whom he'd met at
the University of Georgia. And then some son of a bitch shot him dead on
the beach over near the Hilton. Six weeks ago."

It hit me. I'm sure I must have heard the name of the shooting victim,
but it didn't connect, didn't even make an impression on me. "Shit, Doc.
I'm sorry. I never made that connection."

"He was our only child, Matt. Julie's not doing well. This thing is
about to kill her. She had a hard pregnancy, but wanted Jimmy so bad she
stayed in bed most of the nine months. He came out healthy, and so did
she, but she couldn't get pregnant again. We gave up on that years ago, but
we'd been happy. Now, life is a dismal pit."

"Do you know if the police have any leads on who killed your boy?"

"Not much. A detective, a woman named J. D. Duncan, is working
the case."

"I know her. She's good."

"Yeah. I checked her out. A lot of years on the Miami-Dade police
force, ten years as a detective and toward the end, the vice commander of
homicide. She's good, but she has almost nothing to go on."

"I wish there was something I could do," I said.

"There is. I want you to sue somebody."

"I don't practice anymore, Doc."

"I checked you out, too. You were one of the best trial lawyers
around, practiced a long time in Orlando, and gave it up to come here and
be a beach bum."

That pissed me off. "You checked me out?" I asked, my voice cold.

"Don't get your panties in a wad, L.T. I'm a businessman. I check people out before I get into bed with them."

"And just what kind of business are you in, Doc?" My voice was tinged with suspicion and skepticism.

He chuckled. "You can check me out, Matt. After I got out of the army, I went to Georgia Tech, got a degree in mechanical engineering, and then over the years built a consulting firm that does business in twenty-six states. It's all legit."

I relaxed. "Sorry, Doc. I've had a few rough patches over the last few years. People trying to kill me, if you can imagine that."

He laughed. "I can't. Will you help?"

"Asked the man who saved my life. It ain't like I owe you much, Doc. Whatever you want, if it's in my power to do, I'll do it. Tell me how I can help."

"I understand that you can often prove a case in civil court that you couldn't prove in criminal court."

"That's right. The standard of proof is different. In criminal court, the prosecution has to prove the state's case beyond a reasonable doubt. In civil court, the plaintiff only has to prove his case by the greater weight of the evidence. That's quite a difference in the burden of proof. What are you thinking?"

"And any evidence you dig up can then be used in the criminal system?"

"Yes."

"Good. I'm thinking that if you could use the civil system to gather evidence that the cops can't get to, we may be able to find out who killed Jimmy."

"Then what?"

"I'd want it all turned over to the prosecutors. I'm not going after them, if that's what's bothering you. I learned back in Operation Thanatos that all the killing in the world won't bring back the dead. I just want to see justice done to the bastards who killed my son."

"Do you have any kind of a starting place? Any suspicions about who may have wanted to hurt your son? Or you, for that matter?"

"I've thought a lot about that, but can't come up with anybody. If

Detective Duncan has any persons of interest, I think they call them, maybe you could sue those people and sort some things out that law enforcement can't get into."

"It's a thought, Doc. But we have to have a starting place. We can't just haul off and sue somebody. We have to find a legitimate defendant. Somebody who we think is guilty, that we at least have an outside chance of proving he murdered your son."

"Will you talk to the detective?"

"Sure. She's a good friend of mine. So is the chief of police."

He looked at his watch. "I've got to go. My plane is at the airport, and I have to be in Montgomery for a mid-morning meeting."

"Your plane?"

He grinned. "Yeah. Didn't I mention that I'm richer than hell? I can pay your fees."

"You paid that fee, Doc. A long time ago. Back in the grass."

CHAPTER NINE

Doc left me with my thoughts drifting back to the men I'd served with in Vietnam. I had not kept up with them, and I wasn't sure why. Perhaps it was the fear that they would trigger memories I'd rather forget, bring the past into the present. I could not reconcile those terrible days in a war-torn country with the life I had now, living quietly on an island awash in sunshine and good cheer, with friends and fishing and booze and the occasional pretty girl to share my bed.

A couple of years back, I'd run into my old first sergeant, Jimbo Merryman. He lived over in the middle of the state near Lake Okeechobee and every now and then I'd drive over and we'd take his skiff out for some bass fishing in the lake. He kept up with the guys, but we didn't talk much about those days or the people who had shared them with us.

I wasn't sure about the civil suit that Doc wanted me to file. I owed him a lot, but I also owed my profession something. I wouldn't file a groundless suit, even if the end result could be justice. On the other hand, if I could find someone who I genuinely thought culpable in the death of Jim Desmond, I'd go after him. This wasn't the kind of suit that resulted in money damages for the plaintiff, in this case Doc Desmond. The idea of the suit was that Doc was seeking compensation for the death of his son. But that was subterfuge, what the lawyers call a legal fiction. What we really wanted was to uncover evidence that would lead us to the murderer. We'd turn over whatever we found to the police and the prosecutors and let them proceed in the criminal courts. We'd drop the suit right then. Money was not the object.

I called Jimbo Merryman. "Top," I said, when he answered, "it's Matt Royal."

"How's the boy warrior?"

I laughed. "Hanging in there, Top. How're you?"

"Couldn't be better. You want to come down for a little fishing?"

"Can't right now. I need to ask you something."

"Shoot."

"Doc Desmond showed up at my door this morning."

"I told him where you lived. I hope that was all right."

"It was. I owe him a lot, and it was good to see him."

"He's got a lot of trouble, Matt. Losing his boy and all."

"Tell me about him, Top." I was using the name all army first sergeants are called informally by the men. They were the top sergeants. One of the most important ranks in the armed forces.

"He's made a lot of money over the years. He's done it honestly and by hard work. He's a good man, Matt. I hope you can help him."

"He wants me to file a lawsuit against his son's murderer if we can find him. We would hope to gather some evidence that might be out of reach of the criminal prosecutors and turn what we find over to the cops for prosecution. Do you think he has any ulterior motive for such a suit?"

"No. I think he wants to find a little justice in all of this. His son is dead, his marriage may be dead too if Julie can't rouse herself from her grief. He's grabbing at straws, I think, but he's an honest man, Matt. He's the same guy we knew in Nam. Only richer. A lot richer." He chuckled.

"Okay, Top. I just wanted your take on him. I'll do whatever I can."

"I told Doc he could count on you."

"I'll call soon and we'll go fishing."

"You do that, L.T."

Jimbo was not only the best soldier I'd ever known, he was also the best judge of men I'd ever met. Maybe the two went together. He was a great soldier because he could size up a man in an instant. I'd never known him to be wrong. Maybe this time he was.

I shook my head. I'd put the courtroom and all that it entails behind me. I didn't want to get involved again in the shenanigans that the modern-day lawyer uses. The defendant always pushes for delay. Delay is good for them. They get to bill more hours, make more money with which to stoke the fires of the modern big firm demons. I'd found the tactics stifling, irritating, and detrimental to all the clients on both sides of a case.

The Holy Grail of the judiciary was a clear docket. Judges pushed hard for case closure, but never seemed to understand that by allowing some of the stupidity that bogged down the system, they were not clearing their cases. A closed case was not a billable case. Lawyers didn't like them, but judges lusted after them. It was not a happy forum for litigants with good causes.

I didn't want any part of it, not the other lawyers, not the judges, not the useless paper pushing that was the norm. But I owed Doc, and even if I didn't, I'd want to help. No matter how many years pass, men who forged bonds at war are still brothers and when one is wounded, the others gather round to lend what assistance they can. Doc had risked his life for me. The least I could do was deal with a few idiots for him.

I called J. D. Duncan and asked her to meet me for lunch at Nosh-A-Rye on Avenue of the Flowers.

CHAPTER TEN

The place was almost empty. I took a booth toward the back of the restaurant, but with a view to the front door. I ordered a Miller Lite from the waitress and told her I was expecting a guest. J.D. arrived about five minutes later. She swooped in, hugged me, shifted her gun around to a more comfortable position, and took her seat facing me.

She looked at the bottle on the table. "Beer? At lunch?"

"I'm a sybarite. What can I say?"

"Hmm," she said. "I think something's on your mind."

"I had a visit from a ghost this morning. An old buddy from the war. I haven't seen him since we left Vietnam."

"Ouch. I know you don't like to think too much about those days."

"Yeah. Have you had any luck on the murders?"

The waitress came for our orders. The menu was long and complicated. A lot of dishes were named for movie stars of the '30s and '40s. I knew it was all good, and I ordered potato pancakes and a brisket of beef. J.D. had a salad and a Diet Coke.

"Which murders?" she asked.

I noticed a little crinkle around her eyes. I looked at her, waiting for the smile. She favored me with it and I melted a little.

"Why don't you bring me up to date on all murders on the island in the last three months."

"Does this have something to do with your visitor this morning?"

"Yeah. My pal's name is Charles Desmond. Ring any bells?"

She sat back in her seat. "The dead guy on the beach is your buddy's son?"

"Was."

"Well, yes. Was."

"I didn't make the connection until he came by this morning."

J.D. blew out a breath. "He's a nice guy. I wish I could help him, but we've run into a blank wall on the investigation. He calls now and then, but I never have anything to tell him."

"He wants me to file a civil suit."

"Against the department?"

"No. He thinks you walk on water. He wants to use the suit as a vehicle to help you find evidence."

"I knew he was rich, but I'd think he'd have to have more money than God to get you out of retirement. Who's he going to sue?"

"That's the problem. I don't know where to start. I was hoping you'd share your file with me."

"I'd have to run that by the chief."

"If you're willing to help, I'll call the chief myself and ask him about it. I didn't want to step on your toes."

She grinned. "You were afraid I might react negatively and kick your butt or something."

"There's that. Plus, I want you on board with me."

"If the chief says it's okay, I'm all for it. I'll do whatever I can."

"I'm not getting paid, by the way. Just in case you're interested."

"I didn't think you were. Mr. Desmond must have been a good friend for you to come out of retirement for him."

"A long time ago he put his life on the line to save mine. No matter what you do after that, you cannot repay the debt in full. It's one thing to save a life, like a nurse or doctor, but it's so much more when somebody puts saving your life in front of saving his own."

"That's some motivation you've got there, friend. Be careful that you don't get too close to the fire. You could get burned."

We ate a leisurely lunch, talked of things of little seriousness, laughed a bit, exchanged a couple of jokes. Her cell phone rang. She looked at the caller ID. "Dispatch. I've got to take this one. Sorry."

She left the booth and walked outside. She was back in a couple of minutes, put a ten dollar bill on the table and said, "Duty calls. I've got to interview a lady who lost her watch at the airport in Detroit last March. Says she needs a police report for the insurance company."

I laughted and handed her the ten. "This one's on me."

"Wouldn't that fall under bribing a cop?"

"It might, but you can trust me. I'm a lawyer."

She laughed, snapped the bill out of my hand, and left.

I went from the restaurant to the police station. I stood inside the waiting room and watched the dispatcher finish a telephone call. She rolled her chair over and opened the sliding glass window that separated her from the public.

"Hey, Matt," she said. "Who're you here to see today?"

"Hey, Iva. Is the chief in?"

"Sure. Let me tell him you're here."

She shut the little window and picked up the phone. She said a few words, hesitated, hung up, and motioned me through the door that led to the offices in the back of the building. I walked down a short hall and knocked on the open door of Chief Bill Lester's office. His head was down reading a memo, one of dozens strewn across his desk top.

He looked up. "Come on in, Matt. Damn paperwork gets bigger and bigger. How're you doing?"

Bill Lester was my fishing and drinking buddy and the guy with whom I regularly shared a grouper sandwich at the Sports Page Bar and Grille in downtown Sarasota.

"You gotta come out from under that mess sometime. You want to meet me for a beer at Tiny's this afternoon after work?"

"It's a date. But you didn't just stop by to offer me a beer."

I told him about Doc Desmond and that I wanted his permission for J.D. to show me the police investigative file. I also told him what I wanted to do with any information I turned up.

"Might as well, Matt. We're at a dead end here. Who knows? You might turn up something that we can hang our hat on. Tell J.D. to give you the file and any help she can. I worry that I'm not keeping her busy enough. I know several agencies around here that would jump at the chance to hire her."

"I don't think she's going anywhere, Bill, but I'll put her to work."

"Go for it. Keep me in the loop."

The chief went back to his paperwork and I headed home. I called J.D. and told her what Lester had said and asked if she'd like to drop by my cottage later that afternoon. She said she'd make a complete copy of the file and bring it with her.

CHAPTER ELEVEN

The file was not large, not for a murder investigation. J.D. explained there just wasn't much to go on. Very little evidence. There were statements from witnesses, but none of them were even sure where the shot came from. They had been on the beach and saw young Desmond fall backward when the slug tore into his chest.

J.D. and I were sitting in my living room, the file spread out on the coffee table. I was sipping from a can of Miller Lite and the detective was easing into a bottle of Chardonnay, one glass at a time. It was a little after five in the afternoon. The sun was moving toward the west, toward the sea into which it would soon sink. I looked at my watch. We had about three hours until sunset. The day was clear with a smattering of clouds hanging low over the Gulf. It would be a spectacular sunset, and I wanted to be sitting on the deck of the Hilton watching it.

"You got time for dinner at the Hilton tonight?" I asked. "We could sit on the deck and watch the sunset."

"Sure. Just us and all the other tourists."

I smiled. I loved our sunsets and she always kidded me about it. Said it was something for the tourists to enjoy. I took the position that sunsets were tonics for beach bums and since I was a beach bum we had to watch the sun set.

I pulled some photographs from one of the folders. They were grainy, black-and-white, some kind of security photos probably.

"From the elevator at the Grand Beach condos," J.D. said.

"You're pretty sure that's where the shot came from?"

"Yes. It's the tallest building in that area and we found a filtered cigarette butt and some scuff marks on the flat roof at about where the shot had to come from."

"Did you find the slug that killed him?"

"Yes. It went right through him and hit the sand. We found it with a metal detector."

"Did the bullet tell you anything?"

"Only that it was a thirty caliber."

"Anything else?"

"No. And we couldn't pull any DNA from the butt. We don't even know if it belonged to the shooter. We're thinking it didn't, because it'd been on the roof long enough that the weather had degraded any DNA that might have been there."

"You're sure you've got the right building?"

"Pretty sure. The crime-scene techs were able to figure a pretty good trajectory of the bullet. It fits with the Grand Beach and the scuff marks we found on the roof."

"I'm not sure I understand the significance of the scuff marks."

"We'd had a gully washer the night before. Lots of rain. It would have washed off any marks that had been on the roof. The new ones had to have been made that morning and the maintenance guys were the only ones with keys to the roof. Neither of them had been up there that morning."

I held up the photographs. "Elevator surveillance?"

"Yes. Not much help."

I looked closely at the pictures. Each one had a time stamp in the bottom right corner. Several were taken about an hour before the second group. I separated them out according to the time stamp. I saw a man wearing a light windbreaker jacket made of some dark material, jeans, running shoes, and a ball cap pulled low on his forehead. He never looked at the camera. In all the pictures, he had his head down.

"He knew about the camera," I said.

"Yes. We never got a shot of his face."

"He's carrying a briefcase in all of them."

"We're assuming that was a container for his rifle. He could break it down and it would fit perfectly in the case."

I looked more closely at the pictures. "Are you sure this is a man?"

"Because he's small?"

"Yes. It could be a woman."

"I thought of that, but it doesn't seem too plausible. Women usually aren't professional killers. They have to have some other motive. Jealously, sometimes money, something that rattles their system and makes them angry enough to kill. Besides, most women wouldn't be trained snipers, and we think this guy had to have been well trained in order to hit the target at that range."

I sat quietly for a moment, staring at the pictures. "How did the killer know that Jim Desmond would be jogging on the beach that morning?"

"I don't know."

"Have you considered the possibility that the murder was random? That the killer just went up on that rooftop with the idea of killing somebody, anybody, and Jim came trotting up?"

"We considered that. But there have been no other killings in the past three years in Florida that match the pattern here. I think if it was just random, we'd have had more murders just like this one. A serial killer can't stop with just one."

"What about the killings on *Dulcimer*?" I asked.

"No connection that we can see."

"What if the sheer randomness of all the killings *is* the connection?"

J.D. shook her head. "Doesn't fit. One was a long-range shooting and the others were knifings. The captain was killed by someone skilled in martial arts. Either that, or the killer was very strong. Up close and brutal. And we're pretty sure there had to be a team of at least two people working the boat. One to take care of the captain and another to kill the passengers."

"And you never found any connections between any of the four dead people."

"None."

"If Jim's killing wasn't random, then the killer must have known that Jim would be on the beach that morning. Any thoughts?"

J.D. nodded. "Desmond had been at the Hilton for three days before his wedding. He jogged the beach every morning at about the same time. We think the killer was betting on his being at the same place at pretty much the same time on the day of the murder."

"Do you think there was anything significant about the fact that he was murdered on the day after his wedding?"

"I thought about that, but decided that it was probably a coincidence. If the new wife had been part of it, it would have made sense for her to wait until she was married to have him killed. Then she would inherit."

"Jim came from a wealthy family. Maybe that was a motive."

"Meredith, the wife, has more money than the whole Desmond family. Her grandfather was richer than I can imagine and set up a trust fund for Meredith. She came into control of it on her twenty-first birthday. Even if she inherited the entire Desmond fortune, it would only be a drop in the bucket of the money she already has. As they say, that dog won't hunt."

"I guess not. Didn't you tell me that the couple was leaving that afternoon for a honeymoon in Europe?"

"They were."

"Then if the shooter missed Jim that day, if Jim had not jogged, or gone on the street or the other way on the beach, the killer would have missed him."

"I guess so," she said.

"But if the killing wasn't random, then there must have been a contingency plan."

She was quiet for a moment, sipping her wine. I heard a dog bark in the distance, the screech of one of the peacocks that run wild in the Village, an outboard engine chugging at idle speed up the lagoon where I lived. "Maybe," she said.

"Maybe?"

"The Grand Beach condo building takes up the whole area between the beach and Gulf of Mexico Drive. There are no obstructions on the roof that would have kept the shooter from moving across it. There are a bunch of air-conditioning units up there, but nothing that would stop him from moving from the front of the building to the back. If Desmond had come up the sidewalk on Gulf of Mexico Drive, all the killer had to do was move to that side of the building."

"What if Jim had jogged north on the beach?"

"I see your point. How would the killer have gotten to him? And if he hadn't gotten him that day, then Desmond would presumably have been out of reach in Europe. That's an argument for randomness."

"Maybe not," I said. "Maybe there was another shooter on the roof of another building to the north of the Hilton."

She sat quietly for a beat. "Damn. We never thought about that. There're some buildings to the north that could have hidden a sniper."

"If you're going north from the Hilton," I said, "there are several low-rise buildings, no more than three or four stories high, until you get to the Tropical Condos. That building is eight stories. There are no others that tall all the way up the island."

She pulled out her cell phone. "I'll get a crime-scene unit up there now. It's probably too late, but we've got to check it out."

She made arrangements to meet the crime-scene people at the Tropical in thirty minutes. "If your theory is correct," she said, "there had to be at least two shooters."

"I know."

"I'll meet you later at the Hilton," she said, and was out the door.

CHAPTER TWELVE

July on our key is a time when there are few tourists and we islanders meet for drinks and jokes and stories of other lives, those we lived before we found our paradise on Longboat Key. Some of the stories were probably even true, although we didn't much care and never tried to sort out the truth from the fantasy. Everybody is entitled to start over, and our little island was as good a place as any for that.

I was sitting at the outside bar at the Hilton talking to Billy Brugger who had been slinging drinks in the place for a quarter of a century. He knew everybody, those still with us and those who had departed for other venues, those who had died and those who had simply moved away, perhaps tired of the essential sameness of our lives, bored with the little stimulus that island living provided, needful of the stress they'd left behind in the cities of the Midwest, or simply craving the daily contact of family and the familiar friends of their youths. He knew their secrets, the ones whispered to him over the bar late at night, when the whisperers had drunk too much and were a little maudlin, perhaps thinking of the homes they'd left to chase the sun to Florida. And Billy kept those secrets. He was as closed-mouthed as a sphynx, judicious in his friendships and in many ways a repository of all the island's ills.

I'd stopped by Tiny's after J.D. left. The chief was already into his second drink, chatting with one of the regulars, a commercial fisherman from Cortez. A couple of other locals sat at a table in the corner, intent on the golf game playing on the big flat-screen TV. Bill Lester never had more than two drinks when he was driving. We talked while he sipped on the last one and then headed home. I paid my tab and drove three miles south to the Hilton.

• • •

Billy looked at his watch. "She'll be hitting the water in about five minutes."

He was talking about the sun. He enjoyed the sunsets as much as I did, but would never admit it lest the locals think him as crazy as I. The people who lived on our key figured that when you've seen thousands of sunsets, the beauty pales into insignificance. But not for me. Each one was different from the others, the colors splaying across the water in ever changing patterns, the birds, a new flock each day, flying across the face of the sun on their way home for the night, the small formations of clouds hanging at the edge of the horizon, reflecting the last rays of the day. I was mindful of the fact that perhaps my fascination with the sunsets was that it was the last vestige of Old Florida, the land I'd known growing up, that part of my youth now buried under the condominium towers, parking lots, and thousands of new homes that fed the beast called progress.

"I know," I said. "I can always depend on the sun."

J.D. came up the ramp from the parking lot. "Hey, Billy," she asked, "is he still sober?" She was pointing at me.

"Yeah. You can always tell. He's not nearly as interesting when he's not drinking much."

J.D. took the stool next to mine. Billy poured her a glass of wine. "It's time," he said.

I turned my stool toward the Gulf, my back to the bar. The sun was just beginning to dip into the horizon. I watched as it sank, moving quickly as if glad to be done with this day, seeking a little rest before it started its rise over the mainland in a few hours.

I turned back to J.D. "Find anything at the Tropical?"

"Nothing. But I didn't expect to. Their surveillance cameras are working and they save about six months worth of images on a computer. One of the techs is going through the pictures now, trying to narrow it down to the day of the shooting. See what we get. I'm not expecting much. He'll let me know in the morning."

"You hungry?"

"I could eat a cow."

"How about a hamburger?"

"That's a start. Can I have fries with that?"

"Sure. I'm in an expansive mood."

We sat and ate and talked into the night. Friends stopped by, had a drink, joined the conversation for a bit and moved on to the next bar, the next set of friends. It was getting late and J.D. said she had to work the next day. I pointed out that retired guys didn't even have to get out of bed unless they wanted to. She punched me with her elbow, got up, and pecked me on the cheek. "I'll call you tomorrow as soon as I hear from the crime-scene people about those pictures. If we get anything, I'll bring them by."

The old peck on the cheek. She didn't usually do that. Was it a sign? Was J.D. Duncan having erotic thoughts about me? Sure, Matt. Sure. Delusion is good for the soul. Keep thinking that way. Of course, I'd had more than a few erotic thoughts about her. But we were friends. Nothing more. Never even a hint from her that there was anything more. Well, maybe a hint, or maybe it was just my overactive imagination. I watched her walk down the ramp to the parking lot. She got into her Camry and drove away, waving as she left.

"Billy," I aked, "did you happen to work the Desmond wedding in June?"

"Sure did. Who'd have thought the groom would be dead within twenty-four hours?"

"What was the setup?"

"The wedding was held on the beach just at sunset. We had a big tent covering the deck and the reception was held there. It wasn't a big wedding, but everything was done first class. It wasn't inexpensive."

"Did you see any problems, fights, arguments, anything of that nature?"

"No. Everything was smooth. Why?"

"The groom's dad is an old friend of mine from Vietnam. I'm looking into the murder for him. With J.D.'s help."

"Wait a minute. There was one strange thing that night."

"What?"

"A guy came up to the bar and wanted a drink. He wasn't part of the wedding party, and I told him we were closed. He seemed pissed off about it and mumbled something about rich people taking over everything."

"Anything else?"

"You mentioning Vietnam made me remember him."

"Why?"

"He was Asian. But I'm pretty sure he was American. He didn't have any accent at all. He spoke American idiomatic English. I don't think you get that comfortable with a language unless you grow up speaking it."

"Can you describe him?"

"He was pretty big. Not huge, but bigger than the average Asian. I'd say five ten to six feet tall, maybe one-eighty, one-ninety."

"Did he leave right away?"

"No. He sat for a little while kind of staring at the party. I didn't want to be rude to him, but finally I told him he'd have to move along."

"Did he leave?"

"Yeah. Didn't say another word. Just got off the stool and walked out."

"Have you ever seen him again?"

"No. I'd never seen him before either."

"That means he's probably not an islander. Did you get the idea he was staying here at the hotel?"

"No, but that doesn't mean anything. He may have been a guest here. I didn't ask and he didn't volunteer."

I sipped my beer, talking with Billy about fishing. He was planning to go with Logan and me next time we went out. I finished the beer, paid my tab, shook hands with Billy, and went home.

CHAPTER THIRTEEN

Only I didn't go home. I stopped at Tiny's, the small bar on the edge of the Village that served as sort of a clubhouse for the northenders. It was quiet with only a few people huddled at the bar. I knew them all, the late night denizens of the Village and one mid-key condo dweller, my buddy Logan Hamilton. I hadn't seen much of him lately. He was in love and spent much of his time with his lady, Marie Phillips, who lived in one of the high-rises on the south end of the key.

"You get dumped?" I asked as I slid onto an empty stool between him and Les Fulcher.

"Right. How would she ever replace me? She had one of those girlie things tonight. Dinner at Michaels and drinks at Marina Jack."

"Girlie thing?"

"Yeah, you know. The girls get together and gossip. Marie probably likes to tell them how great I am in the sack."

"Just another group of nice people lying to each other, huh?"

"Well, exaggerating, maybe. Just a little."

I turned to Les. "How's retirement?"

"Lots of fishing."

"Catching anything?"

"Not much."

"I haven't seen you lately. I heard you've been off island for a while."

"Yeah. For two months. Went to Guam."

"Guam? What's a broken-down firefighter doing in Guam?"

"Broken-down my ass. I retired in the peak of health. Still got my youthful glow. I am the epitome of boyish exuberance."

"How's the knee?"

"Gotta get it replaced. I go in the hospital the first of the month."

"So why Guam?"

"I've got a buddy out there and I spent some time fishing and diving."

"When did you get back?"

"Yesterday."

"I guess you heard about the murders we had last month."

"Yeah. I knew Jake Prather, *Dulcimer*'s captain. He used to live next door to me in the Village."

"Sorry about your loss."

"I hadn't heard anything about it until I got in yesterday. I went to see Janice, his widow, this morning."

"How's she doing?"

"She's doing okay, I guess. Jake had some life insurance. Not much, but it'll see Janice through. Did you know them?"

"No. I knew the name and I knew he ran *Dulcimer*, but I don't think I ever met him."

The conversation turned back to inconsequential things. Tiny's owner, Susie Vaught, kept the beer coming and joined in the conversation. It was a pleasant evening on the downside of July, old friends gossiping, trading fishing spots, laughing at the crazy politics of our island. We decided that July was the safest month on the key since the Town Commission didn't meet. All its members were up north somewhere trying to escape the heat.

I was up early the next morning, jogging the beach as the sun rose over the mainland. I ran two miles south and turned for the trek back to my starting place. I left the beach and walked down Broadway and into the Village and home. The peacocks were roaming the streets hunting their breakfast. People were walking their dogs, waiting patiently while the animals sniffed the ground and found the best place to do their business. Full daylight was on us and the air was getting wetter with the humidity that always comes with the sun in summer.

I showered, shaved, put on clean shorts and a T-shirt with the logo of a local restaurant and took my newspaper, coffee, and a muffin to the patio. It was still cool enough in the shade of the overhang to enjoy the outdoors. It was not yet eight o'clock.

My phone rang. J.D. calling.

"The techies came up with some pictures from the elevator cameras at Tropical," she said. "You want to see them?"

"I've got coffee on."

"I'll be there in ten minutes."

I'd moved back inside and the new pictures were spread over the coffee table. The first thing I noticed was that the person in these pictures was wearing the same clothes as the person in the pictures from the Grand Beach elevators. The second thing was the size of the new guy. There was no clear shot of his face. He was wearing the same ball cap as the one from Grand Beach and he kept his head down.

"Did you notice the clothes on this one?" I asked.

"Yeah. They look identical. Like a uniform or something."

"Same briefcase."

"Identical."

"And this is a pretty big guy," I said.

"Yes. You can tell by comparing his size to the elevator door. I'd say he's around five feet ten. Not huge, but bigger than the Grand Beach guy."

"The time stamps match. The one at Grand Beach and this guy were going up and coming down at about the same time."

She took a sip of her coffee. "We've got at least two people involved in this. A hit team?"

"Looks like it. Maybe more than two."

"More than two?" she asked.

"What if Jim hadn't gone jogging that morning. This was their last chance to get him before he left for Europe. There had to be someone else as a backup."

She thought about it, her teeth massaging her lower lip. "Or maybe there was a backup plan. If he hadn't jogged that morning, they may have planned to get him somewhere else."

"You could be right. But why? Who'd want to hit a young guy just out of college?"

"If we answer that question," she said, "we'll probably have an idea of who the shooters were."

"Even if we don't get the shooters, if we can figure out the why and the who behind this, I'll have somebody to sue. We can take it from there."

"Where do we start?"

"The statements from Chaz Desmond and Jim's wife, Meredith, weren't much help. I wonder if I might have a little more luck. Not being a cop, and all."

J.D. bristled a little at this. "You think you can take a better statement than I can?"

"No. Not at all. But Chaz is my old friend and the guy who wants me to proceed with this suit. He can get me to Meredith as part of the family. There just might be secrets there that they would share with me that they'd want to keep out of the public record. And by talking to you they would be afraid that everything would become public sooner or later."

She relaxed, smiled, sat back in her chair. "Good recovery, chum. But I think you're probably right. And there's nothing to lose by trying."

"So it's okay with you for me to talk to them?"

"Sure."

"How about the other witnesses?"

"No problem. Just keep me informed."

"Suppose we set up a new file, one that's not part of the official file. That way I can assure the witnesses that while I'll share the information with you, it'll be completely off the record and that you won't use it without their explicit permission."

She was quiet for a beat, thinking this over. I knew it went against all her training. The rules are specific. Everything goes into the master file. All evidence and statements are to be kept for use in a trial. She would be breaking all kinds of regulations by going off the reservation, as it were.

"I don't know, Matt," she said after a minute or so. "I work for the town. I don't know if I can hide anything from the prosecutors and other cops."

"Think of it this way, J.D. I don't have to share any of this with you. I can claim attorney-client privilege or work product and keep it out of the hands of any of the authorities. But I'd like your help. Besides, you're at a dead end on this case. You've got no suspects, no motive, no nothing. You can't possibly hurt the case by working with me off the books."

"It doesn't feel right."

"Suppose I talk to the chief. If he agrees, will you go along with it?"

"If the chief gives me the okay, I'm in."

"There's a good girl."

"Girl?"

"There's a good detective."

"That's better," she said.

CHAPTER FOURTEEN

After J.D. left, I went to my computer and Googled Charles (Chaz) Desmond. Doc had been a busy man in the years since I'd seen him. There was quite a lot on him, all of it good. He was what he seemed to be. A successful businessman who dealt fairly with his customers and honorably with his competitors. There was nothing apparent that would lead me to believe that he had any enemies.

I spent some time looking up James Ronald Desmond, the dead son. There was very little on him. Most of what I found had to do with his years at the University of Georgia. He'd been involved in the fraternity life on campus and had written a couple of letters to the editor of the university newspaper. He was not happy with the football coach and vented his frustration in the letters in the paper, but that was not something that usually got someone killed by a professional hit team. Especially at the University of Georgia where half the student body was always unhappy about the coach.

I found an engagement announcement in the *Atlanta Constitution* dated two weeks before the wedding. A very short engagement. It did give me one bit of information I didn't have. The maiden name of the bride.

I Googled Meredith McNabb and found pretty much the same stuff from the University of Georgia and a lot of debutante crap from the Savannah newspaper. She came from a very wealthy family whose fortune was several generations old. The only oddity I found was that she had spent a year between high school and college working with volunteers building a school in Laos.

I dug some more and there it was, in the *Savannah Morning News* about five years before. A picture of Meredith McNabb in Laos, standing with a small group of other young people, including Jim Desmond. Their names were all listed in the caption below the picture. The story was about the local debutante who'd left a life of luxury to spend six months in rural Laos, living among people so poor they had never seen indoor plumbing or electricity. God, they looked so young and dedicated and happy. And five years later, one of them was dead and the star of the story was in mourning. Life can be a bitch.

I called Desmond on his cell phone. He answered immediately. "Good morning, L.T."

"Morning, Doc. How're you?"

"About the same. I'm thinking of putting Julie in the hospital."

"Hospital?"

"That's a nice name for the booby hatch. She can't seem to snap out of her grief."

"I'm sorry, Doc. I wish there were something I could do."

"Find the killers, Matt. Just find the assholes who took our boy."

"Tell me about Jim's work in Laos."

"Not much to tell. He wanted a bridge year, I think they call it. A year out of school before starting college. He was aware of the fact that he'd lived an above-average life and felt that he should give something back. Help the less fortunate. He came across this group run by a charity based in Macon that put the so called bridge year kids into projects in the Third World."

"Was the group legit?"

"Far as I can tell. I checked them out. They seem to do very good work and the money they take in is accounted for. Most of it goes into the projects and very little to administration. The volunteer kids who can pay their travel expenses are asked to do so. The ones who can't are funded by the charity."

"Did he like it? Laos, I mean."

"He came home all hopped up about what they'd been doing. He felt like he had helped some people who had no hope."

"Love life?"

Doc chuckled. "Oh, yeah. Meredith was with the same group. They met during the orientation on the Mercer University campus in Macon. That blossomed into quite a romance. Took everything her parents and Julie and I could do to keep them single until they finished college."

"Did Jim ever indicate that there'd been any trouble in Laos?"

"What do you mean?"

"I don't know. Any tension with any of the other students. Anything that could have carried over to the present."

"I doubt it. If there was, I'm not aware of it."

"What about at the university? Any big issues with other students?"

"I don't know of any."

"I'd like to talk to Meredith. Is she in Atlanta?"

"No. She's in Savannah with her parents. I can call her for you. I'm sure she'd be glad to talk."

"I think I'll go up there. Can you set up an appointment in the next couple of days and let me know?"

"Sure thing, Matt. I'll get back to you this afternoon."

CHAPTER FIFTEEN

Savannah is an old city by American standards, founded in 1733 by English settlers led by General James Oglethorpe. This lovely town sits on the banks of the Savannah River and is famous for its twenty-one historic squares, small oases of peace in a bustling city. Meredith met me at a Starbucks at the corner of Bull and East Broughton Streets about halfway between Johnson and Wright Squares.

Meredith had called me the afternoon before, about thirty minutes after I hung up from talking with Doc. She said she was leaving on a trip with her family in a couple of days, but if I could come to Savannah, she'd meet me the next afternoon. We agreed on Starbucks at three o'clock in the afternoon. I called J.D. to let her know where I was going.

I'd driven up from Longboat Key, up Interstates 75, 4, and 95. It's about a seven-hour drive, a little more if you count the stop for a Big Mac. I checked into a hotel out on the interstate and drove into the city for our meeting. Savannah was more humid than Longboat Key, and I had the air-conditioning on the Explorer cranked as high as it would go.

I wasn't too sure about drinking hot coffee on a day like this one, but iced coffee made me irritable. I think it was the combination of caffeine and my distaste for cold coffee. Some things just need to be drunk hot. I ordered a small coffee and sat at a table that gave me a sight line to the door.

I recognized Meredith as soon as she walked in. I'd seen her picture in the newspapers I'd found on the Internet, but they didn't do her justice. She was a tall blonde, with shoulder-length hair, a trim figure, and a face that was still showing grief. She was wearing a pink blouse, white mid-thigh shorts, and white sandals. Her only jewelry was her wedding ring, a simple gold band.

I stood and introduced myself, asked if I could get her a coffee. She declined in a soft voice carrying the accents of the South. I started to explain what I was trying to do and she interrupted me. "Chaz explained it to me. You're an old friend trying to help us. I appreciate that."

"I know you talked to the police. I've seen the statement you gave. I'm hoping there is something that you inadvertently left out, something that will give us a lead."

"I'm willing to do anything I can to help. Whoever killed Jim ruined my life."

"Chaz told me that you and Jim met in Laos."

"Macon, actually. During the orientation before we went over."

"Love at first sight?"

She smiled. "Not really. We became buddies and then sort of drifted into something more. It seemed so gradual and I wasn't sure it would survive Laos."

"Why was that?"

"Oh, you know. Two people with raging hormones isolated in a foreign culture. Things happen and then when you get back to your real life you start having second thoughts."

"Did that happen? Did you have second thoughts?"

"No. I didn't and I don't think Jim did either."

"Chaz said you both wanted to get married before you graduated."

"Yes, but that was because we couldn't live together until we got married. And we desperately wanted to move in with each other."

"Why didn't you?"

"Our moms. They're kind of old South and wouldn't have understood. Neither one of us wanted to disappoint our mothers."

"I found your engagement announcement in the Atlanta paper. Short engagement."

"Very short."

"Any reason?"

"We were planning to get married in the fall, but I got pregnant. We didn't want to embarrass our moms, so we announced the engagement and rushed the wedding."

"Your moms again."

"Yeah," she said, ruefully. "They were college kids during the free love years of the seventies, but I don't think they ever took to it. Or at least if they did, they didn't want their children to know about it."

"Your baby?"

"He's doing fine. I'm due in January. Had an ultrasound yesterday. It's definitely a boy. James Ronald Desmond, Junior."

"Meredith, can you think of anyone who would want to hurt Jim? Or you?"

"No. I've wracked my brain trying to figure that one out. There's no one."

"Nobody at the university?"

"No. Jim got along with everybody."

"How about the group you went to Laos with?"

"No. We were pretty tight. Everybody got along. There was about an even number of girls and boys, and before we came home, almost everybody had paired off."

"No jealously? No fighting over the women?"

"No. Well, there was one problem, but Jim solved it and that was the end of it."

"Tell me about that one."

"There was a Laotian who came down from Vientiane, the capital, three or four times while we were there. He wasn't much older than us, but he was some sort of government minister. Probably a low-level bureaucrat, but the locals treated him with a great deal of respect. He and Jim got into it once."

"What happened?"

"The guy started hitting on me. He spoke English pretty well, and I think he liked my blonde hair. After the third or fourth visit, he grabbed me and tried to kiss me. Jim hit him pretty hard. Knocked him down. There were a lot of the locals watching."

"Did he say anything to you and Jim? Any threats?"

"He screamed something in Laotian that we didn't understand and left. We never saw him again, but a few days later some men came to the village where we were working and closed us down. We had to get the embassy involved before we were able to get back to work."

"Do you know the Laotian's name?"

"No. It was one of the tongue twisters that so many of the Laotians have for names. Lots of syllables. I never could keep them all straight."

"Do you remember an Asian man attending your wedding?"

"No. There were no Asian guests."

"An Asian man came to the outside bar that night and wanted a drink. The bartender wouldn't serve him because of your private party. That apparently didn't sit too well with the Asian guy."

"I wasn't aware of that. The wedding was perfect."

"Do you have pictures of the wedding?"

"Sure. A video and still pictures."

"May I see them?"

"I'll have to send them to you. I have all the pictures and video on my computer. I can e-mail them to you."

I gave her my e-mail address, said goodbye, and went to the River-walk for a cold beer.

CHAPTER SIXTEEN

I was up early the next morning, the Explorer pointed west on Interstate 16, a cup of coffee in its holder on the console, a half-eaten McMuffin on my lap. I was making the two hour drive to Macon for a talk with the director of the Otto Foundation.

I'd called Doc from the Riverwalk the afternoon before and related my conversation with Meredith. I congratulated him on becoming a grandfather. He told me Jim and Meredith met with their parents as soon as they found out she was pregnant. Julie hadn't been too excited about the pregnancy before the wedding, but she had been ecstatic about the baby.

Doc had not heard anything about the problem in Laos with the young man from the capital. It must not have been very important to either Meredith or Jim, since it never came up. He didn't know what, if anything, to make of it.

He told me that the Laotian trip had been sponsored by the Otto Foundation with headquarters in Macon. The executive director was a man named Bud Stanley. I called and made an appointment for nine the next morning.

The foundation offices were in a small and shabby strip center on Riverside Drive. I opened the front door into a room where two women and a man sat at tables peering at computer monitors. The middle-aged man looked up and said, "You must be Mr. Royal."

"I am."

"I'm Bud Stanley. Come on back to my office." He chuckled.

He led me through a door at the back of the room and into a small space that was stacked with office supplies. A Mr. Coffee machine sat on a table, Styrofoam cups stacked next to it. There was a refrigerator in the corner and a scarred wooden table with four unmatched chairs placed around it.

"Nice office," I said.

"Just trying to impress our donors. Can I treat you to a cup of coffee?"

"Yes, please. Black is fine."

He poured two cups and motioned me to the table. We sat.

"Mr. Desmond called me yesterday. Said you were helping solve his son's murder and asked that I give you any help I can."

"Do you remember Jim Desmond?"

"Oh, yes. I remember all our kids. There aren't that many of them."

"Tell me a little about your foundation."

"We are small, funded by an endowment left by a wealthy textile mill owner who died about twenty years ago. He had served in the U.S. government in some capacity during the Vietnam War and was interested in building schools in Vietnam, Cambodia, and Laos. The war and the civil strife that followed had left the countries destitute."

"Is that all you do? Build schools?"

"Yes. We use our endowment and take contributions from people. We send two groups a year to an area to build a school. Each group stays for six months, and in a year we can pretty much complete a building."

"Then what?"

He looked puzzled for a moment. "Oh, you mean what happens to the building after we leave?"

"Yes."

"We have an agreement with the governments that once we have the building built and it is stocked with books, paper, pens, and such, the government will send in a teacher. They promise to staff the school for twenty years."

"Do you supply the books and stuff?"

"No. We coordinate with another charity in Los Angeles that handles that."

"How's it working out?"

"It's been great. In twenty years we've built twenty schools and all of them are still up and running. It's been in the government's interest to have the villagers educated to some extent. We've found that electricity and other infrastructure follows closely behind our schools. It's a win-win situation for the villagers."

"Tell me how you recruit your students."

"We started out with college students who needed or wanted a break. When this bridge year became fashionable, we found that we had a ready-made group of youngsters who wanted something different. Living in a Southeast Asian village without running water, electricity, or sewage is certainly different from what they're used to."

"It sounds like most of your kids would have to come from affluent families to be able to take the time off. Or do you pay them?"

"We don't pay them, so you're right. Most of them come from well-to-do families. We also get a bit of monetary support from the families. For instance, a parent can give us the money for his child's airfare and other incidentals that we pay for and the parent can write it off as a charitable donation. We then buy the airline tickets and provide for the student during the six months they're in country."

"Do you remember a problem that Jim Desmond had with some young Laotian guy that caused the project to be shut down?"

"Oh, yes. That's the only time we've ever run into something like that."

"What can you tell me about it?"

"The Laotian was named Souphanouvong Phomvihana. We called him 'Soupy.' His father ran the biggest poppy operation in the area."

"Poppies?"

"Yes. The area we were working in lies right next to one of the largest poppy operations in Laos. They make heroin out of them and sell it around the world. It's part of the so-called Golden Triangle."

"Tell me about Soupy."

"He was about twenty-five at the time. Jim's group was the second bunch to work on this particular school. Soupy had come around several times to visit the first group, but never caused any trouble. For some reason, he took a liking to Meredith McNabb and apparently got physical with her. Jim gave him a good old-fashioned ass whupping."

"What about the project being shut down?"

"Soupy's dad was one of the most powerful men in Laos. He had an army that protected his fields and kept the competitors out. He was in essence a warlord. Soupy got some of his father's men to go to the village and tell the elders that the Americans had to go. Apparently Soupy had been very embarrassed at having his butt kicked in front of the villagers."

"How did you solve that?"

"We have very good relations with the governments where we work. I called our contact in the State Department, and he had one of the people at our embassy in Vientiane look into it. I think it went all the way to the top of the Laotian government, and somebody there had a talk with Soupy's dad. It seems that Soupy was a hothead and this wasn't the first time he'd used his dad's influence. I heard that the father wasn't happy about it and kind of pinned his son's ears back. Soupy made some empty threats about getting even with Jim, but nothing ever came of it."

"Where's Soupy today?"

"He's the kingpin. His dad died a couple of years back, and Soupy took over."

"So he now controls the army."

"Yes. But keep in mind that the government wants us there, and I don't think they'd ever allow Soupy to cause too much trouble."

"But, Soupy might still have wanted to even the score with Jim."

"That's a possibility."

CHAPTER SEVENTEEN

There was an on-ramp to Interstate-75 a block south of the foundation offices. I drove onto it and headed south to Bradenton. Eight hours later I
was crossing the Longboat Pass Bridge. It was six o'clock in the evening,
and Tiny's was on my way home. I went in, took a stool, and ordered a
Miller Lite. Debbie Messina was behind the bar. She gave me a hug and the
beer and said she'd heard I'd been off-island for a couple of days. Nothing gets past the island bartenders.

It was quiet in the doldrums of summer. The usual snowbirds who
would be found having an afternoon drink in Tiny's during the winter
months, were tucked away in bars in Minneapolis or Chicago or Quechee,
Vermont, or someplace where the humidity was not as lethal as it was on
Longboat Key. I was alone with Debbie for about five minutes when Les
Fulcher came in and took the stool next to mine.

"How's the knee?" I asked.

"Painful. Look, I heard that you're looking into the murder of the
guy who got shot down on the beach last month."

There are no secrets on the island. "That's right."

"I went by to see Janice Prather last night."

"How's she holding up?"

"She's okay. Her daughter lives in Bradenton, so she's there to help
Janice over the rough spots."

"I'm glad she's got family in the area."

"She told me something that I thought was interesting."

"What?"

"On the day Jake died, he told Janice about a man who'd been on
the boat the past three evenings. He didn't eat, but spent the entire cruise

standing up near the bow with binoculars. At first Jake thought he might be a bird-watcher, but he was still there after it got dark. No birds out then. The guy was making notes on a pad and taking snapshots before it got too dark."

"Strange. Did he describe the man to Janice?"

"No. And she didn't ask. It was just one of those odd things that she remembered. I thought you might want to pass that on to the lady detective you're working with. I know she's investigating all the murders."

"Thanks, Les. Probably just a lonely tourist, but I'll let her know."

I finished my beer and left for home. I fired up my computer and checked my e-mail. There was a note from Meredith with a video and about a hundred still pictures of the wedding attached in a zip file. I decided to wait to open it until J.D. and I could look at it together.

I called the detective. "I'm back."

"Man, I'm glad. I missed you something terrible."

"Really?"

"I didn't even know you were gone."

"Some friend. I've been in Savannah talking to Meredith Desmond."

She snickered. "Oh, right. You mentioned that. Did you do any good up there?"

"A bit. And I've got a bunch of pictures and a video from the Desmond wedding. Why don't you stop by and we'll look at them together?"

"I'll be there in about an hour."

I went back to the computer and typed up some notes of my meetings with Meredith and Bud Stanley. I wanted our off-the-record file to be complete in case we ever made it an on-the-record file. Besides, I knew that the notes would better preserve the discussions than my memory would. I e-mailed copies to Doc.

I took a shower, dressed in a clean T-shirt and cargo shorts, and opened a bottle of Chardonnay. I'd read somewhere that you should let the wine breathe before serving it. If you let beer breathe, it goes flat. I like the fact that the only ritual associated with beer is the opening of the can.

The video was like every one you ever saw of a wedding, except this one was on a white sand beach. The members of the wedding party were dressed in tuxedos and gowns, the bride's white dress a confection of beauty. Everybody was barefoot.

There were a lot of still photos, many of the bride and groom, of the entire wedding party, the parents of the bride and groom, and candid pictures from the reception. There was nothing in any of them that raised alarms. There were no pictures of an Asian man. Another dead end.

I gave J.D. copies of the memos I'd written about my conversations with Meredith and Bud Stanley. "Read these and I'll answer any questions you have."

She took a few minutes to peruse the printouts. "Do you think this Soupy could have sent a hit team to take out Jim Desmond?"

"It's not as far-fetched as it sounds. Asians put a lot of emphasis on what they call 'face.' Soupy's a big deal in that part of the world. He might very well have figured that the only way to get his mojo back after Jim whipped him was to kill Jim."

"Mojo?"

"Yeah."

"What's mojo?"

"I don't know. Maybe like machismo."

"I don't think so."

"What do you think mojo is?"

"I don't really care," she said. "How can we dig further into Soupy? Maybe find out if he's the one behind this."

"The whole idea of me getting involved in this was to find a likely target and file suit. The problem here is that I'd never get jurisdiction over Soupy or his organization. I could never show that he was in this country or was responsible for any acts that took place here. Until you get a court to accept jurisdiction, you can't do anything with the case."

"Would it be worth a try?"

"No. Even if we could figure a way to get around the jurisdiction issue, I don't know how we'd serve Soupy with the lawsuit. Even then, if he simply didn't respond, the only thing we could do is get a default judgment entered and then we'd have no reason to take depositions to prove the case. The default would work just as if Soupy admitted to all allegations. There'd be no reason to take depositions, and the court wouldn't let us issue subpoenas. The default wouldn't produce any evidence and would be meaningless in a criminal court."

"We need to find out more about this Soupy guy."

I thought for a minute. "There's always Jock."

"Ah, the magic man. Will he do it?"

"He will if I ask nicely. Probably have to buy him a bottle of wine or something."

"Why don't you call him?"

"I think I'll ask him to come for a visit. He hasn't been here in a couple of months."

"You sure he'll come? It's hot here," she said.

"It's hot in Houston, too."

"You've got a point."

"You want to go to Pattigeorge's for a drink?"

"Sure. Is Sam back from vacation?"

"Yeah. Some vacation," I said.

"Where'd he go?"

"St. Armands. Sat around and drank for a week."

"Wow."

St. Armands was the next island south connected to Longboat Key by the New Pass Bridge. Sam could take the trolley back and forth so he wouldn't have to drive. And as he pointed out, the trolley doesn't make him go through metal detectors to board.

CHAPTER EIGHTEEN

I called Logan and asked if he and Marie wanted to join us at Pattigeorge's for drinks and dinner. They agreed and were pulling into the parking lot just as we arrived. Marie was a blonde in her late thirties with short hair, sky-blue eyes, long legs, and a slender body.

Logan Hamilton was my best friend on the island. He stood five feet eight, weighed about one sixty, and was beginning to lose his hair. What was left was mostly gray. He had retired early from the financial services industry after making a lot of money. He moved to the key about the same time I did, and we became fast friends. I think the fact that both of us had served in Vietnam was the initial attraction. Logan had been an infantryman on his first tour and, after flight school, did a second tour as a helicopter pilot.

We went into the restaurant and were greeted by the bartender, Sam Lastinger, an island legend. Sammy knew all his customers and made sure that any newcomer was immediately introduced to all the others at the bar. He was an institution on the island, a man of cheerful verbosity, a friend, confidant, and ladies' man. He was about forty, a slender, dark-haired guy with a ready grin who seemed to never have a bad day, unless his beloved Florida Gators lost. Women took to him like flies to honey and he always treated them well. He had a lot of ex-lovers who were all still his friends. I never could figure out how he managed that.

The bar was full. We knew everybody there and spent a little time talking before we took our seats at a nearby high-top table. Sam brought our drinks and a menu. We all ordered salads.

Logan looked at J.D. "What's this I hear about you bringing on a junior detective to help sort out the murder on the beach?"

"Just trying to keep him honest," she said. "Find some work to keep him busy."

"Any luck?" asked Logan.

"Not so far," I said. "We've developed some stuff, but I don't know that you can call it a lead." I filled Logan and Marie in on what we'd found out about the Laotian connection, if there was such a thing, and that we were pretty sure there had been a hit team of at least two people who took Jim Desmond down.

Logan sipped his Dewar's. "Any way to run down anything on this Soupy guy?"

"I called Jock," I said. "He'll be here tomorrow afternoon."

"Great," Logan said. "Things always get interesting when Jock shows up."

Marie grinned. "I hope not too interesting. You boys seem to draw trouble."

"Not this time," I said. "Jock's just going to use his contacts to get us some information."

"What can I do to help?" Logan asked.

"Nothing right now," I said. "We're just trying to connect dots."

"Let me know if you need anything."

Our conversation moved on to the things that friends discuss, one of those kinds of evenings when the next day you can't remember just what you did talk about, because the conversations were without substance. Just another quiet evening among friends.

I was up early the next morning intending to jog on the beach. I looked outside to a drizzling rain. It was overcast as far as I could see across the bay. It looked as if the weather was settling in for a wet spell. I decided to head for the beach anyway. A little water wouldn't hurt me, and I hadn't gotten much exercise in the last couple of days.

The beach was deserted. I began my run south, trying to stay on the flatter surfaces. The tide the night before had been higher than usual and there were little hummocks of sand where the water had eroded parts of the beach. I had to be careful not to turn an ankle.

I made it to my turnaround point and headed back north, keeping a steady pace on the sand. The rain was coming a little harder now, and I was soaked. Even in the July heat, I was beginning to feel a little chilled, the sweat mingling with the rain to cause my skin to lose warmth.

I neared the North Shore Road access and slowed to a walk, letting some of the energy drain off. I came to the boardwalk ramp that would take me over the dunes and into the parking lot where I'd left my Explorer.

I mounted the ramp and walked east. I saw a man coming toward me, a plastic poncho covering his head and upper torso. Another inveterate beachcomber, I thought. But the hairs were standing at attention on the back of my neck, an electric tingle moving up into my scalp. Something was wrong. My gut was sending me signals, a recognition of danger that hadn't yet made its way into my consciousness. The man was dressed in jeans and work boots, not the clothes of a runner or a beachcomber. He kept his head down, eyes to the ground. I stopped, waiting for him to pass, every muscle tensed, alert for the unexpected, not sure that the signals my gut was sending to my brain were valid. I wasn't even sure if he saw me and as he closed on the spot where I was standing, I said, "Good morning."

The man looked up as if surprised and then lunged at me. I saw his hand coming out of the pocket of the poncho. He was grasping something. It took me a nanosecond to recognize the knife, a big one, like the KA-BARS the Marines had in Vietnam. His eyes were boring into me, his face a grimace of concentration. He was moving in for the kill.

I reacted without thought, a muscle memory left over from my days as a soldier, honed by my regular martial arts classes in Bradenton. I did just what he didn't expect. I moved into him, sidestepping his thrust, turning my back to him, using my left arm to grasp his knife arm as it slid past me. I caught a bit of the blade in my side. I was aware of it, but the pain had not yet registered. I brought my right arm across my body, clasped his wrist in my right hand, twisted and pushed down hard while using my left arm as a lever to push his upper arm forward. I heard the knife drop to the boards of the crosswalk and at the same instant I heard his elbow snap.

The man screamed in pain. I let go of his wrist, pivoted, and punched him in the solar plexus, using all my strength, aiming for his spine, knowing it would take his breath away. I thought for a second that my fist had gone all the way through him and bounced off his vertebrae, but that was only wishful thinking. He went down, and I stomped his broken elbow. He screamed again. I kicked him in the face, once, twice, backed up, stooped, and picked up the knife. I was going to carve him up like a Christmas turkey. I was filled with rage. The thought that somebody would think nothing of killing me on a rain-cloaked beach on my home island blotted out all my civilized instincts.

I held the knife, dropped back onto the man now writhing on the boardwalk, put my knee in his stomach and the point of the knife under his chin. "Who are you?" I said, my voice sounding in my own ears like a roar. "Who the fuck are you?"

"No," he said. "Don't kill me."

I pushed the point of the knife in farther. He was a dead man. I was going to stick the knife into his brain. Then, like a curtain lifting, the rage dissipated, leaving me, as it always does, emotionally limp and drained. I asked again, this time in a quiet voice, "Who are you?"

"Get off him," I heard a feminine voice say. "Get off or so help me I'll shoot."

I looked up. A woman was standing near the parking lot end of the boardwalk, a large pistol held in both hands, pointing at me.

I didn't move. "If I let him up, you'll still shoot me."

"No," she said. "This is over."

"Tell you what," I said. "You put the pistol down on the boards, and I'll let your friend up. He's not going to be using his left arm for a while, so I don't think he's much of a threat. He and I will walk toward you, and you turn around and walk toward the parking lot. You can pick up the pistol when your back is turned to me. If you try to turn around, I'll stab your friend to death."

"How do I know you won't kill him when I put the gun down?"

"If I do, you'll have time to pick it up and shoot me. When you start walking, if I stab him, you'll have time to turn around and shoot me. I think this will work."

She stooped slowly and placed the pistol on the boardwalk. I noticed that she'd been holding the gun in her right hand. "Turn around," I said, "and pick up the pistol with your left hand."

She did as I told her. "Start walking," I said. I prodded the man with the tip of the knife next to his carotid artery and we began to follow.

The woman walked to a small sedan parked next to my Explorer. She stopped. "This is my car," she said. "What now?"

"Get in the driver's side," I said. "And don't point the pistol at me."

She did as I said, keeping the weapon in her left hand. When she was under the steering wheel, I walked toward the passenger side of my Explorer. I used the electronic key fob to unlock the door. I kept the man in a hammerlock with the knife at his throat. "Okay," I said, "I'm going to release him so that he can get into the car with you. I'll be ducking down as soon as I let him go, so you won't have a shot at me. I've got a nine millimeter in the Explorer and I'll have it in my hand before he gets to your car. We'll have a standoff. You drive off, and I won't shoot."

And that's the way it went down. They were gone in an instant, roaring out of the parking lot and toward the Longboat Pass Bridge about a quarter of a mile away. I memorized the tag number, but knew that by the time the police were alerted, the couple would be across Anna Maria Island and over the Cortez Bridge onto the mainland. There'd be almost no chance of spotting them in the traffic. I called 911 anyway. Told them who I was and what had happened. Said I'd be at my house if they needed to talk to me.

I got into the Explorer and drove out of the lot, across Gulf of Mexico Drive, and headed east on Broadway. My phone rang. J.D.

"I just heard. Are you all right?"

"Yes. Shook up, a minor cut on my rib cage. Nothing else."

"I'll meet you at your house."

"You don't have to do that." But I knew she'd come and that thought put me right with the world.

CHAPTER NINETEEN

I peeled off my clothes as I went through the house toward the bathroom. I showered with water as hot as I could stand it. I looked at the laceration on my side. It was a clean cut, not deep, but it had ruined a good T-shirt. There was little pain, but I knew I'd taken a hit.

I toweled off and put on a pair of shorts. I could hear someone rattling around in the kitchen and assumed it was J.D. I joined her. She had the coffeemaker on and the smell was starting to permeate my senses.

"Let me see where you're cut," she said.

She peered at it, felt around the edges and said, "I don't think you'll need stitches, but we need to get some antiseptic on it and get it bandaged properly."

"You know how to do that? I don't want you to kill me."

"I'm an EMT. I know what I'm doing."

All the Longboat cops had been through the Emergency Medical Technician training and could fill in until the Fire Department paramedics arrived on the scene of an accident or something worse.

"Do you have an antiseptic here? Bandages?"

"In the bathroom. The cabinet under the sink."

She came back bringing the first-aid kit with her. "Lie back on the sofa," she ordered.

I did so and she spread the antiseptic cream on the cut and bandaged it professionally. She ran her hand over the scars on my stomach where the docs in an Army field hospital had pulled shrapnel out of my belly before sending me back to the States for more intensive treatment.

"This isn't your first scrape, is it?" There was a timbre to her voice, sadness maybe, or compassion.

"No," I said. "That's a little reminder of my year abroad when I was nineteen."

"Vietnam."

"Yes."

"You never talk about it."

"No."

"Do you ever want to?"

"Not really."

"I'm a pretty good listener if you ever feel the need."

"Thanks, J.D., but I put all that behind me a long time ago."

"I don't believe you."

"You're probably right."

"Tell me about today. What happened?"

I told her, giving her the details. "I was going to kill the man who came after me."

"Self-defense."

"No. I mean I was going to kill him. After he was disarmed and at my mercy. Before the woman showed up."

"But you didn't."

"No."

"What happened to stop you?"

"The rage went away."

"Rage?"

"Sometimes when I'm in very stressful situations like today, I'm overcome with a rage that comes out of left field. I don't see it coming. It's just there. It turns me into somebody I'm not, or at least don't want to be. Then it goes away. It's like the better part of my brain takes over and pushes the rage back into the gutter where it belongs."

"Does this happen often?"

"No. But sometimes I feel like the rage is there, hiding just beneath my skin, ready to break out if I let my guard down. I have to fight it off. I used to drink it away, but that only caused more trouble. Now I exercise like crazy. Get the endorphins flowing and the rage goes away."

"Do you think the war caused it?"

"No. It was there before."

I was uneasy talking about this and wanted to change the subject. "What else can I tell you about today's attack?" I asked.

"Can you give me a description of the man and woman?"

I stared at her for a moment. "They were Asian."

CHAPTER TWENTY

My doorbell rang. I looked out the window to see Chief Bill Lester's un-marked parked in front of my house. "Door's open," I called.

Bill came in, a worried look on his face. "You okay, Matt?"

"Yeah. A little shook up, but none the worse for wear."

"Morning, Chief," said J.D. "Want some coffee?"

"I could use a cup. Tell me what happened."

I related the facts to him. Including the ethnicity of my attackers.

He frowned. "Does the fact that they were Asians mean anything to you?"

J.D. broke in and told him what we had learned about Jim Desmond's time in Laos, and that we thought there might be an Asian hit team that went after Jim.

Bill said, "You don't think they'd still be hanging around almost two months after the murder."

"No," I said, "but it seems a pretty big coincidence that for reasons I don't understand a couple of Asians tried to take me out."

Bill was quiet for a moment, sipping his coffee. "I wonder why they didn't just shoot you. Why the knife?"

"I've been thinking about that," I said. "There was nobody on the beach or in the parking lot, but you know those North Shore condos are right next to the boardwalk. It was very quiet out there and a gunshot would have drawn attention."

"Not if they'd used a silencer."

"True. I hadn't thought about that. Maybe they didn't have a silencer. Or maybe the guy just likes knives."

"What happened to the knife?" J.D. asked.

"I forgot about it in the rush to get home. It's on the front seat of my car."

"I'll go get it," J.D. said and got up and walked out the front door.

"You know," the chief said, "those folks on *Dulcimer* were killed with a knife or knives. Big ones."

"Was the M.E. able to come up with the kind of knife that was used?"

"Only in general terms. It may have been the same knife or it could have been two different ones. Whichever, they were big knives with straight edges. They could have been KA-BARS, like the ones issued to Marines."

"That's what this guy came at me with."

J.D. came in with the knife wrapped in a cloth. "Maybe there'll be prints on this."

"I doubt it," I said. "After I took it away from him I would have obliterated his prints with mine."

"You said he was hurt," Lester said.

"I'm pretty sure I broke his elbow. Probably ripped up all the tendons. He's going to need medical attention. Soon. The pain has got to be terrible."

The chief's cell phone rang. He answered, grunted into it a couple of times, and hung up. "The car they were in was reported stolen yesterday from a Wal-Mart in Sarasota. They haven't found it yet."

"They're in the wind," I said. "If they were somehow tied to the *Dulcimer* killings, why would they be after me? Unless there's some connection with Jim's murder."

"Even so," said J.D., "I don't understand how they even knew about you being involved in the investigation."

"It's a small island," said the chief. "Word gets around pretty quickly. Maybe Matt tripped over some alarm wires when he was in Georgia."

"Can I see the files on the *Dulcimer* murders?" I asked.

"Don't see why not," the chief said. "J.D. can bring them around later today."

J.D. stood. "I've got to get this knife to the crime-scene investigators. I'll pick up the files and stop back by this afternoon."

"Don't forget that Jock's coming in," I said.

"Shit," said the chief. "Every time Jock shows up, my island goes to hell."

"We'll be careful, Bill."

"Okay. Let's try to grab a beer while he's here. Do you need to see a doctor?"

"I don't think so. Nurse Duncan fixed me up fine."

"Nurse Duncan?" asked J.D., raising an eyebrow.

"Well, you know what I mean."

"Yeah. I'll see you this afternoon."

CHAPTER TWENTY-ONE

I met Logan at the Bridgetender Inn in Bradenton Beach for lunch. The rain had stopped, but it was still overcast. We sat in the bar overlooking the bay, a gray and colorless expanse of still water. The sailboats moored in the lagoon were buttoned up against the weather. I could hear the faint sound of generators humming in the distance, the boats keeping the air-conditioning flowing into the cabins. A large schooner was circling slowly out on the Intracoastal, waiting for the Cortez Bridge opening that was scheduled every twenty minutes.

"I had an interesting jog this morning," I said.

"Yeah? More of those nude people on Beer Can Island?"

I laughed. "No. I think the police have pretty much convinced them that town ordinances don't allow nudity."

"Too bad. Some of the women weren't bad to look at."

"You're a pervert."

"What's your point?"

I laughed again. Logan wasn't nearly as bad as he wanted people to believe. "Somebody tried to kill me on the North Shore boardwalk."

He put down the soda he'd been sipping. "What?"

"Guy came at me with a knife."

"You okay?"

"Little cut. J.D. put a bandage on it."

"What happened?"

I gave him the whole story.

Logan sat back in his chair. "If that guy's elbow was as messed up as you say, he's got to have medical attention."

"Bill Lester's got alerts out to all the area hospitals. If he shows up, they'll get him."

"What do you think the connection is to what you're doing about Jim Desmond?"

"I don't know. I guess somebody doesn't want me knocking around in the investigation."

"But why you? Why now? The cops have been looking into this thing for almost two months."

"I don't know that either, unless maybe my trip to Georgia got some people concerned that we might be closing in."

"Trip wires?"

"Maybe. I've been over my trip and I can't come up with anything unless it was my visit with the Otto Foundation."

"That may be it. They have all kinds of ties with the Laotian government."

"Yes. And the Cambodian and Vietnamese governments as well. The Otto Foundation works in all three countries."

"When is Jock due in?"

"Late this afternoon. He's flying into Tampa and will drive down."

"Maybe he can tell us something about Soupy and his gang."

"I hope so."

It started raining again, great sheets of water washing from the sky. I watched the wall of rain coming across the bay until it got to us and blotted out our view. Lightning flashes seared the dark sky, loud bursts of thunder following closely. Our daily thunderstorm had arrived a little earlier in the day than usual. This much rain would overwhelm the drainage system on the southern end of Anna Maria Island, and by the time we headed south for Longboat, great puddles would be standing on the road that ran beside Coquina Beach.

We finished our meal and the waitress came to offer us dessert or another drink. "Gotta wait out the storm," said Logan.

"We do."

"Scotch would help."

"It would."

"You want a beer?"

"I could handle that."

And so we idled away the afternoon watching the rain, sipping our drinks, and enjoying each other's company. At some point J.D. called to say she had the *Dulcimer* file copied. I told her where we were and that since it was still raining we might be a while. She told me to call if we weren't capable of driving when the rain stopped. She'd come get us.

At four, Jock called. "I'm about to cross the Cortez Bridge. Are you at home?"

"No. We're at the Bridgetender. Come on by here."

"Sounds as if you've been there a while."

"Lunch ran a little long."

He laughed. "I'll be there in five minutes."

I saw him as he crossed Bay Drive, dodging the puddles of water that had accumulated on the old asphalt. He was wearing black; a black silk T-shirt, black slacks, socks, and loafers. He was six feet tall with the wiry body of the runner. His skin had the texture of a man who spent much of his time outdoors. The planes of his face were sharp, his head mostly bald except for the fringe of back hair. He walked with purpose, scanning the street and the outside deck of the Bridgetender, placing every piece of furniture and anybody who was wandering by, setting it in his mind in case he had to react, dodge the danger that he always expected. He was alert, as always, a habit born of many years of clandestine operations, of the need to react instantly to any perceived threat, to be just a little quicker than his adversaries in order to stay alive.

He'd parked in one of the parking places that fronted the little beach on the bay side of the road. I hadn't paid any attention to the nondescript Chevrolet he'd rented at the Tampa airport as it nosed into the space. I didn't see him get out of the car. To my mind, he was just there, crossing the road like an apparition that appeared without warning.

Jock Algren was many things. He worked for one of our government's most secretive agencies, so secret that it had no name. Jock reported directly to the agency's director, who reported only to the president of the United States. He'd spent his adult life, all the days since college, in the service of our country. He was an assassin who killed our enemies when it had to be done. He was a secret agent who infiltrated dangerous cells of individuals bent on destroying America. He was ostensibly an oil company executive, using the cover of that job to move about the world without arousing suspicion. Most of all, he was my best friend since junior high school, more a brother than a friend. Somehow we were Karmically joined at the hip. We were each other's family.

I rose and embraced my old friend. He turned to Logan, hugged him, and said, "Looks like you guys have been at this a while."

I looked at my watch. A little after four. "It's been raining."

I hadn't really had that much to drink. A couple of beers had carried me through the afternoon. Logan had worked the Dewar's with determination, getting a little drunker with each drink, enjoying a day with nothing to do but watch the rain and sip his Scotch.

Jock sat and ordered an O'Doul's, the nonalcoholic beer that he fancied. Other than the occasional glass of wine, he almost never drank alcohol. He once told me that it dulled his senses and a man in his line of work couldn't afford to lose that finely honed edge that kept him alive.

I was the only person in the world who knew that when he came back from an operation, when he had blood on his hands that no amount of soap could remove, when he was questioning his right to live, he would crawl into a bottle of bourbon and stay there for several days. I was usually with him, his keeper as it were, the chaperone who kept him out of harm's way while he cleansed his system with the spirits that came from the bottle. And when it was over, when the guilt and self-loathing had worked their way out of the pores of his skin on the backs of the molecules of alcohol, he would spend a few days in frantic exercise, running, working out in the gym, taking long steam baths, healing his body. Then he'd be fine, the latest bout of conscience finished, and we'd go back to our lives, I to the beach and Jock to the vague trenches that served as the front lines in our war against the terrorists who would obliterate our culture.

"Tell me what's going on," said Jock.

"Do you remember me telling you about the medic who pulled my ass out of the fire in Vietnam at the risk of his own life?"

"Yes."

"He came to see me last week." I spent the next thirty minutes laying out all that had happened since I'd found Chaz Desmond standing at my front door. I ended with the story of my brush with death that morning.

Jock was quiet for a moment, sipping his O'Doul's. "What can I do to help?"

"I'd like to find out more about this Laotian, Souphanouvong Phomvihana and his operation. Can you get anything through your agency?"

"Sure. If he's on the radar of any of our intel groups, we'll have him."

"What if he's not?"

"If he's in the poppy business, we'll know about him."

My phone rang. J.D.

"Are you sober?" she asked.

"I am, but I'm not at all sure about Logan. Jock's here."

"Bring Logan to your house and put him to bed. I'll meet you there with the *Dulcimer* file and we can see if anything turns up. It'll be good to have Jock's eyes on it, too."

I hung up, looked at Logan, said, "Want to go home to bed?"

"Are you shitting me?"

"You look a little under the weather."

"I always look like this. I'm more sober than about ninety percent of the people on this island. What did J.D. want?"

I told him.

"Then let's pay up and get this show on the road." He got up from the table, threw some bills down, and walked toward his car. Steady as a rock.

CHAPTER TWENTY-TWO

We were gathered around my dining room table, the *Dulcimer* file spread out among the remains of the several pizzas we'd ordered from Oma's on Anna Maria Island, the ones delivered by a teenager driving a new Jaguar, an island oddity that amused me and ensured a generous tip. I liked the boy's chutzpah.

We'd been at it for a couple of hours. The day was dying. There would be no sunset this evening, at least not one that we could see. Dark clouds blanketed our island, hanging low and menacing, giving us a slight and unformed sense of dread, a feeling that evil was in the wind that blew from the mainland, a disconnected pathos that often comes on dismal days when the sun stays hidden and our little world is blighted by the grayness of it all. Perhaps it was only I who felt the small depression working up from my gut, the blackness of mood that I knew from experience could engulf me without warning and turn a merely bleak day into a dark abyss from which I was never sure I could escape.

I shook it off, mentally relegating the negative emotions to the oblivion that lurks somewhere deep in our minds where we banish thoughts that can overwhelm and ruin us. But I knew that dark tendrils of dread, like black wisps of some evil cloud, would play for hours at the edges of my consciousness, beckoning me into the pit. Maybe it was only the sequela of my brush with death beside a rain-swept beach on an island paradise that should not countenance violence, but was subject to it because the key was after all connected to the real world by substantial bridges that did not discriminate between predators and prey.

We'd gone over all the documents in the file, including a copy of the Coast Guard accident investigation. Each of us had read the statements of witnesses and the survivors of the dead. Jock put down the last statement, shaking his head. "Nothing much here that makes sense. How many of the passengers did you talk to?"

J.D. said, "As many as we could. There was no passenger list, but we did get the credit card receipts of those who paid that way. If they paid with cash, we had no way of finding them."

"I don't see but a few of the passengers' statements here," said Jock.

"There weren't many," J.D. said. "We talked to each one of the ones we could find, but most didn't see anything or know anything. We transcribed the statements of those who had anything of value, no matter how small the nugget of information. They're all in the file."

Jock held up a handful of statements. "It doesn't look like any of these people ever saw the Hooters girl and the lawyer together."

"No," J.D. said. "All we have is a few people who think they remember seeing them on the boat. We had pictures of both victims and we e-mailed them to the people we talked to if they'd already left the area."

"Were you able to find any kind of connection between the girl and the lawyer?" asked Logan.

"Nothing. Nada. Zip," said J.D. "The lawyer and his wife, Mr. and Mrs. Garrison, were staying at the Colony Beach and decided on the spur of the moment to take the boat. Katherine Brewster was at a B and B on Anna Maria and was following the suggestion of the owner, a Mrs. Jeanette Deen."

"I'd like to talk to Mrs. Deen," I said. "I wonder if she knows more than was in the statement."

"You think she was lying?" asked Logan.

"No. But there are some questions that I'd like to ask. We know more now than the officer who took the statement did at the time."

"What about Katherine's parents?" asked Jock.

"Yeah," I said. "I'd like to talk to them, too. I don't know if there is a connection between the *Dulcimer* killing and Jim Desmond's murder, but that was not part of the thinking when J.D. took their statements."

"You're right," said J.D. "And I took them over the phone. I've never met them."

I was a bit surprised. "They never came down here?"

"No. The body was shipped back to Charlotte for the funeral. There really was no need for them to come here."

Logan said, "Let's think this through for a minute. As I understand it, the only thing we have that might possibly tie the *Dulcimer* events and the Desmond murder together is the fact that the guy who came after Matt this morning was using a knife that was similar to the one that killed Garrison and Brewster on *Dulcimer*. And the only way to tie the attempt on Matt to the Desmond murder is that there may be a connection to some Laotian guy named Soupy who grows poppies for heroin dealers and who may still be pissed off at Jim Desmond for kicking his ass five years ago. That's pretty thin, Counselor."

"Well," I said, "when you put it that way—"

"Logan's right," said J.D. "There's a lot of supposition going on here."

"The fact that the murders all took place on the same day may be important," said Jock.

"How?" asked Logan.

"Don't know," said Jock.

"Coincidence?" asked J.D.

"Doubtful," I said.

"Why?" asked J.D.

"I don't like coincidence," I said.

"Another one of those famous Royal gut feelings?" asked J.D.

"You scoff," I said, "but that gut has kept me out of some bad scrapes."

"And got shot full of shrapnel, too," said J.D.

"Matt been showing his scars around again?" asked Jock.

"Yeah," said J.D. "Just about took my breath away."

"Sarcasm is not healthy," I said.

"Has he shown you the one on his ass?" asked Logan.

"Not yet," said J.D.

"I don't have a scar on my ass," I said.

"Pooh," said J.D. "I thought I had something to look forward to."

"If you're finished having sport with me," I said, "let's get back to the matters at hand."

"Are all lawyers such stuffed shirts?" asked Logan.

"Pretty much," I said. "I think I'd like to talk to Mrs. Deen and then make a trip up to Jacksonville and talk to Mrs. Garrison and on to Charlotte to meet with the Brewsters."

"I think that's a good idea," said J.D. "I'll make some calls. Pave the way with the witnesses."

"When do we start?" asked Jock.

"I'll go see Mrs. Deen tomorrow," I said.

CHAPTER TWENTY-THREE

The bar was in full swing, raucous, the music loud, the smoke-filled air alive with bawdy comments tossed randomly at the topless girls dancing on the elevated runways, writhing on the pole, their garters packed with five and ten dollar bills, giving the guys what they wanted, a fantasy of lust and fulfillment. The men knew it wasn't real, that it was only a mirage of sexuality. Yet a hope fueled by expensive and watered-down booze lingered in their fevered brains, a bare possibility of fulfillment that would be dashed as soon as the lights came up and the bartenders stopped serving and the dancers left with their tattooed boyfriends. The men would file out of the bar and drive to their homes, crawl into their lonely beds, and pass the night in alcoholic oblivion.

The young man glanced at his watch, turning his wrist to catch the minimal light from an overhead fixture. It was late and his friends had left an hour ago. He wasn't sure why he'd stayed, ennui perhaps, a seeming inability to get off his chair and leave. He hadn't drunk much, but had enjoyed the solitude, the anonymity of the bar on the edge of town late at night where no one knew his name. And truth be told, he enjoyed the slope of a well-rounded breast and the flexing of butt cheeks confined only by the single strap of a thong.

His thoughts drifted. He was only two years out of a public high school and much of his worldview was shaped by that experience. He'd known the jocks, the geeks, the dweebs, the preppies, the poor kids, and the rich. He fell into a couple of those categories, rich and preppie. There had never been a question but that he'd go to college and join his father in the family business. But what about the dancers? What had they been in high school? He couldn't place them in any of the categories. What made them become topless dancers? What drove them to undulate mostly naked on a stage and endure the catcalls of drunken men? Why were these pretty girls attaching themselves to men, boys really, who looked like societal dregs? It was all a mystery to the preppie from the suburbs.

He was not a snob. Far from it. He understood that there were people in his world who had not had his advantages, could not look forward to a future of prosperity and community acceptance. He appreciated the fact that he had been lucky to be born into his particular family, the son of a war hero who had become a man of substance and prominence in the city of his birth.

He was twenty years old and had, what, seventy more years to live? What he would do with those years would measure him as a man. Did it really matter that he didn't want the future that had been so meticulously crafted for him? His bridge year, the year between high school and college, half of it spent in Cambodia helping build a school in a place that had no sewage or running water or electricity, had given him a broader view of the world, one not circumscribed by the confines of a medium-sized southern city and its power structure, its flow of people and events little noticed outside its inhabitants' cloistered world.

He was going to have to have the talk with his father, explain his decision to follow a path other than the one ordained for him. It would disappoint the man, but the boy knew he would accept it, even encourage his son to find his own way to happiness and fulfillment.

He signaled for the waitress, paid his bill, and walked toward the entrance. He'd stop on his way home for a late-night burger and fries, maybe a milk shake. He hadn't eaten since lunch and even the little booze he'd consumed was taking a toll on his stomach. A little grease would be helpful.

As he walked toward the door, he was thinking about the next seventy years. He came from a long-lived family, so it was probable that he would live to see ninety. Maybe beyond that. He had a lot of life before him and he'd made up his mind. He'd talk to his father and then set out in the direction he wanted for himself. One that would take him happily through all the coming decades.

When the young man stepped out into the July night, he had less than two minutes to live.

CHAPTER TWENTY-FOUR

Torpor. Malaise. Lethargy. These are descriptions that fit the year-rounders when the dog days of August approach and the heat and humidity hang so heavy over our island that their weight drives us to the ground, turning us into whining creatures who scurry like spider crabs from our air-conditioned homes to air-conditioned cars to air-conditioned markets or restaurants or bars and back again. The key is sparsely populated, with even some of the full-time residents fleeing to cooler climes in northern states or the mountains of the Midsouth. It is a time when few tourists visit our island and those who do are other Floridians who trade the heat of the interior for the anemic breezes that blow from the Gulf of Mexico. It is a time when listlessness stalks the island, when we fall into a kind of stupor that is interrupted only by our need for cold beer and whiskey and boozy comradeship with our fellow sun dwellers, those souls who gladly trade the blissful Florida winters for the harsh summers that drive less hardy mortals into cooler venues to the north.

August had crept up on me with little fanfare. Another month gone, a little closer to mid-October when our weather usually turns gorgeous for its seven month run up to the heat of the summer that comes early in our latitudes.

So, on the first day of August, I drove the Explorer north across the Longboat Pass Bridge onto Anna Maria Island, through the towns of Bradenton Beach and Holmes Beach and into the village of Anna Maria City that perches on the northern end of the seven-mile-long island. The bed and breakfast was a large and rambling Key West-style home that boasted five bedrooms, each with a private bath. It sat on the tip of the island with views over Passage Key Inlet to the Sunshine Skyway Bridge and Egmont Key. A thin beach separated the water from the grass lawn behind the little inn.

A small brass sign on the front door invited me in. I walked into a large foyer with hardwood floors and a staircase ascending to the second floor. A desk sitting near the stairs held a computer and a small bell. A sign welcomed me to the Anna Maria Inn and suggested I ring the bell for service.

A woman came from the back in response to the bell. "Hello," she said, "I'm Jeanette Deen. You must be Mr. Royal. Right on time. Detective Duncan said you'd be by this morning."

I'd read the transcript of the statement a young police officer had taken from Jeanette Deen. I knew she was in her mid-sixties and had bought the Anna Maria Inn with her husband about ten years before when she had retired as principal of an elementary school over in the middle of the state.

The woman standing before me looked to be late forties, perhaps early fifties if you wanted to stretch it. She was trim and fit, her dark hair showing only a few strands of gray. She was smiling and I could see the reflection of the beauty she must have been in her youth. She was still beautiful, but in a more restrained and refined way. She had aged gracefully and because of good genes or good living or both had retained much of her youth far beyond the age when most of us begin to wrinkle and sag.

"It's nice to meet you, Mrs. Deen," I said. "I appreciate your taking the time to speak to me."

"Please call me Jeanette, Mr. Royal. I hope I can be of some help. It was truly tragic what happened to that young woman. Come on back to the kitchen. I've got fresh coffee brewing."

I followed her to the back of the house and sat at a table in a dining nook that was surrounded by glass, giving me the benefit of the view up Tampa Bay to the Sunshine Skyway Bridge. She poured coffee for both of us and took a seat across from me. "How can I help you, Mr. Royal?"

"Please call me Matt, Jeanette. I'm a lawyer and I represent a man whose son was killed on the beach on Longboat Key back in June, the same day as the murders on the *Dulcimer*. We think there may be a connection between the two events."

"I hadn't heard that."

"There hasn't been any press on it. We're not even sure there is a connection, but we're trying to find out."

"Who is 'we' if I might ask?"

"I'm working closely with Chief Bill Lester and Detective J. D. Duncan of the Longboat Key police. Our interests are the same. We're trying to find out who committed the murders."

"How can I help?"

"What can you tell me about Katherine Brewster?"

"Not much, I'm afraid. She'd only been here for a couple of days when she died. I suggested she take the *Dulcimer* cruise that evening. She had a gift certificate for dinner on the boat, but I don't know if she intended to use it. Maybe if I hadn't suggested she go, she'd still be alive."

"You can't blame yourself."

"Oh, I don't. I understand that things happen. If I hadn't suggested she go on the boat that evening, she might have been killed crossing Cortez Road or on the trip back to Charlotte. There's no way of telling, so I know intellectually that I wasn't the cause of her death. But one does wonder at the vagaries of life, doesn't one?"

"One does. I'm convinced that life is a series of random events that somehow come together in some sequence that is beyond our understanding. That sequence, when it becomes a whole timeline, is what we call our lives. It may be fate or the result of a higher intelligence or God. I don't know, but it's there."

"Oh, I think God has a hand in it. I'm not sure just how, but then that's part of the eternal mystery, isn't it?"

I smiled. "It is a mystery, and for some of us it works out very well and that's what we call happiness."

She smiled. "You're a philosopher, Matt."

"Right." I laughed. "Do you know how she chose your place for her stay, or for that matter, how she chose Anna Maria?"

"That's easy. She was given a gift certificate for a week's stay here at my inn. She said she had been asked to bartend at a function in Charlotte, some charity event, and a few days later, she got the certificate in the mail along with a thank-you note signed by the chairman of the event."

"Was the gift certificate one you issued?"

"Yes."

"To whom?"

"To a travel agency in Charlotte."

"Was this unusual?"

"Not really. Sometimes an agency somewhere requests one. They pay me with a credit card less their commission and I send it to them. It's blank, so they can put whatever name they want to on the certificate."

"Would you have a record of the one used by Katherine Brewster?"

"I'm sure I do. It'll be in my computer."

I followed her back out to the foyer. She sat at the desk and clicked at the keyboard for a few seconds. "Here it is. Each certificate is numbered and the one that Katherine used was issued by me to the EZGo Travel Agency in Charlotte on May fifteenth of this year."

"Have you sent them other certificates?"

"I don't think so." She went back to the keyboard. "No. That's the only one."

"Can you check to see how it was paid for?"

A few more clicks. "A credit card. Would you like the number?"

"I would."

I thanked her for the coffee and the information and left.

CHAPTER TWENTY-FIVE

It was nearing noon as I crossed the Longboat Pass Bridge. I'd planned to meet Jock at Moore's Stone Crab Restaurant for lunch. Logan had a morning doctor's appointment and then was going to meet Marie for lunch in downtown Sarasota. J.D. was lunching with the chief to bring him up to date on our evolving views of the cases.

I was a few minutes early, so I swung by my house. I wanted to call EZGo Travel. I dialed information and asked for the Charlotte number. There was no listing. I thought that strange, but then figured it was probably in one of the suburbs. I went to my computer and Googled EZGo. Nothing. Nowhere in the entire country. I went to the North Carolina public records. No listing for a corporation or a fictitious name filing for EZGo. Some of the Charlotte suburbs are in South Carolina, so I checked those records. Nothing.

I called Jeanette Deen. "Hi Jeanette, this is Matt Royal. Sorry to bother you again so soon."

"No bother, Matt."

"Do you have an address for EZGo? The place where you sent the gift certificate?"

"I'm sure I do. Hold on a minute."

I heard the keyboard clicking and she came back on the line. "It was to a post office box in Charlotte," she said, and gave me the box number.

"Thanks, Jeanette. I'll try not to bother you again."

"Anytime, Matt. It's not a problem."

I drove down to Moore's. I usually walked, but it was August and my Explorer had a healthy air-conditioning system. I'm no fool.

Jock was sitting at the deserted bar talking to Debbie, who had been serving drinks there for the past twenty years. She was a good friend and I think secretly had a thing for Jock. I joined them.

"I heard somebody was trying to kill you yesterday," she said.

"News travels fast."

"There's never new news on this island. It's old before it has time to germinate a little. The gossip telegraph works very well, even in August."

"Well, I'm okay. In case you were worried."

"We probably need a better class of killer on this island. You know, somebody who knows what he's doing."

"Ah, Deb. You'd miss me."

"Well, I'd sure miss those big quarter tips you give."

"You're worth it, babe."

She laughed, threw a dish towel at me and went to the beer cooler for my Miller Lite.

"Did you find out anything?" Jock asked.

I related my conversation with Jeanette Deen. "She sent the gift certificate to EZGo Travel Agency in Charlotte, but there is no such business. Just a post office box. I've got the credit card number that the certificate was charged to. Maybe that'll give us some more information."

"You going to ask Deb to check it out?" he asked.

"Yep. We'll save your agency for the hard stuff."

"Check what out?" Deb asked.

"I just need a little hacking job," I said.

"Geez, Royal. There's no such thing as a little hacking job. They're all big. What do you need?"

"Some information on who pays the bills on a certain credit card?"

"You got the number?"

"Of course."

"Give it to me. I'll check it out when I get home tonight."

Debbie was a very competent hacker. She'd taken some computer courses at the local community college just for her own edification. The further she got into it, the more she realized she had a gift. Before long, she was hacking her way into all kinds of databases. It was a hobby for her, and she never took anything of value or shared the information with anyone else. I was probably the only person other than Jock and Logan who realized what she could do. She'd helped us out before.

Back at my house, I typed a note of my conversation with Jeanette Deen into my computer and e-mailed it to J.D. and Doc Desmond. Jock was on his cell phone, which had some sort of encryption that ensured the privacy of his conversations. He was talking to somebody at his agency headquarters in Washington.

"They'll get back to me on Soupy," Jock said as he closed his phone.

"Thanks. We may be chasing wild geese with the *Dulcimer* murders. If Soupy sent a team to take out Jim Desmond why would they kill two people who apparently have no relationship with each other or with Desmond? It just doesn't make sense."

"Maybe Soupy is the wild goose."

"You're thinking that he might not have anything to do with any of this?"

"That's one option. Another is that *Dulcimer* and Jim are just coincidences." He held up his hands. "I know, I know. You don't like coincidences, but sometimes they happen."

"What would you guess the percentages of that are?"

"Near zero, but that doesn't make it impossible."

I shook my head. "You may be right, but I don't like it."

"I agree," said Jock. "Let's keep digging. We'll either hit a complete dead end or we'll turn over a rock somewhere and find our answers."

I thought he was right. I called Mrs. Garrison in Jacksonville. "My name is Matt Royal, Mrs. Garrison. I'm a lawyer in Longboat Key and I've been retained to look into the deaths on the *Dulcimer*."

"I remember you, Mr. Royal. You pulled me out of the water. But who would be looking into that now? I gather that the police haven't been able to find much of anything."

"My client's son was killed on Longboat Key the same day as your husband. There may not be any connection between the murders, but I need to cover all the bases. May I come to Jacksonville to meet with you tomorrow?"

There was a silence on the other end of the phone line, a slow exhalation of breath. "I don't see why not. I've talked to the police twice, so I'm not sure there's anything else I can tell you."

We agreed to a time for me to be at her house and then I called the Brewsters in Charlotte. I told them the same thing I'd told Mrs. Garrison and they agreed to meet with me two days later. It would take me that much time to drive to Jacksonville and then on up to Charlotte.

I called Chaz Desmond to tell him what we'd learned and how confused we were. "I'm going to Jacksonville to talk to Mrs. Garrison and then on up to Charlotte to see the Brewsters."

"When are you planning to go?"

"I'll drive up to Jacksonville tonight and meet with Mrs. Garrison tomorrow. I'll go on from there to Charlotte and see the Brewsters the day after tomorrow."

"I'll send my plane. You can leave in the morning, meet Mrs. Garrison and then fly on to Charlotte. You'll be home tomorrow night."

"That sounds like a plan, Doc. I'll make sure the Brewsters are free tomorrow afternoon."

"Be at Dolphin Aviation at the Sarasota-Bradenton Airport at eight in the morning. My pilot's name is Fred Cassidy."

CHAPTER TWENTY-SIX

I drove the rental car toward the south side of Jacksonville, the quiet of a Sunday morning making me think of that old Johnny Cash song "Sunday Morning Coming Down." The sidewalks, lined by old oak trees draped with moss, were still asleep and I felt a little out of place as if I had suddenly been transported from another dimension to this large southern city cloaked in its Sunday solitude.

Betty Garrison lived in a Georgian-style red brick home fronting the St. Johns River. Apparently her husband Peter had been a very successful lawyer. She answered the door wearing a pair of white linen slacks, a white blouse trimmed in turquoise, and white boat shoes. Her only jewelry was a pendant necklace, a small stone that matched the color of the trim on her blouse. She was a petite brunette with a southern accent that immediately put me at ease.

We went to a family room that had a lot of glass overlooking the river. It was ten in the morning and the sun was already high. A boat with a skier behind roared in near the shore, and the laughter of teenagers floated on the breeze. Far out in the middle of the river a towboat pushed a barge southbound.

The St. Johns is wide as it winds its way through Jacksonville, its languid current pushing toward the sea. It is one of the few rivers in the world that flow northward, and when Jock and I were teenagers we'd spent a lot of pleasant hours on the river's upper reaches near our hometown in central Florida.

Mrs. Garrison offered coffee, which I accepted, and we settled into high-back chairs facing each other. "I hope I can help, Mr. Royal, but as I said on the phone, I've told the police everything I know."

"I know some of my questions will be the same the police asked, but if you'll bear with me I'll be out of your hair real quick."

She smiled. "I've got all the time in the world."

"Tell me how you came to be aboard the *Dulcimer* that evening?"

"My husband and I were taking a little break and had gone to Longboat Key. We were staying at the Colony Beach. We went to the restaurant on the property for dinner. Peter picked up a tourist brochure on the way in and one of the coupons was for the dinner cruise on the *Dulcimer*. We decided to try it the next evening."

"Do you remember seeing Katherine Brewster at all that evening?"

"Vaguely. The police showed me a picture of her. I remember seeing her on the boat because she was so strikingly beautiful and I wondered why she was alone."

"How did you know she was alone?"

"She was sitting at a table for two, but at first no other guest was there. I noticed one man who seemed to be hitting on her stop by, but he left pretty quickly. Then another young man came in and sat with her for a few minutes and left."

"Can you describe either of the men?"

"The young man who sat with her didn't stand out at all. He was in a golf shirt and jeans, brown hair, I think. He seemed a little agitated and didn't stay long."

"What about the man who seemed to be hitting on her? Can you describe him?"

"No. I couldn't even tell you what he was wearing. I just have a vague recollection of a man. He may not have even been hitting on her. Maybe I just assumed it."

"Where was she sitting in relation to you and your husband?"

"There was a line of tables for two set along the windows. She was at the next table, right behind Peter. She and my husband were sitting back to back and I was directly across from him."

"Was there any indication that your husband knew Katherine?"

"I don't believe he did. He spoke to her when we sat down at the table, but nothing else."

"Do you have children?" I asked.

"Two. A boy and a girl."

"Do they live here?"

"No. My daughter is married and lives in Miami. My son is a student at the University of Florida, but he's traveling in Europe right now. He'll be back on campus in a couple of weeks."

"Did you ask if either of them knew Katherine?"

"Yes. I thought of that. She was close to their ages. They didn't know her."

"I understand you went up on deck for a smoke just before the lights went out on *Dulcimer*."

"Yes. A terrible habit, but I was down to about five cigarettes a day. I'm completely off them now."

"Why didn't your husband go topside with you?"

"He was very sensitive to smoke. The least little whiff of it and he'd start sneezing. I always went outside by myself to feed the habit."

"Did you see any Asians that night aboard the boat?"

"Nobody ever asked me that one." She was quiet for a moment, thinking. She shut her eyes as if trying to conjure up a memory, then opened them wide, a look of surprise crossing her face. "Oh my goodness. You're right. I did see somebody. The man I thought was hitting on Katherine was Asian."

CHAPTER TWENTY-SEVEN

Betty Garrison and I talked for another half hour, but she could tell me no more than she already had. Her memory of the Asian man was limited. She knew he was Asian, but she could not describe him. She didn't remember if she ever heard him speak, so she couldn't tell me whether the man had an accent. As far as she knew her husband had never had any dealings with Asians in his practice, but that might not be the case. She wouldn't have known unless Peter made a point of telling her and there was no reason for him to do so. She agreed to check with the managing partner of Peter's law firm and find out about any clients that might have had a beef with him. She would also determine if he'd had any recent clients from Asia.

I'd left Jock at my house. He was working the phones and the computer, running down anything the federal government had on Souphanouvong Phomvihana and his poppy growing operation. He was calling in a lot of favors.

I drove back to Craig Airport and boarded Doc's plane for the trip to Charlotte. I typed my notes on my conversation with Betty Garrison into my laptop and e-mailed them to both Jock and J.D. and a copy to Chaz Desmond.

George and Estelle Brewster lived in a small bungalow in a working-class neighborhood near the rail yards northeast of downtown Charlotte. They were tired people with wan complexions, their bodies gaunt, their hair gray. They were two people beaten into submission by life's dark whims. Perhaps the loss of their only child had been the ultimate defeat visited on them by a world they no longer understood, a loss that deflated them and turned them into the walking dead, those cadaverous beings who look forward to the grave and solace at last, the comforting presence of death providing some measurable meaning to their lives.

I knew from the earlier police statements that the Brewsters were in their fifties, but they looked eighty. Their small house was tidy and smelled of musty furniture that had not been moved in a generation. The living room was spare with only a chair, a sofa, and an old console television set that must have been at least twenty years old. Three photographs sat atop the TV, a portrait of Katherine that was probably her high school senior picture, another of all three Brewsters standing on the front porch of their home, and a third of Katherine and a young man smiling for the camera, low mountains providing a backdrop for what must have been a happy day.

We sat, I on the chair and the couple on the sofa, holding hands, looking glum. "I'm sorry to intrude," I said, "but I'm hoping you can help me solve the murder of your daughter." I'd told them over the phone when I set up the meeting and then moved it up a day what my interest in the case was.

"Mr. Royal, I hope you can figure it out. Kat was our only child. She was a happy girl with a big streak of kindness for everybody," said George.

"Tell me about her," I said.

"She was twenty-five years old. She'd finished the local community college and was working to save some money to finish her education at UNC-Charlotte."

"How long had she worked at Hooters?"

"Almost two years. She was banking most of her money and was going to start school at UNCC this fall."

"Did she ever have any men bothering her at the restaurant? Hitting on her?"

"Oh," said Estelle, "I'm sure that happened often enough, but she let it roll off. She had a boyfriend."

"Who's the boyfriend?"

"His name's Doug Peterson. They met at the community college. They'd been going together for about three years. Planned to get married when they both finished college."

"Had there been any problems with their relationship?"

"No. They seemed very happy," said Estelle.

"Why didn't he go to Florida with her?"

"They really couldn't afford it, and Doug couldn't get the time off," said George. "Kat's trip was free except for the gas money to get down there."

It had not occurred to me to even ask how Katherine had gotten to Anna Maria. I had just assumed she went by air. "She drove down?"

"Yes. She had a Honda that she kept in great shape. All paid for. She bought it used when she graduated from high school."

"How did you get the car back to Charlotte?"

"Doug took a bus down and drove it back," said Estelle.

"Where does Doug work?"

"He works on a lawn maintenance crew over at the university. He's a junior there, planning to be a school teacher. Just like Kat."

"Where did Katherine get the free stay on Anna Maria?" I asked.

"Funny," said George. "It came in the mail. Kind of a surprise."

"Where did it come from?"

"She worked a charity benefit over at the arena back in April. She was a bartender and one of the organizers sent her the certificate."

"Did she know the man before he sent the certificate?"

"I don't think so," said George. "She didn't even recognize the name on the letter that came with the gift certificate, but she appreciated it."

Estelle said, "She said she needed to get away by herself to do some thinking."

"Do you know what she needed to think about?"

Estelle shook her head. "No. She didn't want to talk about it."

"What was the charity event she worked?"

"I don't know," said George.

"Wait," said Estelle. "I think the letter that came with the gift certificate is still in Kat's room."

She left us, disappearing into the back of the house. George and I sat quietly. I watched him stare off into space, saw tears collecting in his eyes. He wiped them away with his calloused hand, sniffed once, pulled a handkerchief from his back pocket, blew his nose, and stared some more.

Estelle returned with a letter-sized paper and two smaller ones. She handed them to me. The first was a note thanking Katherine for helping out at the event and enclosing two gift certificates as tokens of appreciation. One certificate was for the stay at the Anna Maria Inn and the other for a dinner aboard *Dulcimer*. The signature was illegible, but the name typed underneath the scrawl was "Ronald Brumbaugh." The letterhead identified the charity as "Charlotte Learns, Inc." A subheading claimed it as "A not-for-profit corporation that supports public schools in poverty stricken neighborhoods." The smaller sheets were copies of the gift certificates from the Anna Maria Inn and *Dulcimer* issued through EZGo Travel. The certificate for the Anna Maria Inn was for the specific date in June, but the *Dulcimer* certificate was open-ended and could be used at any time at the recipient's discretion.

"Do you know this Mr. Brumbaugh?" I asked.

"No," said Estelle. "And Kat didn't either."

"What about Charlotte Learns?"

"That's a charity that we read about in the paper sometimes. They help our teachers buy pencils and paper and stuff for the poor kids."

"Do you know the name of Doug's supervisor over at the college?" I asked George.

"No," he said. "He worked out of the maintenance department. That's all I know. Why?"

"Don't take this wrong, Mr. Brewster," I said, "but we need to make sure Doug was in Charlotte at the time Katherine died."

Estelle put her hand to her mouth. "He had dinner here that day. With us. Besides, Doug loved Kat. He would never have harmed her."

"I'm sorry I had to ask," I said, feeling a little foolish.

We talked some more without me learning anything new. I got up from the chair, thanked them for their time, and followed George toward the front door. Hanging on the wall between a window and the door was a shadow box with military decorations pinned inside along with the symbol of the U.S. Marine Corps.

"You were a Marine?" I asked.

"Yep. Did six years in the corps. Two tours in Vietnam. Did you serve?"

"Yeah. I did a tour right at the end of the war. Army."

"What branch?"

"Special Forces."

"You guys were tough."

"So were you jarheads. Were you infantry?"

"Yeah. I was trained as a sniper and worked in Force Recon."

"A Marine sniper. The best of the best."

"So they told me."

I shook his hand. "Thank you for your service."

"And thank you for yours."

I left them standing on the porch as dusk enveloped us.

CHAPTER TWENTY-EIGHT

The small jet banked slightly and lined up on its final approach to Sarasota-Bradenton Airport. I looked down at the dark expanse of Sarasota Bay, clearly outlined by the lights of the mainland and the barrier islands. Headlights moved across the Anna Maria Bridge, its superstructure defined by red and green lights. People on their way home or out to eat. A placid scene that reminded me of why I loved my islands so much. It was hard to reconcile this sense of normalcy with the murders that had occurred a couple of months before. I wondered if I would be able to find the murderers, to bring some peace to the victims' families and perhaps to the spirits of the dead themselves.

I'd driven the rental car away from that small house in Charlotte where grief was edging out the good memories of an aging couple who had lost their only child and their remaining hope of happiness. The plane was fueled and ready to go. Two hours later we were crossing the bay on final approach.

During the flight, I'd typed my notes into my laptop and e-mailed them to J.D. and Chaz Desmond. I called Jock and arranged to meet him for a late dinner at the Seafood Shack in Cortez. He was going to bring J.D. I pulled into the restaurant parking lot a few minutes after nine o'clock, walked down the outside deck to the bay side dining area. Jock and J.D. were already seated at a window table. I joined them.

"How was the trip?" Jock asked.

"Quick."

"Did you find out anything?" asked J.D.

"Betty Garrison remembered an Asian man speaking to Katherine

Brewster on the boat the night of the murders." I filled them in on the rest of the trip and what I'd found out. Which wasn't much.

A waitress came and took our orders, and removed the menus. She looked tired. The beauty of the bay would have long ago been lost on her. I guess when one works in paradise every day, one becomes a bit jaded about the scenery that draws the tourists that makes the job possible in the first place. She returned immediately with our drinks, a beer for me, wine for J.D., and O'Doul's for Jock.

"I'm interested in the bogus travel agency," said J.D. "How did the gift certificate from the B and B on Anna Maria end up with Katherine? And why a fictitious travel agency?"

"Debbie called this afternoon," said Jock. "She ran the credit card number on EZGo and came up with a blank. The card was issued to a company named EZGo and was guaranteed by a man named, get this, John Doe."

J.D. laughed. "You're kidding."

"Nope. Apparently the credit card companies aren't very discriminating. The card was used twice. Once for the gift certificate for the Anna Maria Inn and a second time for gas at a service station in Bradenton."

"Did the name Brumbaugh come up in Deb's search?" I asked.

"She didn't mention it to me," said Jock, "and she would have, I think. So I'd say no."

"Anything from your agency on Soupy?" I asked.

"A lot, but I've still got to sort through all the data. He's pretty big in the poppy business and apparently commands a sizable army. He's well known to our intelligence groups as one of the Golden Triangle warlords."

"Any Laotian government involvement?"

"He's right in the middle of it. Most of the warlords have their own people in the various ministries. I don't know how much control Soupy has over what the government does, but he certainly has influence."

"Any indication that he operates outside Laos?" I asked.

"None. I asked our director to query the intelligence agencies. It all came back negative. Apparently Soupy is happy to stay right there in Laos."

J.D. had been sitting quietly. "That doesn't mean he couldn't have sent some goons to take out Jim Desmond."

I shook my head. "The ones who tried to kill me grew up in America. Their English was too good, too idiomatic, to have been learned somewhere else."

"Maybe the ones who attacked you were born here, but their parents are part of Soupy's organization," said J.D.

I nodded. "That's a possibility. I wish I'd been able to hold onto one of them."

Jock said, "I also checked on the Otto Foundation. It's legit. Sends kids to build schools in Southeast Asia. Its director Bud Stanley is another matter."

"What do you mean?" I asked.

"His real name is Robert Charles Bracewell, Jr. Thirty years ago, when he was in his early twenties, he and his dad were involved in a heroin import business in Long Beach, California. The DEA busted them and both went to prison. Senior died there, but Junior, who was called Bud, did his ten years at Lompoc and went on to better things. He legally changed his name to Bud Stanley, went to college at Cal State Northridge, got a degree, and went into the charitable business. He's kept his skirts clean."

"Sounds like a guy who learned his lesson," I said.

"Possibly," said Jock. "But guess who was on the other end of the heroin pipeline?"

"Shit," I said. "You're going to tell me it was Soupy's dad."

"You get the gold star. None other than Soupy's old man."

"No evidence Stanley's still involved?" J.D. asked.

"None," said Jock. "His bank accounts show he's living on his salary from the Otto Foundation."

"Family?"

"Never married. No kids. Mom died while he was in college."

"That's very strange," I said.

"There's more."

I looked at Jock. He was showing a half smile of anticipation. A surprise was coming.

"I'm waiting," I said.

"Bud Stanley has a very nice history. There is no connection to Bracewell. The record of his years before college, the years he was really in prison, is full of jobs that lasted a year or two. All in little companies that no longer exist. He was a typical young man struggling to make a living and then went back to college in his thirties."

"I don't understand," said J.D.

"Somebody manufactured a pretty airtight background for our Mr. Stanley. I even have his high school records, the ones that Cal State got when he applied. He was a mediocre student who did not seem to the advisors to be college material. They're all bogus."

"How airtight is it if you can find out all this stuff in one day?" asked J.D.

"Damned airtight. Nobody would find the connection to Bracewell unless the one looking happens to be an intelligence agency of the United States government."

"So," I said, "Bud had some help. Could he be part of the U.S. Marshal's witness protection program?"

"We checked," said Jock. "The Marshals have never heard of either Stanley or Bracewell."

"Any ideas on how he manufactured such an extensive background?" I asked.

"It's possible he did it himself, but more likely he had help. This was a professional job."

"How did you tie Bracewell and Stanley together?" asked J.D.

"Anytime somebody's doing business with our government in a foreign country, they're fingerprinted. Unless there's some reason, such as a security clearance, to compare the prints to others, it's not done. The prints are just put in a file and can be used for identification if needed. I asked my agency to run Stanley's prints. We got a hit on Bracewell and followed up."

"Did Bracewell just drop out of sight after Stanley showed up?" asked J.D.

Jock grinned. "A death certificate was filed on Bracewell in Los Angeles County about the time that Stanley applied to Cal State. Showed a death from natural causes and burial in a local cemetery."

I knew the look on Jock's face. "What else?"

He laughed. "The only other place that Bracewell's name has shown up in the past twenty years is on a bank account in Switzerland."

"Still active?" J.D. asked.

"Yep."

J.D. frowned. "I understand that there's no way to crack Swiss bank secrecy."

"That's generally true," said Jock. "But there are ways to do it."

"Can we get a look at that account?" I asked.

"My agency has a mole in the bank that holds the account. But, the director doesn't want to use him unless we have something that touches on national security. If we can tie the Desmond murder into a security issue, we can get the information."

"Fat chance," said J.D.

CHAPTER TWENTY-NINE

It was late when we finished our meal, but I wasn't sleepy. Jock and J.D. were ready to call it a day and headed home. I stopped by Tiny's for a beer and a little conversation with friends. The place was nearly empty. Susie, the proprietor, was leaning over the bar talking to Cracker Dix. Two men sat at the end of the bar deep in conversation. The TV above the bar was muted, a baseball game in progress. Somehow the games always seem a little better without the incessant chatter of the announcers.

Susie looked up as I came in. "Hey, Matt."

"Hey, Susie. Cracker."

I took the stool next to Cracker. Susie moved to the cooler to retrieve a Miller Lite for me, brought it back, and set it on a cardboard coaster on the bar. "I heard that Jock was in town."

"Yeah, but the weenie wanted to go home to bed."

"Where's Logan?"

"With Marie. They're having dinner on the mainland. How're you doing, Cracker?"

"No complaints. I heard you've been looking into the murders on *Dulcimer.*"

I chuckled. Everybody knows everything on a small island. Cracker was an expatriate Englishman who'd lived on Longboat Key for thirty years. He'd come with his bride to visit his new in-laws when he was in his mid-twenties and stayed. The marriage didn't last, but his love for our key was as deeply ingrained in his persona as the accent he'd never lost. He stood about five feet eight and his wardrobe seemed to be limited to Hawaiian shirts, beige cargo shorts, and flip-flops, and on cooler days, boat shoes. He wore a thin strand of gold around his neck and a small gold stud in his right ear. He was as bald as an onion and much loved by the islanders.

"Not really," I said. "I'm trying to help an old friend find out who killed his son on the beach the same day as the *Dulcimer* murders. I don't think there's any connection, but I'm checking it out."

"Did you know that Dora was aboard *Dulcimer* that night?"

"No. What was she doing on a tourist dinner boat in June? She's usually in the mountains by then."

"She was late leaving this year and the *Observer* asked her to do a piece on the boat."

"I'd like to talk to her. Do you know how to reach her in Blue Ridge?"

"Don't have to. She's here."

"What's she doing on the key in August?"

"She had to come back for a doctor's appointment or something. She's only here for a couple of days."

"Thanks, Cracker."

The evening wore on. The two men at the end of the bar left, and a few minutes later Tracy Tharp and three other servers from Pattigeorge's came in. Tracy gave me a hug and chatted a few minutes before joining her friends at one of the high-top tables near the bar. A group of workers from Mar Vista arrived for what Susie called the second shift, a time when the restaurants on the north end of the key closed and the workers stopped at Tiny's for a nightcap before heading home.

Cracker was in a storytelling mood, and I enjoyed hearing about his hilarious escapades in Wales, India, Pakistan, and other places that his hippie culture had taken him before he settled down on Longboat. I'd heard some of the stories before, but when Cracker was on a roll, new tales appeared, each one funnier that the last. I often wondered which were true and which were the result of the hyper imagination that rolled around in Cracker's enormous brain. I left Tiny's in a better mood than when I'd arrived, and headed home.

The house was quiet except for the snoring coming from Jock's room. I locked up and went to bed and dreamed of soldiers who had died in a strange land. My soldiers.

CHAPTER THIRTY

Jock and I were sitting on the patio drinking coffee under whirring ceiling fans. The sun was up, the sky cloudless, the bay green and clear. I heard the clatter of a low-flying helicopter and soon spotted it, a Coast Guar-chopper heading north over the bay. An osprey flew low above us, a fish in its talons, gliding toward its nest on Jewfish Key. I was telling Jock about my conversation the night before with Cracker Dix.

"I've met Dora," he said. "She's the small gray-haired lady who comes into Tiny's sometimes."

"Yes. I didn't remember anything being printed in the paper about the killings, so I called J.D. She said there was nothing."

"That seems a little strange. You've got a reporter on the scene of two murders and she doesn't even do a human-interest-type story."

"Yeah. Dora spent a lot of years with major news organizations cov-ering some of the world's hotspots. She'd surely know how to write a story about two people knifed to death on a boat. Why didn't she?"

Jock smiled. "I guess you've got to ask her that."

I looked at my watch. Nine o'clock. I opened my cell phone and di-aled her number. She answered on the second ring.

"Good morning, Dora. This is Matt Royal."

"Good morning, Matt. How are you?"

"A bit perplexed."

"Well, that won't do. How can I help unperplex you?"

"I was talking to Cracker Dix last night. He said you were aboard *Dulcimer* the night of the murders."

"I was."

"But you didn't write a story."

"No."

"Mind telling me why?"

"Not if you'll buy me lunch today."

"Isn't there some law against bribing journalists?"

"Probably."

"Well, you never eat much anyway. I guess a small bribe won't hurt."

"I don't think so. Mar Vista at noon?"

"I'll see you there."

Dora Walters was a petite woman with a cap of gray hair, a ready smile, and eyes that sparkled with the vestige of the beautiful girl she'd been fifty years before. She was in her seventies now, and spent her winters on our key and her summers in the North Georgia mountain town of Blue Ridge. She'd been an internationally known reporter who had semiretired to her job on our local paper. She had traded the reporting of international incidents for taking pictures of self-satisfied partygoers holding drinks and smiling vacuously for her ever-present camera. She always seemed amused by her job and the people she covered. It wasn't the same as reporting on heads of state, but it suited her and she was content to spend her winters slipping into parties and taking pictures and writing stories of this or that charity fund-raiser.

I walked the short distance from my house to the restaurant and was sweating in the August heat by the time I arrived. Dora was just pulling into the parking lot, so I waited at the door for her.

"Matt, you must be nuts, walking in this heat."

"Well, it was only a couple blocks."

"Yeah. In this heat." She walked through the door shaking her head.

We took a seat by the windows overlooking the bay. A waiter came and took our order, a salad for Dora and a burger for me. He brought our drinks a minute or two later and disappeared into the dark reaches of the kitchen.

"Why are you here this time of the year?" I asked. "Aren't you usually still in the mountains?"

"Yes, but I had to come home for a few days to take care of some business matters. I'm headed back tomorrow."

"So," I said, "why no story about the murders on *Dulcimer*?"

"By the time I could write it, it wasn't a story."

"What do you mean?"

"The *Observer* is a weekly. Our absolute drop-dead deadline is Tuesday evening. I was on the boat on a Monday evening. The story would have to be set up on Tuesday to be in that week's paper. It wasn't supposed to be much of a story. And it wouldn't have been without the murders. Just something to fill space during the summer dearth of news on the key."

"Why were you even here? Don't you usually go to Blue Ridge in May?"

"Usually. But I was having some work done on my house and it was taking longer than expected. So I stayed put for an extra couple of weeks."

"So, why didn't you write the story on Tuesday?"

"I was in the hospital."

"What?" I was surprised. I hadn't heard that Dora had been hurt.

"It was nothing. When *Dulcimer* ran aground, I was knocked off my feet. Pete Collandra was one of the medics on the scene and he sent me to the hospital to be sure I hadn't hurt something important. I got out the next day, but it was too late to write the story. By the following week it was old news. Thus, no story."

"What can you tell me about that night on the boat?"

"Matt, you know I'm always happy to talk to you, but why are you so interested?"

"Do you remember that a young man was killed on the beach the same day?"

"Duh. I'm not senile."

"Sorry. The dead man was the son of a friend of mine from my army days. He asked me to look into his son's death. The police are at a dead end."

"I thought that pretty Detective Duncan was in charge of that investigation."

"She is, and she's helping me. We're thinking there might be something that was missed on the first go-around."

"Are you interested in the murder or the detective?"

"Both, I guess, but I'm pretty sure I've got a better chance of solving the murder than wooing the detective."

Dora laughed. "Okay. But what does the murder on the beach have to do with the *Dulcimer* killings?"

"At first, I didn't think there was a connection. But now I'm not so sure. I'm just grasping at straws at this point."

"There's not much I can tell you. It was a pretty normal evening. Nothing out of the ordinary. Just people having fun."

"Did you see any Asian people on the boat that night?"

"Not that I recall. Why?"

"I don't know. I'm beginning to think that some Asians were involved in the killing on the beach. I'm just working back, trying to find a connection."

"Absolutely nothing stood out about the evening until the lights went out and we hit the sandbar."

I thought for a minute, trying to think of anything else to ask her. Then an image jogged my brain. A camera. *I'm an idiot*, I thought. "Dora, did you have your camera?"

She smiled. "I thought you'd never ask."

"Did you get any pictures?"

"A lot."

"What happened to them?"

She reached into her purse and came out with a compact disc. "They're all here. Yours for the price of a small salad."

CHAPTER THIRTY-ONE

Jock, J.D., and I were seated around my desk. I was scrolling slowly through all the pictures on Dora's CD, looking for something that might be of use to us. There were close to a hundred photos of smiling people staring into the camera, engaged in their meals, looking out the large windows of the dining deck.

"There," said J.D. "Isn't that Katherine Brewster?"

I looked more closely. The photo showed a pretty blonde woman seated at a table by herself. Over her shoulder I saw the back of a man wearing a flowered tropical shirt and across the table from him was Betty Garrison. "That's Katherine," I said. "That's the Garrisons sitting behind her."

"Let's see if we have any more of that area of the deck," said J.D.

I scrolled through more pictures. I didn't see Katherine or the Garrisons. But I did see an Asian man, sitting at a table with another man and a woman. "There're our Asians," I said. "Let me see if I can home in on their faces."

I manipulated the photo program, bringing the face of the first man into sharper focus. "I'm pretty sure that's the one who tried to knife me," I said. "Let me get a look at the woman." I played with the mouse, bringing the woman's face into view, blowing it up some, playing with the resolution. "That's her," I said. "She's the one who was with the guy on the boardwalk."

"What about the other guy?" asked Jock. "Do you recognize him?"

I looked closer, manipulating the program some more. "No. I've never seen this one."

"Can you make some prints of their faces?" asked J.D.

"Sure." I fiddled with the program some more, cropping it so that I finally had reasonably good pictures of each of the Asians. I printed three copies of each one.

"Who do you think the third guy is?" asked J.D.

"I don't know. But there had to have been two men involved. One of them broke the neck of Captain Prather, and I don't think the woman would have been able to do that. She could have stabbed Katherine or Garrison, but I don't think she could have gotten both of them."

"You're probably right," said J.D. "From the time the boat veered off course until the lights went out was just a few seconds. I think the murders would have had to have taken place during the first few minutes when the confusion was at its maximum. The one on the bridge wouldn't have had time to get to the dinner deck."

"Let's see what else we can find," Jock said.

I scrolled some more. Nothing. I was at the end of the photographs.

"Do it again," said Jock. "We might have missed something. Let's look for anything out of the ordinary, not just Asian killers."

I started the process again, slowly scrolling through the pictures, stopping at each one, three pairs of eyes scrutinizing each photo, looking for something, anything that would give us a hint of what had happened and who was involved. We found nothing.

"I think," said J.D., "that we need to take a break and then go through them again. There has to be something in all those pictures that we're not seeing. What time is it?"

I looked at my watch. "Three o'clock."

"I need to get some paperwork finished at my office," she said. "Why don't we meet back here at five and take another look."

Logan stopped by at four. Jock and I were still looking at photos on the computer, trying to catch a glimpse of something out of the ordinary; anything that would move us a step closer to understanding any connection between the murders on *Dulcimer* and the death of Jim Desmond.

"Is that porn?" asked Logan as he came through the door.

I laughed and explained what we were doing. "I found the Asians who tried to kill me the other day. They were on the boat that night."

"You want a drink?" Jock asked.

"No, thanks. I've got to get home and pack. We're leaving in the morning."

Logan and Marie were driving to Tampa to start a weeklong Caribbean cruise.

"Be careful, Logan. Too much sun and sex might do you in," I said.

"I'm willing to take that chance. Do you think the Asians are the same people who killed Desmond?"

"No way to tell. Besides, we're not even sure Asians were involved in Jim's death. We've got the connection to Laos and there was an Asian guy at the Hilton the night of the wedding, but that might not mean anything."

"But these guys tried to kill you," said Logan. "If they weren't tied to Jim's murder, why would they be after you?"

"I can't see any other connection," I said. "We hadn't even begun to look into the *Dulcimer* murders at the time they tried to take me out."

"Maybe," said Jock, "they killed Jim that morning and decided to reward themselves with a dinner cruise."

I stared at him, a smile playing at the corner of my lips.

"Nah," he said. "I don't believe it either. They've got to be connected somehow to both Jim and *Dulcimer*."

"Let me see the pictures," Logan said. "Maybe a fresh pair of eyes will see something you're missing."

"Have at it," I said.

I went back to the first photo and started the slow scrolling. I stopped at the one that showed Katherine sitting behind the Garrisons and told Logan who they were. I stopped again at the picture showing the Asians. I scrolled some more.

"Wait," said Logan. "Go back one."

I backed up one picture and held it on the screen.

"Isn't that the Garrisons and Katherine?" asked Logan.

I peered at the photo. It showed the back of a woman sitting across from a man with blond hair, wearing a tropical shirt. Behind the man sat a woman with long blonde hair, her back to us. A young man sat across from her facing the camera.

"You're right," I said. "This one was taken from behind Betty Garrison. We completely missed it."

"Can you enlarge it so that we can get a better view of the guy across from Katherine?"

I used the mouse to crop the face of the man and then enlarged it. I sat back in my chair, surprised beyond words at the image I saw. I'd seen the young man before. In a photograph on the top of a console television set in the Brewster's home. "I don't believe it," I said. "That's Doug Peterson. Katherine's boyfriend."

CHAPTER THIRTY-TWO

By the time J.D. arrived back at my house, Logan had left. He told us he'd be back in a week or so. I showed J.D. the photo Logan had spotted and explained who the young man was.

"How did we miss that?" she asked.

"We weren't looking for anything specific," I said. "And we'd never seen Peter Garrison's face, so we didn't recognize him. I think Logan came in with fresh eyes and picked up on something we'd passed over at least twice."

"We also weren't expecting Katherine to be sitting with her boyfriend," said Jock.

"I thought he was having dinner with Katherine's parents the night of the murders," said J.D.

"That's what the Brewsters told me," I said. "They obviously lied."

"Why would they do that?"

"That's what I want to ask them. I didn't want to call them until you got back."

"I'd like to know how long he'd been here," said J.D. "If he was staying with Katherine, the lady who runs the inn would have mentioned it. I think."

I shook my head. "Mrs. Deen told me that Katherine was by herself. She'd have no reason to lie."

"I can get my people to check into Peterson's travel records," Jock said.

"How long will that take?"

Jock looked at his watch. "At this time of day the only people there would be the night crew. This isn't important enough for them to run with. It'd probably be sometime tomorrow before we could find out anything."

I pulled my cell phone from my pocket. "I've got a better idea."

"Deb," I said when she answered the phone. "I need a favor."

"So what else is new?"

"Don't get testy. Are you at home?"

"No. I'm working."

"Got your laptop there?"

"Of course."

"How'd you like to do a little sleuthing?"

"Now?"

"Good a time as any."

"I'm at work. You know, tending bar, that sort of thing."

"This won't take a minute."

"Okay. Tell me what you want. I'll see what I can do."

I told her and closed the phone.

"Do you still have the Brewsters' number?" asked J.D.

"Sure."

"Give them a call. I can't wait to hear their reason for lying to you."

I opened my phone and dialed the number from the address book. A computer generated voice answered. "The number you have dialed has been disconnected at the customer's request."

"Disconnected number," I said, surprised.

"When did you last use that number?" asked J.D.

"Day before yesterday."

"You think they didn't pay their bill?"

"No. I saw them yesterday and today the phone is off. Too much of a coincidence. Besides, the recording said it was disconnected at the Brewsters's request."

"Do you have a number for Peterson?" asked J.D.

"No, and I don't think we ought to be calling him. This is too strange."

"What then?" asked J.D.

"I'm going back to Charlotte and get in his face."

My phone rang. Debbie.

"Matt, Doug Peterson left Charlotte on a nonstop flight to Tampa that arrived at five thirty p.m. on the day of the murders. He rented a car and returned it early the next morning. He caught a seven a.m. flight back to Charlotte. The car had a hundred ten miles on it."

"Full of gas?"

"Yes."

"Did you think to check his credit cards?"

"I did. No charges for gas. He might have paid cash."

"Okay. I just need one more little favor."

"Geez. This better be good."

"I need to know when the service on this phone number was terminated." I gave her the number.

"I'll get back to you."

"Soon."

"Right." She hung up.

I told Jock and J.D. what Debbie had told me.

"The mileage on that car is just about exactly the mileage from Tampa to Cortez and back," Jock said.

"So he flies in, makes a mad dash for Cortez, boards the boat, kills Katherine, and heads back to Charlotte," said J.D. "It doesn't make sense."

"Why not?" I asked.

"If his plan had been to kill her with the knife while on the boat, he'd have had to plan to do it publicly," she said. "He couldn't have anticipated that the lights would go out and the boat would go aground."

"Unless he had help," I said.

"The Asians," said Jock.

"Then he would have been part of the plan," I said.

"But why?" asked J.D. "And if he just wanted to kill her, why go to all the trouble to get her to Florida?"

"Maybe," said Jock, "he was upset by her coming here alone. He could have decided to kill her on the spur of the moment. When did he make the plane reservations?"

"I didn't think to ask Deb," I said. "When she calls back I'll see if she has that information."

"He would have had to bring the knife with him," J.D. said. "He didn't have time to stop and get one between the time he arrived in Tampa and when he got to Cortez. How did he get it through security?"

Jock nodded. "If he was part of a plan, he would have gotten it from his Asian buddies."

"Why kill Peter Garrison?" I asked.

"Maybe Peter tried to stop Doug from killing Katherine and became collateral damage," said J.D.

My phone rang. I looked at the caller ID. Deb.

"Matt, the phone service was terminated at the customer's request at ten this morning."

"Thanks. Did you happen to note whether Peterson had made advance reservations for his flight?"

"He didn't. He was a walk-up at both airports. No checked luggage either."

CHAPTER THIRTY-THREE

I was up early the next morning, sitting on my patio as the light of a false dawn seeped over the sleeping island. The sound of a boat engine occasionally floated over me, a fisherman headed for the artificial reefs that were submerged a few miles offshore. I heard the distant siren of the Cortez Bridge warning motorists of an impending opening of the draw. Across the bay, the low hanging clouds were taking on the hues of orange and red that preceded the sun's first peek above the horizon. Birds were leaving their nests on Jewfish Key, flying west toward the Gulf and breakfast.

I pondered the odd convergence of events from which we were beginning to discern vague patterns. I had this feeling that someone was dogging our trail, cleaning up after themselves. I had gone to Savannah and Macon, talked to Jim's widow Meredith and Bud Stanley and somebody tried to kill me. My trip to Charlotte was followed by the apparent disappearance of the Brewsters, although it was too early to know if they'd disappeared or had just for some reason cut off their phone. Maybe they'd decided to replace the land line with a cell phone. The termination of their phone service may have been perfectly innocent, but there was a nagging feeling in my gut that whispered danger signals. Why had they lied to me about Doug Peterson having dinner with them on the night of their daughter's murder? What was Doug doing aboard *Dulcimer* on the night of his fiancé's murder? Why had he left in such a hurry if he hadn't killed Katherine?

Questions. Lots of questions, but no answers. I was beginning to think that there was no connection between Jim Desmond's death and the murders on *Dulcimer*. Not if Peterson was involved. Still, there was that Asian connection to Jim through Soupy in Laos, and I had been attacked right after talking to Bud Stanley, who had a connection to Soupy. And the same Asians who attacked me were aboard *Dulcimer* the night of the murders.

I heard the sliding glass door to my living room open and Jock walked out, a mug of coffee in hand. "Want to go jogging? That always clears my head."

"Yeah. Finish your coffee, and we'll head for the beach."

We jogged in silence, pounding the sand, keeping up a pace that would complete the four miles in thirty minutes. The Gulf was flat and serene, the beach deserted, the August heat keeping sane people indoors. We were running along a stretch of beach that was bordered by large houses hunkered behind small sand dunes. We reached the house that marked the end of the second mile and turned back north. An all terrain vehicle, one of those conveyances that seems to be a cross between a four-wheeled tractor and a motorcycle, was coming our way, bouncing over the little hillocks of sand that had been carved out of the beach by last night's tide.

"Uh-oh," said Jock, pointing at the ATV.

"Relax," I said. "The cops are the only ones who use those things on the beach."

"You sure?"

There was something in the way he asked the question, in the timbre of his voice or maybe just the tightening of his face that made me question my assumption that the rider coming toward us was a cop. Jock had been in too many dicey situations for me to discount his intuition.

"Maybe not," I said. "Let's head toward the houses."

The ATV was very near now. We turned to our right, toward the row of homes that lined the beach. Most were empty in August, their owners taking a gentler sun in northern climes. The ATV had the angle on us and I knew we wouldn't get past the dunes and into the yards of the beachfront houses before he caught up with us. He came closer, and I could see that the rider was wearing a motorcycle helmet with a dark facemask, a dirty white T-shirt, jeans, and white athletic shoes.

"Ground," I yelled to Jock.

He dove head first into the sand, sliding as if he were a base runner taking a header into home plate. I was right behind him, diving and rolling to my left. Sand kicked up between Jock and me, bullets fired quickly. There was no report from the pistol, no sound. A silencer. The rider was bouncing on the ATV as it hit the little humps of sand, throwing off his aim.

I rolled to my left a couple more times and reached out for a piece of driftwood partially covered by sand. The gray wood was a tree limb, about the size of my arm, probably from one of the Australian pines that covered the north end of the key and were forever falling into the sea, their shallow roots unable to withstand the gale-force winds that sometimes scoured our island in summer.

The ATV was coming on at a speed that I knew was its maximum. My rolling had taken me ten or twelve feet from Jock, who had maneuvered himself into a squatting position, his hands on the ground, like a football lineman. He was making as small a target as possible, but was ready to launch himself at our attacker as soon as he got a chance.

The driver seemed to be homing in on Jock, ignoring me. I was still lying on my back on the ground, watching him through half-closed eyes, my fingers wrapped around the driftwood limb. Maybe he thought that he'd hit me with one of his errant shots and saw Jock as the more dangerous foe.

The ATV was slowing now as it moved toward Jock, the driver taking aim with his pistol. I had come to rest with my feet pointing toward the Gulf. The ATV was cutting across the sand at a forty-five degree angle to my body, the driver's concentration on Jock, his body tensed, his pistol raised. Jock was staring at the driver as if daring him to take the shot. I couldn't see our attacker's face, but I thought their eyes must be locked. The hunter staring down the prey, going for the kill, knowing there was only one ending to this little ritual of death on the sand.

The ATV closed on Jock. He was about ten feet from me when in one fluid movement I came to a sitting position and heaved the driftwood at the driver. It hit him on his left shoulder almost unseating him. He struggled to stay on the ATV, trying to right himself at the same time that Jock sprang from his squatting position. He took four steps and vaulted over the handlebars, colliding with the driver, both of them tumbling to the ground.

The attacker dropped the pistol as he went over the back of the ATV with Jock on top of him. The ATV sputtered to a stop, its momentum bleeding off as the driver's hand left the throttle.

I rushed to the weapon, picked it up, and turned to the two men in the sand. Jock had the driver in a headlock, one arm around his neck with the other hand grasping the man's chin. Jock was a second or two from breaking his neck.

"Hold up, Jock. We're going to need him."

"No sweat, podna. I'm not going to kill him. Not yet anyway."

"Let's get that helmet off him," I said. I stuck the pistol under the driver's chin and told him not to move as Jock unbuckled the chinstrap.

The helmet came off and the man screamed. Jock had almost taken one or both of his ears with the helmet. He wasn't being gentle.

I was surprised. I was expecting an Asian, but instead I saw a young white man who probably was not yet twenty years old. He had a scraggly goatee and longish red hair that hadn't been washed in a month. His teeth were yellow and crooked and his rancid body odor flooded my nostrils. He was sitting on the sand, his hands in his lap. I kept the pistol pointed at him.

"Who the hell are you?" I asked.

"Don't kill me," he said, his voice trembling.

"I'm trying to decide whether to shoot you or let my friend here break your neck."

"No," he said, his voice trembling.

"Who are you?"

"Clyde Bates."

"Okay, Clyde. Why are you trying to kill us?"

"Two thousand bucks."

"What does that mean?"

"That's what I'm being paid to kill you."

"By whom?"

"I don't know."

I poked the muzzle of the pistol up under his chin, forcing him to raise his head.

"No," he said. "I don't know his name."

"Tell me about him."

"Just some guy that comes into O'Reilly's."

"What is O'Reilly's?"

"A bar over in Palmetto."

"Describe him."

"White guy, about fifty, maybe a little older, gray hair and beard."

"You sure he was white?"

"I think so. He had a good tan, but I don't think he was Mexican."

"Could he have been Asian?"

"Well, maybe."

"What about his eyes?"

"Do you mean were they slanted?"

"Well, yes," I said. "I guess I do."

"I couldn't tell."

"Didn't you look at his eyes?"

"He was wearing sunglasses. I couldn't see his eyes."

"Short, tall, fat?"

"No. He's about your height. He looks like he keeps in shape."

"Accent? Anything like that?"

"He's from the South. You can tell."

"How long have you known him?"

"Just met him yesterday."

"And he decided to pay you to kill us? Just like that?"

"Just to kill one of you."

"Which one?"

"Guy named Royal."

"Why try to kill both of us?"

"I didn't know which one of you was Royal."

"That'd be me," I said. "Who set you up with the guy with the money?"

"Big Tony, the bartender, knows that I do this kind of work sometimes. I think he told the dude I'd handle it for him."

"You've killed people before?"

"No. I just talk about it."

"Talk about it?"

"Yeah. There's some bad biker guys what hang out at O'Reilly's, and I don't want them to think I'm some kind of pussy. So I tell stories."

"Where'd you get the ATV?"

"Stole it from one of the houses up the beach. Fool people left the keys in it."

"How did you know where to find us?" I asked.

"I was watching your house. Saw you come out and head for the beach. I followed you."

"Did he pay you up front?"

"Gave me two hundred bucks. He's going to pay the rest when you're dead."

"Where are you supposed to meet him to get the rest of your money?"

"O'Reilly's."

"When?"

"When you're dead."

"How are you supposed to let him know you've finished the job?"

"He gave me a phone number to call."

"What's the number?"

"It's on a piece of paper in my pocket."

I looked at Jock. "Anything else?"

"No. Let's get the police down here."

I shook my head. "I want to try that other number first."

I turned to my would-be killer. "Stand up, pea brain."

He did.

"Now, reach slowly into your pocket and get me the phone number."

He did.

"You got a cell phone?"

He pulled one out of his pocket.

"Give it to me."

He did.

"I'm going to call your boss. I'll give you the phone and you tell him you've killed me and want to meet him this afternoon to get the rest of your money."

"Okay."

"You blow this and my friend here is going to break your neck."

"Okay."

I used Bates's phone to dial the number. I got a recorded message. I closed the phone and started laughing. "You idiot. There is no such number."

"That's the one he gave me. He wrote it down himself."

Jock laughed. "You've been had, my friend. That two hundred bucks you got is going to cost you about twenty years in prison."

I pulled my cell phone out of a pocket and dialed the Longboat Key Police Department.

CHAPTER THIRTY-FOUR

Officer Steve Carey came walking down the lawn behind the nearest house. I'd been able to give the police an exact address on Gulf of Mexico Drive because the street number was also painted on the seawall that protected the property from the Gulf.

He stopped at the end of the grass and stood surveying the scene. "So Jock, you causing trouble again?"

Jock laughed. "Good to see you, too, Steve."

The cop walked on down to where we had Bates sitting on the sand. "What've you got here?"

I pointed to Bates. "This is Mr. Clyde Bates. He tried to kill us. He's not too smart."

"He can't be too smart if he tried to kill you two."

I told Steve what had happened and what we'd found out from Bates.

"I'm sure Detective Duncan will want some formal statements. She'll be here in a minute."

"You guys okay?" The question was shouted from the lawn. I looked up and saw J. D. Duncan coming our way.

"We're fine," I said.

I watched her make her way down the lawn and over the short seawall. There was a grace about her even when she was wearing the big pistol on her lovely hip. I was not above fantasizing about her, but knew that's all it would ever be. A fantasy. The more time I spent around her, the more the fantasy grew. Ah, the damage we men do to ourselves chasing the unobtainable.

J.D. spent a few minutes talking to Jock and me and then to Bates. He'd ridden his scooter out to the key and parked down the street from my house. When he saw us leave for the beach, he followed. He was going to ride the scooter down the beach, kill us and make a fast getaway. When he was coming down the little road that served as public access to the beach, he saw the ATV parked in the carport of a small house that sat on the access road a couple of hundred yards from the beach. He thought it would handle the sand better. He left his scooter in the carport.

"Where'd you get the gun?" J.D. asked.

"The dude in the bar gave it to me."

"The same one who gave you the two hundred bucks?" she asked.

"Yeah."

"Bullets?"

"They were in the clip in the gun."

"Did you reload them?"

"Why would I do that?"

"Did you?"

"No, ma'am."

J.D. cleared the pistol and dropped the clip into her hand, looked at it. "There're several rounds left in the mag. Maybe we can get some fingerprints."

She turned back to Bates. "Did the man in the bar tell you why he wanted these guys dead?"

"No."

"Weren't you curious?"

"No, ma'am. I wouldn't have done it either, except I didn't want the other guys in the bar to think I was a pu—, uh, chicken."

J.D. smiled. "A chicken, huh?"

"Yes, ma'am."

"Were there other people there when you met with the man who gave you the money?"

"No. Just Big Tony. The bartender."

"Did you just happen to wander in and find them there with a job for you?"

"No, ma'am. Big Tony knows my number. He called me."

"Okay, Steve," J.D. said. "Take him back to the station. I may have some more questions for him when I get through with these victims."

Steve laughed. "I think if ol' Clyde here had any idea who these victims were, he'd have left town."

"That would have been a wise move," she said.

"What do you want us to do?" I asked.

"My car's in the driveway up there," she said, pointing to the nearest house. "I'll take you home and we can get your formal statements. You know the drill."

We drove in silence the short distance to my cottage. I felt like an errant schoolboy being driven home by the principal. J.D. was not happy, but I wasn't sure what Jock and I had done other than almost get killed by a teenager.

We went into the house. "Coffee anybody?" I asked.

"Put some on and come sit down," said J.D., a peremptory tone in her voice.

I went to the kitchen and Jock sat on the sofa, a bemused expression on his face. J.D. took a chair and sat quietly. I put the coffee on and returned to the living room. I sat on the sofa next to Jock facing J.D.

She looked at us for a moment. "I don't want to lose you guys," she said. "You come here and start turning over rocks and something big crawls out and tries to kill you."

"J.D.," I said, "we were jogging on a public beach."

"You know what I mean, Matt. You're not cops. I am. It's my job to turn over rocks. I get paid to do that. You're the amateurs. Civilians."

"Not exactly amateurs," I said. "Besides, you're part of what we're doing."

"I know." she said, "And Jock you have resources I don't have. Matt, you're developing facts that we didn't have before, but this is the second time somebody's tried to kill you."

"The second time this week," I said. "People have tried to kill me a lot more than twice."

She frowned at that. "We cops seem to generally have some immunity. The bad guys are at least reluctant to kill us because then the full weight of cop world falls in on them. But you guys are civilians and don't have the same protection."

I looked at her. "Do you want to end our little cooperative affair?"

"Yes. No. I don't know what I want. But I don't want you dead."

She was looking directly at me as she said this. There was a softening about her eyes and mouth, a glint of tears welling. She looked away, rose, and went into the kitchen. My heart did a little lurch and Jock just sat and smiled.

We sat quietly for a couple of minutes, neither of us saying anything. I rose and went to the kitchen. J.D. was standing at the sink staring out the window to the bay, her back to me. "You want some coffee?" she asked.

"Yeah."

She turned without looking at me, went to the coffeepot and poured a cup, handed it to me, and went back to the living room. Not another word. I followed her. She sat back down in her chair and said, "We've got to go check out Big Tony and O'Reilly's. See if we can get a lead on the man who hired that idiot Bates to kill you guys." The softness was gone. Detective J.D. Duncan was all business.

I nodded. "I'd also like to see if we can get somebody to check on the Brewsters in Charlotte. See if they're still in the house. I'd like to talk to them."

"I'll see if I can get Charlotte P.D. to check on that," said J.D.

Jock looked at his watch. "It's only ten. I doubt the bar's open this early."

"You're probably right," said J.D. "Let's get those statements taken care of. Gotta keep the paperwork in order." She pulled a small tape recorder from her pocket and set it on the coffee table. "Who's first?"

CHAPTER THIRTY-FIVE

Palmetto is a small town that lies just across the Manatee River from Bradenton, its downtown area straddling Highway 41. The place was in the throes of some sort of urban renewal, older buildings being spruced up and new structures coming out of the ground. It was a quiet piece of old Florida where the residents took pride in their town and left most days for work in Bradenton, Sarasota, or St. Petersburg.

O'Reilly's took up the northern end of an old strip center that had not yet been graced with the brush of renewal. The whole place was decaying, most of it empty. It wasn't long for this world. One day soon, the bulldozers would come and wipe it off the map. A new building would take its place and the town would move on into a more modern version of itself.

It was two o'clock in the afternoon and the sun was beating down on the asphalt parking lot, the steamy heat enveloping us, turning the world into a giant steam bath. We walked into the air-conditioned bar, the smell of stale beer and old cigarette smoke assailing our nostrils. The interior was dark, a bit foreboding, but the coolness was welcoming. There were no patrons, the place having just opened for business. A bar ran along the back wall. To the right were doors marked as restrooms. Four or five tables took up the floor space. It was not an upscale tavern.

The bar was low, table height with a row of five wooden chairs placed in front of it. At one end, two steps led down to the area where the bartender worked. It was an unusual arrangement, but not unique. The bartender could still serve his patrons without bending down, but there was no leaning on the bar here. One had to sit in the chairs.

A small man, maybe five foot six, stood behind the bar, a wet towel in his hand. He was getting the place ready for his customers. He had thinning gray hair that had not seen a comb that day and lay like shriveled weeds on his balding head. He had a beard that didn't quite cover his face, as if there were some areas where the hair could not grow. He was wearing a white golf shirt and jeans and a scowl."

"Help you?" he asked.

"We're looking for Big Tony," J.D. said.

"You're looking at him," said the man behind the bar. "What do you want?"

"I want to talk to you about Clyde Bates," J.D. said.

"Never heard of him. Who the fuck are you?" A man clearly out of sorts with the world.

Jock had moved to the edge of the bar, his hand resting on the back of one of the chairs, giving the man a hard look. "Your face reminds me of an old dog I used to have. He got the mange and his coat did the same thing your beard's doing. Looked like shit."

The man reached under the bar, a look of anger flashing across his face. At the same time Jock picked up the chair. The bartender came up with a sawed off baseball bat in his hand and pulled back to swing at Jock. At that instant Jock threw the chair into the man's chest, knocking him backward. He dropped the bat as Jock vaulted over the low bar. In less time that I can describe he had the man by the neck, one hand pushing upward, the other ready to throw a punch into the gut of the little man.

"Everybody stop," said J.D. her voice ringing loudly in the quiet bar. "Let him go, Jock."

Jock removed his hand from the bartender's neck and stepped back two steps. He picked up the bat and held it in his right hand, staring at the man as if daring him to try again.

"What do you want?" the bartender said.

J.D. held out her badge. "I just told you. I want to talk to you about Clyde Bates."

"What about him?"

"About how you and he tried to kill my friends here."

The man blanched a little and held up his hands as if trying to ward off bad news. "I ain't tried to kill your friends."

"You sent Bates to do it."

"No."

"Look, Big Tony. I can run you in right now on all kind of charges. But all I want to do is talk. You help me, we might just forget those laws you broke."

"What the hell are you talking about? I ain't broke no laws."

"Well, there's conspiracy to commit murder, aiding and abetting attempted murder, accessory to attempted murder, assault on a police officer. That's the one that will keep you locked up the longest while you wait for trial. No judge is going to grant bail on the assault charge."

"I didn't assault a cop."

"You tried to hit me with a baseball bat."

"I didn't know you was a cop. Besides, I was trying to hit him," pointing at Jock.

"Well, I thought you were aiming for me," said J.D. "That'll be enough for the judge."

"I didn't know you was a cop."

"Won't matter."

"What do you want to know?"

"Tell me how you got Bates involved in the attempt on my friends' lives."

"I didn't."

"You know, Big Tony, instead of arresting you, I could just let my friends here take you out back for a little discussion. They are not nice men."

The bartender looked from Jock to me and back to J.D. "Okay. Some guy comes in here yesterday and tells me he needs somebody to do some wet work. He didn't say what. I gave him to Bates."

"Who was the man?"

"Don't know."

"Ever seen him before?"

"No."

"You mean some guy comes into your bar and tells you he wants somebody killed and you just set him up with a hit man? Suppose the guy was an undercover cop."

"I didn't set him up with no hit man. I set him up with Bates."

"Bates said you thought that's what he did for a living," said J.D.

The little man laughed. "Bates is always talking that shit, but nobody believes him."

"Then why introduce them?"

"The guy gave me a hundred bucks. I told him Bates was the man for the job. If the guy had been a cop, he couldn't do anything to me because Bates sure as hell ain't no hit man."

"You're not real bright, are you?"

The man looked a little hurt. "I get by."

"What time did the guy come in?"

"About three, I guess. He hadn't been here long when Bates came in. Clyde's regular as clockwork. He comes in at three forty-five every afternoon. He gets off at three thirty."

"Bates has a job?" asked J.D., a little surprised.

"Yeah."

"Doing what?"

"He cleans boats down at the marina," said Big Tony.

"Did you call him?" I asked.

"No."

"He said you did."

"Maybe I did. I don't remember."

"When you introduced the guy to Bates, did they leave?"

"No. They sat over at that table for a little while and then the guy gets up and leaves."

"Has he been back?"

"No. Ain't seen any more of him."

"What did he look like?" asked J.D.

"About six feet tall, gray hair and beard."

"Anything else?"

"No. He wore sunglasses the whole time."

"Did he have an accent?"

The little man thought for a minute. "Yeah. He was from somewhere in the South."

"Think," said J.D. "Close your eyes and think hard. Anything else about the guy that sticks out?"

"He had a great tan."

J.D. looked at us. "Do either of you have any questions?"

"Yeah," said Jock. "Why do they call a little-bitty fuck like you Big Tony?"

"I got a big johnson. People started calling me Big Tony in junior high and it sorta stuck."

"Probably helped you with the girls," said Jock.

"Not so you'd notice," said Big Tony.

"Geez," said J.D. "Let's go. Tony, don't leave town."

"Where the hell would I go?"

CHAPTER THIRTY-SIX

We walked out into the parking lot. I turned to J.D. "Don't leave town? Who are you? Marshal Dillon?"

"I just like to use that sometimes. They always say it on TV and the idiots I deal with all watch a lot of TV. They take it seriously."

"Look," said Jock. He was pointing to a bank building across the street. "See that camera above the front door?"

J.D. and I looked. There was a small box attached to a bracket that extended from the wall above the entrance to the bank. It was making slow sweeps back and forth.

"That's a security camera. It's panning the bank parking lot and probably saving the images on a hard drive somewhere. It may pick up pictures of this parking lot too. We might get a look at the guy who hired Bates to kill us."

J.D.'s cell phone chimed. She answered and listened, occasionally asking a question. She hung up. "That was the shift commander at the Charlotte Police Department. He sent a unit out to the Brewsters. He thinks they're gone. The house is locked up and this morning's paper was still on the sidewalk. One of the neighbors said he'd seen the daughter's boyfriend pull up in a utility van from U-Haul and load some boxes into it. He left and the Brewsters followed in their car."

"They're on the run," I said. "But from whom?"

"You?" asked Jock.

"That doesn't make a lot of sense," I said. "Why would my visit have spooked them?"

J.D. said, "If the boyfriend was the killer, they're protecting him for some reason. Maybe they think you know more than you do."

"Could be," I said. "Or maybe whoever killed their daughter is after them."

"Why don't we get Debbie to check out the van rental?" asked Jock.

I called Debbie.

She answered. "I'm leaving for work. Don't have time to talk to you."

"Just need a little favor, sweetcakes."

"Wow. You call me pet names and my heart goes into overdrive. What do you want?"

I told her and she said she'd get back to me within the hour.

"Now," said J.D., "let's go talk to the bank about that camera."

The bank was local. In addition to the one we were in there was a branch in Sarasota down near the Gulfgate Mall. The manager was pleasant and willing to share his technology with us as soon as J.D. had shown her credentials. He took us to a small room off the main lobby, unlocked it, and asked us in.

"This is the computer where we store all the images from our security cameras. They stay on the hard drive for sixty days and then are automatically erased."

"How many cameras do you have?" asked Jock.

"Six. Two in the lobby, one at the ATM machine, two covering the back parking lot, and the one over the door that covers the front of the building."

"Can we see some footage from the one over the entrance?" asked J.D.

"Sure." He went to the keyboard and pulled up a program, used the mouse to manipulate it and sat back with a little laugh. "There."

The clip he'd brought up showed the three of us walking across the street and into the front door of the bank. "If you'd been robbers, we'd have you," he said.

"The camera gives us a view of the parking lot across the street," I said. I pointed out the parking places that were right in front of the bar. "If the mystery man parked here, we should be able to see him."

J.D. asked the banker, "Can you pull up the video from yesterday afternoon from, say, two to four?"

"Sure." He fiddled with the computer and then sat back so that we could see the monitor. It showed the area running from the front steps of the bank, the street, and the parking lot of O'Reilly's. A time stamp appeared in the lower right corner of the screen. The images were in black-and-white.

We watched for a couple of minutes as cars on the highway drifted by. A woman leading a small boy came into the bank at 2:02. At 2:03 a car pulled into the lot and parked in front of the bar.

"Freeze that," I said. "Can you zoom in on that car there?" I pointed to it with my finger.

The car became bigger until it filled the screen. "Home in on the license plate," I said.

We couldn't read the tag. It was too blurry. The resolution on the video wasn't that good to start with and when it got blown up, it was just short of useless.

"Pull back," I said, "and let's see who gets out of that car."

We watched as a man unfolded from the driver's side. I asked the banker to zoom in on the driver. No go. Too blurry. I couldn't see anything about his features.

J.D. said, "Can you make a copy of those few minutes? I think the Sheriff's office has some sophisticated equipment that might be able to give us a better view of this."

"I'll put it on a flash drive," said the banker.

We drove south on Highway 41, crossed the Manatee River on the Green Bridge, and a few miles farther turned right onto Highway 301 Boulevard and pulled into the Manatee County Sheriff's Operations Center. Debbie called just as J.D. was parking the car.

"Doug Peterson rented the van from a U-Haul center on North Irby Street in Charlotte yesterday morning at eight o'clock. He returned it at six p.m. yesterday. Paid by a credit card in his name. He put a hundred thirty-four miles on it and returned it full of gas. I checked his credit card, and he paid for the gas with the same card he used to rent the van. He also bought lunch with that card at a McDonalds in Hickory, North Carolina. And before you ask, Hickory is about sixty miles from Charlotte."

"You're a doll," I said.

"I know. See you later. I gotta go to work."

"Thanks, Deb."

I related the conversation to J.D. and Jock.

"Sounds as if young Doug took the Brewsters to Hickory," Jock said. "Why?"

"We'll work on that tomorrow," I said. "Let's see if the sheriff's wizards can help us with this video."

CHAPTER THIRTY-SEVEN

We entered the building, identified ourselves, clipped visitor's badges to our shirts, and went to the Audio-Visual Department. J.D. knew one of the technicians and she gave her the flash drive and told her what we were looking for. The tech told us to have a seat and she'd see what she could do with the images.

We'd been waiting for about twenty minutes when the technician came through the door with several photos and the flash drive. She had cleaned the images up pretty good. One showed the man in the parking lot clearly. His hair and beard were gray, just like Big Tony and Clyde had said. Based on the height of the car, we guessed the man to be a bit under six feet tall. Maybe 170 pounds.

The car was a late model Pontiac with Florida plates that we could now read. "Got him," said J.D.

"Unless it's a rental," I said.

"Let's hope not," she said.

We thanked the technician, and left the operations center. J.D. called the Longboat Key Police Station and asked somebody to run the license plate number. She held. Then, "Okay. See if Hertz has anything. Tell them the renter is a person of interest in a homicide. That might wake them up."

She hung up. "The car was a rental from the Sarasota-Bradenton Airport. Those guys are pretty cooperative. We might pick up something out there. Let's go."

We got in the car. I was in the front passenger seat and Jock was in back, pouring over the pictures the technician had given us. "There's something off about this guy," he said. "Look at this picture, Matt. Doesn't it look like he's wearing a wig?"

I took the picture and looked more closely at it. The pictures were in black-and-white, and not the best quality, but I could see what Jock was talking about. "I see what you mean. Looks like different colored hair peeking out from under it."

"If the hair is fake, the beard will be too," said J.D.

We pulled into the airport and parked in short-term parking, walked to the Hertz desk. J.D. showed the clerk her ID and told him she was interested in who rented the car in the photo she was sliding across the counter.

"Your office just called," said the clerk. "My manager told me to give you a copy of the contract." He handed over a sheet of paper. "Do you need anything else?"

"Do you remember this guy?" J.D. asked.

"No. I was working yesterday when he rented the car, but we were pretty busy. All the customers are just a blur."

J.D. looked at the contract. "Damn," she said. "Look at this."

The name of the renter on the contract was John Nguyen.

"That's Vietnamese," I said. "Nguyen is about as common in Vietnam as Smith is in this country."

J.D. turned to the clerk. "Do you remember an Asian man renting a car yesterday?"

"Vaguely. I couldn't describe him, though."

J.D. said, "Let's go find the security chief. The airport has more security cameras than almost anywhere. Maybe we'll get a hit."

J.D. led us to an office off the main terminal area. She introduced herself to the Sarasota police lieutenant who was the chief of the airport security detail. She explained what we were looking for and why.

"What time did your guy rent the car?" asked the lieutenant.

J.D. looked at the copy of the rental contract. "One p.m. yesterday."

"Do you know if he came in on a flight?"

"No idea."

The officer typed onto his keyboard and a schedule popped up on his monitor. "There were only two flights that came in around the time he would have rented the car. His name is not on any of the passenger manifests."

"He could have been using a different name," said Jock.

"I suppose," said the cop, "but let's look at the cameras at the entry points to the airport first. There'll be less traffic there than on the concourses where the flights come in. People don't tend to bunch up at the entrances like they do coming off a plane."

He pulled some video up on the monitor, showing a slice of the driveway that ran the length of the terminal building and the concrete walkway in front of an entrance. "This is the door closest to the car rental booths. I'm starting it at twelve thirty yesterday."

We watched for a few minutes and then Jock said, "There he is."

The officer stopped the video. We were looking at an Asian man who was about the same size as the man we saw on the bank's video. No wig or beard.

J.D. said, "I'd like a close-up of this one."

The lieutenant fiddled with the keyboard and the mouse and a printer whirred to life. Out popped a black-and-white photo of the Asian man entering the terminal.

"That's the second guy on the boat," I said. "The one with the man and woman who tried to kill me."

J.D. looked closely at the photo. "No doubt about it. I want to take this to the clerk at Hertz and see if he can identify this guy. Why don't you two stay here and look at some more video. There might be more Asian men."

She was back in ten minutes. We were still looking at video. No more Asians. She waved the picture. "The clerk said this was the guy who rented the car yesterday."

"So he didn't fly in," said Jock.

"No. I called the station. They're running his name through all the databases. See if anything pops up. You ready to head back to the key?"

We thanked the lieutenant and drove back to Longboat Key.

It was almost five when we crossed the Ringling Bridge. Dark thunderheads were building over the Gulf, the harbingers of our afternoon thunderstorm. I rolled down my window and a whiff of rain tickled my nose. The storm wouldn't be long in coming.

"Anybody want a drink?" I asked.

"I could use one," said Jock. "It's been a long day. J.D.?"

"Sure. Let me stop by the office and check out."

We drove north on the key. Rain drops splattered on the windshield. Lightning slashed the dark sky over the Gulf. Thunder boomed, rolling over us like a low-flying jet. The storm was moving north and a little east, running parallel to the island. It would catch the northern end of the key if it stayed on its course. The worst of the rain was over the water. By the time we got to the police station near the north end a sheet of rain obscured the Gulf, but we were getting only sprinkles.

"I'll be right back," said J.D. She left the car and ran into the station.

Jock and I sat quietly, each absorbed in his own thoughts. J.D. returned. "Where to?" she asked.

"Let's go to Mar Vista," I said. "We can watch the storm."

"There were no hits on John Nguyen," she said. "Not even a driver's license. He must have used a fake one. The numbers don't match anything on file."

"I wonder why he would use a Vietnamese name," I said.

"Maybe to throw us off if we got on his tail," Jock said.

"Could he be Vietnamese?" asked J.D.

"I doubt it," I said. "The Vietnamese and the Laotians aren't generally very compatible. A long history of hatred there."

We parked in the shell lot adjacent to Mar Vista. We sat at a window table, had a couple of drinks, and watched the storm move inland. It came over us and moved across the bay. It was quick, as our afternoon storms usually are. A lot of light, noise, and water, and then it was gone, leaving a bank of dark clouds hovering over the island.

J.D. said, "We've now got three Asians positively identified as being on *Dulcimer* the night of the murders and they just happen to be the ones who have some hand in trying to kill Matt."

Jock laughed. "My feelings are hurt. Nobody seems to think I'm important enough to kill."

"Maybe they're afraid of you," said J.D., winking at us.

"Or," I said, "nobody sees any percentage in killing a weenie."

"I've already got a nice eulogy written for your funeral," said Jock.

"Where do we go from here?" J.D. asked. "Assuming neither one of you gets killed tonight."

"I think Jock and I need to go to Charlotte," I said. "See if we can find young Doug Peterson and get a line on the Brewsters."

"Aren't you getting a little off subject?" J.D. asked. "The connections between the *Dulcimer* murders and Jim Desmond's seem to be pretty thin."

"They're linked," I said. "I don't know how or why, but my gut tells me they're part of the same operation."

"That's not a lot to go on, Matt," said J.D.

"No, but my gut is hardly ever wrong. I want to show the pictures of the Asians to Billy Brugger. See if he can pick out one of them who was at the Hilton the night of the wedding."

"I should have thought of that," said J.D.

"You want to stop by the Hilton before you call it a day?" I asked.

"No. My car's at your place, Matt. Drop me there and you two go ahead. Let me know what you find out."

Jock and I drove south to the Hilton over a rain-slicked Gulf of Mexico Drive. The rain had moved across the bay, but the low clouds still hung over the island, giving it a look of somberness. Night was approaching and I turned on my headlights. We pulled into an almost empty parking lot and nosed into a place next to the ramp leading to the deck and outside bar. A cool breeze blew off the Gulf giving some surcease to the heat.

"Jock," said Billy. "I heard you were on the island. Welcome back."

"Thanks, podna. Good to be back."

We ordered burgers and drinks and took our seats at one end of the bar. A tourist couple in bathing suits sat at the other end. Laughter from children in the adjacent swimming pool floated across the deck. A mother called out to her child to be careful.

I laid the photos of the three Asians on the bar. "Billy, does any one of these look like the guy who came to the bar the night of the Desmond wedding?"

He looked closely at the pictures, pulled some reading glasses from his pocket, put them on, and peered some more. "This one," he said, pointing to the photo from the airport security camera. "That's the one who was at the bar that night."

"You're sure?"

"Positive. I've got a great memory for faces. No doubt about it. That's him."

Jock looked at me. "Your gut's probably right. It's too much of a coincidence to have Mr. Nguyen show up here on the night of the wedding and be aboard *Dulcimer* the next night."

"Not to mention that he hired somebody to try to kill me."

"Or to scare you."

"If that was his intention, he did a pretty good job."

On the way home, I called J.D. and told her that Billy had identified John Nguyen as the man who'd been at his bar the night before the murders.

CHAPTER THIRTY-EIGHT

The University of Virginia campus in Charlottesville was busy with summer school students scurrying from one class to another, lugging books and computers, frowns of concentration on their faces. A few lolled in the grass under the trees that studded the campus, the light from the July sun diffused by the leafy cover.

A U.S. Army first lieutenant dressed in the summer uniform of dark green skirt and light green shirt, black epaulets with the single silver bar of her rank, strolled toward the army's Judge Advocate General Corps School. She was in her second week of learning how to be an army lawyer.

She was a very bright young woman, blonde, fit, and personable. She'd easily finished college and law school, never breaking a sweat while earning top grades. She'd had a number of offers from large civilian firms, but decided to be a soldier, like her dad, the man who'd meant the most to her growing up. She wasn't sure if the army was the ultimate career for her, but the four-year commitment she'd made would give her time to mature, gain some courtroom experience, and serve her country. In a way, she was putting her life on hold, but it seemed the right thing to do. She needed some breathing space before locking into the future.

The JAGC School wasn't particularly difficult. She'd met some nice young people, all with the same interest, law. The class was small and everyone seemed compatible. The only blot on this otherwise idyllic portrait was a student from New York who had attached himself to her on the first day. He had, in a short time, become almost obsessive about her. She'd tried nicely to tell him that she wasn't interested, that she had a boyfriend back home, and that they should just be friends. But the New Yorker was getting worse. There were calls to her cell phone from a blocked number. The caller always hung up when she answered. She'd see him watching her, even in places where he had no reason to be, like the local shopping mall when she was buying clothes the day before.

Only this morning she'd found him waiting outside her quarters when she left for class. She approached him, angry and a bit frightened, and told him that he had to stop following her, that it was creepy and unbecoming for a brand-new army officer. He laughed at her, told her to grow up, that he had a right to be where he was and if she happened by, so be it. He knew that she wanted him and that it was just a matter of time. She told him that if there was one more phone call, one more stalking incident, she would go to the colonel who commanded the school. He laughed and walked away.

She'd thought some more about talking to the administrators of the school, but she didn't want to be tagged as a complainer, a wimp. She was in the army, and that sort of thing was not tolerated. She only had eight more weeks of school before being assigned a duty post. She could handle the harassment until then, and she'd probably never see the guy again.

The day was drawing to a close. She was headed for the library for some book time with her study group. There were four of them, two men and two women, who'd come together in the lounge of the school on their first day. Their backgrounds were varied, different colleges and law schools, hailing from different parts of the country. She was the only northern Californian in the group, although there were a couple of students in her class from the southern part of the state. She'd grown up in a small town in the Trinity Mountains, not far from the Oregon border, in a close-knit family of four. Her sister, older by two years, was married with a baby, living happily within spitting distance of the trim house in which the two girls had lived their entire lives.

A good life, but not for her. She wanted to see some of the world, and the army was a good vehicle for that. Her life was good, her future rosy and exciting. She was looking forward to joining a unit somewhere in the world, to suiting up and going to court, to representing the interests of the army and the United States.

She mounted the steps to the school building, warm thoughts of the years to come suffusing her brain. She walked into the portico and was reaching for the door when a man stepped out of the shadows and plunged a knife into her heart.

CHAPTER THIRTY-NINE

Jock and I were sitting in a rental car outside a duplex near the campus of the University of North Carolina at Charlotte. It was late afternoon, the sun hanging at a low angle over the city, a bit cooler than in Florida, but not much.

A ten-year-old Honda pulled into the driveway and stopped. The young man who got out of it was tall and lanky, a mop of brown hair sticking out from under a ball cap. He was in jeans and a T-shirt stained with sweat. He moved slowly, a man tired after a long day of work in the sun. He walked to the front door and let himself in. He was the man in the photograph I held in my hand, the one of the boyfriend sitting across the table from Katherine Brewster on the night she died.

I'd talked to Debbie the night before, after she got off work and was home and in a less than great mood. I asked her to hack into the University of North Carolina at Charlotte computers and see if she could come up with an address for Doug Peterson. She gave us the duplex.

We'd taken a plane from Tampa nonstop to Charlotte that morning, arriving just after noon. We had open reservations back to Tampa and enough clothes to last us a couple of days if necessary. We'd come looking for information on the Brewsters and we figured Doug Peterson was the one who could enlighten us.

We'd been there for an hour, sitting in the car, watching the neighborhood. It was quiet, most of the people at work or school or somewhere. The area was depressed and depressing, a place for minimum-wage job holders and students struggling to better themselves, to live, or exist, until things looked up for them. Hope kept the residents moving forward, toward a college degree or the next promotion on the job. Hope that the future would relieve them of the necessity of living in a rundown part of town that had seen its best days shortly after World War II.

We had seen no movement in the other side of the duplex. No one home. Jock looked at me. I nodded. We got out of the car and walked to the front door. I knocked. Doug Peterson opened the door, a quizzical look on his face. Probably thought we were Jehovah's Witnesses or something.

Jock stepped past me, put his hand on Peterson's chest, and pushed him back into the house. I followed. "Doug Peterson," I said, "you are in more trouble than you can even imagine. Sit down."

Jock pushed him into a nearby easy chair in front of the TV. Fear was written on the boy's face, shocked by the violent intrusion into his sanctuary. "What do you want?" he asked, his voice trembling.

"Where are the Brewsters?" Jock asked.

"How would I know?" He was making an effort, scared as he was. My respect level rose. He was scared but wanted to protect his friends.

"Because," I said, "two days ago you rented a U-Haul van, packed up the Brewsters, and drove to Hickory with them following you in their car."

He blanched, the color draining out of his face.

"Look, Doug," I said, "we're here to help. I met with the Brewsters three days ago. They couldn't tell me much. We want to know about Katherine's murder and why the Brewsters lied to us."

"That was you who came to their house on Sunday?"

"Yes."

"You said they lied to you. I don't understand."

"You don't have to," said Jock, scowling.

Doug looked at Jock and back at me. "We think you had something to do with Katherine's death," I said.

"No. God, she was my whole life. We were going to get married."

"Why were you on the dinner boat with her the night she was murdered? You didn't go to Florida with her."

"Who are you?" he asked, plaintively.

"I'm a lawyer and this is my investigator. We're looking into the murders on the *Dulcimer*."

"Why?"

"That's none of your business," Jock said, a tightness in his voice. He was playing his role nicely. "Answer the question."

"No," Doug said, "I didn't go to Florida with her. Look, we'd been having a little rough patch. I didn't like her working at Hooters, but she was making too much money to quit. She was going back to school, and as soon as we finished we were going to get married."

"What was your problem with Hooters?"

"Not with the restaurant, with some of the customers."

"What do you mean?"

"Guys were hitting on her."

"Surprise."

"Yeah, but there was this one guy in particular. He was stalking her, calling her cell phone, driving by her house."

"Did she give him her phone number or address?"

"No. I think he got it from one of the other girls, but I'm not sure."

"Did he ever threaten her?"

"Not in so many words. But he'd come into the restaurant and sit for hours staring at her. He told her once that he loved her and would have her one way or the other. That may have been a threat."

"Did she go to the police?"

"No. She thought she could handle it."

"Did you ever talk to the stalker?"

"Once. I saw him at Hooters. Kat pointed him out to me. I went over and told him to leave her alone or I'd kick his ass."

"What kind of response did you get?"

"He just laughed."

"That was it? Nothing else?"

"No. Kat was embarrassed that I'd made a scene. Told me to butt out."

"Did you?"

"Pretty much. That was the cause of our disagreement. I felt like I wasn't protecting my girl, but she wouldn't let me get involved."

"Do you know the guy's name?"

"No. She wouldn't tell me. Said she was afraid I'd do something stupid."

"Do you know anything about him?"

"Just what one of the girls told me."

"What?"

"That he owned a travel agency and traveled a lot."

"What was the name of the agency?"

"EZGo Travel."

CHAPTER FORTY

I looked at Jock. "Now there's a nasty coincidence."

"Yeah. That's the same agency that bought the gift certificate at the Anna Maria Inn."

Doug said, "That's right."

"What do you know about that?" I asked.

"I had dinner with the Brewsters the day Kat was killed."

I interrupted him, an edge to my voice. "Don't lie to me, Doug. The Brewsters already pulled that one on me. You were on the boat with Kat that evening. I've got the picture to prove it."

He nodded. "I was."

I was puzzled. "How do explain having dinner with the Brewsters and still making it to the boat that evening?"

"We finished dinner about one in the afternoon, and I caught a plane out of here a little after three."

"So you had lunch with the Brewsters?"

"Well, yeah. Lunch, dinner, whatever."

The light dawned and I looked at Jock. "We're forgetting our roots, old buddy."

Jock laughed. "That we are, podna."

I mentally kicked myself. The Brewsters hadn't lied to me. In the South, a lot of people still called the midday meal "dinner" and the evening meal "supper." Jock and I had both grown up knowing that dinner was served at noon. Lunch was something your dad took to work in a lunch-box or you took to school in a brown paper bag.

"What made you decide to go to Katherine?"

"I was talking to the Brewsters about her trip. She'd called them and said she liked the area and was enjoying being alone for a little bit. They told me Kat had called the charity that sent her the gift certificate. She wanted to thank Mr. Brumbaugh, the man who sent it to her. The people at Charlotte Learns had never heard of him."

"Didn't they think that was a little strange?"

"Yes. But Kat only called the morning she was supposed to leave, and she really wanted to go. Told her mom you're not supposed to look a gift horse in the mouth."

"But this was the first you'd heard about it?"

"Yes. I asked where the gift certificate had come from and Mrs. Brewster went and got a copy of it that Kat had made for what she called her memory box. When I saw it had been issued to EZGo Travel, bells started going off. I figured the bastard from Hooters was trying to get her to Florida for some reason."

"You thought she was in danger?"

"Yes."

"Did you call her?"

"I tried, but she didn't answer her cell. I called the Anna Maria Inn and a lady there told me that Kat was out. I left a message for her to call me as soon as she got in. The lady said Kat was going on a dinner cruise and it might be late before she got back. Then I checked airline schedules."

"Did you ever hear from her?"

"No."

"How did you know where to find Kat?"

"The lady told me the name of the restaurant the boat left from and the time. I went there and bought a ticket for the boat. I barely made it. I got there just as they were taking the lines off."

"Did you see the stalker on the boat?"

"No. The boat was crowded. He might have been on it, but I didn't see him."

"Why did you run?"

"Run?"

"Yeah. After Kat was killed."

"I didn't know she was dead. She was really pissed when I showed up. Told me to get the hell out of her life. I left. I figured we'd sort it out when she got back to Charlotte."

"Did you tell her about EZGo Travel and the stalker?"

"Yes, but she wasn't concerned. Said the guy wouldn't come all the way to Florida to harm her when he could do it in Charlotte. She thought the gift certificate was just one more ploy on his part to get to see her. She said she might as well enjoy it."

"Didn't you miss her when the boat docked?"

"No. She told me to get lost and that pissed me off. I went to the front of the boat to wait until we landed. When we hit the sandbar, I went back looking for her, but the lights were out and I couldn't see a damn thing. I didn't want to piss her off any more than she was, so I went back to the front of the boat and stayed there until we docked. Then I started for home."

"When did you first find out that she'd died?"

"When I got back to Charlotte. Her mom called me late that morning. The police had called her."

"Did you tell the police about the stalker?"

"I called the Charlotte police and they told me to call the Longboat Key Police Department."

"Did you?"

"No."

"Why not? Didn't you think it important that Katherine might have been set up by a stalker?"

"Yeah, I thought it was important, but it wouldn't bring her back. One of the other girls at Hooters had told me this guy bragged about being part of the mob. If he was, I didn't want them coming after me."

"The mob? What mob?"

"I don't know. I guess he meant the Mafia."

"Where are the Brewsters?"

"They're at a friend's house outside of Hickory."

"Why did they run?"

"When Mrs. Brewster told me about you coming to visit, I thought it might be the mob coming for us all. I told them what I thought about the stalker and the EZGo Travel thing. We decided it would be best if they hid out."

"What about you?"

"I doubt they know who I am. Besides, I've got a job and school. I couldn't just leave town."

What's the name of the waitress at Hooters who told you about the stalker owning the travel agency?"

"Sally. I don't know her last name."

I looked at Jock. "You got anything else?"

"No. I think you covered it, Counselor."

CHAPTER FORTY-ONE

We headed south on I-485, exited, and pulled into the parking lot of a Hooters Restaurant.

The Happy Hour crowd was there, mostly blue-collar types drinking beer and chatting up the waitresses. Jock and I took seats at the bar and ordered drinks, a diet Coke for me and an O'Doul's for Jock. When the bartender brought them, I asked, "Is there a waitress here named Sally?"

"I can't talk about that."

"Did you know Katherine Brewster?"

"Yes."

I handed her a card that showed that I was a lawyer in Longboat Key. "I'm trying to help her family find out who killed her. Katherine's boyfriend, Doug Peterson, told me that Sally might have some information that'd be helpful."

"Let me ask around." She took my card and left.

Jock and I sat and sipped our drinks. In a few minutes a woman in her mid-twenties came to the bar. She had the card I'd given the bartender in her hand. She stood next to me and said, "I'm Sally. Katherine was a very good friend of mine."

"Thank you for speaking with me," I said. "We've just left Doug Peterson. He said you might be able to help us."

"If I can."

"Doug says that Katherine was being stalked by one of the customers here. Do you know who that was?"

"Yes. His name's John Doremus. Or at least that's what he said."

I looked at Jock. "John Doe is the name of the owner of EZGo," he said.

"Yeah," I said. "Sally, do you know anything else about him?"

"Not really. He told me one time he was involved with the mob, but I didn't believe him."

"What kind of mob?"

"I assumed he was talking about organized crime."

"Have you seen him lately?"

"No. He hasn't been in for a while."

"Do you remember the last time you saw him here?"

"No. But I don't think he's been in since Kat died."

"You wouldn't happen to know where he lives?"

She laughed. "No, and I don't want to know."

"Can you describe him?"

"He's about forty years old, dark hair that he parts in the middle. Wears it short, not a buzz cut, by not much longer than that. Has a lot of acne scars on his cheeks, a receding chin, a nose with a little hump on the bridge. He's big, about six feet tall, pretty heavyset, a belly that hangs over his belt. Talks with some kind of Yankee accent, like from New Jersey or New York. His teeth are very white. They might be caps, or maybe he had one of those cosmetic whitening jobs."

"You're very observant," Jock said.

"Gotta be with creeps like that. If I saw him outside the restaurant, I'd run the other way. Do you think he killed Kat?"

"Don't know," I said. "He's what the police call a person of interest. I'd like to talk to him. Do you think there'd be any credit card information on him in your computers?"

"No. He always paid cash."

"How often did he come in?" Jock asked.

"Almost every night. He usually came in late and stayed until closing. I think he always hoped one of the girls would go home with him."

"Did any of them ever go out with him?"

"I never heard of any who did, and I kinda doubt anybody would. He was too creepy."

"Did he seem to take an inordinate interest in any of the girls?"

"You mean other than Kat?"

"Yes."

"He hit on everybody, but Kat seemed to be his favorite. I tried to warn Kat that he could be trouble, but she always saw the good in everybody. Said he was probably just lonely. Maybe her soft heart got her killed."

"Maybe," I said. "Did you ever see him in here with any Asian men?"

"Asian? No. Not that I remember."

"How about an Asian woman?"

"Definitely no. I never saw him with a woman at all."

"How did he dress?" I asked

"What do you mean?"

"Did he wear a suit and tie, casual clothes, jeans?"

"He usually had on a pair of dress slacks and a golf shirt. They were nice clothes. Expensive looking. He seemed to have a lot of money."

"How so?"

"He always flashed a wad of bills when he was paying for his drinks. He was a good tipper and wore a big diamond ring on each pinkie."

"Two rings?"

"Yes. I thought that was a little much, but you know how some guys are."

"Are you sure they were diamonds?"

"No, but they didn't look like glass. I guess they could've been cubic zirconia. I wouldn't be able to tell the difference."

CHAPTER FORTY-TWO

"What now?" asked Jock. We were in the rental car, pointed toward the airport and home.

"I guess we'd better see what we can find on Doremus."

"I guess. But that sounds like a fake name."

"Could be. Can your guys check him out?"

Jock looked at his watch. "A bit late today, but I'll call in the morning. I wonder why he wanted Katherine on Anna Maria?"

"I don't follow you."

"He went to a lot of trouble to get that gift certificate for the Anna Maria Inn. He obviously wanted Katherine to go there. Why?"

"So he could get her alone?" I asked.

"Sure. But why Anna Maria specifically?"

"Good question. Got any ideas?"

"He might have wanted to be somewhere that he was comfortable. Knowledgeable about the area. Wanted to impress the girl. Maybe he has a home in the area."

"That is worth checking out," I said. "Doremus can't be a common name. If we can find that same name on properties in Charlotte and in our area, we'll be able to find him."

"Deb can probably do that as quickly as the agency," said Jock. "We won't get much priority."

I looked at my watch. It was a little after nine. I pulled my phone out and called Deb.

"Where are you?" I asked. "Working?"

"I'm in bed. It's my day off."

"Little early for sleeping isn't it?"

"What makes you think I'm sleeping?"

"What're you doing, then?"

"Duh."

"Oops. Whose bed are you in?"

"My own."

"Who's there with you?

"None of your business."

"Deb, I worry about you."

"Forget it, numbnuts. I'm all alone watching an HBO movie."

"You sure?"

"Yes. I'm sure. What do you want?"

"A little favor."

"I've heard that one before."

I told her what I needed. "If you can't reach me on my cell, it'll be because we're in the air. Leave a message and I'll call you when we land."

We landed at Tampa a little after midnight. We were the last flight in and there were only a few passengers on our plane. The airport was quiet, the little kiosks and restaurants that lined the concourse closed and dark. I turned my cell phone on and checked for messages. One from Deb. I called voice mail, listened, and hung up.

"She found somebody," I said to Jock. "There's a John Doremus who owns a home in Charlotte and a condo on Seventh-Fifth Street West in Bradenton."

"That's got to be him."

"Maybe we should have stayed overnight in Charlotte," I said. "He's not likely to be here this time of the year."

"We've got to check it out."

"Yes. We do. Tomorrow."

An hour later we were home on Longboat Key. I typed up notes on our activities the past two days and e-mailed them to J. D. and Chaz Desmond. Then I went to bed.

J.D. called early the next morning, waking me from a dream that had something to do with beautiful women. "What're you doing?" she asked.

"Dreaming."

"Did I wake you up?"

"Yes. It's okay."

"It's also after nine. You never sleep this late."

"Yesterday was a long day. We got in late."

"I got your memo. Do you think this is the same Doremus who was stalking Katherine Brewster?"

"It's got to be," I said. "That's not a common name."

"Do you want me to go see him?"

"He may be in Charlotte. Why don't Jock and I stop by his condo? If he's here, he might get spooked by a cop."

"Yeah, like he wouldn't get spooked looking at Jock."

"You've got a point."

"Go see him. Let me know what you find out."

CHAPTER FORTY-THREE

Seventy-Fifth Street West is a north-south artery linking Manatee Avenue to Cortez Road. The apartment complex where Doremus lived was only about five miles from the Cortez Bridge that led to Anna Maria Island. It was late morning when I knocked on the door. A black man opened it. He was in his late sixties or early seventies. He had a head full of gray hair, a face that easily wrinkled into a grin when he greeted us, and a voice that was deep and Southern.

"Can I help you gentlemen?"

"My name is Matt Royal. This is Jock Algren. I'm a lawyer on Longboat Key, and I'm trying to find John Doremus."

"You've found him. I'm John Doremus."

"Sir," I said, "the man I'm looking for is white and about forty years old."

He grinned. "You've probably noticed that I don't fit either of those descriptions."

"Do you own a home in Charlotte, North Carolina?"

"I do. Y'all come on in and tell me what you want with a white guy with my name."

The condo was large and tastefully furnished and neat as a pin. The only sign of disorder was the pile of newspapers lying on the floor next to a recliner. It looked like the *Wall Street Journal*, the *New York Times,* and the *Sarasota Herald-Tribune.* Doremus caught my glance at the papers and said, "I like to keep up with what's going on in the world. Have a seat and tell me what I can do for you gentlemen."

"I was surprised to find you here in August," I said.

"I live here year round. My wife lives in the house in Charlotte. We're separated. Seems to make the marriage better." He chuckled.

"We came up with your name by running a property search in both Charlotte and this area," I said. "You popped up, but you're obviously not the man we're looking for."

"Why are you looking for him?"

"Do you remember the murders on the dinner cruise boat about two months back?"

"Sure. That was the big news around here. At least for a couple of days."

"The man we're looking for is a person of interest in those murders."

"What's your interest, Mr. Royal, if I may ask?"

"I'm representing a family whose son was killed the same day over on the beach. The murders may be connected. Jock and I are trying to find this guy named Doremus to see if he can help us out."

Jock stirred in his chair. "Mr. Doremus, can you think of why someone would be using your name in Charlotte?"

"No. Why?"

"It could explain why a white guy has an unusual name, a name that shows up owning property in both areas," said Jock.

"That doesn't make any sense to me," said Doremus. He was silent for a beat, then, "Can you describe the white guy?"

"Six feet tall, heavyset with a belly, short, dark hair that he parts in the middle, acne scars, a receding chin, northern accent, very white teeth. He wears diamond rings on each pinkie."

"Crap," said Doremus. "That's Chick Mantella. He's sort of my nephew."

"Nephew?" I was surprised. As far as I knew the guy was white.

"Sort of. Thirty years ago my brother Arthur married a white woman who had a small son from a previous marriage. That was Chick. Arthur raised him, gave him a good home, but Chick turned out to be an asshole. Never could hold a job for more than about three months."

"Is Chick his given name or a nickname?"

"His real name is Chesley Ambruster Mantella, Jr.

"No wonder they call him Chick," said Jock.

"Where does he live?" I asked.

"Charlotte, but he comes here a lot. Stays in my spare room. He's not a bad guy, just full of shit."

"Why do you put up with him?"

"His mother's a sweetheart. My brother's been ill for a long time and she's hung in there. Takes great care of him. Putting up with her son is a little bit of payback for all she does for Arthur."

"When was he here last?" Jock asked.

Doremus thought for a moment. "He was here when the murders took place. I remember, because he left abruptly. Didn't even say goodbye. I was out with a lady friend that evening and when I got home, he'd packed up and gone. Left a note saying he had to get back to Charlotte."

"Have you heard anymore from him?"

"No, but I talk to his mom regularly. I know he was back in Charlotte living with her."

"Does he work that you know of?"

"I don't think so. His biological father died about two years ago and left him a bunch of cash. That's when he bought those gaudy rings. Hasn't hit a lick at a snake since."

"Mr. Doremus," I said, "I know Chick is kin and all, but can I ask you not to tell him about our visit?"

"Not to worry, Mr. Royal. I don't like the kid much, and I sure don't want to have anything to do with a man who's involved in a murder."

"We don't know that he is. We just want to talk to him. Can you find out if he's still in Charlotte?"

Doremus hesitated, a look of resignation on his face. "I don't want to, but I know the family you're representing must be hurting. I'll call his mom tonight and let you know."

I gave him my card, shook hands, and left.

CHAPTER FORTY-FOUR

Jock and I were having lunch at the Seafood Shack when his cell phone rang. He excused himself and walked out to the marina dock next to the dining room. He was back in a few minutes.

"Matt, I hope you're not going to be pissed at me, but I need to tell you something."

I looked at him, puzzled. I made a come on gesture with my hand.

"I had Chaz Desmond checked out."

"Why would I be pissed about that?"

"He saved your life."

"I checked him out too, Jock. As best I could on Google."

"Glad you're okay with it, because we got some curious information when we ran him through the systems. Did you know that he was sending money every year to a man in Vietnam? A lot of money."

"I didn't know that. How much?"

"Two hundred grand."

"That is a lot. Who's the recipient?"

"A man named Tuan Nguyen."

"Tuan Nguyen? That's mighty close to John Nguyen, the guy from O'Reilly's."

"That's what I thought," said Jock.

"Chaz just writes him a check?"

"No. The scheme is a little more sophisticated than that. Chaz owns Desmond Engineering Consultants, Inc. Every year, according to the firm's tax returns, a two-hundred-thousand-dollar donation is made to a charitable foundation named Evermore. Evermore has only one beneficiary, this guy Tuan Nguyen."

"Is the foundation recognized by the Internal Revenue Service as a charitable organization? Are the contributions deductible?"

"Yes on both counts. On the other hand, the IRS doesn't check into these things very closely. Almost anybody can set up a foundation and get a tax-deductible certificate."

"I'm guessing that you found the man behind the foundation."

"Right. Charles Desmond."

"So," I said, "his firm contributes to a charitable foundation that he controls and the money always goes to the same person. How long has this been going on?"

"This is the fifth year."

"Blackmail?" I asked.

"I don't know. I suppose if somebody was blackmailing you and you wanted to save a little money, you could do it by making a tax-deductible donation to a charity and running the money that way."

"How does the money get from the foundation to Nguyen?"

"Wire transfer," said Jock. "To a bank in Ho Chi Minh City."

"And from there?"

"We don't know. I've got my computer geeks trying to break the encryption on that bank. They'll be able to get in sooner or later, but you know we're still a low priority."

"Can Deb help us?"

"Something like this is way above her head. If she tried to get in, she could leave footprints that could be traced back to her. That might put her life in danger."

"Then I guess we'll just have to wait until your guys can help us out."

"This case is getting stranger and stranger," Jock said.

"Maybe the guy at the airport *was* Vietnamese."

"But why would he be interested in killing you?" asked Jock. "You're working for Desmond."

"I don't know, but I think I need to talk to Jimbo Merryman.

At eight that evening, Doremus called. Chick Mantella had moved out of Charlotte and was living in a condo in downtown Orlando.

CHAPTER FORTY-FIVE

The air smelled of rain and dying fires and unwashed bodies. The tinge of coffee boiled too long wafted over me, the need for caffeine roiling my gut and reminding me that I'd missed breakfast. Smoke drifted over the campsite that puckered like a boil on the prairie near the Myakka River. Horses whinnied and snickered in the nearby stand of trees. The sun had not yet shown itself through the overcast that had settled on the camp, its filtered light giving everything a gray pallor as if disease had taken over the world.

Men in the gray and butternut uniforms of the Confederate States Army moved like ghosts through the campfire smoke that hung low to the ground, dodging the tents where they'd slept the night before. Bacon was sizzling in pans held close to cook fires. Voices were muted, low, conspiratorial in the heavy air that presaged rain. I wondered if there was fear in those voices, fear of the coming battle, of the death that some of them would certainly endure on this day. A semblance of death anyway.

I walked through the camp angling toward the command tent. I saw a squat man, five feet eight maybe and 220 pounds of muscle, standing at the entrance sipping coffee from a tin mug and talking to a small group of officers. The man with the coffee wore the three stars of a Confederate colonel on his collar, tall riding boots, a cavalry saber, and a slouch hat favored by horsemen. A small flag fluttered from the top of the tent identifying it as the headquarters of the Fourth Georgia Cavalry.

"Morning, Jimbo," I said as I approached the knot of officers.

"Matt. What the hell are you doing out here?"

"I called Molly last night. She said you'd be here reenacting the Battle of Olustee. Kind of far south, aren't you?"

"Yeah. Lot of the guys can't get enough time off to travel all the way to Lake City."

"I ran into a bunch of Yankees just down the road," I said.

"Yeah. That's some of Butler's troops."

"Butler? I thought Seymour was the Union General."

"He was. I'm talking about Billy Butler. He's a pharmacist at the Walgreens over in North Port. But how did you know that Seymour commanded the Union troops?"

"Well, Colonel," I said, "I know a lot about the Battle of Olustee. My great-grandfather, Harmon Royal, was a trooper in the Fourth Georgia Cavalry commanded by Duncan Clinch."

"I'm impressed. But what brings you way out here?"

"I need to talk to you about an old friend. Privately."

"Would you excuse us, gentlemen?" Jimbo asked the assembled officers.

They saluted and we walked a few yards away from the headquarters tent.

"It's about Doc Desmond," I said.

"What's going on?"

"Do you have any idea why Doc would be sending two hundred grand a year to some guy in Saigon?"

"Wow. No. What's this all about?"

"A man named John Nguyen, an American apparently of Asian descent, tried to kill me a couple of days ago. Then yesterday, Jock's agency's magic computers spit out the information that Doc is using a charity he set up to send money every year to a man named Tuan Nguyen in Saigon or Ho Chi Minh City or whatever the hell they call it these days."

"That's very strange. How long has it been going on?"

"Five years. I'm wondering if it's some sort of blackmail scheme."

Jimbo shook his head. "That doesn't make a lot of sense. If it's tied to the war somehow, you'd think he'd have been paying it long before the past five years."

"Unless something happened then and the blackmailer just found Doc."

"I guess that could have happened. The five years coincides with about the time Doc started making the real big bucks."

"Tell me what you know about that."

"He had a pretty good business going for a number of years," Jimbo said. "He had an office in Atlanta and one in Orlando and I think another one in Miami. Then all of a sudden it exploded. He moved into other states and in five years had a really big outfit."

"That sounds a little odd, don't you think? All that growth that quickly."

"I don't know, Matt. I've never understood business and I never wanted to. Doc always seemed on the up-and-up to me."

"I called a friend last night and asked her to see what she could find on his company. She's a pretty good hacker. Apparently he owns it by himself. No partners or other stockholders. But I'd think the expansion would have taken a lot of money, and she couldn't find any specific influx of dollars except for some legitimate loans from banks."

"Maybe that was enough."

"Maybe, but then why the payments to some guy in Vietnam? And why would an Asian man with a suspiciously similar name want me dead?"

"I don't know, Matt, but keep in mind that Doc was one of us."

"I know, Top. And he saved my ass that day in the grass. I can't forget that. But I'm afraid it might get in the way of my seeing Doc as he is today, not as he was in Nam."

"Matt, I know you'll do what's right. Now I've got to go attack some Yankees."

"Good luck, Colonel. If you hear anything about Doc, let me know. And keep this conversation under your hat."

I drove back to Longboat Key in a mood that matched the weather: dismal. What the hell had Doc gotten himself into? Was he being blackmailed? If so, did it have to do with his service in Vietnam, his business affairs? If he was being blackmailed, could his son's death be tied into it somehow? But if that were the case, why would he want me to look into Jim's murder? Did Doc think the death was part of whatever he was involved in with the man in Ho Chi Minh City? Did he expect me to be able to turn over some rock that would give him leverage against his blackmailer? Lots of questions and no answers.

I drove northwest on Highway 70, the sky ahead getting darker. A storm was coming in from the Gulf. I looked at my watch. Not yet nine o'clock. When summer storms came in the morning, they were usually big ones and brought a lot of rain. Before long, I was in it, the windshield wipers working overtime, pushing the waves of water, barely clearing my view ahead. I had my headlights on and had slowed, driving cautiously. By the time I crossed the Cortez Bridge, the rain had slackened, but the dark clouds hovered like an omen. A slight chill ran up my spine. I didn't think the rest of the day would be a lot of fun.

CHAPTER FORTY-SIX

I was antsy as I drove onto Longboat Key, out of sorts, confused, and more than a little bit pissed. I was concerned that my friend Doc wasn't what he seemed to be, or perhaps was more than he seemed. We had odd threads running through the investigation, some leading to a man in Ho Chi Minh City and perhaps a killer in Bradenton, another to a Laotian warlord, a third to a creepy guy named Mantella who now lived in Orlando. And we weren't even sure the *Dulcimer* murders were related to the death of Jim Desmond. I was beginning to think that Doc knew more than he was telling me and maybe was using me in a way that played on my moral debt to him. Could he be that callous? It did tend to piss me off.

Jock was at my desk, his head buried in the computer monitor when I walked in. "Any coffee left?" I asked.

"In the pot. Been there a while. Can't vouch for its taste."

"I'll make some more. You want another cup?"

"Yeah, if you don't mind."

"What're you looking at?" I asked.

"Trying to run down some more info on your buddy Doc. Did Jimbo have anything?"

"Not really, but he did tell me that Doc started making the big money at about the same time he started sending those checks to Vietnam."

"I've been thinking about that," said Jock. "I had the guys in Washington send me the information they got on those transfers. The payments were all made in April. Except for this year. The payment didn't go out until early July. And that one was for three hundred thousand. An extra hundred grand."

"I wonder why."

"Suppose that Doc *is* being blackmailed and for some reason he decided to stop making the payments. Maybe whoever he was paying off decided that murdering his son would be an object lesson and the money would start flowing again. The extra hundred may be interest."

"Why kill his son?"

"I don't know. Maybe the message was that Doc's wife would be next, or maybe his daughter-in-law, if he didn't pay up."

"And add a little vig to the payment," I said. " Say, a hundred grand."

"Right."

"But if they're blackmailing him, why not just release whatever evidence they have that he had done something crooked or whatever it is they're holding over his head."

"Because that would kill the goose that lays the two hundred grand eggs. By killing his son, the bad guys would send a powerful message and keep the money rolling in."

"We need to bring J.D. up to date," I said.

I called her cell phone. "You busy?" I asked when she answered.

"On my way to the Village. Another murder investigation."

"What?"

"Two deaths. Poisoning, I think."

I was concerned. I knew practically everybody in the village. "Who?"

"A couple of peacocks."

"Geez, Duncan. That's cruel."

"I thought so. Poor birds."

"Right. Can you have lunch with Jock and me?"

"Sure. I'll be through with the peacocks by then."

"Meet us at Moore's"

"This is one weird investigation," said J.D.

We were sitting in the dining room at Moore's Stone Crab Restaurant at a table next to the windows that provided a view twelve miles down the bay to the city of Sarasota. It was usually a breathtaking vista, but today the drizzling rain and low clouds obscured it. I'd filled J.D. in on what we knew, what we suspected, and what we surmised. I told her about my confusion at all the threads of the investigation, none of which seemed to coalesce into any coherent whole.

"Maybe," she said, "we can start eliminating suspects. The last one standing is probably the culprit."

"I don't have any idea how to go about that," I said.

"We could start with Mantella in Orlando," said Jock.

"Or," said J.D., "you could just call your buddy and ask him straight out about the payments to Vietnam."

"I don't think so," I said. "If he suckered me into this in some way, he's not going to tell me the truth. If he says he's not dirty, I wouldn't believe him at this point."

Jock said, "You've been sending him all the memos on what we're doing, so if he's up to something, he knows pretty much everything we know."

"Yeah, one more reason for me not to call him. I think we'd better find out more about his operation. Maybe when Jock's agency people get back to us with the information on the Ho Chi Minh City bank account, we'll know more."

J.D. looked at Jock. "Any idea when that'll be?"

"No," he said. "I'll call the director and see if we can light a fire under somebody. I'd bet they already have a back door into that bank's computers, so it shouldn't be too big of a job."

"Can you call him today?" asked J.D.

"As soon as we get through eating," Jock said.

"Maybe you could do it while we're waiting for our food," she said.

Jock grinned. "Maybe I could." He got up and left the table.

When he returned, he said, "They've got some sort of big emergency going on up there that all the computer geeks are working on. The director assured me he'd e-mail me everything we need by noon tomorrow."

"Maybe we should go talk to Mantella," said Jock.

And that's what we decided to do. As it happened, I relearned the lesson that snap decisions often don't work out too well.

CHAPTER FORTY-SEVEN

We drove I-75 north to I-4 and then east to Orlando. Just past Disney we ran into the traffic jam that always starts building at mid-afternoon. It was almost five when we parked in front of a high-rise condo building on Rosalind Avenue in downtown Orlando. This was the address we had for Chick Mantella.

We'd decided that the best place to find him was his condo, but we didn't want to confront him there. He didn't know us, and if we casually bumped into him at a bar, we might have a better chance of getting the information we needed.

We left the car and scouted the building. There were several entrances. One was the main entrance into a lobby that faced Rosalind Avenue and the four floors above of parking garage, each with its own exit from the elevator lobby on that floor. J.D. had run Mantella's name through Florida and North Carolina databases until she found a car registered in the name of Chesley Ambruster Mantella, Jr. It was a black Mercedes with a North Carolina license plate.

There was no doorman at the main entrance, but the door was locked and controlled by a card key. We walked around to the ramp leading to the garage. It was open. Jock took the second floor garage and I took the third. I was halfway down the first row of cars when I saw Mantella's Mercedes. I called Jock on my cell phone and met him back at my car. We drove around to Robinson Street and parked in a bank parking lot that gave us a view of the ramp to the garage.

"We know he's home," I said.

"Unless he went out with somebody else."

"There's that. Hope for the best."

We sat for twenty minutes, listening to NPR on the Explorer's radio. The black Mercedes came down the ramp, made a left turn onto Robinson, and drove west. The driver was alone. "Looks like our guy," said Jock.

"It does." I pulled out and followed our quarry. He crossed under I-4 and took the on-ramp for the westbound interstate.

"Where the hell is he going?" asked Jock.

"Beats me. Let's hope it's not far. I've got to pee."

Chick didn't go very far. He took the Conroy Road exit, turned left onto Vineland Road, and then another left onto Kirkman Road. In a few minutes we pulled into the parking lot of a Hooters Restaurant.

"I think he's in a rut," said Jock.

"At least we can get something to eat. I love their chicken wings."

The place looked pretty much like every Hooters I'd ever been in. There was a U-shaped bar jutting from the back wall and a large dining area with booths and tables. Chick had planted himself at a table near the bar, his pinkie diamonds assuring us that we had the right guy.

We sat at the bar, on the side that gave us an unobstructed view of Mantella. I ordered the wings and a diet Coke and Jock asked for a salad and water. The place was filling up with the after-work crowd, an eclectic group of hard hats, business suits, and a few sunburned tourists wearing Disney and Universal Studio T-shirts.

Chick seemed to be in constant conversation with any one of several waitresses. They would bring him a drink, each one a dark amber whiskey over ice in a cocktail glass, linger for a few minutes, laughing and working on their cuteness, and then move on. He knocked back the drinks with alacrity, quickly as if trying to get drunk, or just maybe encouraging the next waitress to return with another drink and a little company.

"You know, Jock," I said, "that is one sad bastard there. I almost feel sorry for him. I guess this is his life, sitting in Hooters, talking up the girls that wouldn't give him the time of day without the big tip."

"Yeah, and he may have murdered one of them."

"I know. You just wonder what drives people."

We watched for a while longer. Chick was drinking quickly, ordering another, and quaffing that one. The more he drank, the louder he got. When we judged him pretty well potted, I walked over to his table.

"Aren't you John Doremus?" I asked.

He looked at me, his eyes squinting, his concentration skewered by the booze. "Who're you?"

"I'm Ed Hollingsworth. We met in Charlotte a couple of months back. At Hooters."

"Don't remember you." His speech was slow, his enunciation careful, the drunk's attempt to hide the extent of his inebriation.

"I'm the stockbroker. You were telling me you'd inherited some money and wanted some advice on where to invest it."

"Oh, sure. How are you?"

"Great. Small world, huh?"

"Yeah."

"Hey, did you ever get some of that waitress you were working up there?"

"I got a lot of them."

"Yeah, but this one was special. What was her name? Kitt, Kate, Kat? That's it. Katherine."

He squinted again, concentrating on me, suspicious now. Maybe I'd overplayed the hand. "What's your name?"

"Ed Hollingsworth."

"What do you know about Kat?"

"Nothing. I was just wondering. You seemed pretty focused on her that night."

"I think you have me mixed up with somebody else."

"You are John Doremus, aren't you?"

"Yes, but I don't remember anybody named Kat. Why don't you go on back to your seat. I like being alone."

"Okay. Nice seeing you again."

I walked back to the bar and sat. I looked over at Chick's table. He was staring at me, a hard look with no warmth. He waved one of the waitresses over, pulled out a wad of bills, gave a few to her, and walked out. Jock had paid our tab while I was talking to Chick. We followed him out to the parking lot.

The wind was up, but the rain had stopped. Night had fallen and shadows danced on the asphalt, the palm fronds stirred by the breeze diffusing the glow from the security lights. Chick was walking toward his car as we came up behind him.

"John," I called.

He stopped, turned, and showed us the pistol in his hand. "Who the fuck are you?"

I stopped dead, raising my hands. "Whoa, friend. Stay cool. What's this all about?"

"You come around asking me about a dead girl and I'm supposed to stay cool? Who are you?"

"I told you. I'm Ed Hollingsworth."

"Bullshit. I saw you following me from my condo, watched you come into the bar. You waited until you thought I was drunk before coming over. What kind of fool do you take me for?"

"Obviously you're not as big a fool as I thought, Chick."

He laughed. "How in the hell did you find me?"

"It wasn't hard," said Jock. "We're cops."

That seemed to rock Chick a bit. "Let me see some ID."

Jock pulled a small leather case out of his back pocket, held it up and took two steps toward Chick.

"Stop right there," said Chick. "Toss it over here."

Jock was maybe four feet from Chick when he threw the case toward him. It landed at Chick's feet. He bent over to pick it up and Jock launched himself, covering the four feet in a split second. He caught Mantella while he was bending over to pick up the case, the force of his body taking Chick back onto the asphalt. Jock quickly disarmed him and stood. "Stay on the ground," he said, pointing the pistol at Chick.

"You're not cops."

"No."

"Don't kill me."

"I wouldn't think of it," said Jock. "Let's get him in your car, Matt. I don't want anybody calling the real cops."

I pulled a pair of flex cuffs out of a bag in the back of the Explorer. We secured Chick in the backseat and Jock and I sat in the front, turned so that we could see him.

"What do you want?" Mantella asked.

"Tell us about EZGo Travel."

"Shit. Nothing to it."

"You formed the business, right?"

"Yes. But it never got up and going."

"You used it to lure Katherine Brewster to Anna Maria Island. Why?"

"You don't understand. We were in love. I had to get her away from her boyfriend so we could be together."

"You sick fuck," I said. "She didn't want anything to do with you."

"Yes she did."

"She told you to leave her alone."

"That was just for the boyfriend's benefit. She didn't really mean it."

"Why Anna Maria Island?" I asked.

"It's romantic."

"Did you meet her there?" I asked.

"No. I was going to, but I got delayed in Charlotte."

"Why the delay?"

"Come on, man. I don't want to talk about this."

"I'm going to shoot you if you don't," said Jock.

"Okay, but it's kind of embarrassing," Chick said.

"I don't know what can be more embarrassing than laying dead in a Hooters parking lot," I said.

"I got a dose of clap," Chick said, resignation in his voice.

"Clap?" I asked. "Gonorrhea?"

"Yes."

"From one of the Hooters girls?" I asked.

"No. I paid for a whore one night. I started having burning when I peed and went to the doctor. He shot me up with penicillin, but it took a few days to clear up. I didn't want to give it to Kat, so I stayed in Charlotte getting the treatment."

"Geez," Jock said. "You're some piece of work."

"Hey. How was I supposed to know the bitch had the clap? Cost me a hundred bucks. You'd think for that price you'd get one who wasn't diseased."

"You went to Anna Maria eventually, didn't you?" I was thinking about the gasoline he bought in Bradenton on his EZGo credit card on the night of the *Dulcimer* murders.

"Yes."

"Did you talk to Katherine?"

"No."

"Why not?"

"I went to the inn where she was staying and parked outside waiting for her. She came out but got in her car before I could say anything. I followed her to the restaurant where she went on the boat."

"If you were in love, why didn't you just call her and tell her you were on the island?" I asked.

"You don't understand. She had to keep up appearances for the boyfriend. I couldn't just call her. I had to bump into her somewhere. Like in a bar."

"Did you get on the boat?"

"No."

"Why not? Couldn't you have bumped into her there?"

"I saw the boyfriend buying a ticket."

"Doug?"

"Yeah, whatever his name is."

"What did you do?"

"I went to the bar in the restaurant. I figured I'd wait for the boat to get back and talk to her then."

"What happened?" I asked.

"When the boat docked, I saw the boyfriend. He was one of the first to get off and he went directly to the parking lot and got in his car and left. I waited for Kat, but she never showed up."

"Did you stay around?"

"For a while. There was a coast guard boat docked right behind the dinner boat. I heard the dispatcher say over its radio that they'd found a couple of bodies and that one of them was Katherine. I was devastated."

"I bet you were," said Jock, his voice dripping sarcasm.

"Don't make light of my grief."

"Why did you leave?" I asked.

"I figured her boyfriend did her because she was going to leave him for me. I didn't want him to find me anywhere near Kat."

"Where did you go?"

"I stopped by my uncle's house and got my stuff and drove back to Charlotte."

"How did you know we were following you?" I asked.

"I've got some problems. I have to be careful."

"What kind of problems."

"The mob kind."

"What does that mean?"

"You know. The mob. They're after me."

"Look, dipshit," said Jock, "you can pull that mob stuff on waitresses, but I'm not buying it."

"It's real. Honest."

"Tell us about it," I said.

"The mob's out to get me."

"Why?"

"I used to live in New Jersey."

"And?"

"Well, they didn't like the fact that I moved to Charlotte."

"Were you involved with the mob in any way?"

"No."

"Then why would they care if you moved to Charlotte?" I asked.

"You'd have to ask them."

I looked at Jock, who rolled his eyes. I thought I'd try one more time.

"Why did you use your uncle's name in Charlotte at the Hooters?"

"The mob's not after him."

"Then why did you use your own name in Orlando?"

"There's no mob in Orlando."

I gave up. I looked at my watch. A little after nine. I held up my cell phone and used the camera application to take a picture of him. I stepped out of the car and called J.D. "I'm sending you a picture. Can you go through the pictures Dora took on *Dulcimer* and see if this guy is there?"

"The pictures are still on your computer."

"This is important, J.D. My house isn't locked. Let yourself in and check it out for me."

"Is this the guy named Chick?"

"Yes. He says he wasn't aboard, and I tend to believe him. He's a real loon, but I don't think he killed anybody. I just want to make sure he's not in any of those pictures."

"He could have been on the boat and not in the pictures," J.D. said.

"I know, and the fact that he's not in the pictures won't prove anything. But if he is there, it'll prove he's lying."

"When do you need this?"

"Jock and I are holding him in Orlando. I don't want to take too long because he is one pain in the ass."

"Okay. I'll get back to you."

I clicked a button on the phone and sent the picture of Chick Mantella to her.

We drove aimlessly for an hour, chewing up time, awaiting J.D.'s call. We didn't want to let Chick go if we thought he was involved in the murders. If he wasn't in any of the photos taken by Dora, we'd take the chance that he was telling the truth. I didn't think the *Dulcimer* killings could have been handled by one person. There had to be at least one other man to take out the captain. Nothing fit. Chick was a loner, paranoid and delusional. I could see no plausible scenario whereby he could have killed three people on a boat that he said he was not on.

The car had been quiet for most of the drive. Chick muttered something every once in a while, but Jock would tell him to shut up or he'd shoot him. The message finally got through, and Chick sat sullenly in the back. After most of an hour had passed, I said, "Chick, I've got somebody looking through a lot of pictures that were taken on the boat the night Kat was killed. If we find out you've been lying to us, if a photo shows that you were on that boat that night, we're just going to pull off into some woods and shoot you."

"You won't find a picture of me on the boat." He sounded adamant, and I thought he was pretty well convinced that we might just shoot him for the hell of it.

A few more miles went by and my phone rang. J.D.

"No sign of him in Dora's pictures. Can I go to bed now?"

"Thanks, J.D. Jock and I'll be home late. I'll fill you in tomorrow."

We took Chick back to Hooters, cut the flex cuffs, and left him standing next to his black Mercedes.

CHAPTER FORTY-EIGHT

"So, we've ruled out the stalker," J.D. said.

"Guy's a nut job," said Jock.

We were having lunch at Rotten Ralph's on the Bradenton Beach Pier. A few tourists were seated at the outside tables, but we were cheerfully ensconced in the air-conditioned area. The sun was high and brutal, the heat index worse than usual. The humidity had followed the storms of the day before and descended on us like a layer of sweat.

We'd driven back to Longboat Key after leaving Chick in the parking lot. I'd typed up my notes that morning and mailed them to J.D. For now, I was keeping them from Chaz Desmond. If he was involved in this thing in some way, I couldn't figure it out. And until I did, I wanted to keep him out of the information loop.

"Jock," J.D. said, "did your people come through with any information on the bank in Vietnam?"

Jock looked pained. "No. I got a call from the director this morning. He was very apologetic, but whatever is going on up there is real big and he just can't spare the manpower to handle our problem. He said he'd get to it as soon as he could, but he couldn't tell me when that'd be."

"Is Clyde Bates still in the county lockup?" I asked J.D.

"Yeah. He's being held on two attempted murder charges. The bail is a lot more than he can make. Why?"

"I'm curious," I said. "Why would John Nguyen hire that numbnut to hit somebody? For that matter, why did he even go to O'Reilly's in the first place? That isn't exactly the kind of place I'd go looking for a hitman."

"I've been thinking about that myself," said J.D. "Maybe there's more to O'Reilly's than we know."

"I bet David Sims would know," said Jock.

Sims was a Manatee County detective who had helped us in the past. He was a former Secret Service agent who had been on the county force for almost thirty years. He knew just about everything that went on in Manatee County.

"J.D.," I said, "do you want to call him?"

"Why don't the three of us go see him," she said.

"It's Saturday. He's probably off fishing somewhere."

"Try him," said Jock. "You've got his cell number."

I called Sims and caught him as he was putting his boat in the water at the ramp next to Annie's. I told him that Jock was in town and we needed to see him.

"If you can meet me at Annie's in the next thirty minutes," he said. "After that I'm going to be sitting on my boat out next to those grass flats on the east side of the Sister Keys."

Thirty minutes later, we were at Annie's, a small wooden structure built on pilings over the bay at the mainland foot of the Cortez Bridge. It housed a combination bait shop, bar, restaurant, and fishing supply store. It had a fuel dock and some of the best hamburgers on the west coast.

We sat at a small table on the deck overlooking two long piers, one of which held the fuel pumps and the other various commercial boats, a Jet Ski rental concession, and a parasail boat that pulled tourists on a parachute attached to a long line.

"This can't be good," Sims said, shaking his head. "Every time you guys show up, something is about to go off the rails."

"We're just looking for a little information," I said. I pointed to J.D. "You can see we're on the law's side here."

He laughed. "Either that or Detective Duncan has gone over to the dark side. What can I help you with?"

"Are you familiar with O'Reilly's bar in Palmetto?" I asked.

"Yeah. Big Tony DeMarco owns the place."

"Any crime going on there that you know about?" J.D. asked.

"There's always some penny-ante stuff happening, but nothing serious."

"Like what?" asked J.D.

"Card games, betting. Big Tony fronts for a bookie, but it's all small-time stuff."

"You've never busted him?" I asked.

"No. We keep an eye on the place and if anything got serious we'd move in. But Big Tony knows that and stays mostly clean."

"What about running a clearinghouse for hitmen?" I asked.

Sims laughed. "You're kidding."

I told him about Bates and John Nguyen and how Big Tony arranged for them to get together.

Sims laughed some more. "Clyde Bates? Cleans boats over at the marina? That's precious."

"He came after Jock and me," I said.

"That shows you how stupid he really is," said Sims. "Coming after you two."

"What do you know about Bates?" J.D. asked.

"He's kind of a joke around Palmetto. He works at the marina on the north side of the river. Been there for a couple of years. He's a local boy. Dropped out of high school and worked at the marina ever since. He lives on an old houseboat that the marina owner keeps back in the work area on chocks. Boat hasn't been in the water in years."

"So, you're telling me he's not really a hitman," said J.D.

"Not even close. I heard he goes down to O'Reilly's most nights. Gets a little buzz on and tells the bikers he's a tough guy who kills people for a living. Nobody believes him, of course, but he's harmless so they put up with him. Treat him sort of like a mascot."

"Doesn't sound like anybody with good sense would hire him to kill somebody," said J.D.

"Maybe," said Sims, "this Nguyen guy was just trying to send a message."

"How would that work?"

"Hire the unlikeliest hitman in the area. Nguyen would know Bates couldn't pull it off, but it might just be enough to scare you off, Matt. He apparently doesn't know Jock is in the picture, so he points Bates at you, and Bates screws it up, and you've gotten the word that you should back off of whatever you're doing or a real hitman might just be coming your way."

"That has a certain logic to it," said Jock.

"Yeah," I said, "but the guy with the knife made a real effort. He wasn't fooling around."

"Are there any Asian gangs operating in this area?" Jock asked.

"No," said Sims. "We've got Mexican gangs, Russian gangs, a number of others, but no Asian gangs that I know of."

"Then," I said, "who the hell are these people?"

"Let me know if you find out," said Sims.

We were crossing the Cortez Bridge when Jock's cell phone beeped. He pulled it out of his pocket, opened it, and said, "Text from the director. The information on Desmond was just e-mailed to my computer."

CHAPTER FORTY-NINE

The documents were spread over my kitchen table. They held rows of figures and names, indicating checks written from the account and to whom they were written. The names of the recipients were written in the Vietnamese writing system known as *quoc-ngu*. The English equivalent of each name was typed in an adjacent column. One U.S. dollar was equal to ten thousand Vietnamese dong, which made the amounts in dong dispersed from the account seem huge. Fortunately, the U.S. equivalent was also typed in an adjacent column. I assumed the translations were part of the computer program the agency used when deciphering foreign documents.

Each year, in April, two hundred thousand dollars was deposited in the account, except for this year. There was no deposit in April, but a three hundred thousand dollar one was made in July. The deposits came from the Evermore Foundation and were the only deposits ever made to the account.

"I wonder what these checks were for," said J.D. "There seem to be a lot of smaller checks to different people, a lot of them companies. The same people and companies appear over and over."

I looked at the list of payees. "Most of the ones to individuals are for the same amount and are paid each month."

Jock riffled through a stack of documents. "We have copies of the checks, but they don't say what they were written in payment of."

"Wouldn't our Internal Revenue Service want to make sure that the money going out of Evermore was for a charitable purpose?" I asked. "Wouldn't Evermore have to provide proof to the government that it wasn't just laundering money somehow?"

"I'd think so," said J.D.

"They seem pretty lax about charitable organizations," said Jock. "I can probably get the IRS records, but it'll be the first of the week. Not much is going to get done by our agency geeks on the weekend unless it's an emergency. Even when we get the records, there probably won't be much in them."

"Maybe the best thing to do," I said, "is to talk face-to-face with Chaz Desmond."

"You going to Atlanta?" asked J.D.

"No. I'd like to have him come here. I'd also like to have our old first sergeant Jimbo Merryman with me. He's a good judge of men and maybe if it's just three old soldiers talking, Chaz will come clean."

"Can you do that this weekend?"

"Jimbo's out in the woods killing Yankees. I can probably get him to come here on Monday, and that'll give Doc time to get here as well. Plus, I want to look through these documents some more."

"Sounds like a plan," said Jock.

I called Chaz Desmond early in the afternoon. "Doc, I need to see you. Can you come to Longboat on Monday?"

"What's up, Matt? Have you got some leads?"

"Yeah. We've learned quite a bit, but I don't want to talk about it on the phone. We need to meet."

"I'll be there. What time?"

"Can you make it to my house by late morning, say eleven o'clock?"

"See you then."

I called Molly Merryman, Jimbo's wife, and asked her to have Jimbo call me when he got in on Sunday afternoon. She'd explained to me the first time I'd called that Confederate soldiers didn't carry cell phones. They did have one for emergencies, but it was considered less than authentic to use it for anything short of a life-threatening event.

We spent the rest of the day pouring through the bank documents. Nothing really jumped out at us, but we did get a list of the regular recipients of checks out of the account and a time line for the disbursal of the money. All the checks were payable to names we'd never heard, except for the ones that the accountant Tuan Nguyen wrote to himself each month for an amount equal to about a thousand dollars.

J.D., Jock, and I drove to the Sandbar Restaurant on the north end of Anna Maria Island, sat on the deck overlooking the beach, and ate a late dinner and watched the sunset. A bright and beautiful display as always. It was almost as eye-catching as the detective sitting across the table from me.

Sunday was a quiet day, a time to catch up with the energy expended over the past two weeks, to contemplate the next few days, and wonder if my buddy Doc was mixed up in some dark scheme that had somehow led to the murder of his son and two strangers on a dinner boat.

I was convinced that the deaths on *Dulcimer* were tied to Jim Desmond's murder, but I didn't understand why. What was the connection between Jim on the one hand and the dead people on *Dulcimer* on the other? There had to be one, but what was it? And was there a connection between the lawyer Garrison and the Hooters waitress Katherine Brewster? Was one of them just collateral damage?

I was beginning to suspect that Katherine was the target, and somehow Peter Garrison got in the way. Maybe he tried to protect Katherine. If Garrison had been the target, I doubted that Katherine would have intervened, and if she had, the murderer could probably have overpowered her without killing her.

We now knew that Katherine's boyfriend was not the killer and we were pretty sure that her stalker wasn't either. That left us with the Asians. The only connection to them was Doc's annual payments to a guy in Ho Chi Minh City. But that left us without an explanation for Katherine's death. It was a conundrum and it gave me a headache.

It was almost noon. Jock had curled up on the sofa with a book and fallen asleep. I didn't bother him. I was hungry and decided to drive down to St. Armands Circle for lunch at Lynches Pub and Grub. The sisters who owned the place had been friends of mine since I first came to the island. In those days they'd owned a popular bar and restaurant at mid-key on Longboat. The building was now gone to the wrecker's ball, and the Lynch girls were in business on St. Armands.

I called J.D. to see if she wanted to join me. She declined. Said she was catching up on some stuff, reviewing the paper work in our file, enjoying a down day. She'd see me on Monday.

The day was clear and hot and humid. The cerulean sky was devoid of even a wisp of cloud. The Gulf lay flat and still, its aqua color soothing. Far out, near the horizon, a boat cruised south, its sails full, catching the wind and moving at a good clip. A day like this chased away the dark concerns about murder and Asian assassins and other hobgoblins of the mind.

Our island was a lush tropical paradise. The condo complexes and mansions that lined the key's main road were hidden behind flowering plants and shrubs. The commercial areas were rare and well maintained. Yet the island was changing. A number of the bars and restaurants had died because they could not survive the summer doldrums when tourists didn't visit. There just weren't enough year-rounders to keep them in business.

People died or ran out of money and moved back North or tired of the island's lack of excitement and moved to the mainland. It was a continuous loss to those of us who would live nowhere else, but new people moved in and new friends were made and the cycle began all over again. I think most communities are this way. We mourn the loss of what we had once been while looking forward to what we will become. The human condition. It always amazes me.

Lunch was quick, chicken wings and French fries washed down by Miller Lite. I stopped at the Chinese restaurant next door and got several kinds of take-out for Jock. The owners were always glad to see him and Logan come in. They never could make up their minds about what to eat, so they ordered one of everything. The proprietors loved it and always asked me about my friends when I came in alone.

Jimbo Merryman called me late in the afternoon. I told him what we'd found in the documents, and that I was going to confront Doc about the Evermore Foundation. I thought it would go a lot easier if Jimbo were part of the conversation. He said he'd be at my place before eleven the next morning.

CHAPTER FIFTY

Jimbo Merryman knocked on my front door a little before ten on Monday morning. Jock had left a few minutes earlier, bound for the Starbucks on St. Armands Circle. He said he'd sit and drink coffee and read a book until I called.

Jimbo and I sat and sipped our coffee. I was filling him in some more on what we'd turned up in our investigation and my suspicions about Doc. "I don't like to feel this way, Top. I owe the man my life."

"Matt, I think there's got to be some explanation. A man like Doc doesn't just decide one day to get dirty."

"Money is a powerful magnet, Jimbo, and sometimes good men cave at the thought of a lot of it."

"Doc and I've kept up with each other for a long time. He was doing pretty well, making a lot of money, and living the good life for most of that time. I'm not saying it was huge money, but it was enough that he had pretty much everything he wanted. Then he decided to expand. Part of that was the timing. He was in the right place at the right time. He bought up a couple of small firms and then kept adding to the business. Sometimes he'd open a new office in another city and other times he'd buy an existing firm. It was an orderly progression and the big money started to flow."

"What about the businesses he bought? Was there any animosity between him and the people he bought out?"

"I don't think so. He paid a fair price and then turned the offices very profitable by getting rid of the deadwood. Some of the employees had been there for years and weren't producing. Doc changed the culture of those businesses."

"If he fired a bunch of people, there'd be some mad folks."

"I don't think so. He gave them great severance packages and helped them find work in different fields where they would do better."

"What about the change in management? Did that create problems with the staffs?"

"Not that I'm aware of. He brought in a lot of vets to take over management. Most of them were Corps of Engineer officers who'd commanded troops in the field. He said if a guy could manage under fire, he could sure as hell manage in a civilian environment. He gave them each a bonus structure based on results and worked that kind of system into all the employees pay packages. The results are a lot of happy workers and an awful lot of money for Doc."

Eleven o'clock came and went. We sipped more coffee. At noon I called Doc's cell phone. No answer. Not even voice mail. I called his office in Atlanta, identified myself, and asked to speak to Charles Desmond.

"I'm sorry, sir," said the receptionist, "but Mr. Desmond is on vacation."

"Do you know where he is?"

"No, sir."

"Do you know how I can reach him? It's vitally important."

"I'm sorry, sir, but I don't have that information."

"Who's in charge when Mr. Desmond is out of the office?"

"That would be Mr. Macomber, the vice president."

"May I speak to him?"

"He's in conference, I'm afraid."

"Tell you what," I said, a bit of frustration creeping into my voice, "interrupt Mr. Macomber and tell him that Mr. Desmond's personal lawyer Matt Royal is on the phone and needs to speak to him about an urgent matter."

"I'll see what I can do, sir."

In a moment a deep voice came on the line. "Mr. Royal? This is Paul Macomber."

"Mr. Macomber, I'm an old friend of Chaz's and I'm handling a legal matter for him. I really need to get in touch."

"I know who you are, Mr. Royal, and I know what you're doing for Chaz, but I don't have any idea where he is."

"Isn't that odd?"

"Oddest damn thing that ever happened around here."

"Did you know he was supposed to meet me in Longboat Key, Florida, this morning?"

"No, I didn't. He called me last night and told me to cancel all his appointments for this week. Said he and Julie were going on a vacation. He didn't want to be bothered. For anything. He was adamant about that part."

"What time did he call you?"

"It must have been around ten. I was getting ready for bed."

"I tried his cell phone and got no answer. Not even voice mail picked up," I said.

"I had that phone cut off first thing this morning. Chaz's orders."

"Did you try to call him at home this morning or on his cell before you cut it off?"

"Yes to both. No answer at all."

"Did he take the plane?"

"No."

"Are you sure?"

"I'm supposed to fly down to Jacksonville this afternoon and the captain just called to say the plane was ready anytime I wanted to leave. So I'm assuming Chaz didn't take it."

"Mr. Macomber, this is very important. If you hear anything from him, ask him to call me immediately."

"I'll do it, Mr. Royal."

I turned to Jimbo, puzzled, and not a little bit worried. I told him what happened and who I'd talked to.

"I know Paul Macomber," said Jimbo. "He used to run a bank in Jacksonville, and Chaz hired him away. Paul handles all the negotiations with customers and handled all the buyouts of other firms. He's a finance guy and a big part of the success of the firm. Been with Chaz a long time."

I called Jock on his cell phone, told him what happened. "I'm worried, Jock. This doesn't sound like Chaz. He takes off without letting anybody know where he's going and apparently decided to do so after he talked to me."

"Let me see if I can get my agency to put some traces on his credit cards. If he uses one, we'll know where he is. I'll be on back out to the house in a few minutes."

I hung up and looked at Jimbo. "I don't like this, Top. Taking off like that tells me he's guilty of something."

Jimbo nodded. "Or maybe he's dead."

Jimbo waited around to see Jock. They'd met before and after a few minutes of catching up with each other, Jimbo left for home.

"Did you get Doc's credit cards on a watch list?" I asked Jock.

"Yeah. If he uses one, we'll know it within seconds."

"I've got a bad feeling about this."

"I do too. It doesn't make sense that he'd run. Even if he thought you were closing in. I doubt that he killed his son, and he sure as hell wouldn't have any reason to kill the other two. If he's being blackmailed, whatever is the basis of it would have to be terrible to make him run."

"Do you think he's dead?" I asked.

"Don't know. Maybe somebody took him."

"We need to get J.D. over here, and see if the Atlanta police can give us a hand."

J.D. did not answer her cell so I called the police department. I identified myself to Iva the dispatcher and asked to speak to J.D.

"Matt, we don't know where she is."

"What do you mean?"

"She didn't check in this morning. She's not answering either her cell or her home phone. I sent an officer by her condo, but she wasn't there. The manager let him in, but there was no sign of her. Her gun belt and badge were still on the sofa and the bed wasn't made. A full pot of coffee was on the burner. Her car is in its parking space. We're worried."

"What's going on?"

"We don't know. I'm calling all her friends. I left you a message on your home phone. Did you get it?"

"No. I haven't checked messages this morning. You must have called while I was in the shower. Keep me posted, Iva."

I hung up. "J.D.'s missing," I said to Jock. "What the hell is going on?"

CHAPTER FIFTY-ONE

I was stunned. J.D. was missing, and it didn't sound as if she had left her condo willingly. She wouldn't have left a coffeepot on, nor would she have left her gun out in plain sight. It always went into the safe when she got home and only came out when she was headed for work.

I didn't know what to do. J.D. was more than a friend. She had become an important part of my life in the few short months since she'd come to the key. I sat, my mind wandering, afraid that I was somehow responsible for whatever had happened to her.

"Matt," said Jock, "Gear up, buddy. Lock and load. We're going to find her."

"I don't know if I have the energy, Jock."

"The Army didn't give you the Distinguished Service Cross back in Vietnam for sitting on a sofa and staring at the bay. Off and on. Isn't that the old Army saying? 'Off your ass and on your feet.'"

I laughed sourly. "Yeah, and 'drop your cocks and grab your socks.' You have a plan?"

"Not yet. We'll figure it out as soon as you stop feeling sorry for yourself. Then we'll go get the bastards and bring J.D. home."

Jock was the most deadly serious man I'd ever known. When his country or his friends were in peril, he was a force of reckoning. The only way to stop him was to kill him. And a lot of men had tried to do just that. None of them had survived the encounter.

I mentally shook myself, like an old dog just out of a bath. Jock was right. We didn't have time for me to sit around mired in self-doubt. There was another old army saying that fit the situation. "Mount up," I said, and we began to draw up a plan to slay the dragons and rescue Fair Guinevere.

CHAPTER FIFTY-TWO

Chief Bill Lester came through my front door, a look of concern on his face. I'd called him fifteen minutes before and asked if he could stop by. "Nothing," he said. "Not a goddammed clue as to what happened to her."

"Take a load off, Bill," said Jock. "We're trying to figure this out and there are some things you need to know."

"What?"

"I don't know how much you've been paying attention to what we've been doing on the Desmond and *Dulcimer* murders," said Jock.

"Not much. I figured J.D. would tell me anything I needed to know."

"We think there's a chance that Chaz Desmond is dirty," said Jock. He told the chief all that we knew about Doc and the Evermore Foundation. "We'd decided to confront Desmond, and Matt asked him to come to Longboat for a meeting. He was due here at eleven this morning. He didn't show. Matt called his office and it looks like Desmond disappeared sometime last night."

"You think it's connected to J.D.'s disappearance?"

"Be quite a coincidence if it wasn't."

"Any ideas?" asked the chief.

"There's one big loose end," I said. "Bud Stanley in Macon. The guy who runs the Otto Foundation."

"I'm thinking we ought to pay him a visit," said Jock.

"We think J.D. was taken this morning," said Lester. "Her condo looks as if she was getting ready to go to work. Her gun belt and clothes were laid out, coffee on, her cell phone next to her gun. When the crime-scene techs went through the condo they found a pastry in the microwave. Looked like she was fixing a quick breakfast."

"Did the techs find anything that would be helpful?" I asked.

"Nothing. They got a lot of fingerprints, but so far we're just turning up people who would have reason to be in her condo. Friends and such."

"None of the neighbors saw anything?"

"No. The place is almost empty. Most of the owners are snowbirds and it's quiet during the summer. She was probably gone before the maintenance manager came to work."

"I don't know what else to do," I said. "If we go to Macon, maybe we'll find something."

"That's a long drive," said Lester.

"I've got an idea." I picked up my phone and called Desmond's office in Atlanta. I identified myself and asked to speak to Mr. Macomber. I was put right through.

"Did you hear anything?" he asked.

"No, but there's a police officer here on the island who has been working on Jim's murder and she's missing too."

"You think they're connected?"

"Don't know, but there is a man in Macon I need to talk to very badly."

"Okay."

"I need a plane to get there and back."

"Okay."

"I was thinking about yours. When are you going to Jacksonville?"

"I'm leaving for the airport in a few minutes."

"How long are you going to be there?"

"Overnight."

"Can you send the plane to Sarasota to take a friend and me to Macon and back?"

"I'll have to run that by Harry Anderson."

"Who's that?"

"Our general counsel. If he says it's okay, I'll send the plane on down."

"You'll let me know?"

"Five minutes." He hung up.

I fixed some more coffee while we waited. It was almost one o'clock and I was getting hungry. The phone rang.

"The plane will be at Dolphin Aviation in Sarasota at three thirty. You can have it until midnight tonight. After that the pilots are going to have to take a break. If you need the plane tomorrow, I can get back to Atlanta on commercial."

"That's great, Paul."

"Anderson said Chaz would blow a gasket if we didn't help you out."

"Sounds like a smart lawyer."

"Sometimes," he said and hung up.

CHAPTER FIFTY-THREE

Jock and I were at the airport a little after three. We'd picked up some sandwiches at Harry's Continental Kitchens Deli and drove directly to the airport. We were standing on the tarmac just outside the small terminal when Desmond's jet taxied up. A window opened on the pilot's side of the aircraft and Fred Cassidy, the same pilot who'd flown me to Jacksonville and Charlotte a few days earlier, stuck his head out.

"I'll let the stair down, Matt. Come on aboard."

Jock and I climbed the steps to the cabin and belted ourselves in. Fred stuck his head into the cabin and said, "We're ready to go. Should be in Macon in about an hour. There're some soft drinks in the refrigerator."

We took off to the northwest, out over the bay and the barrier islands that defined its outer boundaries. We flew up the coast for a short time and then turned back to the northeast on a track for Macon, Georgia. I reached for my cell phone to call ahead and reserve a rental car. No phone. I'd left it sitting on the coffee table in my living room. I mentally kicked myself and borrowed Jock's phone. When we landed in Macon an hour later, a car was waiting for us.

By five, we were sitting in the parking lot of the strip center on Riverside Drive that housed the offices of the Otto Foundation. Two women came out and one turned to lock the door. We sat and waited.

"Maybe he's already gone," said Jock.

"One way to find out." I used Jock's cell phone to dial the number of the foundation. Bud Stanley answered on the third ring. I hung up.

"He's in there," I said.

"Unless he forwarded the phone to someplace else."

"No. I saw some movement behind the big window. Probably Stanley moving across the room to answer the phone."

"Okay."

We sat some more. At five thirty, Stanley came out of the front door, locked it, and walked to a gray Toyota Camry parked in front of the building. He pulled out of the lot and drove southeast on Riverside Drive. We followed, Jock driving. He let two cars get behind Stanley before he entered the southbound traffic. We didn't have far to go. Stanley took a right onto College Street and drove a couple of miles before turning onto a residential street lined by renovated Victorian homes. He pulled into the driveway of one in the middle of the block and parked in the detached garage. Jock drove by slowly. I saw Stanley leave the garage and walk into the house.

Jock parked the rental on the street three houses down from Stanley's. We stayed on the sidewalk on the opposite side of the street. We were walking through a neighborhood that had been there for a hundred years or more. The houses all had been lovingly restored, and it was obvious that these weren't just modern knockoffs.

"Looks like a pretty expensive neighborhood," Jock said.

"Yeah. Pretty high on the hog for a charitable foundation administrator."

"What's your plan?"

"Don't have one. Put on your ugly face and let's see what happens."

He scowled at me, grimacing, his lips tight, his nose a bit flared. I said, "You look like you're constipated. Try something else."

We mounted the steps onto a large porch that wrapped around the house. I knocked on the door and we waited. In a minute, Bud Stanley opened it and looked at me. Recognition dawned.

"Mr. Royal, this is a pleasant surprise." He made no move to invite us inside.

"May we come in?"

"I'm sorry, but I'm off to a function. I don't mean to be rude, but your timing is bad."

"We need to talk," I said.

Stanley looked from me to Jock. "Who's your friend?"

"He's not a friend. Let's just say he's an associate."

"Well," Stanley said, "I wish I had time to be hospitable, but as I said, I have to go."

He started to close the door. I reached out and stopped it. He glared at me.

"We just want to talk," I said.

"Do I have to call the police?"

"I don't think you want to do that, Mr. Bracewell."

Stanley looked at me for a moment. I could see his resolve drying up, but he wasn't going to give it up easily. "Who the hell is Bracewell?"

"Robert Charles Bracewell, late of Lompoc Prison."

"I don't know who you're talking about."

"Okay. Call the police. Maybe we can get them to run your fingerprints. The very least that's going to do is really fuck up your evening."

He gave it up then. His face seemed to sag, deflate a little, his shoulders slumped almost imperceptibly, and he backed up pulling the door open. "Come in," he said.

He led us to a living room just off the entrance foyer, told us to take a seat. He sat in a recliner that was situated so that its occupant had a direct view of a large flat-screen TV sitting in an entertainment center against the opposite wall.

"Get up, Mr. Stanley," Jock said.

"What?"

"Get your ass out of that chair. Now. And keep your hands where I can see them." Jock was holding a .38-caliber pistol, pointed at Stanley's chest.

"What is this?" A note of indignation rode the rising voice.

"Now," said Jock. "I'm not asking again."

The man stood, hands in front of him, palms out, a sign of peace or of surrender. Maybe both.

"Matt," said Jock, "check the cushions on the sofa. I don't want to find any weapons there."

I pulled the cushions and checked down the sides of the sofa. "Nothing," I said.

"Okay, Stanley," said Jock. "You sit there. I'll take the recliner."

"I don't have any weapons," said Stanley. "Who are you people?" He made himself comfortable on the sofa. I took a chair across from the sofa and Jock sat in the recliner, his pistol pointed at Stanley.

"I'm looking for some friends," I said, "and I'm hoping you know where they are."

"Who?"

"Chaz Desmond and a Longboat Key detective named J.D. Duncan."

"How am I supposed to know where they are?"

"They've disappeared. You're a bad guy. Maybe you had something to do with it."

"I'm not the same guy who was in Lompoc. I've turned my life around."

"Maybe."

"I know Desmond, but I have no idea who Duncan is. Besides, what does any of this have to do with me?"

"We think your friend Soupy was responsible for the murder of Jim Desmond. Now Chaz has disappeared and so has the detective who was investigating the murder."

"I told you before, I don't know anything about that. I doubt that Soupy would be involved."

"Are you still running drugs for him?" I asked.

Stanley's face changed, suddenly, like a light going off, or maybe on. I thought I saw a trace of fear cross his eyes, a subtle tell that a good poker play would never allow. I'd hit a weak spot, a punch that he hadn't seen coming.

"I don't know what you're talking about," he said, blustering.

"I know that you and your dad were in the drug business with Soupy's dad. It isn't much of a stretch to think that you're still involved. You just happen to have a nice little charitable organization that sends kids to Laos where Soupy is one of the biggest growers of poppies. I'm thinking that somehow you use the kids to bring the drugs into this country."

"Nice try, Mr. Royal." The voice came from the entry foyer, a deep rumble with a southern accent. I looked to my left and saw an Asian man, a stranger, standing in the doorway, a double-barreled twelve-gauge shotgun pointed in my direction. "Tell your friend to drop his pistol or I'll blow your head off."

I glanced at Jock. He was looking at the Asian, but his pistol was pointed directly at Stanley. "If you pull that trigger," said Jock, "Stanley dies."

"So does Royal," said the man with the shotgun.

"If I put the pistol down what assurance do I have that you won't kill us?"

"This blunderbuss will be heard in the next block if I fire. I don't want the trouble. You let Stanley go and we'll leave quietly. No fuss, no blood."

Jock thought about it for a beat and then laid the pistol on the floor.

"Use your foot to push the pistol to Stanley," the Asian man said.

Jock did so, the pistol sliding easily on the hardwood floor. Stanley picked it up, pointed it at us, and smiled.

The Asian man spoke to Stanley in a foreign language. Stanley responded in the same language, rose from the sofa, and went past the Asian into the back of the house. We sat still as stone, no one moving. I heard the car in the garage start and come down the driveway. The horn beeped and the Asian backed out of the foyer, his shotgun pointed our way. He reached the front door, turned the knob, and rushed outside. Jock and I moved quickly to the window, just in time to see the Camry disappear down the street, two heads showing in the front seats.

We ran to the rental, but by the time we got it moving, Stanley and his friend were gone. There was no chance of following them.

Jock looked a bit perplexed. "I didn't think to check out the rest of the house. I must be slipping. It never occurred to me that Stanley would have a Laotian houseguest."

"He didn't," I said. "The guest was speaking Vietnamese."

CHAPTER FIFTY-FOUR

"That didn't work out too well," said Jock.

"Let's go back to the house. We might find something there."

"Might as well."

"What if somebody calls the police?" I asked.

"Good point. Let's get in and out in a hurry."

We didn't find much. The house had three bedrooms, one of which appeared to be Stanley's and another where the Asian guy had been staying. There was a suitcase sitting open on the bed, but there was nothing in it other than the normal things a person carries when traveling.

"Looks like he was only visiting," I said.

"Yeah. Let's see if there's a passport or some other kind of identification."

We didn't find anything that would tell us who the visitor was. Just some clothes and toiletries. We found a computer in the master bedroom and another in a small office off the living room. I took the hard drives from both and we left the house. We hadn't been there more than ten minutes.

"What now?" Jock asked.

"There are two women who work in the Otto Foundation office. I'd like to talk to them."

"Do you know how to find them?"

"Let's get into the office. There's got to be some kind of records there that'll lead us to them."

"Breaking and entering is a felony in Georgia, right?" asked Jock.

"Yep."

"Okay. Just checking."

We drove back to the Riverside Drive office. It was dusk by the time we got there. Nobody was around. The small stores that took up the rest of the space in the center were closed. No cars in the lot.

"Can you pick the lock?" I asked.

"Sure." He pulled a small case from his wallet, extracted his picks.

I parked the car right in front of the office and kept it running in case we had to make an emergency exit. Jock went to the door and opened it as quickly as if he'd had a key. I guess he'd had a lot of practice with that sort of thing.

I got out of the car and went inside. I remembered the table where I'd found Stanley when I'd visited the week before. I turned on the computer and ran into a screen requesting a password. Damn. I thought about for a few beats and then typed in "Bracewell." Nothing. Just a blinking message telling me that was not the right password. I thought some more and typed in "Lompoc." Same result.

I didn't have a lot of time to fool with this. I didn't want to get arrested for breaking and entering. I thought some more and tried an old trick Debbie had once told me about. I typed in "copmol" the name of the prison spelled backward. Bingo. I was in.

I did a quick search. Nothing other than what appeared to be normal business files. The bank account statements showed several large checks being written each month to various corporations and foundations. The Otto Foundation seemed to have plenty of money, but I thought it curious that it was sending so much to other entities. Maybe there was some sort of cross-pollination between the foundations and the corporations were supplying goods or services that helped in building the schools.

I found the payroll account. Apparently a local bank handled the payroll, withholding, and whatever else was needed. A monthly report was sent to the foundation. The report included the names and addresses of the employees Bud Stanley, Judy Avera, Maude Lane, and Nigella Morrissey along with their social security numbers and rates of pay.

"This is odd," I said. I pointed out the payroll entries.

"Probably her dad was Nigel and they wanted to feminize it."

"I'm talking about the payroll, not the lady's name."

"What?"

"The foundation pays Bud a hundred twenty thousand a year, which is probably pretty standard. It pays two of the women thirty thousand a year and the third one, Nigella Morrissey, the same thing Stanley makes."

"What's Morrissey's job title?" asked Jock.

"Don't know. None of them has a job title."

"Get their addresses. We'll need to talk to them."

"No address for Morrissey, but the other two are here," I said. "Let's go pay a visit. See if they know anything."

I used a coin to unscrew the back of the computer and removed the hard drive. Might as well take it. I didn't think Mr. Stanley would be coming in to work the next day.

Jock plugged Judy Avera's address into the GPS system on the rental. We followed the directions given by the voice of that annoying woman who seemed to run every GPS system in the world. We crossed the Ocmulgee River and turned into a middle-class neighborhood. It was dark now, and the streetlights cast circles of light at every corner, leaving the rest of the street in shadow. We pulled up in front of a house in the middle of the block.

I looked at my watch as we walked up the sidewalk to the small front porch. Almost nine. A little late for a social call, but too early for an emergency worker to be knocking on the door. I rang the bell and in a few moments I saw a shadow move across the peephole. Somebody was taking a look at us. A woman's voice came from the other side. "Who is it?"

"It's Matt Royal, Mrs. Avera. I was in your office a couple of weeks ago visiting with Mr. Stanley."

"Just a minute."

I heard a lock turn in the door, and one of the women I remembered from the office was standing there. She was in her fifties or maybe a little older. She obviously took good care of herself. She was wearing a loose housedress, her light brown hair tied in a knot on the top of her head.

"Come in," she said. "My husband and I are having our one after-dinner drink. Can I get you something? A drink? Coffee?"

I could smell the rich aroma of freshly brewed coffee wafting in from the back of the house. It'd been a long day. "I wouldn't mind a cup of coffee, if it's not too much trouble," I said. "This is Jock Algren, a friend who is helping me investigate the murder of Jim Desmond."

She led us into a living room. A man sat in a chair, his feet on a hassock, a glass of red wine in his hand. He stood, shook hands, and sat back down. Judy motioned us to chairs and we sat. She left the room and returned in a couple of minutes with two steaming mugs of coffee. She took a chair next to her husband who had not uttered one word in her absence.

"Poor Jim," Mrs. Avera said. "Bud told us you were a lawyer trying to help his family find the murderers."

"That's correct," I said.

"How can I help?"

"Did you know Jim?"

"Yes. I meet all the kids. I usually work some with them out on the Mercer campus while they're in orientation."

"Have you worked for the foundation for a long time?"

"About six years," she said.

"Did you know Bud Stanley before you went to work there?"

"I'd met him a time or two at social functions, but we weren't friends or anything. I heard he was looking for an assistant and I applied for the job. My kids were grown, and I wanted something to do to keep myself busy."

"Do you know any of these people?" I asked, showing her the pictures of John Nguyen and the other two Asians who were aboard *Dulcimer* the night of the murders.

She studied the pictures for a few moments, then pointed to one of them. "I've seen this one recently. He had a cast on his arm. Ran from his shoulder to his wrist." She was pointing at the picture of the man who had tried to knife me on the North Shore boardwalk.

"When did you see him?" I asked.

"He was in last week. Thursday, I think. Maybe it was Wednesday."

"Had you ever seen him before?"

"No. Well, maybe once, but I'm not sure."

"When would the other time have been?"

"If it was the same man, it was probably back in May or June. Do you think he had something to do with Jim's murder?"

"We're not sure, Mrs. Avera. We're just looking at all possibilities."

"Did you ever hear the man speak?" Jock asked.

"Yes."

"English?" Jock asked.

"Oh yes. That's the only language I speak. He talked to me when he first came in."

"Anything distinctive about his accent?" asked Jock. "Heavy accent?"

"No. He spoke American English. Sounded Southern, too. I think he's from around here."

"Did he tell you his name?"

She was quiet for a moment. "Now that you mention it, I don't think he ever did."

"Do you remember what you talked about?" I asked.

"Nothing really. Just passing the time of day. Bud was on the phone, and I was just being nice to him."

"Was it unusual to have Asians come into the office?" I asked.

"Not at all. We deal with three countries in Southeast Asia, so it's not unusual to have Asians stop by."

"What is their business here?"

"I don't know. Bud always talks to them privately. Back in the break room."

"Did you ever ask about any of them?"

"No. It's none of my business. Once, last year, I mentioned to Bud that I thought it a little funny that some of them came around so often. It really made him mad. He told me it was none of my business and that I should keep my nose out of it. So, I do."

"Was that outburst unusual for Bud?"

"Oh, yes. He apologized later and even sent flowers here to my home. It never happened again."

"Did you ever hear the name Robert Charles Bracewell?" I asked.

"No, not that I remember."

"Who handles the money that comes in from donors?"

"Bud does all that."

"Does he keep a list of donors?"

"I'm sure he does. Probably on his computer. Neither Maude nor I have access to the list, but Maude does the routine bookkeeping."

"What about Nigella Morrissey?"

"Who?"

"Nigella Morrissey."

"I don't know her."

"Doesn't she work for the foundation?"

"No. There's only the three of us, Maude, Bud, and myself."

"Could she be some sort of outside recruiter or fund-raiser or something like that?"

"I would've met her if she worked for the foundation. We didn't recruit other than to put flyers out in high schools around the state. The only fund-raising that I'm aware of is what Bud gets from some of the parents of the kids who go to Asia. The foundation supports most of our needs."

"How big is the principle of the foundation?"

"I have no idea. I'd guess it's pretty big to put as much money into our operation as it does."

"Do you know how much money comes in every year from the Otto Foundation?"

"Not a clue. But it isn't cheap to send those kids to Asia and pay for their upkeep."

"Does Bud handle all those disbursements?"

"Bud and sometimes Maude. It's all handled electronically. I never see any of that."

We were quiet for a few moments, sipping the rich coffee. I asked, "Do you know of any other of the kids who were ever part of the program who have died?"

"There was one boy from Hahira who died of cancer a couple of years back. And, of course, Andy Fleming."

"What happened to Andy ?" I asked.

"Poor boy. Somebody shot him."

Alarm bells were banging inside my head. "When?"

"A couple of weeks ago."

"Where?" I asked.

"Over in Alabama. Outside a bar. I think it was just his being in the wrong place at the wrong time."

"Was he on the same trip as Jim Desmond?"

"Oh, no. He was there last year. He had just finished up his freshman year at Auburn when he was killed."

The bells were subsiding. Young Fleming's death didn't fit any pattern I could discern. I'd check it out, but it was probably not connected. "Do you remember the name of the town where Andy was killed?" I asked.

"I think he was in his hometown. Birmingham."

The clock on the wall told me it was almost ten. "We'd like to talk to Maude Lane, too. Do you think she could meet us early in the morning before she goes to work?"

"Maude's a night owl. She only lives two blocks from here. I'll call her. She'll probably see you tonight."

A streetlight illuminated the front of Maude Lane's small white clapboard house. Marigolds lined the bricked walkway to the front door. Azaleas flanked the front stoop and lights on either side of the doorway were on. I knocked on the door.

A lady in her seventies opened it. She had a wrinkled face split by a smile of welcome. Her gray hair was in a bun pinned at the back of her head, a pair of reading glasses perched on her nose. I recognized her from my brief visit to the Otto Foundation offices two weeks before. "Mr. Royal," she said. "Do come in. This must be Mr. Algren."

The house was neat and clean and forty years old. The furnishings were of excellent quality, but a bit out of style, as if they'd been there for a lot of years. I smelled freshly brewed coffee as we entered the living room. The caffeine jolt I'd gotten at Judy Avera's wasn't enough to dampen my need. I hoped Mrs. Lane would offer us some more. She did.

"Take a seat, gentlemen. I'll get us all some coffee."

She returned with a sterling silver set, pot, tray, creamer, and sugar bowl. The cups were porcelain with small blue flowers and a gold band around the rim. "We used to do this every night," she said. "My husband, Karl, and me. Late coffee never seemed to keep either of us awake. He's gone now."

"I'm sorry," I said.

"Thank you, Mr. Royal. He was a good man, but the cancer ate him up, and it was a relief when he passed on. He was in such pain. But the years go by and the memories fade and every once in a while, like now, they come bounding back with a force that surprises me. But you didn't come here to talk about me. Judy said you're looking into Jim Desmond's death. How can I help you?"

"I appreciate your seeing us so late, Mrs. Lane," I said. "We're beginning to think there was an Asian connection to his death. Mrs. Avera said there were a lot of Asians in and out of your office. Can you tell me anything about them?"

"No, I'm sorry. Bud never introduced any of them to us. He always took them into the back room."

"Do you remember any of them speaking?"

"Only to say hello or that they were there to see Bud if he was in, something like that."

"Were they all speaking English?"

"Yes."

"Any accent?"

"Not a foreign accent. A couple of them sounded southern."

"Did you ever pass the time of day with them?"

"No, but Judy did have a conversation with one recently. I wasn't paying much attention."

"Do you know Nigella Morrissey?"

"I don't think I do."

"Did you ever hear the name around the office?"

"Not that I remember."

"If I told you that she worked for the Otto Foundation, would that help?"

"What kind of work? It's just the three of us in the office."

"I don't know, Mrs. Lane, but we think she was employed by the Otto Foundation in some capacity."

"Well, that's news to me."

"I understand you make some of the disbursements. Nigella's name never came up?"

Maude shook her head. "I authorize some electronic funds to be sent to some of our suppliers, but only when Bud tells me to. He always gives me a list of the ones to send."

"Have you worked for the foundation for a long time?" I asked.

"About ten years. After Karl died, I needed something to keep me busy. We never had any children and my family is scattered, so when I got the opportunity to work for the Otto Foundation, I jumped at it."

We talked for a bit longer, but there was nothing else to learn. We finished the coffee and drove toward the airport. I was in a bleak mood, my mind churning with worry about J.D. We hadn't come up with anything that would help in finding her. We'd chewed up a day and had very little to show for it. Images of her kept flashing through my brain like a slide show, pictures of her smiling on a spring day on my boat, or in a favorite restaurant on the key, or over a glass of wine in my living room. And then would come another slide, a picture of her tied to a chair somewhere, her face a rictus of fear.

Jock broke into my melancholy reverie. "What do you think?"

"I don't know. We've got an obvious connection to Stanley now. The one who tried to kill me was in the Otto Foundation offices. We don't know whether he's Laotian or some other variety of Asian. But then we get the thug with the shotgun in Stanley's house speaking Vietnamese. That could tie him to John Nguyen and maybe to Tuan Nguyen in Ho Chi Minh City."

"Or maybe they're all Laotian and one of them speaks Vietnamese."

"That's a possibility."

"Do you want me to get those hard drives you stole off to my tech people in Washington?"

"That'll take too long. Let's get them to Debbie, see if she can make any sense out of them. If not, we'll get them to your people first thing in the morning."

"It'll be midnight by the time we get to Longboat," Jock said.

"Debbie's a night owl and if she knows this might tie in somehow to J.D.'s disappearance, she'll work all night."

•　　　•　　　•

We flew through the night to Sarasota. I asked the pilot if he could wait until he heard from me in the morning to decide whether to go to Jacksonville to pick up Macomber, or to ferry us around some more. He was agreeable. He'd spend the night at the Sarasota Hyatt Regency and talk to me in the morning.

I called Debbie and told her what I wanted. She said to stop by her condo in West Bradenton and she'd take a look at the hard drives.

By the time we got home, it was almost one in the morning. Jock and I were exhausted. It'd been a long day. Jock said goodnight and headed for the guest room. I found my cell phone right where I had left it. I looked at the display. I had a missed call. I didn't recognize the number on the caller ID. The call had come in at 3:15 that afternoon, just about the time Jock and I were lifting off from the Sarasota airport. Whoever had called left a voice mail. I dialed the message center and punched in the pin number. The voice in the mailbox made my heart sink

"Matt," said J.D. "I'm scared, but I'm okay. Tell the chief—" The message stopped. Dead. The phone just cut off. I didn't think she'd hung up. Something or someone had interrupted her cry for help.

CHAPTER FIFTY-FIVE

Jock was on the phone to Washington. I was pacing. Less than fifteen minutes had elapsed since I'd heard J.D.'s voice. Jock was trying to get a trace on the call that had come in to my phone. The techs at his agency were running it down. They had resources that were beyond anything I'd ever heard of. Jock hung up.

"I don't know if this is good news or bad news," he said. "The call bounced off a cell tower in Fort Lauderdale. The phone number is for one of those you buy at convenience stores. It was bought this morning at a store in Sarasota. Yesterday morning now, I guess. It was rung up in the cash register at six twenty-five a.m. Paid cash."

"Lauderdale's only a three hour drive from here and the call came in at 3:15. If somebody left here with her before eight this morning, where the hell has she been?"

"Maybe she wasn't able to call earlier. I don't like the idea that she was cut off like that. Maybe she got hold of the phone somehow and called and was found out by whoever kidnapped her."

"Goddammit Jock. We've got to do something."

"We are, podna. I've got the address of the convenience store where the phone was bought. Let's get a couple of cops and go over there. They probably have some kind of security camera."

I called Chief Bill Lester. I knew he always slept with his cell phone next to his bed. My name would show up on his caller ID.

"This better be good, Royal. I was having a wonderful dream."

"I heard from J.D." I told him what we'd found out so far.

"Good ol' Jock and his resources. I'll get a couple of Sarasota cops headed to the store. I'll meet you there."

•   •   •

The convenience store hunkered on the Tamiami Trail in a forlorn block of buildings near the Ringling School of Art and Design. It was not part of a chain, but an independent store that catered to the people who made their living in the shadows of the night; streetwalkers, drug dealers, pimps, and winos. The cashier stood behind a bulletproof glass. Patrons shoved their worn bills into a tray and the attendant sent back the change. The front door could only be opened when the clerk behind the glass pushed a button releasing an electronic lock. No one could get in without the blessing of the cashier, and no one got out without paying for the beer or cigarettes or chips or whatever small item they needed to see them through another night.

Jock and I pulled into the parking lot just behind Bill Lester. A marked Sarasota Police Department patrol car with two uniformed officers was waiting for us. Everybody climbed out. The cops recognized Lester and he introduced us as his associates. We were buzzed into the store.

The attendant behind the thick glass was tall and thin and wore a scraggly beard that barely covered his chin. His hair was colored some godawful shade of green. A small spike pierced his bottom lip and another went through his right eyebrow. He was probably still in his teens.

"I'm Chief Lester," Bill said. "We need to see your security tapes from the last twenty-four hours."

"No can do," said the skinny kid.

"What's that supposed to mean?" Lester asked.

"The owner is the only one who can let you have those."

"Call the owner," said Lester.

"No can do."

"Why not?"

"He's gone home."

"Call him at home."

"No can do."

"Look, dickhead," said the chief, "you say that one more time and I'm going to engage in a little police brutality. Why can't you call him at home?"

"He went to his home in Pakistan for a couple of weeks. Left me in charge."

"Then you can give us the security tapes."

"Not without the boss's okay."

"What's your name?" asked Lester.

"Duke."

"You like to travel, Duke?"

"Can't say yeah or no. Ain't never been anywhere."

"You ever hear of Guantanamo?"

"That place in Cuba where they lock up terrorists?"

"That's the one," said Lester. "You're pretty close to earning yourself a free trip down there."

"Whoa. What're you talking about?"

"We're involved in a national security operation. You're involved. If you don't give me that tape right now, you'll be on your way to Cuba within the hour."

"Who says?"

"I do," said Jock. He pulled a leather ID case from his pocket, held it against the glass partition. "Can you read that?"

The kid looked closely, squinted some. "It says you work for the president of the United States and have police power in every jurisdiction. Some other stuff, too."

"What that means," says Jock, "is that I can have your ass on a plane to Cuba before the sun comes up. Get the fucking tape."

"Yes, sir." He disappeared through a door behind him.

One of the uniformed cops looked at Lester and said, "Where'd he get that?"

"From the president," said Lester. "Mr. Algren is a federal agent. With more power than any of us ever thought of having."

"Shit fire," said the cop.

The kid returned with a compact disc, unlocked the door to his cubicle, and handed it to Lester. "This is the one that started at midnight last night. We put forty-eight hours on each disc, and the boss keeps them for a month or so."

Lester took the disc. "We'll bring this back in a few minutes."

We went to the patrol car, inserted the disc into the computer bolted to the dash and fast forwarded through the time-stamped images until we came to the one showing 6:00 a.m. the day before. The camera was above the cubicle where the clerks worked so we had a pretty good shot of the entrance and the area right in front of the cubicle. We slowed it and watched a man come through the front door. He wore a baseball hat pulled low over his face. He kept his head down. He was aware of the security camera. He went to the counter and said something to the attendant, a different kid with wild hair. The images were in black-and-white, so I couldn't tell the hair color this one was affecting.

The customer passed some cash through the slot in the window and the clerk sent a phone back. The man tested it and apparently satisfied that it was in working order, turned to leave. "Stop it," I said. Lester complied. "Now back up slowly." The images peeled backward. "Freeze it," I said.

We were looking at a man in profile. The ball cap obscured most of his face from the front, but the angle of the camera as he turned away caught a full right-side likeness.

I said, "I know that man. He was the copilot on Desmond's plane last week. Took me to Jacksonville and Charlotte."

Jock said, "Not the same one we had this morning. That guy was black."

"Do you know his name?" asked Lester.

"I don't recall. The pilot introduced me, but I don't remember his name. Fred Cassidy would know and he's at the Hyatt Regency."

"Who's Cassidy?"

"The pilot," I said.

"We need a print of that picture," said Lester. He looked at the uniformed cops. "Can one of you send this to the station and ask them to print it? I'll stop by on my way to the Hyatt and pick it up."

Jock and I arrived at the Hyatt Regency at three a.m. and parked in the circular driveway that flanked the entrance. We had come directly to the hotel and were waiting for Bill Lester to arrive with the photograph.

The place was quiet, nobody around. The lobby was empty except for a night clerk behind the registration desk. "Can I help you gentlemen?" he asked.

"We need to see a guest," I said. "Fred Cassidy. The police will be here in a few minutes to talk to him."

"Are you police officers?"

"No, but we're working with them on a case."

"I think it'd be better to wait for the cops," he said.

"Okay. The chief will be here soon. You wouldn't happen to have any coffee around, would you?"

The clerk grinned. "I've always got a pot going in the back. You're welcome to it."

He returned with two mugs of steaming brew just as Bill Lester entered the lobby. "Did you get Cassidy?" he asked.

I gestured to the young man behind the reception desk. "He wanted to wait for the police," I said.

"Probably a good idea," said Lester. "You two don't exactly look wholesome." He pulled out his ID and showed it to the clerk.

The clerk gestured toward a phone at the end of the counter. "If you'll pick up that house phone, I'll connect you to his room."

Cassidy answered after several rings, the remains of a deep sleep in his voice. "Fred," I said, "this is Matt Royal. I'm sorry to bother you, but there have been some developments that we need your help with. Can you come to the lobby?"

"Developments? In the disappearance of Mr. Desmond?"

"Yes."

"I'll be right down."

We were seated in a group of chairs in the lobby overlooking the swimming pool. Bill Lester showed Fred the picture from the security camera at the convenience store. "Do you know this man?"

Fred took the picture and peered closely at it. "He looks like a guy who flew with me last week for a couple of days."

"Who is he?" asked Lester.

"His name is Tom Telson."

"How do I reach him?"

"I don't know. He doesn't work for our company."

"Then why was he flying with you?"

"He was a fill-in. My regular copilot, the one upstairs asleep, was out sick and Federal Aviation Regulations require that I have a copilot. I called an agency that supplies pilots and he showed up. Had the proper licenses and type ratings. He just worked with me for two days until my regular guy came back."

Lester asked, "What's the name of the agency Telson works for?"

"Pilots on Demand. They're based in Atlanta. We use them occasionally if one of our regulars is sick or on vacation."

"How many regular pilots does Desmond have?" I asked.

"Just the two of us. It's usually not a problem, but we keep a working relationship with Pilots on Demand in case we need a fill-in."

"Do you have a phone number for Pilots on Demand?"

Cassidy pulled out his cell phone and scrolled through the phone book. He gave us the number. "I doubt anybody's there this time of the morning," he said. "There's an answering service that you can use in emergencies, but it doesn't work too well. It still takes about three hours to get a pilot out of bed and to the airport. If you need one sooner, you're screwed."

The chief said, "I don't think we can do much more tonight. You guys get some sleep and we'll start again first thing this morning."

"Fred," I said, "what time do you have to let Macomber know whether you're going to pick him up?"

"No later than nine o'clock."

"Okay. I may need you to take us to Birmingham. I'll get back to you before nine."

"What's in Birmingham?" the chief asked.

"That's what I want you to find out," I said.

CHAPTER FIFTY-SIX

"Another one of the Otto Foundation kids was killed a couple of weeks ago in Birmingham," I explained to the chief. We were standing outside the hotel breathing in the humid air. The traffic on Tamiami Trail a block to the east was light, the city quiet in the wee hours as if resting before plunging into the tumult of another hot day in August. "He was shot in what might have been a bar fight. It's probably nothing, but I'd like to talk to the detective investigating the case."

"You think there's a connection between Desmond's murder and this boy in Birmingham? Did they know each other?"

"Probably not, on both counts. I doubt there's a connection and the boys probably didn't know each other. Jim Desmond was in Laos five years ago and this kid in Birmingham, Andy Fleming, was there last year. He might not even have been in Laos. He could have been in Cambodia or Vietnam. I didn't think to ask Mrs. Avera about that. But it's a loose end that I'd like to tie up."

"I'll call Birmingham P.D. Nobody's going to roust the detective from bed this time of morning, so why don't you guys go home. I'll call them at eight. They're an hour behind us, so I'll probably catch them right at shift change. I'll let you know. Now go home."

Much to my surprise, I slept hard. The jangle of the phone brought me out of a deep sleep. I looked at the bedside clock radio as I reached for the phone. It was a little after eight. I'd slept for almost four hours. I looked at the caller ID. A blocked number. I answered.

A man's voice dripping an Old South accent said, "Matt Royal?"

"Yes."

"This is Detective Bagger Dobbs, Birmingham P.D. Your chief called mine and mine told me to call you on the Fleming case."

"I appreciate the call, Detective. Did your chief tell you what our connection is?"

"Only that it might have to do with a kidnapped cop."

"This may be a wild-goose chase, but what can you tell me about the case?"

"It's pretty cut and dried. The kid was at a titty bar called The Booby Hatch. It's a rough place out on the edge of town. Bad neighborhood. He was walking out of the bar when he was shot in the back."

"I had the impression there was some sort of altercation at the bar."

"No. Nothing out of the ordinary. It looks like the kid was on his way home. He'd had a couple of drinks, but his blood alcohol was only zero point three. He was shot just as he was opening his car door."

"What kind of gun?"

"A rifle. Big slug. We think a thirty-caliber."

"We had a shooting here on the island. Used a thirty-caliber rifle. Did you find the bullet that killed Fleming?"

"Yeah. It was embedded in the front seat of his car. Went clear through him."

"I'd like to see if the slugs match up as coming from the same weapon," I said.

"I'll send the information down to Chief Lester. He'll have it in the next few minutes."

"Thanks. Any other leads?"

"We have one witness, but he's not much help. He was pretty drunk coming out of the bar, but he said he saw a car rushing out of the parking lot right after he heard the shot."

"I guess he didn't get a tag number."

"No," said the detective, "he didn't even notice the make of the car. All he could tell us was that the driver appeared to be Asian. Maybe a woman."

CHAPTER FIFTY-SEVEN

Jock and I were sitting in a small office in the Birmingham police station at ten o'clock central time, three hours after my telephone call from Bagger Dobbs. I'd called Fred Cassidy and told him we needed to go to Birmingham. We lifted off at nine and landed in the Alabama city an hour later. A rental car took us downtown.

We were sitting on folding chairs that had once been part of a set that likely included a card table. The detective was behind a metal desk painted a pea-soup green. Probably military surplus. There were no windows and no wall decorations. A fan hung from the ceiling, barely turning the air that smelled of old cigarette smoke.

Dobbs was a big man, befitting his voice. He was in his early fifties, burly, brusque, and black. He was intrigued by the possibility that the Fleming and Brewster murders were tied together and that they somehow had a bearing on the disappearance of J. D. Duncan. I told him everything we had unearthed so far.

"I got a call from Chief Lester about the time we landed here," I said. "The slugs that killed Fleming and Desmond likely came from the same rifle. He also got an address for the copilot who we think bought the phone. The Atlanta police are trying to locate him."

"Any ideas as to why some Asian dudes would be killing young men who'd helped build schools?"

"Maybe. Did the name Souphanouvong Phomvihana ever come up in your investigation?"

"That's a mouthful. But, no."

"How about Soupy?"

"No."

"What can you tell me about Fleming's family?"

"His dad's a big-time lawyer downtown. Mom spends most days playing tennis at a local country club. They show up at charity balls, get their pictures in the papers. Two other kids, both older than Andy. The oldest one is a man who practices law in his dad's firm. The other one is a woman who is married to a lawyer in the same firm. They kind of keep it in the family. Andy was planning on law school after he finished at Auburn."

"We need to talk to Andy's father," I said. "How can I get hold of him?"

At eleven o'clock we were sitting in the corner office of Harrison T. Fleming, Esquire. Dodd's office would have fit into a small corner of this one. The expansive windows on two sides gave us a view of downtown Birmingham and the surrounding hills. One wall had a large oil painting of General Lee marching through Hagerstown, Maryland, on his way to his Waterloo, Gettysburg, Pennsylvania. The other wall was filled with diplomas and awards.

Jock and I had been shown in by a professionally dressed woman who identified herself as Mr. Fleming's assistant. She brought us coffee and assured us that someone would be in shortly. He was finishing up a meeting in the conference room.

I was idly scanning the ego wall, discovering that Harrison T. Fleming had graduated from the University of Alabama and its law school and had been editor in chief of the law review. He was admitted to the Alabama Bar and several federal courts including the United States Supreme Court. My eyes moved over the rows and then stopped, backed up, and homed in on one framed set. I got up and walked to the wall to get a better view. It was actually a shadow box that contained the brass insignia of the U. S. Army Special Forces and the shoulder patch showing the familiar blue background with a gold sword and three gold lightning flashes diagonally across the sword. The Airborne and Special Forces rockers topped the patch. Below that were the three golden chevrons of the U.S. Army sergeant, a blue-and-silver combat infantry badge, and ribbons denoting combat service in Vietnam.

The door opened and a tall man entered. He wore a worsted wool suit, blue with a subtle pin-stripe, a red-and-silver regimental tie, a head of iron-gray hair, and a big smile. "Sorry I'm late, gentlemen. I'm Martin Caine, Mr. Fleming's law partner. Unfortunately, he isn't in this morning and I haven't been able to reach him by phone. He's out West somewhere playing golf. When Detective Dobbs called his secretary, she assumed he'd be in today."

I was still standing by the wall, my back to it now. I'd turned when I heard the door open. Jock had risen from his chair. "I'm Matt Royal," I said, "and this is Jock Algren and Detective Dobbs." I returned to my chair. Caine took the chair behind his desk.

"Mr. Caine," I said, "I'm a lawyer in Longboat Key, Florida, and I'm looking into a murder down there for the family of the victim. There are some troubling aspects of both that murder and the murder of Andy Fleming. There seems to be a connection, and it's important that we talk to Mr. Fleming today."

"I'm sorry, Mr. Royal, but I don't know how to get hold of him. He hasn't been himself since his son's murder. He called me Saturday evening and told me that he would be out of the office this week and that I should see that his calendar was cancelled. He said something about a golf trip out West, but that's all he told me. Apparently, I wasn't clear to his secretary that he would be gone all week. Otherwise, she wouldn't have made the appointment for you to come in this morning. Perhaps I can help. I was Andy's godfather and we were very close."

I told him about the bullets probably being from the same rifle and the fact that we have identified some Asians who may have been involved in the shooting in Florida. He knew about the Asian seen leaving the scene of his godson's murder.

I asked, "Did you ever hear the name Souphanouvong Phomvihana or maybe Soupy?"

"No. I think I'd remember that name."

"Andy went to Southeast Asia with the Otto Foundation last summer."

"Yes."

"Where did he go?"

"Cambodia."

"Did he get to Laos at all?" I asked.

"Not to my knowledge. I think he stayed the whole six months right in the little village where they were building the school."

"Can you think of any reason some Asian person would want to kill Andy?"

"None," he said.

"A lawyer from Jacksonville, Florida, named Peter Garrison was killed in Longboat the same night as my client's son. Do you know that name?"

"Never heard of him."

"Can you think of any connection that there might have been between Andy and the Desmond boy?"

"Did you say Desmond?" he asked.

"Yes. He was twenty-three and was killed the day after his wedding."

He paused for a moment, then shook his head. "I'm sorry. I wish I could help. I'd give everything I have to find the bastard who killed Andy, but I can't see the connection between the two murders. The rifle makes it seem pretty open and shut, but as far as I know, Andy never met the Desmond boy."

I pointed to the wall. "I see that Mr. Fleming did a little time in Southeast Asia."

"Yes. We both did. A lifetime ago."

"Do you know where he was?"

"Pretty much all over. He doesn't like to talk much about it. Did you serve?"

"Yes. Fifth Special Forces out of Camp Connor at the tail end of the war."

"That's when I was in-country. A grunt in the First Cav," he said, rising from his chair.

We were being dismissed. He shook hands with us and we turned to leave. As we reached the door, Caine cleared his throat. "Mr. Royal," he said, "thank you for your service."

I turned, looked at him and said, "Welcome home, brother."

CHAPTER FIFTY-EIGHT

While Jock drove us to the airport I called Bill Lester. I told him what we'd learned in Birmingham, or perhaps more precisely, what we hadn't learned. "Anything on Telson?" I asked.

"According to Pilots on Demand, he's not working. But he hasn't been home in a couple of days. His wife said he flew out on a trip two days ago and she hasn't heard from him since. Said the trip isn't unusual, but he always calls at least once a day. His cell phone goes directly to voice mail. He's in the wind."

"We're on our way back to Sarasota. Should be landing about two o'clock your time. Let me know if you hear anything."

Jock asked, "What now?"

"I don't know. We're not any closer to finding J.D. than we were this time yesterday."

"We know she has to be with Telson. That's something."

"Not much."

"She said she was okay. That means something."

"She also said she was scared," I said.

"Look, we know now that the same rifle was used to kill both Desmond and Fleming. We can be pretty sure that both murders were carried out by Asians. The only connection between the two victims was the Otto Foundation. We know that Bud Stanley is dirty and that he has a lot of Asian visitors. We know that one of his goons speaks Vietnamese."

"But the Fleming boy was in Cambodia. That sort of leaves out the Soupy connection."

"Maybe there never was a Soupy connection," said Jock.

I thought about that. "But there was a Soupy connection to Stanley."

"Right. But it might not have anything to do with Desmond."

I thought some more. "Suppose Stanley is still running drugs for Soupy. Maybe he's using the kids somehow to bring the drugs into the country. The Otto Foundation could be the way to launder some of the money."

"And if Stanley is using the kids to bring in the drugs," said Jock, "maybe both Fleming and Desmond tripped over something that alerted them and they had to be taken out."

"That makes some sense, except that Desmond had been home for four years when he was killed. He apparently didn't have anything to do with the foundation after he came home from Laos. If he'd found something earlier, I'd think he'd either have been taken out before now or gone to the cops."

"When's Logan due back?" Jock asked.

"He's supposed to dock in Tampa early tomorrow."

"I'd like some new eyes looking at the evidence. Logan's pretty good at that."

"Jock, did you notice anything strange about Caine when I mentioned Jim Desmond's name?"

"He seemed a little taken aback, but his reaction didn't ring any alarm bells."

"Not in me either. But there is a coincidence here. All three of the fathers of the murdered young people served in Vietnam at about the same time."

Jock was silent for a beat. "Where're you going with this?"

"I don't know. It's like trying to grab a handful of cloud. I can see the shape, but I can't get hold of any substance."

"Didn't you say that Brewster was a Marine?"

"Yeah."

"And Fleming and Desmond were both army."

"Yes. And there were still a lot of people in-country during that time. I doubt they would have known each other. It's just a little loose thread that needs to be tidied up."

I called Debbie. "Did you find anything on those hard drives?"

"Not as much as I would have thought, but some interesting items."

"Talk to me."

"It seems that a lot of money is being transferred out of the Otto Foundation accounts to other banks. The transfers are always relatively small, but they add up to quite a bit."

"Overseas banks?"

"No. All in this country."

"Have you got a list of the banks?"

"All of them. Everything is done electronically."

"Were you able to find out where the money goes after it's transferred into the other banks?"

"Not yet. But I've got the names of the accounts in those banks. Their security might be too much for me. I was hoping Jock's people could get into them."

"I'm sure they can. Was there anything on Nigella Morrissey?"

"Yes. I got into the foundation bank account records. She shows up on the payroll the first time when the payroll account was opened with the bank about five years ago. The payments were being sent to a bank in Macon, but in mid-June of this year, that changed. Her pay is now electronically transferred to an account in a Sarasota bank. Ten thousand dollars a month. The last payment was transferred overnight Sunday. It was in the account at the opening of business yesterday."

"You're sure? Sarasota?"

"Yes. I ran her Social Security number through the databases. I wanted to see what else I could turn up on her. The number was never issued to anyone named Morrissey. Turns out it was issued to a friend of ours."

An icy chill ran up my spine, an augury of dread, the presage of knowledge I didn't want. "Who?"

Debbie let out a long slow breath. "I'm sorry, Matt. The Social Security number belongs to Jennifer Diane Duncan."

CHAPTER FIFTY-NINE

I closed the phone. I sat quietly, staring at the passing cityscape, trying to get my thoughts in some sort of order. J.D. couldn't be dirty. Not the J.D. I knew. She was a professional law enforcement officer, a woman of strong ethical and moral values, a strength of character that glowed like luminous radium, somehow always letting the world know that she was an upright human being with no character defects.

"What's up?" asked Jock. "You look like somebody died."

"It turns out that the elusive Nigella Morrisey is J. D. Duncan."

"I don't understand."

"Debbie tells me that Morrissey's paychecks go into an account in a Sarasota Bank. Morrissey's Social Security number is identical to J.D.'s."

"Uh-oh. That's not good."

"Something's not right. J.D. isn't dirty."

"I want to agree with you, podna. But we'll have to follow the facts."

"Deb says she has a number of banks where the money has been shifted from the Otto Foundation account. Can your people get those records?"

"Shouldn't be a problem."

By the time we reached the airport Jock had called his agency and then called Debbie and asked her to e-mail the bank information to an agency geek who would get into the accounts and find out where the money went. Jock told the computer guy to look first at the Sarasota bank and an account in the name of Nigella Morrissey.

We landed at Sarasota a little after two o'clock. Fred Cassidy said that he and the copilot had been instructed to lay over at the Hyatt Regency again in case I needed the plane. Jock called his contact in the agency office in Washington while we drove back to Longboat Key.

He closed his phone. "It doesn't look too good, Matt. Morrissey's account gets nine thousand two hundred thirty dollars each month. That's the ten grand less the Social Security and Medicare withholding. She doesn't withhold any income taxes. There have only been three checks written out of the account, each one on the day after the money is transferred in and each one for exactly nine thousand dollars, payable to J.D. Duncan. The checks are cashed at the bank on the same day. The last one was cashed yesterday morning at nine forty-five."

"That's pretty neat," I said. "If the checks are cashed for less than ten grand the bank doesn't have to report it to the government. I wonder if the bank has security cameras that can identify the person who cashed the checks."

"Bill Lester can get that for us."

"I don't want to involve Bill in this just yet. He'll have to take some action and then the word will get out that J.D.'s on the take. Even after we prove she's not, the stain will still be there."

"Look, podna," Jock said. "I know you've got feelings for J.D, but you can't let that cloud your judgment. Things don't look so good for her right now. Bill's your friend and J.D.'s boss. He needs to know about this."

"I don't want to lie to Bill, but what he doesn't know can't hurt him."

"Unless J.D. is dirty, and then a load of crap is going to fall on the chief."

I was quiet for a moment, thinking it over. Bill truly was a good friend, to both J.D. and me, but he also had responsibilities to his department and the town that paid his salary. He was an honorable man and the duty he owed his fellow officers and the people of Longboat Key would likely override his emotional attachments to a couple of friends. On the other hand, if J.D. were truly dirty, I would be putting Lester's career in jeopardy.

"I'll keep that in mind," I said, more sharply than I meant to.

Jock drove in silence for a few moments. "Let me make some calls."

We pulled into a Crispers Restaurant on Cortez Road. We hadn't eaten since a quick breakfast on the way to the airport that morning. I went inside, leaving Jock in the car with his cell phone. He came in a few minutes later and joined me in the ordering line.

"My director is calling the bank president. National security concerns open a lot of doors."

"How's this going to work?"

"The director will tell the banker that I need to look at his security tapes from yesterday morning. That we're tracking a terror suspect and we think he might have been in the bank yesterday. No names, no fuss, just a routine follow-up by a field agent. Me."

We ate our lunch in silence. Jock's phone rang, he answered, said "okay" and hung up. "We're in," he said. "Let's finish up and get to the bank. The president is expecting us, and he'll have the tape ready."

The bank was a small independent establishment, one of those set up by entrepreneurs who get funding and grow the deposits with the hope of selling out at a big profit to one of the large chains. The president came to the lobby to greet us and took us back to his office. Jock flashed his credentials and introduced me as his associate. The banker plugged a flash drive into the computer on his desk.

"This starts at nine a.m. when we open the doors," he said. "It goes until noon. If you need more tape, we can get it for you."

"This should do fine," said Jock. "We appreciate your cooperation."

"Always glad to help. I don't like the thought of a terrorist in my bank."

"It's probably nothing," said Jock, "but we have to follow up any lead."

"Okay. I'll leave you alone."

Jock and I huddled behind the desk reviewing the security tape on the monitor. It was a small bank and there were only two teller windows. One of them was closed. The camera was placed behind the tellers so that we could see the faces of the customers. We had a clear picture of the bank lobby and the entrance.

Just before nine forty-five, a woman came through the entrance. She was a brunette, her hair shoulder length. She carried herself with that assurance that cops adopt, not exactly a swagger, but a stride of confidence that hinted that she was in charge of her surroundings. As she neared the counter her face came into focus. I told Jock to stop the video. We had a fairly close-up view of the woman cashing the check. No doubt about it. The lovely face, the one that could break into a smile that lit up a room, belonged to Detective J. D. Duncan.

CHAPTER SIXTY

We went to the lobby to talk to the bank president. Jock said, "I noticed that your teller had the person cashing the check make a thumbprint."

"Yes, we do that for security. We check ID, but that's easy to fake. We have to cash checks on our customer's accounts, so we require the thumbprint. If the ID was fake and we gave cash to a somebody other than the payee on the check, we'll have a way to find them and prosecute."

"Could we get a copy of the print on a certain check?" asked Jock.

"Yes, but the checks have already been sent to the processing center. I can probably get somebody there to find it for you, but it'll be at least tomorrow morning before I can get it back."

"I'd appreciate it if you'd get right on that," said Jock.

I held up the flash drive with the security video. "We're going to need a copy of this."

"Take that one," said the banker. "We're giving blank flash drives away to new customers. I've got a boatload of them in the storeroom."

"Do you want to bring Lester in on this now?" Jock asked. We were driving back to the key. I felt as if a dark cloud was slowly engulfing me, turning me into block of stone, unable to think or move or feel. Was J.D. really dirty? It seemed so.

"Not yet," I said. "I know this woman, Jock. She's not capable of something like this."

"The money started flowing right after Jim Desmond was killed. Maybe she came across something in the investigation and is being bought off."

"That'd be a logical conclusion if I didn't know her. She's not capable of that kind of betrayal of all of us."

"You weren't involved until very late in this. Maybe she wouldn't do it to you, but by the time you got interested it was too late to back out."

"She wouldn't betray Bill Lester and the department. Or her own values. Something is wrong with the picture we're getting."

"I hope you're right."

"We need to dig deeper," I said. "Can your people dig up some information on a top secret outfit that ran something called Operation Thanatos back at the end of the Vietnam War?"

"If there's information on it, I'm sure we can get it. What's this about?"

"Doc Desmond left our unit and went to a group made up of special ops types, Army Special Forces, Marine Recon, Navy SEALs, CIA. They were super secret and were used to assassinate Viet Cong leaders."

"Do you think that had anything to do with Jim's murder?" asked Jock.

"Probably not, but we ran into a Vietnamese speaker, another guy with a Vietnamese name, the Evermore Foundation, and the fact that Doc was in Vietnam and is probably being blackmailed."

"You think Desmond's service in Vietnam is tied to the murder of his son in some way?"

"I don't know, but it occurs to me that Brewster was a Marine sniper who was in Force Recon and Fleming was Special Forces, just like Doc."

"That's pretty thin," said Jock.

"I know. There were a lot of men in all those units, but I'd like to check them out just to be sure."

"How big was Operation Thanatos?"

"I don't have any idea, but I'd think it'd have to be fairly small because of the secrecy."

"I'll see what I can get." He unfolded his encrypted cell phone and touched a speed-dial number. He told somebody on the other end of the conversation what he needed and hung up. "He says if they exist he can get them, but it may take a day or two. He'll send the documents to my laptop."

"Who were you talking to?"

"The director."

"Can you get him back on the phone, see if his geeks can run down anything on Nigella Morrissey?"

CHAPTER SIXTY-ONE

I was dead tired. My watch told me it was five o'clock, but it seemed much later. I had been pushing myself all day on less than four hours of sleep, and we were no closer to finding J.D. Jock did not seem to be affected by the lack of sleep.

I put a pot of coffee on and sat at my computer to check e-mail. Among the usual spam and mundane notes were e-mails from two addresses I didn't recognize. I opened the first one. The time stamp said it had been delivered at 2:12 that afternoon. It said, "Trust me. J.D."

I hit the reply button and typed, "Where are you?" I waited for a minute, two, hoping that I'd get a response. Any response. I did. It was from something called mail delivery subsystem with the message "Delivery to the following recipient failed permanently" with the address J.D. had e-mailed from. Dead end.

I opened the next message that had arrived at 4:17. It said, "Look at Marsh LLC, a Florida limited liability company." That was all. Again I hit reply and wrote, "Who are you?" I got the same message from the mail delivery subsystem. No such address.

I got a cup of coffee and sat thinking about the messages. I knew that you could set up an e-mail account through one of the free service providers without much hassle. You'd get an e-mail address and the right to use the account. You didn't have to give a real name or address. However, the service that set up the account would have the electronic address of the computer from which the account originated. With the cooperation of the service provider you could find out where the message came from.

If you set up an e-mail account, sent one message, and then closed the account, a person replying to you would get the same message I got from the mail delivery subsystem. I didn't know what the Marsh LLC message was all about, but either J.D. was trying to reach me or somebody was playing a stupid game. I didn't think it was the latter.

Jock came out of the bathroom wearing a pair of shorts and a T-shirt with the logo of the Houston Astros. He poured himself a cup of coffee and joined me in the living room. I showed him the messages and the replies.

"I'll get my techies on this. They should be able to run down the locations of the computers that sent the e-mails without much trouble."

"Let me call Bill Lester. See if he's had any developments."

"You ready to tell him about the bank accounts?"

"Not yet."

Within the hour we had some information that didn't make a lot of sense. Lester hadn't heard anything. All their lines of inquiries into J.D.'s disappearance had hit dead ends. She had no family since her mother had died the year before, so there was no one to call with bad news.

Jock's people had quickly run down the electronic addresses of the computers that sent the two e-mails. The one about Marsh LLC was sent from a computer in a public library in Decatur, Georgia. The one from J.D. could not be found. The message had bounced around the ether through a number of servers, some in Eastern Europe. It was just impossible to track it.

I called Debbie's cell phone. "You at work?"

"No. My night off."

"You alone?"

"Not that it's any of your business, but what if I am?"

"You are alone."

"Sadly, yes."

"Good. I need a little favor."

"Here we go again."

"I need you to take a look at the Florida Secretary of State's online records and see if you can find out anything on a limited liability company named Marsh LLC. I'd be surprised if the names on the paperwork are real, but see if you can follow it back to its source. I'd like to know who's behind it."

"You need this when?"

"Now."

"Geez. I'll see what I can do." She hung up.

"You think Marsh is connected to this in some way?" Jock asked.

"Don't know, but I can't think of another reason why anyone would be sending me that message from a library computer."

Jock had checked his e-mail on his laptop while we sipped coffee. There had been nothing, but he'd left the computer open on the dinette table. It pinged to let him know he had an e-mail coming in. He went to the computer and opened the e-mail. "The director came through. Nigella Morrissey is alive and well and living in Tampa. I've got her address and phone number and a whole lot more information. She's a lawyer. The ten thousand bucks that was going to her account at the Macon bank was being sent on to an account in Nigella's name in a Tampa bank."

"I think we need to pay her a visit. Tonight."

He was peering at his computer screen. "I agree. Listen to this. They've tracked a lot of the money from the Otto Foundation bank account that went to other corporations and foundations. Those accounts are in banks all over the country, but they have one thing in common. The money that comes in is almost immediately transferred out to a single account."

"Let me guess," I said. "It goes to Nigella's account in Tampa."

"Right. And that account is her law firm trust account."

"So that's money that is not going to be reported on tax returns because it's theoretically not her money. It belongs to her clients."

"Right. And those clients are all corporations that have never filed a tax return."

"That's slick," I said. "The Otto Foundation simply files its tax returns showing expenses paid out to other foundations and businesses. I'll bet that none of those entities really exist or if they do they're just shells."

"Right."

"And the money is transferred from the corporate accounts into a lawyer's trust account and then to other corporations that are probably just shells."

"Okay."

"Nigella doesn't file any kind of a tax return on the trust account, because she's not required to, and if the Florida Bar ever audits the trust account, it'll balance perfectly."

"So what about the corporations that get the money from Nigella's trust account?"

"Those accounts are probably controlled by Bud Stanley, or more likely, his alter ego, Robert Charles Bracewell."

"I love the way your mind works. You're either a hell of a lawyer or a crook at heart."

"Logan would say they're one and the same," I said. "Can you get your geeks to see what they can find out about the corporations that Nigella is sending the money to?"

"Sure." He typed for a bit and then waited, watching his monitor, and then peering more closely. "Done. They'll have the data for us by this time tomorrow. Logan needs to see this stuff. You're sure he's due in tomorrow?"

"Yeah, but he may not be at his best. A week on the cruise with all that food and booze would be way too much temptation for Logan."

"Let's go find out what makes our girl Nigella tick," Jock said.

That turned out to be easier said than done.

CHAPTER SIXTY-TWO

We were driving across the Sunshine Skyway Bridge that spans lower Tampa Bay and connects Manatee and Pinellas Counties. The sun was low on the horizon, but it still had a couple of hours before its daily descent into the Gulf of Mexico. A large ship, probably a phosphate carrier, was inbound, riding high, its Plimsoll Line showing far above the surface. It would load at the Port of Tampa and return to sea heavy with phosphate that would be turned into fertilizer for use around the world.

Few of the people who wintered on the gilded coasts of Florida knew that just a few miles inland a very different world existed, one of working men and women who mined the earth for phosphate, ran cattle, harvested citrus and vegetable crops, hunted deer, and fished the fresh-water lakes and rivers for food. A land of large Indian reservations and scrub and swamp and sinkholes and alligators and panthers, a land where man was an intruder and where life was cheap and dismal and desperate.

In the center of the state, near Orlando, the top tourist destination in the world, home of Disney and Universal Studios and SeaWorld and numerous other attractions, lay a single working cattle ranch that comprised three hundred thousand acres. Florida was a working state as well as a retirement mecca. And like every other state, we had our share of crooks and scam artists and other assorted criminals. Ours were just flashier and sometimes funnier than those of most any other place.

I'd called Nigella's home phone just before we left my house. She answered and I apologized for calling a wrong number. She was home, and hopefully would still be there when we arrived.

I had also logged onto the Florida Bar website to see what I could find on her. Not much. She'd graduated from the University of Tennessee and Vanderbilt Law School. She'd been admitted to the Bar five years before. Her office address was listed as a post office box in Tampa. She had no ethical grievances filed against her.

Nigella lived in a large house on Bayshore Drive near Hyde Park with an expansive view of Tampa Bay. The house was long and slender, built on a narrow lot in the style of Charleston, with the front door on the side. It was still daylight when we knocked. It was opened by a woman with a definite Asian appearance, but the softening of the epicanthic folds and the lighter skin tones told me that Caucasian blood flowed through her veins. A Eurasian. She was about thirty, tall and slim and beautiful, her black hair pulled back into a tight bun, diamond studs in her earlobes. She was wearing a white shirt, white shorts and shoes, and held a tennis racket in her hand.

"Can I help you?" she asked.

"I'm Jock Algren, Ms. Morrissey. I wonder if we could talk to you for a few minutes."

"Make it quick. I'm on my way to play tennis." Her voice was edgy, suspicious.

"May we come in?" asked Jock.

"We don't have time for that. What are you selling?"

Jock put his hand on the tennis racket and wrenched it from her grip. He used his other hand to push her back into the house, holding onto her arm with one hand, with the racket in the other. I followed. We were in a foyer with a living room opening to our left. Jock continued pushing Nigella, until she backed into a sofa and sat down.

"What the hell do you think you're doing?" she asked, her voice loud and strained, pissed.

"We're here about Bud Stanley," said Jock.

"Who?"

"Bud Stanley. You know, the one who sends you all that money."

She sat perfectly still, staring at us. Silent.

"Matt," Jock said, "check out the house. I don't want another surprise with a shotgun."

I pulled out my thirty-eight-caliber police special and went to search the house. Most of the downstairs was taken up by a kitchen, formal dining room, living room, and foyer with a staircase leading to the second floor. There were four bedrooms, each with its own bath. Only one of the rooms looked as if it had been used. The beds were all made, there were no clothes or suitcases or any indication of life in other than the master bedroom.

I came back downstairs. Jock and Nigella were sitting still, staring at each other. "All clear," I said.

"Ms. Morrissey," Jock said, "you're going to answer some questions for us. We can do this the hard way or the easy way, but sooner or later you're going to tell us what we need to know."

"Go to hell."

The movement was so fast I wasn't sure I saw it. Jock lashed out and slapped her face with his open hand. It didn't appear to have much power behind it, but Nigella was thrown back against the sofa. Tears welled in her eyes, but she just stared at us. No sound, no words, not even a sigh.

"Lady," Jock said, "my friend here gets a little queasy when I get rough and I'd hate for him to start throwing up on these beautiful rugs. But we're about to get serious here."

"Go to hell."

Jock sighed. "Take off your clothes."

"What?"

"You heard me. Get naked."

"You sick bastard. No fucking way."

Jock pulled a large knife from a scabbard at his ankle, one that had been covered by his trousers. "If you don't take them off, I'm going to cut them off, and I might get a little careless. You know, cut some of that beautiful skin, maybe your face."

"What do you want to know?"

"Where is Bud Stanley?"

"I don't know."

Jock brandished the knife. "That's not very helpful."

"I really don't know. He left Macon yesterday. He called and said he'd be in touch with me."

"Did he say when?"

She hesitated. Jock moved quickly and put the tip of the knife under her chin. Nigella paled and backed away from the weapon. The back of the sofa restricted her moves. She wasn't able to go far.

"Yes," she said. "Tonight. He's supposed to be here before midnight."

Jock pulled back on the knife. "That's better. Where's J. D. Duncan?"

"I don't know."

Jock waved the knife in the air near her face.

"Really," she said. "I don't know." Her voice carried a pleading tone.

"Do you know J.D.?" I asked.

"I know she's a cop down on Longboat Key. That's all."

"Does she somehow work with you and Stanley?" I asked.

"I don't know, but I think so."

"What's her job?" I asked.

"I don't know anything about that, either."

"Do you know how your name ended up with her Social Security number at a bank in Sarasota?" I asked.

"I don't know anything about that."

"Nigella," said Jock, "we're going to be here with you until Stanley shows up. If I find out tonight or later that you've lied to us, I'm going to carve you into little pieces and feed you to the fish out there in the bay. It won't matter where you go. I will find you. Just like I did today."

"I'm not lying. I just don't know."

"Tell us about the Otto Foundation," I said.

"What about it?"

"Are they in the drug business?"

"Yes. Of course. That's where the money comes from."

"Where do the drugs come from?"

"I don't know. My job is simply to launder their money."

Fear of Jock had loosened her tongue. She was talking rapidly, taking shallow breaths, glancing at him every few seconds. He was sitting quietly in a chair he'd pulled up to the sofa, his knees almost touching hers, the knife still in his hand, a scowl on his face.

"Do you know how the drugs get into the country?" I asked.

"No."

"Are you familiar with the name Souphanouvong Phomvihana?"

"Sounds Laotian, but I've never heard that name."

"What is your ethnic background?"

"Irish dad and Vietnamese mother."

"Where are your parents?"

"I have no idea about my father. His name was Nigel Morrissey, but he disappeared when I was an infant. He left me his name, nothing else. My mom lives in Chattanooga, Tennessee."

We talked for another hour, sporadically asking her questions, getting no answers. I thought she was too frightened of Jock to lie to us. Maybe we'd gotten all we were going to get out of her. She didn't seem to have a lot of knowledge about the drug business, insisting only that she was used for laundry and was paid very well to do so.

Shortly after dark, I heard footsteps coming up the walkway that led to the front door. I pulled my pistol from my pocket and stood by the door. A key was inserted into the lock from outside. Before the key turned, I swung the door open, my gun pointing right into the very surprised face of Bud Stanley.

CHAPTER SIXTY-THREE

"Do come in, Mr. Stanley," I said, opening the door wider.

He stood there, stunned, not sure what to do.

"If you run," I said, my voice hard, "I'll shoot you in the back. Get your ass in here. Keep your hands where I can see them."

He walked in, his hands in front, palms turned outward. He saw Nigella. "Are you okay?" he asked her.

"Yes."

"What's going on?"

"You left in a hurry up in Macon," I said. "We weren't finished with our visit. Sit down."

He sat at one end of the sofa, Nigella at the other. Jock had a nine-millimeter pistol trained on him. "Where's J. D. Duncan?" asked Jock.

"I don't know. I didn't know she was missing."

"Look, dickhead," said Jock, "I don't have time to fool around. If you don't tell me what I need to know, I'm going to shoot you. First in the foot, then the other foot, then the knee and so on until you decide to talk to me."

Stanley blanched. "Look," he said, "if I knew where she was, I'd tell you."

"You know who she is," Jock said, a statement, not a question.

"Yes. She's the Longboat Key cop who was investigating the Desmond killing."

"Tell me about the money going into her account," I said.

"What money?"

"Shoot him, Jock," I said.

"No. Wait. I don't know what you're talking about."

I stared at him for a moment. "You sent three payments of ten grand each to a bank account in Sarasota in the name of Nigella Morrissey but with J.D.'s Social Security number. It shows up in your records as payroll."

"That's not possible."

"Believe me, asshole, it's in the records."

"I swear to you, I had nothing to do with that."

"Who besides you had access to the Otto Foundation bank accounts?" I asked.

"Nobody other than Maude Lane."

"Tell me about your connection to Souphanouvong Phomvihana."

"I told you in the office that day. I don't have a connection with him."

"You and your dad worked with Soupy's dad."

"Yes, but I gave that up when I got out of prison."

"You're still dealing drugs," I said.

He was quiet for a beat, then exhaled, and said, "Yes."

"Where do they come from?"

"From the same area of Laos. But not from Soupy."

"Look," I said, "I'm not really interested in the drugs. I'll let the Drug Enforcement Administration deal with that. Right now I want to find J. D. Duncan. That's my only interest."

"I don't know anything about that. I'd tell you if I did."

In the end, we didn't get any more information. I tended to believe Stanley when he said he didn't know anything about J.D.'s disappearance. He and Nigella were too scared not to tell us the truth.

I called the DEA office in Tampa. It was late now, after ten, so I got a duty officer. "This is Matt Royal," I said. "I need to talk to Special Agent Dan Delgado."

"He's gone for the day, sir."

"Can you reach him?"

"Yes, sir."

"Tell him to call me on an urgent matter. He knows who I am." I gave him my cell number.

"I'll call him, sir."

Dan Delgado had worked with Jock and me on another problem we'd run into a few months back. He was the special agent in charge of the Tampa office of the DEA.

My cell phone rang. "Matt, you running drugs or something?"

"Not exactly, Dan. Jock Algren and I are holding some people at gunpoint who I think you'd love to talk to."

"If Jock's there, we probably have a huge mess. Where are you?"

I gave him the address.

Twenty minutes later Delgado showed up with two other agents. They were wearing windbreakers with POLICE printed across the back in block yellow letters. Below that was the agency name. Dan shook hands with Jock and me and we explained who we had and what kind of evidence we'd accumulated. We asked him to hold them separately and incommunicado until we were able to dig further into J.D.'s disappearance. Dan knew J.D. and was most willing to help out. Nigella and Stanley were carted off in handcuffs.

"What now?" asked Jock as we got back into the car.

"I don't think there's anything else we can do tonight. I need sleep. We'll start fresh in the morning."

CHAPTER SIXTY-FOUR

I woke feeling like a regiment of infantry had walked across my head during the night. Tired as I was, I hadn't slept well. Images of J.D. flashed through my sleep, vivid dreams of her in a dark place from which she could not escape. Still, I'd stayed in bed long past my usual time. It was almost nine when I rolled out.

I showered, shaved, and stumbled into the kitchen. Jock was there drinking coffee and reading the morning paper. He looked as if he'd slept through the night without any worries. I thought it must be a habit he'd learned during all those years of clandestine operations.

"Got a question," I said. "Were you really going to strip the clothes off Nigella last night if she hadn't started talking?"

"You're a pervert."

"I'm just asking."

"No. I wouldn't have touched her. I just wanted to scare the hell out of her. I think I succeeded. Why?"

I grinned at him. "Just wondering."

"Right. You were thinking about her naked."

The man had a point. He went back to his paper. I grabbed a couple of packaged pastries and popped them into the microwave. Such was breakfast when I didn't have time for the Blue Dolphin. I got a cup of coffee and joined Jock at the table.

"The director got a lot done on Thanatos," he said. "It was waiting for me this morning when I opened my e-mail."

"What've you got?"

He went to the living room and returned with a sheaf of printouts. "The most interesting part of this is the makeup of the teams. There were twelve men in each and there were only three teams. They were dubbed, Team Alpha, Team Beta, and Team Charlie. Desmond was part of Team Charlie. Look at the roster."

"Damn," I said. "Desmond, Brewster, and Fleming were all part of the same team. This isn't a coincidence. But there are only seven names here. What about the others?"

"Five of them are dead."

"Any information on the living members?"

Jock handed me another sheet of paper. "Names and current addresses."

I looked at the list. "Are you sure the other five are dead?"

"Yeah. I checked. Two were killed in Vietnam before the end of the war, one died in a car wreck a year after he came home, and two died of cancer."

"Why are the team members kids being killed?"

"Don't know, but I'd like to find out if any of the others have had deaths in their families."

"I'll get Bill Lester onto this. He can query the police departments in the towns where they live. Maybe something will turn up."

"We need to warn these guys. Somebody is targeting them."

I called Bill Lester and gave him the names and addresses of the men who'd served on Charlie Team in Operation Thanatos. "It can't be a coincidence that the children of three men who served on the same team are now dead," I said.

"I'll get right on this and get back to you," said the chief. "And before you ask, the answer is no. We haven't made any progress in finding J.D."

I hung up and my phone rang again. Debbie.

"Good morning, sunshine," I said. "You're up early."

"I spent most of the night on Marsh LLC. I thought you'd want it first thing this morning."

"What'd you find?"

"It's a tangled mess. Marsh LLC is owned by a company incorporated in Ohio called BriteSun, Inc. That corporation has only one officer, the president whose name is Victor Chaffin. The office address is a post office box in Columbus."

I interrupted. "What about the registered agent for service of process?"

"Both Marsh and BriteSun use one of those companies that serve as registered agents for lots of corporations all over the country."

"Okay. Go on."

"BriteSun does not seem to have any business operations, and other than the listing on the Ohio Secretary of State's website, there's nothing on it anywhere."

"Then why the hell was somebody trying to get me to look into Marsh?"

"There is one thing I found that may have some bearing on this mess."

"What?"

"Marsh LLC is shown as the owner of a piece of property in the Bahamas."

"How did you ferret that out?"

"BriteSun was incorporated in Ohio about twenty years ago. The check that was written for this year's annual corporate fee was drawn on a bank in Columbus. The signature on the check was illegible and there was no printed name on it. I hacked into the bank's computers and found the account. It was set up by the same person who is shown as the president of BriteSun, Victor Chaffin."

"That's interesting."

"There's more. That checking account is only used once a year to keep BriteSun active. That is until recently when somebody put a million dollars into the account. It's listed as 'capital infusion.' Marsh was formed a couple of days later, the million dollars was transferred by check to Marsh. I got the routing numbers off the endorsements on the back of the check and traced that to a bank in Atlanta."

"And you hacked their computer."

"Damn right. Marsh wrote a check to the trust account of a law firm in West Palm Beach for guess how much."

"One million dollars."

"Bingo."

"And you found out what it was for."

"Law firm computers have notoriously bad security. This one closed on the Bahamian property for Marsh LLC."

"Where is the property?"

"It's a house in Marsh Harbour. In the Abacos." She gave me the street address.

"Damn, you're good," I said.

"That's not all I got. Victor Chaffin died five years ago. He's listed in the Social Security death index, and I found his obituary in the Columbus *Dispatch*. He was the founder of Chaffin Consultants, an engineering firm that was one of the first bought by Desmond Engineering Consultants when it started expanding."

"I'll be damned."

"Bye." She hung up, and I related the conversation to Jock.

"If she's able to hack into bank computers, she's better than I thought," he said. "The agency's hackers are the best in the world and they have trouble with bank computer security. Does she have any particular training in this stuff?"

"No. It's just something she got into and developed a real talent. She's usually too wired to sleep when she gets home from work, so she stays up and trolls the Internet. I think she's made some friends who spend their entire lives breaking into other people's computers. It's like a big game. Get in and get out. As long as they do no damage, they figure it's all in fun."

"But they can find a lot of private information on people. That could be dangerous if they mess with the wrong folks."

"I agree, but she doesn't listen to reason sometimes."

"Maybe because you're the enabler," he said. "You seem to ask her for help on a regular basis."

I got another cup of coffee, sipped it. "You may be right. I'll be more careful about what I ask her to do in the future. But for now, what the hell is the connection between a house in the Bahamas and what we're looking into?"

I went to my computer and put the Bahamian address into Google maps. I found the place, but it wasn't in Marsh Harbour proper. The house sat alone on a small island off the northern tip of the peninsula that held the town. The only access to the island would be by boat. It was isolated and secure. A good place for people who didn't want to be bothered.

My computer pinged, letting me know that an e-mail had arrived. I opened it. The message was: "I'm OK. Your buddy Tripp would love this place. Trust me."

"Jock," I said. "Look at this."

"Damn. At least she's okay or says she is. Who's this buddy of yours, Tripp?"

"Tripp Harrison. He's an artist. I've never met the man, but I love his paintings."

"I don't get it."

"I've got three of his works, two limited-edition prints and one original oil. They're all here in the house. J.D. likes them as much as I do."

"I still don't get it."

"All three of the paintings are of scenes in the Abacos."

CHAPTER SIXTY-FIVE

"She's in that house," said Jock. "If we knew who sent you the e-mail about Marsh LLC we'd know a whole lot more."

"None of this makes sense. Why would J.D. be in the Abacos and who the hell is she with?"

"And there's also customs to worry about," said Jock. "If she landed in the Bahamas, she had to clear customs. There'll be a record."

"Can you run that down?"

"Real quick," he said as he opened his cell phone.

When he finished his conversation, he said, "Apparently they're real slow about getting information into computers at Bahamian customs. We might not get the information for several days."

"If somebody took her there against her will, I doubt they're going to want to be anywhere near a customs officer."

"What about going by boat? You've made that trip several times."

"It'd be a pretty easy trip. You're supposed to stop at the first port of entry and clear Bahamian customs, but boats go there all the time without stopping. There're so many American boats in Bahamian waters during the summer that the Defense Force can't keep up with them."

"It'd be a pretty long trip, wouldn't it?"

"Not that bad. If I were taking a big go-fast boat over, I'd leave from Lauderdale, stay north of Bimini into the Northwest Providence Channel, skirt the southern tip of Abaco, and come into the Abaco Sound at Pelican Harbour. That's only about fifteen miles from Marsh Harbour."

"How long would the trip take?"

"It would depend on the seas. The distance is only about a hundred seventy-five miles. If you average forty miles an hour, which those big cigarette-type boats can do without breaking a sweat, you'd make it in less than five hours with fuel to spare."

"So, the cell call from J.D. came in at three fifteen from Fort Lauderdale. If they were leaving then, on good seas they'd be in Marsh Harbour before dark. Can you check to see what the weather was like on Sunday?"

"Sure," I said.

I logged onto the National Oceanic and Atmospheric Administration's website and looked at the weather conditions for the last couple of days. "Weather was good," I said. "West winds five to ten miles per hour, seas less than two feet. It would probably have meant flat seas, and even if there was a little chop, with the west wind it would have been a following sea. Nothing for a big go-fast with a captain who knows what he's doing."

The doorbell rang and I heard the front door open. "I smell coffee," said Logan as he walked into the living room.

"In the kitchen," I said. "Help yourself."

"You know I never drink that noxious brew."

"There's tomato juice in the fridge."

He kept talking as he walked into the kitchen, poured a glass, and returned. "Did you guys miss me?"

"You been gone?" asked Jock.

"Docked in Tampa early this morning."

"You got some sun," Jock said.

"Yeah. All over, too. We had a balcony and just hung out there in the nude."

"That is not an image I want to contemplate this early in the day," I said.

"Eat your heart out," said Logan. "I went to the Dolphin for breakfast and heard that J.D.'s missing. What's going on?"

Jock and I spent thirty minutes filling Logan in on everything that had happened since he left for his cruise. "You got any ideas?" I asked.

"Why don't we look at this as two or three different issues? The first is that Doc and J.D. disappear at about the same time on Monday. A pilot who flew occasionally for Doc is seen buying a cell phone in Sarasota early that morning. Later you get a call from the same cell phone and it's J.D. And the pilot is nowhere to be found. You get an e-mail message from J.D. on Tuesday telling you to trust her. The same day you get an e-mail from an unknown someone in the Atlanta area telling you to look into Marsh LLC. It turns out that Marsh owns a house on an island in the Abacos. And the guy who is president of the corporation that owns Marsh LLC is dead, but it was a subsidiary of an engineering firm that Desmond now owns. Then you get another e-mail from J.D. that cryptically tells you she's somewhere in the Abacos. They probably didn't fly there because that would alert customs. But a fast boat could have taken them there without a lot of hassle. It sounds like J.D. and Doc may both be in Marsh Harbour."

"Where's Telson, the pilot?" I asked.

"Doesn't matter. He may have flown Doc here to pick up J.D. and then on to the east coast. They took a boat from there. He's probably home in Atlanta."

"Okay," I said. "That's makes sense except for one thing."

"What?" asked Logan.

"Why would Doc kidnap J.D.?"

"Maybe he didn't. Maybe she went willingly."

"But why?"

"We'll just have to find that out."

"Another thing bothering me," said Jock, "is why J.D. went to the bank to cash that check."

"Well," said Logan, "we could assume she's dirty and that she's shacked up with Doc. But we all know that's not the case."

"Alternative?" I asked.

"Maybe they just wanted to put some pressure on whoever set up the account in J.D.'s name. Let them know that J.D. was on to them."

"How did she find out about the account in the first place if she wasn't part of it?"

"Another good question, Counselor. We find J.D., we find the answers."

Jock said, "You only discussed one of the issues. Want to tackle the ones dealing with the dead kids of Thanatos team members? Or the attempts on Matt's life? Or Stanley's role in all this?"

"I'm going to have to think about those. Let me see the security video of J.D. cashing that check."

I put the flash drive into a port in my computer and got the tape rolling. Logan watched it with growing interest, his eyes riveted to the monitor, his hand manipulating the mouse, varying the speed of the tape. He went through it twice and then paused it at a point where J.D. had turned to leave. He pointed to a man in the picture. "This guy seems to be pacing around the lobby during most of the tape. Do you know who he is?"

I peered more closely at the tape. The camera had caught J.D. just as she was passing by a man in a suit. They were right next to each other. She going toward the exit and the man was standing there, mouthing some words. "He's the bank president."

"He must be pretty tall," said Logan. "What? Six three or so?"

"No," I said. "He's about my height, a little shorter maybe. Five ten or eleven."

"Look closely. This guy towers over J.D. He's got at least six inches on her. She's what, five nine?"

My pulse quickened. "Yes. Damn. This woman's several inches shorter. But it's J.D. I got a full face shot of her at the teller's window."

"Look again," said Logan. He backed up the tape, slowing it as he hunted for a particular shot. He stopped it again. This time the picture was of a smiling J.D. talking to the teller.

"Look at the front tooth," Logan said. He pulled the picture in tighter. "See anything?"

"I'll be damned," I said. "There's a small chip in the right front tooth. J.D.'s teeth are perfect."

"Look some more," Logan said. "There's a lot you can do with makeup, but some things can't be changed. The width between the eyes, laugh lines, shape of chin. Have you got a picture of J.D.?"

"There're some on the computer. Go to my photo folder and you'll find them."

I pointed Logan to the right place in the computer files. There were a number of photos of friends enjoying the slow lifestyle of the key. One had a full face shot of J.D. sitting with Logan and Marie on the beach at Egmont Key, her big smile brightening the day. He cropped the picture and printed it. He then pulled up the security tape and held the printed picture of J.D. up to the monitor.

The pictures were very close, but there were subtle differences. On the security tape, the smile wasn't quite right, the curve of her cheek a little different, the eyebrows a tad thinner. "That's not J.D.," I said. "Damn. How did we miss that?"

"At some level," said Logan, "you and Jock were thinking J.D. had changed sides. The picture confirmed your worst fears. Even though your brains were telling you that she wasn't dirty, the evidence was pretty convincing at the subconscious level."

"Why would somebody go to all the trouble to convince us that J.D. was the one cashing that check?"

"I don't know," said Logan, "but it worked."

I was feeling guilty for doubting her, and relief that my dark suspicions had been wrong. But she was still in trouble, still missing without explanation. I had to find her.

CHAPTER SIXTY-SIX

"We need to get to the Abacos," I said. "J.D.'s been gone two days. That can't be good."

"Does everybody agree that she's probably there?" asked Jock.

Logan and I nodded.

"We've still got Doc's plane," I said.

Logan said, "If Doc is holding J.D. against her will, why would he allow you to use his plane?"

I hadn't really thought about that one. I picked up the phone and dialed Fred Cassidy's cell phone. When he answered, I said, "Are you in communication with Chaz Desmond?"

"No. I don't think anybody knows where he is."

"Who authorized you and the plane to stick around to help us?"

"That'd be Paul Macomber and the company's lawyer, Harry Anderson."

I hung up and called the offices of Desmond Engineering Consultants and asked to speak to Macomber. "I'm sorry, sir," the receptionist said, "but he's in Charlotte today."

"Then may I speak to Mr. Anderson."

"He's out sick today."

"Can you give me his home phone?"

"I'm sorry, sir, but it's against our policy to give out home numbers."

"He's probably in the book," I said. "Can you tell me what town he lives in?"

"No problem, sir. Decatur."

"Decatur, huh? Thank you."

I hung up, my pulse quickening. "There are a lot of suburbs around

Atlanta," I said, "so was it just a coincidence that Anderson lived in the town whose library computer generated the e-mail alerting me to Marsh LLC?"

Jock looked at me. "There are no coincidences, not in a case like this one. There are only a few people who know Doc hired you to look into his son's murder. Anderson is one of them."

He was using his fingers to tick off his points. "He lives in Decatur. He's Desmond's lawyer. He probably knows about Marsh LLC and the house in the Abacos. He's been a close friend of Doc's for many years. They've built a company together. He wouldn't do anything against Doc's interest unless he thought it was better for Doc if you knew about the house."

"The answers are in Marsh Harbour," I said. "Logan, you up for another trip to the islands?"

"Can I take my gun?"

"I think that'd be a good idea. I'll call Cassidy and let him know where we're going."

I called Bill Lester as I was walking out the door. "Bill, Jock and I are on our way to the Bahamas. We have a lead on J.D."

"Talk to me."

"We think she's safe and hiding out with some friends near Marsh Harbour."

"You think she's okay?"

"Yeah. She's with Doc Desmond."

"Okay. Keep me posted. I've found out something else that is very odd."

"What's up, Bill?"

"I followed up on the list of names you gave me. The Thanatos group. We know about Desmond, Brewster, and Fleming, but there were four more still alive. One of them owns a small garage in a town in North Dakota up by the Canadian border. His only son was shot to death a few months back. Another member of Team Charlie lives in Northern California. The sheriff there told me that there'd been no murders in the county in the last couple of years. I asked him if he knew the team member. He did. Then he told me that the guy's daughter, an army officer, was murdered in Charlottesville, Virginia last month."

"That pretty much seals it. Somebody is definitely targeting the children of the members of Team Charlie."

"There's more," the chief said. "The other two men and their families have disappeared."

"Shit. Are you sure?"

"Matt, J.D. had already talked to each of the cops I spoke to. They'd looked into this thing for her. They were kind of curious as to why I was calling them."

"When did J.D. talk to them?"

"Sunday. The day before she disappeared."

CHAPTER SIXTY-SEVEN

The islands lay like brown amoeba floating on an ocean of ever-changing hues. Dark blue over trenches, light green covering the sandbars and shallows, brown where the reefs poked toward the surface. Puffy clouds dotted the horizon, cotton candy daubed on a cerulean backdrop. A kaleidoscope of pastels imprinted on a tropical canvas. This was the Bahamas from twenty thousand feet, a country of seven hundred islands and twenty-five hundred islets and cays covering a hundred thousand square miles of Atlantic Ocean.

We landed at the Marsh Harbour Airport and checked in with the customs officer stationed there. Like most things in the Bahamas, the arrival procedures are relaxed and cursory. Logan had been apprehensive about bringing our weapons to the Bahamas, but Jack had assured him that the authorities were not likely to examine our bags. They didn't really care what we brought in as long as we paid the fees. Jock was right.

We showed the man our passports, paid the arrival fee in cash, got a signed document attesting to the fact that we'd cleared customs at a government port of entry, and were told to enjoy our stay. Our pilots were headed for a hotel they knew that catered to executive aircrews laying over while their bosses enjoyed whatever it was they did on the island.

Jock, Logan, and I retrieved our bags from the plane and took a taxi to a marina that rented boats. I'd made a reservation online before we left my house.

J.D.'s interest in the other dead children of Team Charlie members was another anomaly in our theory of what was going on. We'd only gotten the information on Team Charlie from the director that morning. How did J.D. find out about it before we did? How did she know to start making calls on Sunday? Did she have a source that she wasn't sharing with us? The facts just kept getting fuzzier. One minute I thought we were on the right track and the next minute the fog of doubt rolled in and obscured the picture that was taking shape in our minds. It was maddening, like a jigsaw puzzle that was beginning to come into focus and suddenly some of the pieces changed shape, causing me to rethink what I'd begun to accept as truth.

Our plan wasn't well formed. We were going to take our time surveilling Doc's house on the island, seeing what level of security he had in place. We were going to storm the property just after dark, rescue J.D., and get back to the plane. It wasn't much of a plan, as Jock pointed out. But we couldn't come up with anything better.

We were anchored about three hundred yards off the little island that contained the house Desmond had built. A dock ran out from the front of the place about sixty feet. Two go-fast boats, each at least thirty-five-feet long with big twin Yamaha outboards hanging off the transoms, were moored on either side.

We were decked out for fishing, large floppy hats covering our heads and shielding our faces, trying to look like three guys spending a day doing not much of anything. Our boat was a twenty-three-foot center-console Grady-White, a fishing platform. Jock, Logan, and I sat with rods and reels, casting now and then. I had a pair of binoculars and checked for activity at the house every few minutes. It was quiet.

Our guns were stored on the floor of the boat in the duffels we'd used to transport them. We had three M4 military assault rifles and three nine-millimeter Glock 19s. The bags also held camouflage paint, black clothing, and extra rounds for the weapons.

We were waiting for dark, hoping to get a better idea of what was on the island before we launched our attack. I didn't expect to see J.D., but I thought Doc might be roaming around, checking his security. Old habits don't die, and an old soldier in hiding would make sure he was secure.

The sunlight was fading when my cell phone vibrated in my pocket. I pulled it out and saw that the call was from a blocked number. I answered.

"Matt," J.D. said, "you guys come on up to the house."

"J.D.," I said, "are you all right?"

"I'm fine. Look at the dock, the one right in front of the house."

Shit. I held the phone away from my mouth, said in a whisper, "They're on to us."

"Matt," J.D. said, "I can hear you. I'm fine. I'm standing on the end of the dock. Bring the boat on in, and I'll help you with the lines."

I picked up the binoculars and looked toward the dock. J.D. was standing at the end of it. Alone. She was dressed in shorts and a golf shirt and seemed relaxed. If she was under duress, there was no sign of it. "She wants us to bring the boat to the dock."

"I don't think we have much choice," said Jock. "We sure as hell didn't surprise them."

"She looks okay," said Logan. "J.D. wouldn't let a little thing like the threat of getting shot make her throw us to the wolves."

Logan was right. J.D. would not let herself be used as bait. I put the phone to my mouth. "Okay. We're coming in."

I closed the phone. "Get the weapons out of the bags," I said. "Don't let them show above the gunwales. They've probably got glasses on us."

I used the windlass to raise the anchor, cranked the engine, and moved toward the dock. J.D. waved at us as we came closer. Jock and Logan were at the bow and stern with lines. I eased the boat into the dock and J.D. caught the bowline from Logan. Jock jumped off the stern and wrapped his line around a cleat. I shut down the engine and climbed off the boat.

J.D. hugged me and then Jock and Logan. She looked at the floorboard of the boat and smiled. "You won't need those," she said, pointing at the guns.

"What the hell is going on, J.D.?" I asked.

"Come up to the house. Doc's there with some other people you'll want to meet. He's got one heck of a story to tell you."

"How'd you know we were here? I thought these floppy hats would hide us."

She laughed. "I'd know you guys anywhere. Besides, Doc had a GPS beacon hidden on his plane. He could follow it on the Internet. We knew the plane had landed at the Marsh Harbour Airport, and we were pretty sure you were aboard. I thought you'd get my hints."

"I figured them out, but why? If you're here voluntarily, why didn't you just tell me that?"

"Come on up to the house. Doc will tell you everything."

I was a little steamed. She'd worried the hell out of me and now she was telling me that the hints as to her whereabouts were part of some kind of game. "I don't find any of this very amusing," I said.

She hugged me again, put her mouth to my ear, and whispered, "Matt, I'm so sorry to have worried you. It was necessary, and I knew you'd find me." She kissed me on the neck, just below my ear. "Thank you."

I was still a little pissed, but the kiss, the first one ever that was more than a friendly peck on the cheek, was quickly washing away my anger. I hugged her back. "I'm so glad you're okay," I said. "These have been the longest three days of my life."

"Come on. Let's go up to the house," she said and led the way.

CHAPTER SIXTY-EIGHT

The house was large and rambled over most of the little island. There was a tennis court on one side of the structure, a guesthouse on the other, and an infinity pool in the rear, the boat dock in the front. J.D. led us through the front door into a large entryway and on back to a great room overlooking the pool and Abaco Sound. The room was filled with middle-aged men. Doc was there and so was George Brewster, and to my astonishment, Paul Galis, a Key West detective I'd met the year before when I was trying to find my former wife's stepdaughter. There were four other men whom I'd never seen. Doc introduced them to me as Don Lemuel from North Dakota, Conrad Dixson from California, Ben Wright of Kentucky, and Harrison Fleming.

I'd brought the duffel containing the weapons with me. I didn't think leaving them on an open boat was a good idea. I set the bag on the floor.

"These are the remains of Team Charlie," said Doc. He looked at the group arrayed in a semicircle of stuffed chairs and two sofas. "I used to work for Matt, back when he was a Special Forces shave tail running our A team out of Camp Connor. He's tougher than he looks. He took a bullet in the leg and later a gut full of shrapnel while earning the Distinguished Service Cross, the army's second highest award for valor. He's also a lawyer, but he doesn't take it too seriously."

Doc pointed to Jock. "This has to be Jock Algren, a guy you don't want to know much about, but I'll vouch for him because Matt and J.D. do. I don't know this other gentleman."

"Logan Hamilton," I said. "A Vietnam airborne Ranger grunt who did a second tour flying helicopters. Owns a Silver Star. He's okay." I looked at Galis. "Good to see you, Paul."

"Same here, Matt."

I could see a visible relaxation on the faces of the men in the room. We'd passed the first test. We were soldiers who'd tasted combat and acquitted ourselves well. That made us part of the brotherhood.

I'd met Paul Galis in Key West and was aware that he'd been a Special Forces trooper in Vietnam toward the end of the war. We hadn't talked about his experiences there, because that's not what old soldiers do. Still, it was a shock to see him with this group.

"What's going on here, Doc?" I asked.

"This thing runs deep, Matt. It started coming to a head over the weekend, and I had to make some quick decisions. I left you out of the loop on purpose. You were part of my misdirection strategy."

"I'm not sure I like the sound of that," I said.

"Take a load off," said Doc, pointing to four empty chairs. "I'll rustle up some drinks. What do you want?"

We all ordered water and in a few minutes Doc returned with bottles for all of us. "Okay," he said. "Let me start with Team Charlie's last operation."

The story was as old as war, and as necessary. There have always been bands of assassins tasked with taking out the leadership of the opposing forces. The theory was that if the leaders were killed, chaos would ensue and the killers' side would have the advantage for at least a short time. Often that is all that's needed in battle. It was a good theory and had been a part of the American war machine since the Colonial sniper Timothy Murphy killed British General Simon Fraser in 1777, a death that led directly to the American victory at Saratoga.

"We were a band of killers," said Doc. "I don't think any of us would ever have robbed a bank or stolen a loaf of bread, because we saw ourselves as honorable men. But we believed that by killing the Viet Cong leadership, we were shortening the war and saving American lives."

Team Charlie had drawn from all the military special ops groups, Army Special Forces, Marine Force Recon, and Navy SEALs. There was a team leader and an assistant leader, both civilians, both Central Intelligence Agency operatives. The other ten men were military, and though they wore no rank insignia they were given the courtesies of noncommissioned officers.

The team had been operating for about six months without any losses. They'd hunted and killed Viet Cong leaders targeted by intelligence operatives sitting in Saigon. On the night when it all fell apart, they were sent to the village of Ban Touk near the Laotian border. The word came down that there was a meeting of high-level Viet Cong cadre and the commanders of North Vietnamese Army units hidden just across the border.

"It was the treasure trove," said Doc. "The plan was that we'd take out a lot of the enemy leadership, maybe wounding them so deeply that they'd head back north. But it didn't go that way."

The names of the CIA personnel assigned to Thanatos were kept secret. The operatives were known only by a nom de guerre, each one a gemstone. The Team Charlie leader, known to the men as Opal, issued the orders just before the operation began. The team was to surround the village and open fire on his order and then move in and set the huts on fire. Nobody was to leave there alive. That was important, he'd said. One hundred percent casualties. All dead. No exceptions.

The men crept through the dark. They were in heavily forested mountainous terrain, moving quietly, staying away from the trails that traversed the area, humping it through the woods, silent as the night. They came to the village, if you could call it that. It was just a cleared area with five or six huts, formed into a tight circle. An area of flat ground served as the centerpiece of the community. There were four black-pajama clad men standing around in front of the huts, shifting nervously from foot to foot, their rifles slung over their shoulders. Team Charlie fanned out, surrounding the small assemblage of huts and setting up intersecting lines of fire.

Opal, the team leader, ordered the men to open fire. The soldiers in the clearing were cut down immediately and the rifle and machine gun bullets began to cut into the huts, chopping them to splinters. No fire was returned. Not a single round.

"Get in there and fire those huts," Opal ordered.

The men moved in, one carrying a blowtorch. "What about documents?" he asked. "Shouldn't we check that out before we burn the place down?"

"No. Fire the fucking huts," said the leader. "Now."

The man with the torch, a Marine named Brewster, stopped over a dead VC soldier, shined a flashlight into his face. He shrugged and moved toward the second hut, blowtorch in one hand, rifle in the other, pointing ahead. He went to the door of the hut, used his rifle barrel to push aside a curtain, shined a flashlight inside. A foolhardy move, and one that surely would get him killed. Nothing happened.

"Doc," Brewster said, "look at this."

Desmond moved swiftly up behind the man, looked over his shoulder. Inside were women and children and two babies, all dead. He went to the shattered bodies to see if his medical skills could save any of them. They were all dead, killed by American bullets. The worst part was that they were gagged and tied to stakes driven into the ground. They could not have ducked had they tried. They were set up.

Brewster said, "Those guys out there in the black pajamas were about twelve years old. I don't think they were VC."

"What the fuck are you doing?" shouted Opal. He was standing in the door of the hut. "I told you to burn this fucking place."

"Look here, sir," said Doc, "these aren't VC or NVA. They're women and children. I'm going to check the other huts."

"No, you're not," said the leader. He was pointing his rifle at Doc. "I'll blow your fucking head off if you don't follow orders."

"Sir," said Doc, "do you hear what I'm telling you? There are no bad guys. We just killed a bunch of innocent people."

"They're fucking gooks, Desmond. It doesn't matter."

"You knew, didn't you?" asked Doc.

"This is war, Desmond. Sometimes there's collateral damage."

"When did you know?"

"All along. We think the men from the village are being held across the river. But if we hadn't attacked, we'd have blown our source. If the VC knew that we knew about there being only women and children here, we'd have lost valuable intelligence."

"And the VC guards?" asked Brewster.

"Kids from this village. They were told to act like guards. If they didn't, their families would be killed."

"Why didn't you say anything to us?" asked Doc.

"If you'd known would you have come on the mission?"

"Hell, no."

"There you have it, soldier," said Opal, a hard edge to his voice, his rifle still pointing at Doc. "You follow your fucking orders now and fire up this place."

"I have a question," said Brewster.

"What?"

"Did Topaz know about this?"

"Of course. He's the assistant team leader. If I couldn't have led tonight, he would have."

Brewster shot the leader through the chest. "Oops. More collateral damage," he said and walked out of the hut. Doc didn't bother to check the leader's pulse. If he wasn't dead, he would be soon, and that was good enough for now. He followed Brewster out into the clearing. The other men had heard the exchange and were just standing there, numbed by what they'd learned. They were soldiers, not murderers.

"Where's Opal?" asked the assistant leader.

"Dead," said Doc.

"You killed him?" Panic rode his voice. "You murdering bastard."

"You knew there was nothing here, just women and children waiting to be slaughtered," said Doc. "We just committed a war crime. At your orders. With your full knowledge of what we were doing."

"It was necessary," said Topaz. "This is war."

"No," said Brewster, "this is murder."

"Well, fuck you, Brewster," said Topaz. "Your ass will be in a sling when we get back."

"You're not going back," said Doc.

"What?" a hint of fear brought a quiver to Topaz's voice.

"I think you're about to be killed in the line of duty."

"Hey, wait a fucking minute." Topaz started backing up, hands in front of him. Doc looked at the other men, one at a time. Each one nodded. Once. Each raised his rifle. Pointed it at the assistant. Doc and Brewster joined them.

"No," screamed Topaz. "You can't do this."

Doc nodded. The men fired one volley, killing the assistant team leader with ten bullets.

Doc sat quietly, drained by the story and the memory. "I've never told this tale to anyone. I could still be prosecuted for murder, I guess, but it was the right thing to do. At least that's what I've always told myself."

"What happened after you left the bush?" I asked.

"We all swore an oath of secrecy. Never tell anybody what happened. If one of us went down, we'd all go down. We got back to base camp and reported that we'd run into an unexpected firefight. Opal and Topaz were in the lead and were killed by the first shots fired from ambush. The brass didn't believe us, and we were interrogated by CIA types, over and over for the next week. We all stuck to our story, so there was nothing they could do. They knew we were lying, because they knew what the operation was really about. But they couldn't break any of us."

"What happened to the bodies?" I asked.

"We put Opal and the Topaz in one of the huts with the other bodies. A night wind was blowing and it fueled the fire. They went up very quickly. We told the CIA that we'd been unable to recover their bodies after the firefight, but that we'd carried out our mission. None of those guys were about to hump back into the bush to check out that village. They knew, but they couldn't prove a damn thing."

Jock said, "My agency sent me a list of the team members the director got from somewhere in the bowels of our intelligence network. I didn't bother to follow up on the dead team members. Doc, do you know who they were?" He handed the list to Doc.

"I knew the three who died after they came home. They were good men. The two you show as killed in Vietnam were obviously the team leaders, Opal and Topaz."

"You never had any idea of who they really were?" Jock asked.

"No. We knew they were CIA. That's all. When we weren't in the field, they disappeared. I always assumed they went back to Saigon to report in and enjoy a little time at the officer's club."

"We need to find their names," said Jock. "Once we know who they are, I may be able to backtrack and find out who their friends were and if any of those friends still work for the CIA. It's a start, but it may take a while."

"I don't think we have that kind of time," said Doc.

"What about the teams?" asked Logan. "What happened to them?"

"They were all disbanded, I think. Team Charlie sure was. We were sent home and discharged within a week of the operation. We had to sign a lot of paperwork swearing ourselves to secrecy about the whole Thanatos thing. As far as I know, not one of us ever talked about it, and not one of us has had any contact with any of the other team members. Not until last weekend, anyway."

CHAPTER SIXTY-NINE

On Saturday afternoon, Doc had been playing golf in Atlanta with the manager of his Birmingham office. The manager happened to mention that a friend of his in Birmingham had lost a twenty-year-old son a couple of weeks ago. Shot to death in the parking lot of a bar. By a sniper. Said his friend was a prominent lawyer and wondered if Doc knew him. Harrison Fleming. Doc lied and told him he didn't know the man.

Doc, of course, knew Fleming, a member of the team, a man he hadn't seen since he left Vietnam. He thought it too big a coincidence that two members of Team Charlie had lost sons to snipers in the space of a couple of months. He needed to talk to Fleming, see if any of the other team members were in danger.

Doc was concerned that somehow the past was coming back to exact vengeance. He didn't know who the perpetrators were or why they would kill the team members' children rather than the members themselves. But the CIA has a long memory, and the teams had been run by young men. Their friends would now be in the upper echelons of the agency and maybe they'd decided to seek revenge. Take care of the team members who'd killed their buddies. Maybe the children were just the first casualties.

Before the team had been split up and sent home, the men had agreed not to seek each other out except in a dire emergency. In that case, they had a code phrase that would immediately alert the members: Opal is on the move.

Doc called Fleming at home on Saturday evening. When the phone was answered, he heard party noises, soft music, the hum of conversation, distant laughter. "Flem, this is Doc. Opal is on the move. Go to a pay phone and call this number." The number was assigned to a disposable cell phone Desmond had bought months earlier.

Ten minutes later it rang. "Doc, you okay?"

"I'm fine, Flem. I heard about your boy. I'm sorry. My son was killed by a sniper on a beach in Florida a couple of months ago."

"Geez, I'm sorry, man."

"Thanks. I don't think their deaths are a coincidence. I'm not sure what's going down, but it's probably connected to the teams. Can you get your family to safety? Tonight? To a place nobody would think to look?"

"Yes. There're all at my house for my other son's birthday. I can have them gone in an hour. My son-in-law's family has a home in Colorado. Lots of security. They can go there."

"Good. Get them moving, by car preferably. Airline tickets are too easy to follow-up on. Can you borrow a car from somebody?"

Fleming knew not to waste time asking questions. They weren't needed. The directions would come. "Sure. My next door neighbor."

"I want you to drive to the Chattanooga Airport. Park the car in the long-term lot, and walk across to the general aviation area. You'll see a Cessna 172 parked on the ramp nearest the parking lot. A man will be standing by the plane wearing a red T-shirt with a Sloppy Joe's Bar logo and a ball cap with the Tampa Bay Rays logo. His name is Tom Telson. He'll fly you to the Charlie Brown Airport in Atlanta and put you in a hotel near the airport. He'll use a credit card with the name of a company I own but nobody knows about. Don't give out your real name. Don't use your credit card. Don't call anybody. Don't tell even your family where you are. I'll be in touch."

It was getting late, close to ten, but Doc had one more call to make. Detective J. D. Duncan.

CHAPTER SEVENTY

"Jock," Doc said, "I owe you an apology."

"For what?" Jock asked.

"I knew from the memos Matt was sending me that you were helping out with the investigation. I checked up on you, but could only find out that you worked for an oil company and had ties to some innocuous federal agency. I knew those are often covers for CIA operations. I was concerned that you might be one of those guys."

Jock grinned. "Now you *have* insulted me. Accusing me of being CIA."

"Yeah. J.D. straightened me out on the way over here."

"Apology accepted, Doc."

"I called J.D. late Saturday night," Doc said. "Told her what I thought was going down, but that I needed her police credentials to check up on the other team members. I had always kept their names and addresses current in case anything like this popped up." He looked at me. "I told her not to call you."

"Why, Doc?" I asked. "I thought we were in this together."

"I was afraid that somebody was tracking us pretty closely. I didn't want to tip them off if you were somehow being watched. Besides, if they thought you were going about business as usual, they wouldn't be too worried about what I was doing. And I didn't want Jock to know."

"And what were you planning to do?" I asked.

"Disappear. J.D. didn't want to do anything without your okay. I didn't tell her I didn't trust Jock, but I finally convinced her that if she got in touch with you about any of this, it would put your life in danger."

J.D. said, "Matt, I was afraid that any direct contact with you after I left on Monday morning could lead somebody to us or put you in more danger. That's why I used the rather cryptic messages on the e-mail."

"Doc," I said, "I think your lawyer Anderson sent me an e-mail that led me to the ownership of this house."

"He did, at my request. If that e-mail had been intercepted, I don't think anybody would have traced it to me or even thought it had anything to do with me."

"What makes you think somebody was tracking us?" I asked.

"I got to thinking about the attempts on your life. Both came right after you'd made a connection to the Laotians. The first attempt happened the day after you initially met with Stanley in Macon, and the second the day after you connected the Asians to the *Dulcimer* and the murders of Katherine Brewster and the lawyer from Jacksonville.

"I didn't connect Brew's daughter to the *Dulcimer* murders," Doc continued, "until after I heard about Flem's son. Then it hit me in the face. The connection between somebody trying to kill you and your discoveries about the Asians and the link to Soupy in Laos. Add to that the fact that the murder attempts didn't seem too professional, and I thought they might be some sort of misdirection."

"They seemed real enough to me," I said.

"Think about it," said Jock. "The first guy used a knife when he could have shot you. The beach was deserted, no one around. It never quite made sense to me that the guy didn't use a gun. And that idiot Clyde Bates would be the last person a professional would hire to take you out."

J.D. chimed in. "If we're dealing with the CIA and they thought you were chasing Laotians, it'd be in their interest to keep up the charade. The only thing tying the Longboat murders to Soupy was the fact that Asians were aboard *Dulcimer* at the time of the murders, and we thought there might be a connection to Soupy because of his fight with Jim Desmond. We didn't know about the Thanatos connection."

I nodded. "Okay. But what about Stanley?"

"We got off on a tangent," said J.D. "Stanley was dirty, but not because he was involved with the killings. He was just a dope pusher who'd had some connection to two of the victims. There are such things as coincidences, whether you believe in them or not." She smiled.

"Then why were you on their payroll?" I asked.

"What? Whose payroll?"

I laughed. "Okay. I know you're not, but somebody went to a lot of trouble to convince us you were playing footsy with Stanley." I told them the story of the bank accounts and what we'd found out.

J.D. sat back in her chair, a look of consternation on her face. "Does Chief Lester think I'm taking bribes?"

"He doesn't know about the bank account," I said.

"You didn't tell him?"

"No."

"Matt, he needs to know."

"Why? You didn't do anything wrong."

"But suppose I had? Bill Lester is a good cop. He wouldn't let this slide."

"That's exactly why I didn't tell him."

"Call him, Matt. Now. Bring him up to date."

"Okay," I said. "I'll call him tonight."

She frowned. "Why in the world would someone go to all that trouble to implicate me?"

"More misdirection," said Logan. "It'd be no big deal for the CIA to tap into the computers at the Otto Foundation and their bank. They could have set up the whole thing so that it looked as if Nigella was receiving money into that account for months. Then, suddenly the money started going to the Sarasota bank and J.D. was withdrawing it. They just added J.D.'s Social Security number to the mix to make it seem more authentic."

I shook my head. "But that would presuppose they knew that we'd get into Stanley's computers and follow up on the bank's."

"No big deal," said Logan. "They'd pointed you at Stanley and could guess that you and Jock would follow up and stumble across the drugs and the accounts. The CIA, or whoever, must have known that you knew about Stanley being Bracewell."

"I don't see how anybody could have picked up on that information," I said. "It was kept pretty close. Just the memos to J.D. and Doc and to my own file."

"Maybe they hacked into your computer," said Logan.

"I think I can explain it," said Doc. "My office computers had been compromised. Somebody set them up so that everything was being mirrored on an off-site computer."

"I'm not sure I understand," I said.

"A month or so ago we upgraded our entire system. An outside vendor came in and spent a couple of weeks reworking things. I think one of their people fixed our system so that anything that was on it was being seen on another computer somewhere else in the world. All my e-mails would have been intercepted."

"Including the memos I sent you."

"Right. I didn't think about that until Saturday afternoon late. I rousted our IT guy and had him check out the system. He spent all night working on it and found the back door or whatever the hell they call those things. He couldn't track where the signal was going. I figured it had to be CIA."

"Can you trust your IT guy?" asked Jock.

"Yes. He's been with me from the beginning. He'll keep quiet about what he found."

"So," said Logan, "the CIA or whoever was reading your memos, Matt."

"I don't believe it's the CIA," said Jock. "There may be a rogue element that's involved, but the agency itself wouldn't take a chance on getting caught up in something like this."

"And," I asked, "who are the Asians we keep bumping into?"

"There're only five of them that we know about," said Jock. "The guy whose elbow you broke, the woman he was with, and the guy who hired Bates to kill Matt. The three of them were aboard *Dulcimer* the night of the murders. The fourth one is the guy who held a shotgun on us at Stanley's house in Macon, and of course, there's Nigella Morrissey. Nigella's Vietnamese and the guy at Stanley's house spoke Vietnamese. Maybe the other three are Vietnamese, too."

"Vietnamese working for the CIA?" I asked.

"The four that anybody heard speak English, including Nigella, are probably American born or at least have been here most of their lives," said Jock. "Maybe they've been recruited by some rogues in the agency."

"Or maybe," said Logan, "this is personal."

"What do you mean?" asked J.D.

"Maybe the ghosts of Ban Touk are coming home to roost," Logan said.

I thought he might be right. Avenging angels riding a dark wind blowing from the village. A wind not unlike the one that fueled the fire and consumed the dead on that fateful night so many years before.

CHAPTER SEVENTY-ONE

Dinner was a simple affair. Doc had a large grill built into his patio, a summer kitchen I think it's called. He grilled fresh grouper steaks for eleven; Jock, Logan, J.D., me, and the seven surviving members of Team Charlie. Harrison Fleming tossed the salad and heated the bread in the built-in electric oven. The wind was up so the small bugs that like to bite were kept away. We ate the steaks, salad, and bread and drank some very good wine around a big table next to the pool, overlooking the clear water of the sound. We talked of things of little importance, putting off the serious stuff, as if by agreement, until we finished dinner.

Doc cleared the plates and stashed them in a dishwasher under the counter. He brought more wine from the interior of the house, and we settled in for an evening of decision. We were stumped as to who was after us and what we could do to protect ourselves and the families of the team members.

I learned some more about how we ended up at this house in the Bahamas. On Sunday, J.D. had made the calls to police officials in all the towns where the surviving members lived, working from the list Doc had given her the night before. She discovered the deaths of Don Lemuel's son in North Dakota and Conrad Dixson's daughter on the campus of the University of Virginia. Neither Galis nor Wright, who lived in Kentucky, had suffered a loss.

J.D. called Doc before noon and gave him the information she'd found. Doc called each of the team members and using the code told them of the danger. Each of them had contingency arrangements in case something like this happened. They sent their families to the prearranged places and started making their way to Fort Lauderdale.

Doc had remembered Telson and called him at home on Saturday afternoon when things started coming apart. He told him he'd like to hire him for a few days to do some top-secret work. The work involved his company and secrecy was of the utmost importance. The job would involve flying, perhaps out of the country, but Doc couldn't tell him anything else. The pay was equal to what Telson would earn in six months working regularly.

Telson had rented an executive jet in his name, telling the owners that he had a copilot lined up to help him fly the craft. He lied, but since he was paying cash and had all the proper licenses and certificates from the Federal Aviation Administration, they let him have the plane. Doc didn't think anyone would ever connect him to Telson since their dealings had in the past always been through the company Telson worked for.

On Sunday, Telson flew the jet he had rented to Lexington, Kentucky, where he picked up Ben Wright. From there they went to North Dakota, to the airport at Minot and picked up Don Lemuel. Then to Charlotte to fetch George Brewster and back to Atlanta. It was late in the afternoon by the time they parked the plane on the tarmac at Charlie Brown Airport. Wright, Brewster, and Lemuel were put in separate hotels and told they'd be contacted by Doc later in the evening.

Conrad Dixson came by a more circuitous route. He left his home in Northern California on Saturday evening and took a bus to Medford, Oregon, paying cash. At the bus station in Medford he caught a cab to the airport where he checked into the private terminal using a false name. He was met by a man wearing a uniform of black trousers and a white short-sleeve dress shirt with the four stripes of a captain on his epaulets. "I understand we're going to Fort Lauderdale," the captain said.

"That's right," said Dixson.

"Okay, sir. My name's Miller. My copilot's name is Nick. We're ready to go."

They walked to a small jet, the cabin constructed for groups of only three or four executives. "We'll have to refuel in Denver and again in Memphis, but we'll have you there by about ten in the morning Eastern time."

The plane had been chartered by Doc using one of his many companies, one that hopefully wouldn't be traced to him.

Paul Galis had driven to Fort Lauderdale from Key West in his assigned unmarked police cruiser. He told his boss he was going to Miami to investigate a case he was working on.

Each of the men was staying at different hotels under assumed names.

Early on Monday morning, Telson picked up the team members stashed in the Atlanta hotels and took them to Charlie Brown Airport. Doc was there, waiting with the plane. The greetings were effusive, lots of hugging and backslapping. Old soldiers returning to the fray.

They flew directly to Sarasota, and Doc asked Telson to rent a car and go to the nearest convenience store and buy a disposable cell phone. When Telson returned, Doc drove to Longboat Key to J.D.'s condo. It was a little after six and J.D. was up, preparing to report to work at seven. She was surprised to see Doc at her door and concerned about the urgency in his demeanor. She invited him into the condo.

"We've got to get you out of here. Right now," he said.

"What's going on, Mr. Desmond?"

"Call me Chaz or Doc. Did Matt fill you in on Thanatos?"

"Thanatos?"

"It was a top-secret operation near the end of the Vietnam war. Teams were set up with twelve men each. Their only job was to assassinate enemy leaders."

"Okay. Can't say I'm surprised."

"I was on one of those teams. So were the three men whose children were killed recently. The ones you found out about yesterday. All the names on the list I gave you were part of a Thanatos team."

"What's your connection?"

"I was on the same team."

"I thought you were one of Matt's men."

"I was. But after Matt got wounded the first time, I volunteered for Thanatos. It's a long story and I'll tell you later."

"Why do we have to leave?"

"I found out last night that my computers have been compromised. I think all my e-mail is being read by somebody who is killing our children. The memos Matt sent had your name all over them."

"I still don't see what this has got to do with my going with you."

"If I'd thought about it the way I should have on Saturday, I wouldn't have asked you to make those calls. I'm beginning to think the CIA is involved in this."

"You're crazy, Doc. Are you seeing boogie men under the bed, too?"

"I know that sounds a little nuts. But Thanatos was a CIA operation, and we killed the two CIA men who were assigned to our teams. I think it's time for a little revenge."

"This is too much," said J.D. "I still don't see how I'm involved."

"If the CIA is involved, they've got very sophisticated methods to track the team members. I'm afraid I've put you in the crosshairs by asking you to follow up on the murders."

"Let me call Matt."

"No. You can't do that."

"If I'm in danger, so is he."

"He can take care of himself."

"So can I. Either I talk to Matt, or I'm staying right here."

Doc pulled a pistol, pointed it at J.D. "I'm sorry about this. But you're going with me."

J.D.'s belt with pistol, mace, stun gun, and cuffs was resting over the back of the sofa. Doc got her cuffs, threw them to J.D. and said, "Put these on. Hands in front."

"No way. You won't shoot me. That'd defeat your purpose. You tell me you're trying to get me out of harm's way, yet you'd shoot me? Doesn't make any sense at all."

"Then I'll make a phone call and have a very good marksman kill Matt."

J.D. held out her hand. "Cuff me. This isn't over. Not by a long shot."

Doc cuffed her hands, pulled off his jacket, and placed it over the cuffs. They took the elevator to the first floor where Telson had pulled the rental car near the door. They got in and headed for the airport. They rode in silence, J.D. seething with anger, and Doc troubled by what he'd done to her.

At the plane Doc introduced her to Wright, Lemuel, Fleming, and Brewster. "I'm going to take the cuffs off now. You're free to go, but I'd like you to listen to these men before you make that decision."

"You bastard. You threatened to kill Matt Royal."

"I would never do that, J.D. Not in a million years. I owe him my life."

"I thought it was the other way around. He told me about you taking him out of a fight when he got wounded."

"He probably didn't tell you about the times he pulled my ass out of trouble."

"No."

"Twice. One time he pulled me out of a ditch while he was taking direct fire from a sniper. Matt would probably have been killed if Jimbo Merryman hadn't gotten the sniper. And I would have been dead meat if Matt hadn't come to get me and drawn the sniper's attention. Another time I was pinned down by four NVA regulars and was about out of ammo. Matt came in with his M16 on full automatic, threw a couple of grenades, and hauled me out of there. No, ma'am. I'd never hurt Matt Royal."

J.D. turned to the other men. "I'm listening," she said.

And when they finished with their stories of the grief they felt at losing their children and the fear they had for the surviving members of their families, J.D. was convinced she could be of more help going with them than she could staying on Longboat Key.

On the short flight to Fort Lauderdale, Doc told J.D. of his fears of Jock's ties to the CIA. She told him that he was wrong, that Jock worked for another agency entirely, and that Matt was the closest thing he had to family. "Jock would die for Matt," said J.D. "And Matt would die for Jock. It's that simple. The fact that you saved Matt's life means that you're forever on Jock's short list of people he'd die for. And I think he'd be the hardest person in the world to kill."

"We're taking a boat from Lauderdale to Abaco," said Doc. "When we get on the boat and are safely on our way, you call Matt and let him know you're okay."

"Thanks, Doc. I'll feel better not having him worried."

They landed in Lauderdale at a little after nine in the morning. Telson rented another car and went to the hotels to pick up the remaining members of the team. They all met in a suite Doc had rented at a large hotel with a marina. The suite was in Telson's name. Doc and Telson went to buy a boat identical to the one Doc kept at his house in the Bahamas. Doc paid cash and put the title in Telson's name. Doc drove the boat back to the marina and moored it at one of the docks.

Shortly after two in the afternoon Doc eased the boat out of its slip, fully loaded with the six other survivors of Team Charlie and Detective J.D. Duncan. They idled under the Seventeenth Street Bridge, passed Port Everglades, and turned east to transit the inlet. The sun was high and hot, the seas calm, not even a breeze to ripple the surface. Doc put the powerful boat on plane and headed for the Bahamas.

CHAPTER SEVENTY-TWO

The evening was winding down. The plates had been cleared, the last of the wine drunk. The men were reminiscing about their tour with Team Charlie, telling stories of the good times, the days when they had stood down and weren't hunting and killing the enemy, remembering the drinking bouts when they tried to wash away the reality of what they did for a living. Laughing, ribbing each other about real or imagined foibles, never touching on the killing and what it did to them.

Jock and Logan were standing with a small group of the old soldiers, involved in their memories. I sat on the sofa, the voices swirling around me. I was sipping a beer, my first and only one of the evening. J.D. sat in a chair next to me, immobile, quiet, pensive, an empty wine glass in her hand. It had been a tough three days for her.

I was still a bit unsettled. The solutions to our puzzle seemed a little too pat, too tidy. If the Asians involved were Vietnamese and were somehow tied to the destroyed village, where did Nigella fit into the picture? She was clearly working with Stanley, and if our discovery of his operation was merely a misdirection ploy and not part of an overall plan of retribution by the survivors of Ban Touk, what was a Vietnamese woman doing with Stanley?

Then there was the Evermore Foundation. I wanted to get Doc alone before I raised that issue. Why was he funneling money to a man in Vietnam who happened to have a name very similar to the man who set up the second attempt on my life? What was the connection?

Doc's theory that the attempts to kill me were not serious rang true, but could that be because Doc was behind them? If so, why? Why would he ask me to look into the murder of his son and then try to scare me off? It didn't make sense.

Was this meeting on a Bahamian island with the members of Team Charlie, the secrecy surrounding it, and the disappearance of J.D. from Longboat Key all another misdirection ploy? Was Doc somehow involved in the murders, in the drug trade? Where did his start-up money come from, the cash he used to buy up engineering firms in half the states of the country? Was his approach to me just part of an effort to steer any investigation away from him? Maybe he hadn't counted on my relationship with Jock and Jock's ability to see through layers of obfuscation because of his ties to the intelligence community.

But then, as far as I knew, there was no investigation targeting Doc. He'd come to me because his son had been murdered and the law couldn't find the killer. If he had pointed me at Stanley's group it didn't make sense that Doc was part of it. Maybe Doc was involved in another drug smuggling group and he wanted me to disrupt Stanley's outfit.

And why had someone pointed me toward J.D.? Why the attempt to make it appear she was part of the conspiracy involving Stanley's group? The puzzle was getting more out of focus, the pieces dissolving into different shapes, refusing to fit together. I could not see through the fog of deception that had been surrounding me for days.

The old soldiers were tired. It had been a long day of planning, thinking, and, in some cases, grieving. They were milling about the room, finishing their drinks, saying good night. J.D. was still sitting in her chair, staring at me. "What?" I asked.

"Nothing," she said. "I was just thinking about you as Sir Galahad, rushing off to rescue me."

I laughed. "You don't need rescuing. I knew you could take care of yourself."

"Probably, but I'm glad you came."

"You're not going to make a habit of this are you? Disappearing, I mean."

"Are you afraid you wouldn't be able to find me?"

"Yeah. I'd miss you."

She looked at me for a moment, quietly. There was a seriousness about her that I had seldom seen. "I'd miss you too, Matt," she said and rose from the chair. She came and sat on the sofa next to me.

I was only sure of my friends, J.D., Logan, and Jock. I looked around and realized that other than those three, I could not trust anyone in the room. It was a sobering thought, and one that raised the hairs along the back of my neck, sending a tingle through my brain, a warning that all was not as it seemed, and that my friends and I needed to be very careful.

I leaned into J.D., whispered, "I want you to sleep with me tonight."

She drew back, a shocked expression on her face. "Matthew," she said.

I chuckled. "Let me rephrase that. I want you to sleep in the same room with me tonight. There are two beds in there. I've already told Jock and Logan to bunk in together as well. I'm not sure I trust these guys, and it'd be better if we stick together."

She smiled. "Well, shoot," she said. "I thought maybe you were just getting a little frisky."

"And if I were?"

She was quiet for a moment, staring at me. "I couldn't settle for just frisky."

I felt a lurch in my chest, down where my heart is. She was opening a door, I thought, a door to a relationship. Maybe. But now was not the time to explore it. "I couldn't either," I said. I looked at her for a beat, smiled, and left the sofa.

I pulled Jock out of the group he was chatting with, got him out of earshot. "We need to find out the names of the two CIA guys Team Charlie killed, Opal and Topaz."

Jock looked at his watch. "It's late. I doubt the night-shift wonks can pull anything for me."

"What if the director lit a fire under them?"

"That'd get the job done. Is it that important?"

"I think so. If there are men in the CIA who've gone rogue and are pursuing this, we may be able to backtrack and find out who Opal and Topaz were buddies with in Saigon."

"I'll call him, but I have a question."

"Okay," I said.

"Why do I have to sleep in the room with Logan while you get J.D.?"

"Because I'm the guy making the room assignments and Logan snores. A lot."

Jock grinned and went to make his phone call. I walked out to the patio in search of Doc. I found him talking to Fleming. "Excuse me, Flem," I said, "but could I have a word with Doc?"

"Sure," said Fleming. "I'm on my way to bed. See you guys in the morning."

"Doc," I said when Fleming had gone, "tell me about the Evermore Foundation."

I saw his face change, a look of surprise crossing it. He was silent for a moment, then shrugged his shoulders. "Not much to tell, really. I set up the foundation to funnel money to the survivors of Ban Touk."

"Explain it to me."

"Several years ago, I began to make more money than I'd ever dreamed of. I didn't just want to spend it on bigger and bigger houses and cars. I'd never been able to get those dead women and children out of my mind, the Ban Touk people. I assumed that some villagers had survived, mostly the men who had been taken into Laos by the people who set us up.

"I began to make inquiries. I wanted to see if I could find any of those who might still be alive. I hired a lawyer in Ho Chi Minh City, using a false identity. He came highly recommended by a couple of the executives in a company I'd recently acquired. They'd been involved in some infrastructure projects in Vietnam and had used this guy."

"What was his name? The lawyer in Ho Chi Minh City."

"Tuan Nguyen."

"What did you tell him?"

"Just that I was aware of a massacre that had taken place at Ban Touk and I wanted to see if any of the people were still alive."

"And?"

"This lawyer had some sources in the Vietnamese intelligence agency. He found some of the records concerning the massacre. They didn't say that it'd been set up by the North Vietnamese and Viet Cong, only that some Americans had killed all the women and children. Many of the men from Ban Touk were still alive, and Nguyen found some of them still living in the same area where the village had been. They had rebuilt and started new families. A few of the women and children of the village had survived, those who were somewhere else when the men were moved into Laos. None of these people knew that their families had been staked out like goats for the slaughter. They just knew the Americans killed their families."

"Why did you want to remain anonymous? You were doing a good thing."

"The only reason I would even know about the massacre was if I was there. It was never made public. I didn't want anyone to tie me to it, so I set up the foundation with a couple of layers of insulation. I'm surprised you figured it out."

"Jock can do wonders."

"I guess."

"You've been putting two hundred thousand dollars a year into the foundation until this year, when you didn't pay into it until after Jim was killed. Then you put in an extra hundred thousand. Why?"

Doc massaged his forehead, taking a minute to think. "I just didn't have the money in the spring. I had bought two more engineering concerns and it took all my cash. I knew a big influx of money was only a couple of months away, so I e-mailed Nguyen and told him the foundation would not be able to make the donation in April as usual, but that a larger donation would be sent during the summer."

"What does Nguyen use the money for?"

"He gets a small percentage as a fee, but the rest of the money is doled out for all kinds of things the villagers need. Generators for electricity, wells for running water, sewage disposal, and scholarships for the village kids. Just enough to help out, but not enough to sap their work ethic."

"Are you sure Nguyen is using the money like you want?"

"Yes. The foundation gets copies of all checks and I have an accountant in Ho Chi Minh City who follows up and makes sure the money is being used properly."

"Doc, I hope this is on the up-and-up," I said.

"It is. My way of giving back something to those I took so much from."

A low buzzing sound filled the room. The men were instantly alert, all movement stopped. "We've got visitors," said Doc. "That's the perimeter alarm. Grab your weapons."

CHAPTER SEVENTY-THREE

The men moved quickly, their age not slowing their soldier reflexes by much. They picked up rifles that were stacked in a corner of the great room. I hadn't noticed them before because a tapestry was draped over them, giving the appearance of just another piece of furniture. I unzipped the duffel and passed the M4s and Glocks to Jock and Logan.

The men and J.D. moved to prearranged positions. Apparently they'd planned for this before we got to the island.

"What's going on?" I asked.

Doc picked up the TV remote control and pointed at the large flat-screen monitor hanging on the wall at the end of the room. Pictures came up, greenish looking squares covering the screen. "Those are the security cameras operating with night-vision technology," Doc said. "Each screen covers a quadrant of our little island. They overlap so we don't have any blind spots. If the intruders get closer, they'll cross the next line of defense and a siren will go off and floodlights will come up."

"What do you want us to do?" Jock asked.

"Sit tight for now. We've got all the lines of fire covered. If we need to shoot, we're in good shape."

Nothing moved on the screen. Maybe it was some kind of animal, an innocent incursion. Then I saw movement, a man crawling up from the beach. He was wearing black and in the eerie glow of the night-vision lenses, it looked like neoprene. A wet suit. He must have swum in and now was moving quietly toward the house. I pointed him out to Doc.

"I see him," said Doc. "Everybody stay quiet. There's only one man. Somebody is probing our defenses. Let's not give anything away."

We watched for a couple more minutes as the man made his way closer to the house. The old soldiers stood quietly, positions manned, rifles at the ready. It was the infantryman's lot. Hurry up and wait. The fire discipline ingrained in them so many years before was still there. They watched the man on the beach come onto the lawn slithering through the grass.

"We need to find out who he is," said Jock.

Doc nodded. "He's getting close to the point that sets off the lights and siren."

"I'll go," said Jock. "I don't want the alarms to spook him."

"Want company?" I asked.

"No. Better if I go alone." He moved to the door on the opposite side of the house from where the intruder was working his way toward us. He pulled a black windbreaker from a peg at the entrance, put it on over his jeans and white shirt, zipped it to his chin, and let himself quietly out the door.

I turned back to the TV monitor. The intruder was still making his way slowly toward the house. Moments passed. The room was quiet, all attention focused on the man in the wet suit. He was crawling toward a depression in the lawn, a swale, used to direct excess rainwater toward the sea. He had just reached the lip of the swale when an arm reached out and encircled the man's throat. He was pulled violently into the depression, Jock's forearm never leaving his throat. Within seconds the intruder went limp. Dead? Knowing Jock, I doubted it. He'd want information.

Jock hoisted the limp body onto his shoulders in a fireman's carry and walked toward the house. Doc went to the nearest door and let him in. Jock brought the man to one of the sofas and tossed him like so much linguine onto the cushions. I got a look at the intruders face. He was Caucasian. I was surprised that he wasn't Asian.

"He'll wake up in a few minutes," said Jock.

"He's not Vietnamese, that's for sure," said Fleming. "Any ID on him?"

Jock ran his hands over the wet suit. "Nothing but a cell phone in a waterproof bag."

"Let me see that," said J.D. Jock handed it to her. She opened the phone and pushed a couple of buttons, looked closely and said, "This is probably a disposable phone. There's only one number programmed into it and that's on speed dial."

The intruder was stirring on the sofa, his eyes open and trying to focus. Jock slapped him gently in the face, once, twice. The man shook his head and then his eyes focused on the armed men in the room.

"Who are you?" asked Jock.

The man just stared, lips pressed tightly together, and shook his head.

"Do you speak English?" Jock asked.

The man shook his head again.

Jock turned to Doc. "Take this piece of shit out back and shoot him. He can't help us."

Doc reached for the intruder's arm. The man shook him off, sat up. "Wait," he said. "I speak English." There was a slight hint of the islands in his voice, the way that many of the white Bahamians speak, more American than Caribbean, but distinctive.

"What are you doing crawling around on my island in the dark?" asked Doc.

"Can't tell you that," the man said.

Jock put a nine-millimeter pistol to the guy's forehead, right in the middle, just inches above the bridge of his nose. "I'm going to ask you some questions, dipshit, and you're going to answer them or I'm going to kill you where you sit."

"That wouldn't be very smart," said the intruder.

Jock laughed. "Smart or dumb, you're still dead."

"I'm an officer in the Bahamian Defense Force," he said. "My people are waiting for me to call," he said. "If they don't hear from me," he paused, looked at the large chronometer on his wrist, "in ten minutes, they're going to storm this island with heavy weapons. One of our boats is just offshore."

"Yeah," said Jock, "and I'm Captain Kirk of the *Starship Enterprise.*"

The man on the sofa stared at Jock. He wasn't afraid, or if he was, he didn't show it. "You guys don't want to get into this. Running drugs is one thing. Killing a Bahamian military officer is a much bigger deal. You won't leave this island alive."

Jock removed the pistol from the man's forehead. "Drugs?" he asked. "You think we're running drugs?"

J.D. stepped in front of the man, holding her ID case so that he could see. "I'm a detective in Longboat Key, Florida. What makes you think we're running drugs?"

"A boatload of men comes into our country without clearing customs and ends up on this island. A couple of days later a private jet lands at our airport and clears customs. But they don't declare a large duffel bag that could hold weapons. An airport worker sees them sneaking the duffel off the plane. They rent a boat and come to the same island where the people on the boat landed. What would you think, Detective?"

"A fair assumption," J.D. said. "How do we verify your identity?"

"Call Chief Constable Bram Gilmore at the Marsh Harbour police station. He's aware of our operation."

Doc went to the phone, looked up a number in the book, dialed it, and asked to speak to Gilmore. The conversation was short. Doc hung up, turned to the intruder. "What's your name?"

"Lieutenant Thomas Llewellyn." He pronounced it "leftenant," in the British fashion.

"He's legit," said Doc. "Can I get you a drink, leftenant?"

CHAPTER SEVENTY-FOUR

Llewellyn looked at his watch. "You've got five minutes to convince me that I shouldn't have my men blow this place off the map."

Jock said, "Call your men. Tell them to back off for another fifteen minutes. That'll give us time to explain what's going on."

"It'll also give you time to get ready to kill my people."

"We're already on alert, Lieutenant," said Jock. "Look around you. These might be middle-aged men, but they were the most capable soldiers of their generation. They can still take out your men. Our position is fortified and you will have to stage an amphibious landing. That didn't work out too well for you alone. It's not going to work out for your men. If they come in now, they're dead. If they come in later, they're dead. But if we're legitimate, everybody goes home alive."

Llewellyn thought for a beat, nodded, picked up his phone, and punched a button. "Stand down. I'm in the house with the people here. I need about another half hour to verify some stuff. If you don't hear from me by then, or if you hear gunfire, light this place up."

He closed the phone and looked at Jock. "Okay. Convince me."

"I'm a U.S. intelligence agent," said Jock. "Detective Duncan is with the police. These other men are businessmen from the States. We're here hiding out for a few days. We're not on an operation. These men are my friends and I'm lending a hand, unofficially."

"Who are you hiding from?"

"We don't know. But somebody's trying to kill us. They've already killed three grown children of some of the men in this room."

Llewellyn looked around him. "These aren't your everyday civilians," he said. "Not the way they handle those weapons."

Jock nodded. "They're all former Special Operations soldiers. From the Vietnam war."

"What's going on?"

"I'd rather not get into that," said Jock, "but I think I can prove myself to you so that you'll accept my word that the only thing any of us has done wrong is ignore Bahamian immigration laws."

"How are you going to do that?"

"Call your commanding officer. Have him get in touch with the Bahamian ambassador to Washington. Tell him to ask the ambassador if you can trust the word of Jock Algren." He handed his ID to Llewellyn.

"It's late," said Llewellyn. "The ambassador might be asleep."

"He'll get up for me," said Jock.

Llewellyn walked out onto the patio and made his call. He was only gone for a few minutes before he returned to the room, a big smile on his face. "The ambassador remembers you well and sends his regards. He said we could trust you with anything."

The movement was quicker than lightning. One nanosecond Jock's right hand was hanging loosely by his side and the next it was a fist plunging powerfully into Llewellyn's gut. I was standing a few feet from Jock and Llewellyn, the other men spaced about the room in no particular order. I sensed confused movement, a murmuring. One of the men said loudly, "What the hell?"

"Stand down," I ordered. "Jock knows what he's doing."

"You heard the L.T.," said Doc. "Stay tight."

Jock had Llewellyn by the throat, his palm pushing on the man's chin. Llewellyn was sitting on the floor, his back against a sofa, Jock on top of him. Llewellyn was trying to catch his breath, breathing in short gasps.

"Who the fuck are you?" Jock said, his voice low, full of menace.

"I told you," said Llewellyn, making a mighty effort to breathe. "I'm with the Bahamian Defense Force."

Jock grinned. "You stupid bastard. I have no idea who the Bahamian ambassador to the U.S. is, but I know he never heard of me. You're CIA. And this is not a sanctioned mission."

I could see resignation on Llewellyn's face. He'd been had and he could see no way out. I watched him work it out, his brain functioning, sorting all the possibilities. There was only one. Give it up. Jock saw it too, and released him.

"You're right," he said, all trace of the Bahamas gone from his voice. "I'm CIA and I report to some very senior people. You work for the government. You don't want to mess with this. You ass is about to be grass."

"Son," said Jock, a genuine smile on his face, "nobody in government is senior to me, except for the president of the United States. And I can have him on the phone inside a minute, no matter where in the world he happens to be. Your superiors are finished. They're going to end up under lock and key in some godforsaken outpost where nobody will find them. You need to call your men off. Tell them the mission is aborted and they're to go back to wherever the hell they came from."

Llewellyn looked at his watch. Laughed. "You're full of shit. In about five minutes those men are coming ashore. You're going to be dead in ten minutes."

"And you'll be dead the minute they come into our perimeter. Your guys don't stand a chance, son, and I'll kill you the minute we hear them coming ashore."

Llewellyn stared at Jock and perhaps at his own mortality. He understood that it didn't matter if anything else Jock had told him was true. The real truth was that Jock would kill him. That fact alone took precedence over everything else.

"Okay," he said. He picked the phone up from the floor where it had dropped when Jock punched him. He opened it, pushed a button, and said, "It's over. Stay where you are for now. I'll get back to you." He closed the phone.

"Good show," said Jock. "You're a gutsy guy. Now, tell me who you really are."

"If I don't?"

"I'll kill you." The statement was flat, toneless. "And if you lie to me, I'll find out and then I'll kill you. And you're going to be in my custody while I check out everything you tell me."

"Okay. I don't know much. You have my real name. Tom Llewellyn. You're right. I work for the CIA. My boss is Barry Nitzler. He organized the operation. I don't know if it's sanctioned by the higher-ups, but Nitzler did okay it."

"Tell me about Nitzler," Jock said.

"Not much to tell. He's been with the agency since Vietnam. Married to a Vietnamese woman he got out just before the fall of Saigon. Lives in Virginia. No children that I'm aware of. He's an assistant deputy director in charge of clandestine operations. I'm not giving anything away. He and his title are listed in public records."

"What were you supposed to do here?" Jock asked.

"I was told to reconnoiter, see if I could determine if Mr. Desmond was here with some other men. If so, I was to arrest them and bring them back Stateside."

"Where were you to take them?"

"To one of our safe houses in Miami."

"Do you know who these gentlemen are?"

"No. I was told they're some sort of terrorists or terrorist sympathizers."

"How did you find us?"

"I'm not entirely sure, but I understood that the agency had most or all of the men under loose surveillance. By late yesterday Nitzler had figured out that all of them had disappeared. He put out an urgent request this morning to all the airports in the U.S. and Bahamas to be on the lookout for Desmond's plane. We got two hits this afternoon. One from Sarasota and the other from Marsh Harbour."

"How did you get here so quickly?"

"My team and I were flown in from D.C. in an agency jet. Nitzler or somebody cleared us with the chief constable in Marsh Harbour and he knew what to say if the operation went balls up."

"What did you tell your men when you called from the patio a few minutes ago?"

"Just that I thought we had you all together and I thought I could arrange for them to come in without firing a shot."

"What did you tell them about me?" asked Jock.

"Nothing. What was I going to say? That some guy with a fake government ID wanted me to call the Bahamian ambassador to Washington?"

"Do you believe me now?"

"I believe you'll kill me."

"Okay, son. This could go a couple of ways. If I find out you've lied to me, you're dead. If I find out you've been completely truthful, I'll square things with your boss."

"Nitzler will have my ass for screwing this up."

"If what you're telling me is the truth, Nitzler will be in jail. I'll talk to the director of the CIA. He and I go way back. He'll listen to me."

I watched Llewellyn's face. I'm not sure he entirely believed Jock, but I think I saw a bit of hope dance across his features. Maybe he wouldn't die tonight, and maybe he'd salvage his career.

Jock asked, "Llewellyn, how many men do you have out there?"

"Five."

"Doc," I said, "can we take five more guests?"

"No problem."

"Llewellyn, call your men. Tell them to come to the dock at the front of the house, on the south side of the island. Tell them to leave their weapons in the boat and come up the dock unarmed. You'll meet them there."

Llewellyn made the call and in a few minutes we heard a boat approaching the island at high speed. Doc turned on the outside floodlights that lit up the dock and the surrounding water. We watched as the boat came off plane, settled in the water, and idled toward the other moored boats.

"Llewellyn," I said, "you go stand at the land end of the dock. Jock will have an M4 trained on you, and if he sees anything suspicious, he'll kill you. These men will cover those on the dock. If I so much as see a gun, they're all dead. If some smart SOB decided to drop a couple of men on the other side of the island, we'll know it as soon as they come ashore. You with me?"

"Yes, sir."

"Go."

Llewellyn stood at the head of the dock and waved his men in. They all came onto the dock, no weapons in hand. There were five of them and they followed their leader to the grass where several old soldiers showed themselves, armed and ready.

When the CIA team saw the men with the guns, their hands went up. There was some grumbling, but Llewellyn silenced them. They all walked to the house where Doc greeted them.

"Gentlemen," said Doc, "please come in. You'll be our guests for a couple of days. No harm will come to you, but you will be held incommunicado. We have plenty of good food and enough spirits to make your stay enjoyable. All your questions will be answered in due course."

CHAPTER SEVENTY-FIVE

The white C-130 aircraft with the red stripe and seal of the U.S. Coast Guard set down on the single runway of the Marsh Harbour airport and taxied to the ramp. The surviving members of Team Charlie and our little band from Longboat Key stood sweating in the early morning sun. Llewellyn and his five men were sitting with their hands cuffed behind them, their backs against the wall of a small hangar,

"Mr. Algren," Llewellyn called, "if you've got the juice to get hold of a coast guard plane, I'm ready to accept that you're who you say you are. Can you uncuff us?"

"I'm not convinced you're who you say you are, Mr. Llewellyn," said Jock. "We'll sort it out when we get to Miami."

Jock had made the call the night before. I didn't ask who he could call who had the power to send us a government aircraft, but then I'd long since given up trying to discern the breadth of his power. It seemed to be almost unlimited.

Bahamian customs was turning a blind eye to our little group and the cuffed men in our custody. We'd put our weapons in duffel bags, but I doubt anybody would have thought they were tennis rackets. We'd land at Opa Locka airport near Miami and our captives would be taken to a safe house in Miami owned by Jock's agency. They'd be kept there incommunicado until we figured things out.

Llewellyn had become very cooperative the night before as he began to perceive that Jock might be exactly who he said he was. He called the man overseeing his operation and told them that he had taken control of the situation at Doc's house, but that he would have to hold the men until daybreak. The Bahamians were getting a little squeamish, but everything was under control. He was in charge and would bring the people he'd arrested out at first light.

We left before dawn, but not as Llewellyn had indicated to his superior. We took our rented boat back to the marina and used the other two boats to transport our men and our prisoners. The marina was deserted and we tied the boats to the docks and disappeared into the darkness. Two vans were waiting on the road that ran next to the marina, courtesy of Chief Constable Gilmore and Tom Llewellyn. We were taken directly to the airport.

The sun was well up by the time we landed at Opa Locka. The August heat beat down on us, a relentless fact of summer in Florida. We were met by two men from the Miami office of Jock's agency. Neither spoke a word, just nodded as Jock gave orders. One handed Jock a large envelope, and loaded the CIA men into another van and left the airport.

Because his plane in Marsh Harbour was too small to accommodate all the passengers, Doc had arranged for Tom Telson to bring the rented jet from Atlanta to Opa Locka to pick up the men of Team Charlie. They would fly back to Atlanta and check into hotels, taking a reluctant J.D. with them.

My phone call to Bill Lester the night before had not been exactly pleasant. I told him everything we'd discovered in Marsh Harbour. He was relieved that J.D. was safe and he understood the implications of the involvement of rogue CIA agents. Finally, I took a deep breath and told him about the bank account and the fact that J.D.'s name was on it.

His voice was cold. "When did you find out about the account?"

"Yesterday."

"And you're telling me about this now?"

"I'm sorry, Bill. I knew J.D. wasn't involved, but I also knew that you'd have to take some action, give the information to the town manager at the very least. It would inevitably get out, and J.D.'s career would be over. The fact that she was innocent wouldn't be a factor in the story."

A stony silence ensued. Then a sigh. "You're right. I couldn't report what I didn't know. But you ever do something like this again and I'll put your ass under the jail. Are we clear?"

"We're clear, Chief. And I'm sorry."

"Forget it. You did the right thing. I'll square her disappearance with our people."

He was going to tell them that J.D. had been on an undercover operation that he could not disclose and he was sorry to have worried them. They would be a bit pissed, but in the end would accept her disappearance as just another burp in a cop's routine.

When everybody was gone, Jock, Logan, and I went into a small office in the coast guard hangar. The air-conditioning was working overtime, blowing a steady stream of cold air into the small space. I had already sweated through my shirt and welcomed the relief the coolness brought. Jock sat at a desk and opened the envelope given him by the agent.

He studied the contents for a minute, shuffling through the pages. "Looks like the director came through. These are dossiers on the Thanatos teams and Nitzler."

He passed me a sheaf of papers. "You guys take a look at the teams. I'm going to dig into Mr. Nitzler. I think his career is over."

I began to read the pages, passing each one to Logan when I finished it. The report, written in dry bureaucratic speak, couldn't obscure the drama. The war in Vietnam was winding down. Nixon's Vietnamization of the war was in full swing. The only problem was that the South Vietnamese could not win. Their government was corrupt and the people had lost confidence in it. The Viet Cong, supported by the north with money, weapons, and regular troops, were in the ascendancy. The outcome was inevitable. The south would fall. The only thing the Americans could do was prolong the agony in hopes of salvaging some strategic position. Thanatos was born of desperation. It was an attempt to slow the advance of the Communists by assassinating their leaders. While it had some successes, it was in the end, a failure. The teams were disbanded, their members threatened with prosecution if they ever disclosed what they'd done during the last few months of their service.

I read on, absorbed in the futility of the operation, the needless deaths of good soldiers who'd joined the teams, angered by the perfidy of the intelligence agencies that were fighting a war they could not win, killing with no purpose other than to engage in a paroxysm of vengeful murder, as if saying, "Yes, you beat us, but many of your leaders won't live to enjoy their victory." There was nothing about the massacre at Ban Touk. The only reference was that "a successful assault was made upon a refuge of senior Viet Cong commanders and two men from Team Charlie were killed in action."

I reached the last page of the dossier. It was a list of names. All the men who'd been engaged in Operation Thanatos. "Shit," I said, "Nitzler was the guy running the teams from Saigon."

Jock looked up from the papers he was reading. "Yeah, it's here in his file. He was what the military used to call a barnburner, a man on his way up. He was young to have the job, but he ran Thanatos. Apparently the operation lasted less than a year, and Nitzler came back to D.C. a hero. The fact that the teams didn't accomplish a damn thing seemed to have no effect on his career. They killed a lot of people and that's what was important. Vietnam was just a body-counting exercise and the figures were always inflated."

"There's more," I said.

"What?"

"Remember Opal? The team leader that Doc and the guys killed?"

"Right."

"His name was Nigel Morrissey."

CHAPTER SEVENTY-SIX

"Damn," said Jock. "That's obviously Nigella's dad. What are we missing?"

"We're only missing one piece of the puzzle," said Logan.

"How do you see that?" I asked.

Logan held up his index finger. "If we drop the one missing piece into the puzzle, we'll see the whole picture. There has to be something that connects Nigella, Nitzler, and Stanley. Soupy and the Laotians are not a part of this. They were just part of the misdirection."

"I think we can connect Nitzler and Morrissey," I said. "They were both CIA and worked on Operation Thanatos. They were probably buddies, and now Nitzler is taking his revenge for the killing of his pal."

"How does that connect Stanley and Morrissey's daughter?" asked Jock. "And how are Nigella and Stanley connected to Nitzler?"

Logan was quiet for a moment. "I would guess that Nitzler has some relationship with Nigella. She's the daughter of his buddy. I just don't see how Stanley and his drug operation work into the picture."

"Maybe DEA has something," said Jock. "Delgado had all day yesterday to work on Stanley and Nigella."

"It's worth the call," I said.

Jock phoned the DEA office in Tampa and asked to speak to Delgado. The conversation was short and mostly one-sided. Delgado did all the talking. Jock hung up. "He wants to see us as soon as possible. Says there's a lot we need to know and he can't talk about it over the phone. He's also sending one of his guys to the bank in Sarasota to pick up that check with the thumbprint. It'll be interesting to see who was cashing those checks."

I looked at my watch. Not quite nine in the morning. "If Doc's plane's still in Marsh Harbour, can you square it so that he can bring it here to Opa Locka without worrying about customs and a lot of bureaucracy?"

"I'll talk to some people," said Jock. "You call Fred Cassidy. See if he's left the Bahamas yet."

"What about Nitzler?" I asked. "We've got to get to him."

"Nitzler's in a safe place. My agency guys picked him up on his way to the office this morning. He's in one of our safe houses in Virginia. My director called the CIA director and told him that Nitzler was a security risk and that my agency would take care of it. Nitzler won't even be missed at the office this morning.

I reached Cassidy at the airport in Marsh Harbour. He was about to leave for Atlanta. He agreed to fly directly to Opa Locka and pick us up. Jock handled the bureaucrats and by eleven o'clock we were in a taxi in Tampa on our way to the DEA offices.

Dan Delgado, the special agent in charge, met us in the reception area and led us back to a small conference room. He offered coffee and Jock and I accepted. Logan asked for a bottle of water. A middle-aged woman brought the coffee and water and closed the door on her way out.

Delgado drew a deep breath and said, "Gentlemen, we have a big problem here. You've stepped all over one of our investigations."

"What do you mean?" Jock asked.

"The Otto Foundation has been bringing drugs into the country and sending money out. The DEA office in Macon was on top of it and was about to bust the entire operation when you guys showed up."

Jock said, "This goes deeper than the drug running, Dan. There's a tie-in to some murders and probably some rogue CIA types. We don't have the whole picture yet, but we're zeroing in on it."

"You think the CIA was involved in the drugs?"

"I don't have any idea," said Jock. "At least one very senior guy in the CIA is involved in the murders. I don't know anything about the drugs, except that we stumbled over Stanley's operation. Have you sweated anything out of Stanley?"

"No. He's our guy."

"What do you mean?"

"He's a confidential informant for us."

"I don't get it," I said. "He's the guy in charge of the operation."

Delgado shook his head. "Stanley runs the foundation charitable operations. Maude Lane runs the drug side of the operation."

I sat back in my chair. Stunned. "Maude Lane? The grandmotherly type who works at the foundation?"

Delgado laughed. "Some story, huh?"

"That doesn't make sense," said Logan.

"She's worked there for ten years," I said. "Has the drug running been going on all that time?"

"No," said Delgado. "Stanley approached the Macon police at the end of last year. Said he'd noticed some funny things going on with the bank statements. Apparently Maude Lane ran the bookkeeping side of the operation. Stanley had done an audit of sorts at the end of the year and couldn't account for money coming in and going out to people and corporations he'd never heard of. The police smelled drugs, because the Southeast Asian connections the foundation had, and called us in."

"Did you know that Stanley had a prior conviction for dealing drugs?" asked Jock.

"Yes. He came clean at the first meeting. He really is a guy who turned his life around. He does a lot of good with that foundation and he's very proud of it."

Jock said, "We ran a background check on him. He had some very professional help in setting up his new history. Do you know anything about that?"

"Yeah. I looked into it. Our agency set that up for him after he got out of prison. He gave us lots of leads that ended up with us disrupting a number of drug-importation operations on the West Coast."

"What did your people find when you looked into the Otto Foundation?" I asked.

"It appears that somebody with a lot of computer savvy went into the foundation's computers and made some changes in the accounts going back a couple of years. They also hacked into the bank computers and brought them into compliance with the foundation records."

"Why would they do that?"

"We think it's a smoke screen, set up so that if anybody started looking closely at the records they'd see that the funny money had been going
in and out for several years. Actually, it started last fall."

"When Jock and I confronted Stanley in his house in Macon, an
Asian man speaking Vietnamese pulled a shotgun on us."

"That was Jack Minh. He's one of our agents. His job was to protect
Stanley if any of the drug people decided to take him out."

"Where does Nigella Morrissey fit into this?" Logan asked.

"Nigella," said Delgado, "is Maude Lane's niece. Maude's brother,
Nigel Morrissey, was killed in Vietnam, but he left a Vietnamese wife and
infant daughter. They were evacuated from Saigon before the fall."

"Maude's your missing puzzle piece, Logan," I said.

"I think you're right," Logan said. "Dan, how did a nice old lady like
Maude Lane get involved in drug smuggling?"

"We've never quite figured that out. We know that Nigella was the
one who talked Maude into using her ties to the Otto Foundation to turn
it into a drug operation, but we don't know why. Nigella isn't talking. She's
invoked her right to remain silent. There's nothing we can do."

"What if," asked Jock, "I told you this was a national security issue
and that Nigella is a target of a national security investigation?"

"I know who you are, Jock," said Delgado. "If you tell me that
you need her for a national security investigation, I'll turn her over to your
custody."

"I may want to do that," said Jock. "Let me think about it. Where is
she now?"

"She's in the county lockup, held in a secure area under our jurisdiction. No visitors, but I'm afraid she'll be seeing her lawyer this afternoon. I can't hold that off any longer."

"Can you have her brought here so that I can talk to her?"

"Sure. I can have her here within the hour."

"Dan," I said, "do you want to speculate, based on everything you
know about the drug operation, as to how Maude got roped into this by
her niece?"

Dan was quiet for a moment, stroking his chin. "I think there is somebody way up the food chain who is in charge of this thing. These ladies didn't come up with this sophisticated an operation on their own. We were trying to work our way up the chain when you guys showed up."

"I've got an idea about who was in charge," said Jock. "But I'm going to have to do a little digging. I don't have some of the legal constraints that you guys do."

The phone on the table buzzed. Delgado picked it up, spoke into it, and then listened. He hung up. "I do have a little package for you. Mary Jennings."

"Who's Mary Jennings?" I asked.

Delgado smiled. A big happy, gotcha kind of smile. "A young lady who works for Hillsborough County and managed to leave her thumbprint on that check at the Sarasota bank. She's a part-time actress. Does commercials and amateur plays and looks uncannily like a certain Longboat Key detective we all know."

"I'll be damned," I said. "Is she here?"

"Yep. Scared shitless and in the interrogation room. You want to talk to her?"

"Bet your ass," I said.

"Be my guest, Counselor."

CHAPTER SEVENTY-SEVEN

Mary Jennings was sitting in a small room with bare walls. The only furniture was a table with a chair on either side. A video camera hung from a bracket high in one corner. A one-way mirror was built into one wall so that agents standing in the next room could watch the action.

She appeared to be about thirty years old and wore her light brown hair in a French twist. She was dressed in a navy business suit, white blouse, and low-heeled pumps. She sat alone at the table, her nervousness showing in her body movements. She crossed and uncrossed her arms, then her legs. She looked around the room, obviously uncomfortable, nervous, concerned. I watched her for a few minutes through the one-way mirror. At first glance there was no resemblance to J.D. Duncan. She was not as tall as J.D. and carried a little more weight, but when I looked closely at her face, I could see how some makeup and a dark wig could transform her enough to fool the bank security camera. And me, as it happened.

I walked into the room, shut the door, and stood quietly, staring at the woman at the table. She looked at me and finally said, "What is this all about?"

"Ms. Jennings, my name is Matthew Royal. You do realize that you're in a Drug Enforcement Administration facility, don't you?"

"Yes, but I don't know why."

"We're looking at drug charges as well as some very nasty national security matters."

"I don't have any idea what you're talking about."

"Let's start with the name J. D. Duncan, a bank in Sarasota, and a monthly withdrawal."

She opened her mouth as if to say something, thought better of it, and shut up. She took a deep breath and said, "I want a lawyer."

"It doesn't work that way, Ms. Jennings. You can't have a lawyer."

"I know my rights."

"Those rights are suspended during national security investigations." I was lying, but I didn't think she'd know that.

She paled, blinked rapidly, sat back in her chair. "National security?"

"Yes. You're in a lot of trouble here, and your best bet is to come clean with us and tell me everything you know."

"Who is 'us'?" She wasn't going down easy. A smart woman.

"Let's start with the fact that federal security agencies are involved and I'm working with them. That's all you need to know."

She seemed to deflate, the fight going out of her. "There's nothing to tell. I was hired to do an acting job and I did it."

"Tell me about it."

"I got a phone call from a man who identified himself only as 'Gemstone.' He told me that he needed an actress to pose as somebody else and cash some checks in a bank in Sarasota."

"Didn't you think that might be illegal?"

"I raised that issue. He said it was okay, that the money was his, but that he couldn't get to it because an ex-wife was hounding him for back alimony."

"What were you supposed to do?"

"He sent me a picture of a woman named J. D. Duncan. Said it was his sister and she was helping him dodge the ex-wife. The problem was that the sister lived in Idaho, and he needed somebody to cash the checks at the bank in Sarasota."

"That sounds pretty thin," I said.

"I know, but he was going to pay me five hundred dollars for each trip to Sarasota. I couldn't pass it up."

"Why the disguise?"

"Gemstone said that his ex-wife had a lot of friends in law enforcement and could possibly get hold of security tapes from the banks. He wanted me to look as much like his sister as possible."

"You know that this makes no sense at all."

"I know. But at the time it seemed like an easy way to make a few bucks."

"What did you do with the cash?"

"I took out five hundred dollars and mailed the rest to Gemstone at a post office box in Tampa."

"Did you have any other contact with Gemstone?"

"He'd call every month and tell me to go to the bank. That was all. A total of three or four calls."

"Did he ever tell you why the money was in a bank in Sarasota?"

"No."

"And you never asked?"

"No. What's going to happen to me?"

"I'm going to turn you over to the Sarasota police. Let them work out the charges."

She teared up. "I'll lose my job with the county."

"Yes, but you got five hundred bucks for each run to Sarasota."

"That's not fair."

"Neither is what you tried to do to an outstanding police officer."

"I don't understand."

"You don't need to."

I got up and left the room, leaving a small-time actress to contemplate her immediate future. I felt no sympathy for her at all. She'd given no thought to what grief she may have caused someone while she earned her five hundred bucks. I hoped they put her away for a while. A little prison time might give her a new outlook on how to use her talents.

"That wasn't very productive," I said to Jock as we stood outside the interrogation room.

"I don't think she was a part of anything bigger than what she thought was a small-time scam," he said.

"I agree."

"I thought it interesting that the man she dealt with identified himself as 'Gemstone.'"

"I caught that. The CIA guys in Operation Thanatos were all named after gemstones. What I don't understand is why they went to all this trouble to implicate J.D.?"

Jock shrugged. "It was probably part of the misdirection and maybe a safety valve in the event that J.D. started closing in on them. They could always implicate her in their scheme and discredit her investigation. The checks started coming in her name about the time she began her investigation. "

"Maybe you can get something out of Nigella," I said."

CHAPTER SEVENTY-EIGHT

Nigella Morrissey was in the same interview room that had held Mary Jennings. I stood with Logan and watched her through the one-way mirror. She was wearing an orange jumpsuit, the kind that jails and prisons all over the country issue to their inmates. She sat with her back straight, arms resting on the table, her wrists cuffed, shackles around her waist secured to a U-bolt cemented into the floor. She didn't move except for an occasional involuntary blink of the eyes. She seemed unconcerned about her situation.

Jock walked in the door and stood quietly next to the table. Nigella looked up and smiled. "Ah," she said. "The thug returns. Got your knife? Want to cut my clothes off?"

"I just want to chat for a bit."

"Get me my lawyer."

"You don't get a lawyer."

"Bullshit. I'm a lawyer. I know my rights."

"This is a national security matter."

"So?"

"So you don't get a lawyer."

"That's not the law."

"Maybe not, but you still don't get a lawyer."

"I'm not saying a thing without one present."

"That's exactly what your aunt Maude Lane said."

Nigella flinched, an almost imperceptible movement. "Maude Lane? Don't know her."

"That's odd," said Jock. "She's your dad's older sister, helped pay your way through college and law school. Works for the Otto Foundation. Juggles the money for you."

Nigella shook her head, whether in denial or resignation, I couldn't tell.

"She's on her way to Egypt," said Jock.

"Egypt?"

"Surely you've read about the whole rendition thing."

"What do you mean?"

"You know, where the government sends national security risks to other countries that don't have the legal constraints we do against torture. It helps get the prisoners talking. Been going on since the early years of the Clinton administration."

"I know about rendition. What have you done with my aunt?"

"So, she *is* your aunt."

"Yes, you bastard. What have you done with her?"

"She's in jail in Macon, Georgia, waiting for a government plane to come get her."

"I don't believe you."

"Don't count on Barry Nitzler to stop it. He's in custody in Virginia."

"Bullshit. He's way up in the food chain."

"I'm higher."

"I don't believe you."

"Do you have a number that you can call and he'll always answer? In case of emergency?"

"Yes."

"Have you called it before?"

"Yes."

"Always able to get hold of Nitzler?"

"Yes."

Jock handed her his cell phone. "Call him now."

"Then you'll have the number."

"I already have it."

"Bullshit."

Jock took the phone back, pushed a couple of buttons and showed Nigella the small screen. "Is that the number?"

She nodded, dialed the number, listened, closed the phone.

Nigella sat back in her chair, a look of defeat replacing the defiance she'd shown before. "No answer," she said.

"Tell us what we need to know and I'll guarantee that your aunt won't be sent out of the country," Jock said. "She'll go into the criminal justice system just like any other drug dealer."

"Can I have a glass of water?"

"Sure. As soon as we've finished talking."

"Okay," Nigella said, "okay. My dad was a CIA operative in Vietnam at the end of the war. He met and married my mom and they lived in Saigon. I was born there. When I was just a few weeks old, my dad was killed by some American soldiers who were part of a team he was leading."

"How do you know this?"

"My uncle is Barry Nitzler. He told me."

"Your uncle?"

"Yes. His wife and my mother are sisters. He and my dad were best friends. They'd met in college and joined the CIA together."

"When did he tell you this?"

"A couple of years ago. He'd just been promoted to an important position in the CIA. He went into the records and found the names of the men who'd killed my dad."

"How did you get involved in the drug business?"

"I was practicing with a firm in Tampa. Barry suggested that I set up my own shop and work to launder some drug money. The profits from the drug business would be used by Barry to take revenge on the ones who'd killed my dad."

"How did he plan to get that revenge?"

"I don't know. He never said and I never asked."

"How did the operation work?"

"Barry said that the Otto Foundation would be the perfect front and since Aunt Maude worked there, maybe we could get her to handle that end of things."

"Did you talk to your aunt?"

"Yes. Barry and I went to see her in Macon early last year. He'd known her for years. He told her that he now had the documents that proved that some American soldiers had killed my dad and another CIA man. He wanted her help in getting even."

"Did you set up the scheme then?"

"No. She wanted time to think about it. She called me a few days later and discussed the procedures, how it would be done. Barry would provide her with a computer whiz who would help her set things up and hack the bank computers."

"How did it work?"

"The money would go from the foundation to several dummy companies that Barry set up. Then the funds would be wired from those companies into my trust account. I'd then send money back to an account that Barry controlled."

"What was the money used for?"

"I don't know."

"Murder?"

"I don't know. I didn't ask, didn't want to know."

"What did you think Barry was going to do with the money? How was he going to exact his revenge on the soldiers?"

"I supposed he was going use the money to set up whatever he needed to get the job done. To kill them."

"You weren't bothered by that?"

Nigella's voice rose. "These guys killed my dad. I never knew him because those bastards took it on themselves to kill him. They deserved whatever they got."

"Do you know about Ban Touk?"

"What's that?"

"A village in Vietnam, near the Laotian border."

She shook her head. "Never heard of it."

Jock's voice became harder, edgier. "How about a massacre of civilians? Women and children. Ever hear of that?"

"My Lai? Everybody's heard about that."

"No. Ban Touk. It happened much later. At the same time that your dad was killed."

"I've never heard anything about it."

"Did you know what your dad was doing in Vietnam?"

"Only what Barry told me. That he led a team of soldiers who killed Viet Cong."

"Did he tell you why he thought your dad was killed by the soldiers?"

"Just that it was some sort of mutiny. I don't know if he even knew the details."

"Are you aware that four of the adult children of men in your dad's team have been killed in the last three months?"

"No. Why would Barry kill the children of those men? That doesn't make any sense. I can see him killing the murderers, but not their kids."

"Who are the Vietnamese men and women involved in what Barry Nitzler is doing?"

"I have no idea. I didn't know there were any Vietnamese involved."

"Nigella, we're going to be doing some more digging. I told you the other night that if you lied to me I'd kill you. I won't do that, but if what you've told me turns out to be untrue or incomplete, you'll be on that flight to Egypt."

"What about my aunt?"

"She's in the Bibb County Jail in Macon with a DEA hold. She's not going anywhere, and assuming you've been truthful with me, she won't be sent to Egypt."

"Barry's not going to let anything happen to her or to me. Even if you've got him in custody. He's got lots of friends in D.C."

"Barry will be dead by the end of the day. Once he's been wrung dry of information, he'll have some sort of fatal accident. The CIA doesn't take kindly to its people going off the reservation."

"You'll never be able to use any of this evidence against me."

"Don't need to," Jock said, as he rose and moved toward the door.

"What do you mean?" Nigella asked, a note of alarm sending her voice up a register.

Jock looked directly at her, was quiet for a beat. Then, "I think you know, Nigella." He left the room, closing the door softly.

CHAPTER SEVENTY-NINE

"Was she telling the truth?" I asked.

"I think so," said Jock, "but maybe not all of it."

"Where did you get that telephone number you showed her?"

"One of our guys who's interrogating Nitzler sent it to me this morning. They're making progress with him. He's scared shitless, wants to cooperate and get out of this with his life. I don't think that's going to happen."

"You were serious then in telling Nigella he won't survive?"

"Yeah. I don't know for sure, but I don't think it would be in the best interest of the intelligence agencies for him to live."

"What now?" I asked.

"We wait. I should be hearing something from D.C. shortly."

"Look," said Logan quietly, "I think you took the starch out of her, Jock."

Nigella sat slumped in the chair, her head in her hands. She was sobbing. I could almost see the waves of despair rolling across her consciousness. It wasn't a pretty sight. A beautiful woman had been reduced to a quivering mass of regret.

"I didn't enjoy that," said Jock, "but I want her nervous. We may need to get more out of her. I'm not sure she told us everything she knows."

"What'll happen to her?" asked Logan.

"She'll go to prison," said Jock. "Probably get twenty years, unless she's implicated in the murders. Then she'll do life, or if Florida tries her, maybe get a ride on the needle. Everything she owns will be confiscated by the government. She'll lose her law license."

"That's pretty harsh," said Logan.

"Better than what Jim Desmond and those other kids got," Jock said.

The three of us left the DEA offices and went to a small café down the block. We ate a leisurely lunch, idly chatting about the case and how things were starting to come into focus. I still had a lot of questions, but they'd have to wait until we got a clearer picture from D.C.

We were on our way back to the DEA office when Jock's phone rang. The conversation was short. Jock closed his phone. "We're going to Washington," he said. "They're about finished with Nitzler, but they're giving us a shot at him in case we have any questions."

"What about the killers?" I asked. "The Asians."

"They were thugs involved with the drug runners that Nitzler hooked up with. They're being rolled up by the police this afternoon. They'll all be in custody before dark."

"What can we learn in Washington?" Logan asked.

"Maybe the truth," said Jock.

CHAPTER EIGHTY

Doc's jet landed at Washington's Reagan National Airport in the late afternoon. We were met by somber men in a black SUV and driven into the Virginia countryside. We took a lane off the main highway and drove for a few minutes past big homes set back from the road. Horses were pastured in the large expanses between the houses. Finally, we came to a driveway leading off the lane. We turned in and drove across some rolling hills to a large house set well back from the street. It was a fairly new house, built in the antebellum style of the Old South. There were long porches and columns in front. The building was clapboard, or an imitation thereof, and painted white with black shutters. An imposing and isolated place.

We were shown into a living room where a tall man slouched in an upholstered chair, sipping from a tumbler of amber whiskey. He was wearing a white dress shirt, a red-and-white tie that was askew on his chest, dark pants, and wingtip cordovan shoes. His hair was gray and a lot of it was missing. He looked up and his face broke into a large grin. "Jock," he said, and stood to embrace his visitor.

"Dave," Jock said, "this is Matt Royal and Logan Hamilton. Gentlemen, my director, Dave." No last name. I wasn't surprised. Jock's agency didn't exist publicly. It's funding came from some black bag dollars that were funneled through the CIA. While there was a lot of cooperation between the agencies, Dave answered only to the president of the United States.

"At last I get to meet you two. God, you've gotten my buddy here involved in some strange stuff the last couple of years."

We shook hands. "Can I get you a drink?" asked the director.

"I wouldn't mind a little Scotch if you have it," said Logan.

"I'll take a beer," I said.

"O'Doul's," said Jock.

The director disappeared and returned with our drinks. It had been a long day that started before dawn in Marsh Harbour. It was still daylight outside, but I felt like I'd done a hard day's work and midnight was closing in. The beer tasted good, cold and plain good.

"What have you got for us, Dave?" asked Jock.

"Nitzler gave it all up, I think. He was using the drug connection to ensure his retirement. The killings were just a sideshow. He'd always wanted to get the men who'd killed his buddy Morrissey, but he'd never had the ability to get at them. His new position in the CIA and his drug connections cleared that problem."

"Can we talk to him?" Jock asked.

"He's in the basement. Help yourself."

We finished our drinks and Dave summoned another agent to take us to Nitzler. We found him sitting in a room with no furniture except the chair he sat on. He was wearing navy pinstriped suit pants, a white dress shirt, no tie, no belt, no shoes. He was shackled to a chair that was bolted to the floor. When we entered, he looked up. He was sweaty, tired, the lines of his face etched with exhaustion. "Who're you?" he asked.

"I'm Jock Algren."

"I know your name. Who're these guys?"

"Matt Royal and Logan Hamilton."

"Shit."

Jock squatted down to eye level with Nitzler. "You want to tell us what the hell you were doing killing people you had no beef with?"

"No reason not to at this juncture," Nitzler said. "I know the drill. I won't be going home."

"Then a little truth won't hurt you," said Jock.

"It was part of the misdirection. I figured if the kids were killed, and they were killed by Vietnamese, then if anybody got onto us, they'd think it was the survivors of Ban Touk exacting revenge by killing the children of the men who killed their children."

"That's kind of far out, isn't it?" asked Logan.

"Yeah, but I also wanted those bastards who killed Nigel to feel the same kind of pain I've felt since his death. If they were just killed, there'd be no pain. This way, they got to suffer before I took them all out."

"You're a cold-blooded son of a bitch," I said.

"You have to be to do the kind of work I've done for the past thirty years," he said.

"Tell me about your efforts to kill me," I said.

Nitzler laughed, a dry cackle that made him appear to be unbalanced. "The first time I wanted you hurt bad, scared, out of my face, but not dead. I figured you'd think it was the Laotians and you'd close up shop and forget about us. I didn't count on you breaking my man's arm."

"And the second time?" I asked.

"Misdirection. I figured you'd backtrack the dummy we sent and begin to wonder what kind of fools we were. I didn't count on you finding out who hired the idiot."

"John Nguyen," I said.

"Yeah."

"How did you know we found John Nguyen?"

"Your fucking interrogator told me. That's how you first started to connect the dots and gave up on the Laotian connection."

"That's right," I said. "You screwed up on that one."

Nitzler looked at Jock. "The guy from your agency also told me you were Royal's buddy and had gotten yourself involved. I've heard tales about the great Jock Algren for years. If I'd known you were involved we would have played this thing differently."

"How so?" I aked.

"I don't know. But I would have taken his contacts in the intelligence community into consideration."

"Did you hack into Desmond's computers?" asked Jock.

"I did. I read all your memos. Very informative. When you guys got the bright idea that Laotians were doing the killing, I thought I'd just let that be. You were going off in the wrong direction so that suited my purposes."

"What about the drug money?" asked Jock. "Where did that go?"

"Some of it went to pay for the Viets I hired to kill those kids. The rest of it went into my bank account in Switzerland. In the name of Robert

Bracewell. Dave and his boys are already on it. I'm sure that money will be in an agency account before the end of the day."

"Pretty slick," I said. "How did you know about Bracewell?"

"I came across the connection when I was checking out Stanley."

"Why Stanley and the Otto Foundation?" I asked.

"Simple. Maude Lane was Nigel's older sister. She already worked there and it didn't take much to convince her to help us get the men who killed her brother."

"Why try to implicate Detective Duncan in your operation?" I asked.

"Standard procedure. When she started the investigation into the murders, I set her up to take a fall if she happened to stumble over something that would implicate me or the agency."

"Why lure Katherine Brewster to Anna Maria Island to kill her?" I asked. "Why not do that in Charlotte?"

"I had nothing to do with her going to Florida. I was getting my team in place for the Desmond boy's wedding when that idiot Mantella set up his scheme to get her to Florida. It seemed only natural to set them up to take out the Brewster girl at the same time. I thought the chances of law enforcement tying the killings together were slim."

"How did you find out what Mantella was doing?"

"I'd had the Brewster's phone tapped. We got the girl telling her boyfriend about the gift certificates and her planned trip to Florida. I had EZGo Travel checked out and we tracked it back to Mantella."

"Why kill Garrison?" I asked.

"The lawyer?"

"Yes."

"Collateral damage. He tried to save the Brewster girl."

"How did you know Katherine would be onboard *Dulcimer* that evening?"

"We didn't. I knew she had a gift certificate for a cruise. I had the team aboard every night, with one of them standing in the bow to take care of the captain when the time came."

"Where does Llewellyn fit into this?" asked Jock.

"He's a good man. Follows orders. Doesn't ask questions. He was handy when I got word that Desmond's plane was in Marsh Harbour. He and a team went straight there, figured out that you'd be in the house on the island, and went to see what was up."

"How'd he know about the house?" Jock asked.

"He didn't. Not until he got to Marsh Harbour. He found out that Royal had rented a boat and the dockmaster told him that he saw the three of you anchored and fishing in the area of the house. I told Llewellyn to slip up to the house after dark and make sure it was Desmond before he raided the place. I guess we didn't count on your security measures."

"Why?" Jock asked.

"Why what?"

"Why did you do it? Betray your country, your agency."

"I didn't betray my country. I just wanted a nice nest egg for retirement and when I came across the smuggling ring during another operation, I figured I could get the money and take out the bastards who killed my buddy. A little retribution."

"What about those women and children killed at Ban Touk?" asked Logan.

"What about them?"

"You don't think they deserved some justice, like maybe the execution of the guy who ordered them killed? Opal or Morrissey or whatever his name was?"

"Fuck 'em. A bunch of slopes. Wrong place, wrong time. We were in a war."

"Just collateral damage," Logan said.

Nitzler looked at Logan, a hard, defiant look. "Damn straight, bucko."

CHAPTER EIGHTY-ONE

On the last day of August, J.D., Jock, Logan, Doc Desmond, and I sat at a table on the covered patio at the Mar Vista pub. The sun had sunk into the Gulf an hour before and a slight breeze blew off the bay chasing the worst of the heat away. The big ceiling fans circulated the air so that the evening was more pleasant than I had expected.

Jock had arrived on a commercial flight from Houston about an hour before. Doc came from the airport where he'd parked his private jet. The meeting had been arranged the day after we left Virginia. We wanted to give it a couple of weeks for the agencies involved to sort out their options. Somebody would let Jock know the outcome and he would tell us.

After our talk with Nitzler, the three of us had bedded down in rooms on the second floor of the safe house. We were exhausted from our long day and sleep came easily. The next morning we had called Doc's pilot Fred Cassidy at the hotel where he'd spent the night, and he flew us to Atlanta. We met with the remnants of Team Charlie and told them that the danger was over, that they could bring their families home, get back to their lives. They wanted to know more, but all we could tell them was that they'd be told everything in due time, no more than a couple of weeks.

Cassidy had flown us back to Sarasota, and the next day Jock left for Houston. Our adventure was over. J.D. was ribbed by her fellow cops about turning into a fed, but she just laughed them off. The story Bill Lester put out, one that was backed up by Dan Delgado, the special agent in charge of the Tampa office of DEA, was that J.D. had been seconded to the DEA for help in an undercover operation. It had been so hush-hush that the only story anybody could come up with to explain her absence from the key was that she'd disappeared. Lester apologized to his men for the deception and life returned to the desultory tempo of the island summer.

Jock had been completely briefed by his director and given permission to tell us all that he knew. He didn't actually have a lot to add. We had learned the gist of the Nitzler operation, as we were now calling it, from Nigella and Nitzler. But the story was not complete, and Jock had come to flesh it out. He reiterated what we already knew, giving Doc more information than we'd given him in Atlanta when we met with Team Charlie.

"Who were the Vietnamese involved in this thing?" asked Doc.

"They were part of a drug cartel operating on the Mississippi Gulf Coast. There are a lot of Vietnamese fishermen in that area. Most are scrupulously honest and hard working, but a few of them decided to make a killing importing drugs in their fishing boats."

"Kind of like those guys down in Everglades City a few years back," said J.D.

"Same thing," said Jock. "The Vietnamese fishermen would offload drugs from a mother ship way out in the Gulf and bring the drugs in. Sometimes the money is too easy to resist."

"How did Nitzler get involved with them?" Doc asked.

"He was running an operation against one of the Mexican drug cartels and he stumbled onto the Vietnamese connection in Mississippi. He had the ones involved picked up and told them they would be put in prison if they didn't cooperate with him. They began to funnel some of their money into the Otto Foundation. It was essentially protection money paid to Nitzler to keep him from putting them out of business. When Nitzler needed some people to handle the killings, the leaders supplied a few of their enforcers."

"Are they still running drugs over there?" asked J.D.

"No," said Jock. "All the evidence was turned over to DEA and they made the busts."

"What about the enforcers working for Nitzler?" asked J.D.

"There were only three involved in the killings," said Jock. "One, the woman who was there at the first attempt on Matt's life, was the sniper. She took out Doc's son, the Fleming boy, and young Lemuel up in North Dakota. The other one, the slasher, killed the Dixson girl at the University of Virginia and tried to take out Matt on the beach. The third guy was the one we knew as John Nguyen. He broke the *Dulcimer*'s captain's neck."

"Where are they now," asked Doc.

"Unfortunately, they died in a car wreck," said Jock. "They were found in a sedan that ran off the road and submerged in a lake in North Carolina. They were passengers in a car driven by a CIA officer named Barry Nitzler. The driver had a blood-alcohol content of about three times the legal limit. All four had been dead for a couple of days when the car was found."

"What did they do about Llewellyn?" I asked.

"He's fine. The CIA took him back. He was following orders of his boss and had no reason to suspect anything illegal. Neither did any of his team members. He's probably in for some ribbing, but otherwise his career is safe."

"What about the rest of them?" Logan asked.

"Nigella pled guilty to the money laundering and all charges relating to the murders were dropped. The prosecutor would have had a hard time proving that Nigella had anything to do with them. She's going to be in prison for the next fifteen years. Her aunt, Maude Lane, got the same sentence. She'll probably die behind bars. The other Vietnamese who were involved are going to prison on a whole raft of charges. They'll probably never get out."

Doc shook his head. "All these years and that damn war isn't over yet."

"It may never be over," I said. "At least during the lifetimes of those who fought there."

"Just think," said Doc, "one man with an agenda, a ruthless bastard named Nitzler caused all this. The deaths at Ban Touk, our kids, and now Nitzler himself, the man who started it all. In a way, he set up his own death that day in Vietnam when he decided to have us kill those women and children. Logan thought the people after us might have been the avenging angels of Ban Touk. Turns out it was just the same pissant who ordered the deaths of those poor people."

"Maybe in the end," said Logan, "we were Ban Touk's avenging angels."

"I guess we were," said Doc. "I guess we were."

CHAPTER EIGHTY-TWO

Logan, Jock, and Desmond said their goodbyes. Logan was going to drive the other two to the airport. J.D. and I sat alone in the quiet of the late evening, savoring the gentle breeze wafting in from the bay. She was sipping a glass of wine as I worked on my last beer of the evening. We were quiet for a few minutes, lost in our own thoughts.

I felt her hand rest lightly on top of mine and looked up into those startling green eyes. She was smiling, a bit sadly perhaps. "Matt," she said, "I'll never forget that you came to find me in the Bahamas."

"I—"

"No," she interrupted. "Don't say anything."

I nodded, sat quietly, my hand still under hers on the table.

"You are very special to me," she said. "More so than I would like. I've made it for years, since my divorce, without any special entanglement. There have been men in my life, but nothing serious. It's been kind of a rule with me. It keeps me from doing something stupid like I did when I married that jerk who tried to beat on me. You could be the exception to that rule. It scares me."

She sat quietly then, her eyes fixed on my face. "J.D.," I said, "I've only been in love once in my life. To the woman I married. I messed that one up about as much as your husband did your marriage. She left me and then she died. You've stirred feelings in me that I thought were gone for good. But I'm not sure that I'm man enough to live up to your expectations, to be the man you deserve."

"You remember in the Bahamas I said I couldn't just accept friskiness as a reason for sex?"

"Yes."

"Maybe I was wrong."

My heart did that little jig that J.D. seems to be able to trigger. I smiled. "Where does that leave us then?"

"I don't know."

"Do you want to go home with me?"

"Yes. But I won't. Not tonight anyway."

I was actually a little relieved. I felt that we had achieved some sort of delicate balance in our relationship, an equilibrium that was more than friendship, but not quite that of lovers. Maybe it was best to keep it that way for a while.

I raised my mug of beer and in my best Bogart imitation said, "Here's looking at you kid."

She laughed, that wonderful laugh that made my heart want to jump out of my chest and run around the patio in pure joy. "Man," she said, "you've got to work on that some."

I smiled. Yes, we had a number of things to work on and we had the long months in the sun stretching before us to figure it all out. There was a hint of romance floating on the air coming off the bay, and there was no better place than our small island to let it develop at its own pace. J.D. and I would be fine, and perhaps soon, we would be better than fine.